More praise for Terri Brisbin's
A LOVE THROUGH TIME

"A treat! *A Love Through Time* is a mystical, magical adventure you won't want to miss. Terri Brisbin is a welcome new voice in time-travel romance."
—Susan Wiggs

"Terri Brisbin's exciting first novel will teach everyone a new lesson in how to love. An afternoon delight. You won't want this one to end."
—Shirley Hailstock, author of *Whispers of Love*

"Terri Brisbin's *A Love Through Time* gives new meaning to 'what I did on my summer vacation.' Tender and poignant, this debut novel marks Ms. Brisbin as a talent to watch!"
—Deb Stover, author of *Another Dawn*

DON'T MISS OTHER EXCITING TIME PASSAGES ROMANCES,
AVAILABLE FROM JOVE!

Terri Brisbin

A LOVE THROUGH TIME

A Jove Book / published by arrangement with the author

PRINTING HISTORY
Jove edition / November 1998

The Penguin Putnam World Wide Web site address is
http://www.penguinputnam.com

ISBN: 0-515-12403-6

A JOVE BOOK®
Jove Books are published by The Berkley Publishing Group,
a member of Penguin Putnam Inc.,
375 Hudson Street, New York, New York 10014.
JOVE and the "J" design are trademarks
belonging to Jove Publications, Inc.

PRINTED IN THE UNITED STATES OF AMERICA

10 9 8 7 6 5 4 3 2 1

I dedicate this book, my first published novel, to the very special people who have been and still are my best supporters:

—to my husband, Chris, and sons, Matthew, Dru, and Mike, who left Mom alone enough times to finish the book;

—to the real Pol and Rachelle, Paul and Rochelle Adler, and to all my dental office colleagues, who listened, corrected, and never failed to encourage me;

—to my first and longtime best friend, Cindy, who asked why romance writers never use the ''p'' word (It's here, just once, for you!);

—and finally to all the members, past and present, of the Prodigy Romance Novel BB who pointed me in the right direction, and to the members of NJRW who walked with me along the way: Colleen, Terri, Chelle, Jenn, Lyn, Rainy, Elaine, Shirley, Anne, the Susans, Mary, Beth, Mary Lou, and all who I haven't mentioned by name.

Thank you all for what you've given to me.

Author's Note

Because Scottish Gaelic is difficult for most of us to read and pronounce and because it doesn't even sound as it looks, I chose to use a form of Scots English in this story. It has the characteristic accent usually associated with the Scottish language, but it is recognizable and readable to those of us who speak English. Reading it aloud will give you a real taste of Scotland, as it were.

To aid in your reading, here are some of the commonly used words and their translations:

amna = am not
doesna = does not
haes = has
hiv = have
maun = must
willna = will not
wi', wi'in, wi'oot = with, within, without
ye = you
dinna, didna = did not
haid = had
haesna = has not
hivna, havna = have not
no' = not
weel = well
yer = your, you're

This list is not complete but is a sample of the words I use in the story.

'S e am gum bidh an dearbhadh de gaol siorruidh.
'Tis time that will be the proof of love everlasting.

Prologue

DUNNEDIN, SCOTLAND

FOR GENERATIONS, MACKENDIMEN clan lore has it that the stonecutter's simpleton son was to blame. Centuries ago, after stumbling off the path that led to the quarry, the boy got lost while looking for more stone to fit his father's requirements. Confused, weary, and hungry, the boy wandered through the lush forest searching for the quarry or home.

Wending his way through the woods, he lurched into a small clearing where he found an ancient circle of stones. Not realizing the importance of such a ring, he decided that he would use some of the perfectly sized and smoothed boulders to meet his father's demands. Shortly after, the boy found his way back to the path and used the stones as he had made up his mind to do.

The stones, fashioned into an archway in a new wall around the MacKendimen keep, caused peculiar things to occur. Strange, unidentifiable noises emanated from the archway. Sometimes unusual lights and shadows filtered through from one side of the arch but not the other. When people seemingly disappeared through it, the laird of the time reached his limit. He ordered the arch to be filled in with stone and the rest of the construction left unfinished.

Generations later, Cormac, the MacKendimen at that time, commanded that a larger keep be erected a distance away from the original location and it was. Eventually, the walls of the deserted castle, robbed of stone for the new fortress, began to deteriorate. After many centuries, there were only ruins left behind to mark the spot . . . and one complete archway. By the late 1900s, the stones and mortar placed in the arch all those years before had crumbled. It was open again.

And the magic waited.

NEW JERSEY—PRESENT DAY

"You're going *where*?"

The entire room instantly quieted and all eyes and ears were on Maggie Hobbs. Everyone in the teachers' lounge waited for her answer. Usually, they were involved in their own conversations, but Pat's startled exclamation grabbed everybody's attention.

"You heard me," Maggie replied, clearing her throat and waiting for the silence to die down. "Scotland. I'm going to Scotland."

"But who are you going with?" Pat's voice was a little quieter this time. "You can't be thinking of going on your own."

"I showed you the brochures from the tour group months ago, Pat. Didn't you think I was serious?"

"I didn't think you meant *this* summer or by yourself."

Pat's tone, full of worry, warmed Maggie with the sense of protection and concern that she felt as they talked. But Pat sometimes forgot that they were both teachers and almost the same age. Maggie was not one of the second graders in the classes they taught.

Maggie leaned back in her chair and pushed her long auburn curls back over her shoulders. Looking around the crowded room, she noticed that almost everyone had gone back to their own discussions. She spoke in a normal voice to Pat now.

"You know how much I've wanted to go to Scotland, and you know how long I've wanted to do this. This is the first summer I'll have the time to go."

"You mean, now that you've broken off with Don, there's no one to stop you?" Pat raised her eyebrows at the end of the question, almost daring Maggie to lie.

"No. This is the first time I'm not taking any summer classes." Maggie glanced at Pat, making eye contact, before continuing. "And, the first time there's no one to interfere with *my* plans."

"Is that what Don did . . . interfered?"

"That, among other things." Maggie sighed loudly. "Don had his ideas about where our relationship was going, and they were very different from mine. Breaking up was the best thing that could have happened to us."

"Are you sure?" Pat asked.

Maggie reached across the table and patted her friend's hand. "Yes, the best thing that could have happened. We'll both be happier with other people."

"So you're going to Scotland. When do you leave?"

"Not until the middle of July. I'm joining a group tour that visits mostly historical sites. I'll spend a week in England and two weeks in Scotland." Picking up her lunch tray and carrying it over to the counter, Maggie laughed over her shoulder. "Maybe I'll pick up a Scottish accent by the time I get back."

"Knowing you, you'll pick up the accent the first day!" Pat followed Maggie into the hallway now filled with lively and loud students.

"I dinna ken what ye are blethering aboot," Maggie answered in an exaggerated Scottish brogue.

"You've been reading too many Scottish romance novels, my girl. And you do know what I mean. Just don't be too friendly with the natives over there."

"Aye, aye, ma'am."

After offering Pat a crisp mock salute and a mischievous wink, Maggie took her friend's arm and guided her into the crowded corridor. She decided to wait until she was ready to leave to give Pat all of the details of her trip. That delay would give Pat less time to worry about her and less time to harass her into changing her plans. *O, Scotland, bonnie Scotland, here I come,* she thought. But for the moment, she headed for her classroom.

"Excuse me? You're going *where?*" Nancy Hubbard asked, her voice barely below a scream.

Alex MacKendimen pivoted to face the irate woman whose questioning voice was a few decibels short of ear-piercing. He took one look at her turbulent expression and braced himself for the coming storm.

"This really shouldn't be news to you, Nancy. You've met my aunt Jean and heard her talk about her trip home."

Clenching her jaws, Nancy glared at him. "Well, I may have heard her discuss *her* trip, but I never realized that it included you!"

Alex crossed the room and placed his hands on Nancy's shoulders, unsuccessfully trying to draw her into an embrace. He decided not to fight her resistance and dropped his arms to his sides.

"Aunt Jean is the last of my father's family still alive here in the States. She asked me to take her to this festival. It's only held every five years, and she's worried that she won't be around for the next one. Please understand . . ." Alex reached for her again, but she backed away.

"I'm sorry, Alex, I don't understand. You have put me and our vacation off for too long. First it was your damn commitments at work and now this."

"Nancy, we can still go. I'll be back by the end of July, and I have plenty of time accumulated at work that I can use for us. Or . . ."

"Or what?" Nancy's voice and the frown on her face showed her suspicions.

"You could come with us." Alex waited for the explosion. Nancy enjoyed the finer things in life. Traipsing around the wilds of Scotland or attending the MacKendimen clan gathering in a town far away from any glamour that Scotland might offer in its larger cities did not fit her concept of a vacation.

"That is not an option," Nancy replied quietly. "I don't think this is going to work." She picked up her purse and faced him.

"It could work, if you'd join us." Even as the words left his mouth, Alex knew they weren't talking about the trip any longer.

Nancy fumbled in her purse and then threw something at him. He caught it one-handed and looked at it. He shook his head as the realization hit him: She was returning his house key.

"Nancy, wait . . ."

"Good-bye, Alex. I hope you and your aunt have a nice summer in Scotland." Nancy's voice grew loud and shrill as she stalked over to the stairs. "And don't bother to call me when you get back."

The pounding of her shoes on the bare steps and hallway echoed through the foyer as she made her way to one of the bedrooms. Alex walked over to the doorway and listened to her progress through the room, opening and closing drawers and doors. After a few minutes of rampaging through his upstairs rooms, Nancy stomped her way down the steps dragging a suitcase.

Pausing on the lower landing, she gifted him with her most furious scowl yet. Then, without another word, she yanked the door open, dragged the suitcase through it, and slammed it closed behind her.

His mind reeled. He watched through the window as Nancy hurried to her car, threw the luggage in, and climbed in after it. The roar of the engine and the squeal of the wheels as she pulled out of the driveway were loud enough to hear through the closed window.

How could she so misinterpret this trip? Why was she so angry? Of course he had commitments at work. She knew how close he was to securing the partnership and her part in it. Wait a minute . . . She had broken up with him? He breathed in deeply a few times, trying to clear his head.

He paused and waited for the anger or hurt to hit him in the gut. But, in a single moment of internal recognition, he only felt relief: deep, soul-lifting relief. She was gone, and his life was his own again, to run as he wanted. Alex strolled into the living room and dropped on the couch. Sliding down and pulling a designer pillow behind his back, he rested his feet on the glass cocktail table . . . something that would have driven Nancy crazy. He leaned his head back and looked around, smiling at the quiet.

It felt good.

Chapter 1

THE BUS PARALLELED the course of the Western Highlands Rail Line, hugging the curving coast and presenting extraordinary views of the rugged Highlands on one side and the deep chasms and valleys worn by rivers rushing toward the turbulent Atlantic Ocean on the other. Their next stop was Oban before turning inland and heading for Loch Lomond and then on to Glasgow.

"So, Maggie, what's been your favorite place so far?"

"Well, Mrs. Ludlam, I don't think I have just one favorite place. In England, I enjoyed York and the Jorvik Viking Center. So far, in Scotland, every castle we've visited has impressed me more than the last one." Her elderly roommate had the energy of someone forty years younger and kept pace with the busy itinerary without a problem.

"Didn't you like London?"

"Of course. The shops were fun." Maggie leaned closer to the woman sitting next to her on the motorcoach. "I may still have some pound notes in my purse for the rest of the trip." They laughed at her comment and both women turned their eyes back to the incomparable vistas spreading out around them.

The tour guide announced a rest stop and Maggie collected her things, stuffed them in her backpack, and left the bus. At the last moment, she grabbed her camera in the hopes of capturing just a few more spectacular photos. After using the privies, Maggie decided to walk a bit to stretch her legs before reboarding the bus. A gift shop across the narrow street caught her attention. A few minutes later, she was browsing through the aisles and looking at postcards. On the off chance that those pictures might be more appealing than her own photos, Maggie selected several to save as reference points of her journey.

Walking out into the scenic town, she checked her watch. Since there was still a half hour left on their break, Maggie strolled over to a viewing area that overlooked the verdant farmland surrounding the town. Looking down at the rolling countryside, memories already made came flooding back.

She'd been in Scotland for over a week and was halfway through her trip. Western and southern England still lay ahead, but Scotland was almost finished. She found the magic here that she had dreamed of all those years. Touching ancient walls, walking through historic castles and palaces, and visiting centuries-old battlegrounds sent shivers into her soul. She would never forget the colors of Scotland. Green fields and forests. Purple meadows of heather. Blue-misted mountains against a deep pink sky. Nothing would ever come close in comparison with the scenery of Scotland.

Maggie sighed deeply and looked around her. Mrs. Ludlam approached, waving to get her attention. Maggie stood and walked toward the friendly woman, another facet of her trip she would not soon forget.

''Maggie, it's time to leave.''

''Thank you for finding me. Although,'' she added a wink for emphasis, ''I don't think I'd mind being left behind.'' The older woman wrapped her arm around Maggie's and walked toward the waiting tour group.

''I agree,'' Mrs. Ludlam responded. ''After seeing some of the men here, even I wouldn't mind staying behind.''

They climbed aboard the bus, found their seats, and waited for the departure to Oban. *Three more days, just three more days,* Maggie thought. She planned to enjoy every minute she had left in this country of her dreams.

The next day, after the bus passed through Dalmally, rattling noises interrupted the usually tranquil ride. Stopping in the center of a small town, the travelers eavesdropped on a heated discussion between Ms. Buchanan, the extremely efficient tour guide, and Mr. MacTavish, the driver.

Then Ms. Buchanan's voice came over the speaker: ''I'm afraid there's a problem with the motorcoach that needs the attention of a professional repairman.'' After the groans of dismay died down, she continued. ''We're near a small village that is hosting a clan gathering, which you may enjoy while we''—her sharp glance landed on the driver—''take care of the problem. We will drop you off here at the edge of the gathering and we will pick you up''—again her eyes turned accusingly to Mr. MacTavish—''at half past six. I'll see to arrangements for this evening, and we'll make it to Glasgow almost on schedule. Thank you for your cooperation.'' The microphone clicked off, and the passengers started talking.

The chattering grew as the tourists gathered their belongings. Maggie sorted quickly through her bag and threw anything she might need for a long day of sightseeing into her backpack. Her carry-on bag would be secured with the other luggage until they reboarded the bus at the end of the day.

''Are you sure you need all of that?'' Mrs. Ludlam waved her hand at the growing pile on Maggie's lap.

Maggie scooped the various bottles, containers, and packages into her bag and zipped it up.

"Well, Mrs. L., ye niver ken when ye might need something ye dinna hiv." She laid the brogue on thick, and Mrs. Ludlam laughed.

"By the time we leave here, you'll be sounding just like the natives. Come to think of it, you do already!"

The day that looked so threatening a while before had turned into a glorious one. Sunshine poured from a near cloudless sky onto the fields surrounding the ruins of the old castle belonging to the Clan MacKendimen. The touring group was enjoying a clan gathering that was held every five years and drew family back from all parts of the world. As Maggie made her way through the tents and pavilions, she also heard that the "true but dispossessed" heir of the clan was here. Drawn by the scrumptious aromas of food and promises of a story yet to be told, she found a food counter nearby and purchased a hot meat pie and beverage. Glancing around the tent, she found a place filled with tables and benches and sat by a crowded one to try to find out more. She didn't wait long.

"Have ye seen him yet, Cora?"

"Nay, Alison, I've not. How aboot ye? Do ye know what he looks like?"

"Nay, only that he's from America and his name is Alex."

"Does he carry his faither's looks?"

"Aye, he does!" A new voice entered the conversation. "Tall and handsome with the MacKendimen blue eyes, too."

"Ye saw him, Rose? Did ye meet him as weel?"

Maggie watched as the young woman named Rose preened in the attention her boast had gained her.

"He was much more polite than I expected of a foreigner, ye ken? He took my hand, even kissed it, he did."

Rose held out her hand as though remnants of the kiss could be seen by all.

"Sounds as though he haes his faither's charm as well."

A dreamy sigh followed that comment, but Maggie shifted on her bench. *Charming.* A shiver, like icy fingers, skimmed up her spine. That's how everyone described Don. That's how *she* described Don before she knew his charm was just a diversion to keep you from seeing the real manipulator underneath.

The mouthful of rich, well-seasoned meat pie that moments ago stirred up her appetite now turned dry as dust in her mouth. She forced the food down in a convulsive swallow. Don followed her even to Scotland. She shook her head, clearing the negative memories. He would not ruin *this* vacation. Maggie focused back on the lively conversation still going on at the next table.

"Weel, let's look aboot. He carries the clan sword, which should be hard to miss, even in this crowd."

The women stood, and Rose obligingly pointed in the direction where she had last seen the "heir o' the clan." They separated and headed off in different directions on a mission to seek out the rightful laird. *This could be interesting, after all,* Maggie thought. A clan festival and the makings of a scandal. The Scots loved a good scandal. She made a mental note to try to see this pretender to the clan's seat sometime during this day. Her attention turned to the cheering crowds close by, and Maggie finished her pie and followed the shouts to the next clearing where huge men tossed even bigger cabers through the air like they were twigs. She found a place to sit and enjoyed watching the muscle-bound men throwing telephone pole–length trees. Their physiques were amazing, from their arms and shoulders all the way down to their . . . feet!

"You make a fine Scotsman, Alex. Your father would be proud."

"Would he, Aunt Jean?" Guileless blue eyes turned up

to look at him as Alex MacKendimen waited for her answer.

"Your father chose to leave his clan and heritage behind him when he came to America. That's no reason for you to ignore your family background, lad." Her words carried a hint of bitterness.

He knew his father's reasons for leaving. Better opportunities awaited in America for him. His father was willing to give up all he held dear to move to the land of opportunity. His future family deserved a chance for the good life in the United States.

Unlike Aunt Jean, who held onto her heritage, Gordon MacKendimen left it all behind. He refused to speak Gaelic or wear the clan colors. He refused to return to his homeland. Then his death made a return impossible. Aunt Jean didn't understand these things, but Alex did. His own success in life, bought by his father's separation from all he knew, was the only thing important in his life. Alex being made the youngest partner in his firm would have made his father proud and that meant more to Alex than anything he might have missed in his pursuit of success. More than anything.

He had jeopardized his career once, when Nancy's father found out about their breakup. In spite of her insistence that it had been her idea to end their engagement, her father, a senior partner in the firm, seemed reluctant to consider Alex's bid for a partnership position after the split. Many months of "kissing up" and getting back in good graces had put him in line for the next opening. It would finally be his—providing he made an attempt to reconcile with Nancy. Not too big a price to pay for finally fulfilling his father's dream.

Alex shrugged and looked at the traditional Scottish costume he wore and the clan sword he carried in a scabbard on the heavy leather belt. Aunt Jean made sure one and all knew of his relationship to the present laird. Actually, his uncle Calum had taken Aunt Jean's announcement of the presence of the real heir to the clan pretty well. Of course, that was after he stopped choking and coughing on the whiskey he had sipped just as Aunt Jean spoke. And, after half the people in the room had slapped him on the back to clear his throat. And . . . well, maybe he had not taken it so well, after all.

Alex strolled through the festival grounds with Aunt Jean, smiling at all who greeted him. Thank God for his corporate schmoozing experience—he'd have been lost in this situation without it. He now knew how beauty pageant contestants must feel: always on, always smiling and gracious. He relaxed his facial muscles and pulled his aunt to a stop beneath some shady trees.

"You enjoyed seeing Uncle Calum suffer, didn't you?"

"Me? Your poor, defenseless Aunt Jean?" His sixty-years-young aunt had the nerve to bat her eyelashes at him like a teenager.

"Ha! He never stood a chance against you, and you know it! He and Dad teased you unmercifully when you were young, didn't they? So, this is your revenge?"

Aunt Jean gasped loudly at his assessment of the sibling relationship. "How did you know?"

"You weren't the only one who told stories about the good old days."

"Your father?" Her voice lowered to a whisper.

"Yes, Dad told me how much of a trial you were to your older brothers from the day you were born. Now, I'm your target."

"Not my target, Alex," She looked horrified at the thought. "I just wanted you to see the real Scotland and the rest"—she gestured at the people attending the gathering—"the rest of your family, before it's too late."

"Too late? Don't give me that 'I'm not going to live much longer' routine. You'll probably outlive all of us."

Alex leaned down to her and touched his lips to her cheek. They began walking again. "Well, who else do you want to show me off to?" He joined his favorite relative in some hearty laughter as they explored the clan festivities, his cell phone packed securely in his sporran. Only in Scotland, he thought, could men wear skirts and pocketbooks and get away with it.

"Come in, lass. Come inside and sit for a wee bit."

For some reason, Maggie did just as the old woman asked. Usually cautious about strangers, she surprised herself by feeling so comfortable here at this fair. She even traded her street clothes at one of the tents that rented authentic costumes for the gathering participants. What would Pat have to say about this?

Now, dressed in the garb of a medieval peasant—plain woven skirt, matching bodice and a linen chemise underneath, with only her modern backpack out of sync—she accepted the stranger's invitation. As she entered the small tent, the hubbub behind her faded and a quiet calmness surrounded her.

The old woman was wearing a shawl of the blue, red, white, and deep green plaid the MacKendimens now called their own. The gray hair pulled into a bun at the nape of her neck and the wrinkled skin on her face, neck, and hands showed her many years. The twinkling, deep-set blue eyes bespoke of wisdom and kindness.

"I am said to hiv two sights, lass. And my second sight tells me yer here to meet yer destiny."

"Second sight?" Maggie asked, raising an eyebrow. She ignored the unexpected tingle that shot through her at the woman's words.

"No need to be afraid, lass. I dinna see that yer's is a bad future. Nay. I see one filled wi' good fortune and love."

"Don't you have to read my palm or something?" Maggie held out her hand, but the woman shook her head.

"I've waited for ye, lass. I dreamed of ye and yer tie to the clan MacKendimen."

Curiosity overcoming her natural caution, Maggie crossed to the table and dropped onto the small bench. "Who are you?"

"My name is Mairi."

"Well, Mairi, I hate to disappoint you, but I have no connection to this clan." Maggie shook her head for emphasis. Mairi only nodded serenely, looking as if she'd chosen to ignore Maggie's words. "Maybe you were dreaming about someone who looked like me," Maggie finally suggested when the woman made no further response.

"Nay, yer the right one." Mairi took a deep breath and let it out slowly. Maggie held her own breath, waiting. "Ye teach the wee ones and ye've been sent to teach one of our own."

Maggie's lungs refused to obey her command to breathe. How did this woman know she was a teacher? She had not mentioned her profession to anyone at this gathering. And who was she supposed to teach in Scotland? She tried to laugh to show her disbelief, but the laughter died in her throat when her eyes met Mairi's intense, enigmatic gaze.

"Relax, lass. Breathe nice and slowly." Mairi took Maggie's hand in hers and massaged her palm with a soft, almost hypnotic stroke. "Ye hiv nothing to fear from me." Another shiver crept along Maggie's spine.

"What do you want from me?" Maggie looked around at the tent, and everything appeared hazy. A buzzing sound invaded the quiet of the tent, and Maggie cocked her head, trying to locate the source of it. She realized the sound came from inside her head, and she shook it, trying to clear her vision and her hearing.

"Nothing, lass. I ask nothing of ye except that ye be ready to teach a MacKendimen when the time comes." Mairi rose from her seat and, firmly but gently, led Maggie to the opening of her tent. As Maggie stepped over the threshold of the enclosure, Mairi continued to speak.

''A MacKendimen needs to learn about the power of true love, Maggie, and yer to be his teacher.''

Maggie, surprised that the woman knew her name, tripped over the canvas lip of the tent and stumbled forward. She turned back to ask a question, but the tent was empty.

Completely empty.

Chapter 2

ALEX FIRST NOTICED the ruins while he escorted Aunt Jean through the festival. They caught his eye again later when he was going to the food tents for some lunch. And now, he felt their pull even more strongly as he walked toward the field where the contests of strength were held. Alex decided that now was as good a time as any to explore the oldest part of the MacKendimen property.

Tugging on the kilt as he walked, Alex also rearranged the sporran and thick leather belt around his waist. He could never get used to wearing one of these . . . plaids. He kept it on only for Aunt Jean and the look of love and longing on her face when he entered the room wearing it. When she saw him, her eyes filled with tears and she whispered his father's name. The family resemblance was strong, he knew, but the emotion on her face and in her voice made it seem more real to him.

Pride swelled in his soul when his uncle handed him the clan sword to complete his dress. Uncle Calum told him, as he hooked the heavy belt and scabbard around his waist, that this sword was presented to the laird of the Clan MacKendimen by none other than the Bruce himself.

Nevertheless, the damn thing was heavy and cumbersome to someone unused to carrying its weight and length. Alex readjusted it for the umpteenth time and squinted into the bright afternoon as he walked steadily toward the ruins. He could gain some privacy there and call the office on the cell phone. *Thank God for modern conveniences,* he thought as he picked his way over the rocky path.

Maggie wended her way carefully through the tumbled and crumbled stones strewn across the field. These ruins were much older than the present castle, which was built in the 1600s. Several decaying archways stood in silent watch over their surroundings, but most lay in broken sections on the ground. Bits and pieces of a clan legend were talked about by the attendees at the festival, but Maggie didn't know the whole story.

She approached one of the structures, closed her eyes, and placed her palm on the stones. The urge to actually touch history had grown in her as she toured England and Scotland. Every time Maggie entered a building or walked through a hallway, she felt this compulsion to absorb the history of the place, using all of her senses, especially touch. These ruins drew her to them like metal filings to a magnet.

Maggie suddenly jumped, literally shocked, as a jolt traveled up her arms and through her body. It reminded her of an electric pulse, but there were no power lines here. She moved her hand to a different place on the arch, and still the unseen power surged. She stepped away from the arch and held her hand above her eyes to shade them from the sun so she could see the whole structure. Looking at the other arches, she realized that this was the only one still intact. Well, the frame was intact, but the stones and mortar inside its curve were gone, all but a short pile that formed a wall.

Maggie sat back down and kept her hand in contact with the arch. The sensation, warm and tingling, was almost pleasant, once she got used to it. Almost as pleasant as watching the approaching Scot.

Maggie slowly got to her feet as she realized the Scot was heading directly toward her.

"Hello," he said as he came closer, "and which of my lovely Scottish cousins are you?"

He stepped nearer and caught her hand, pressing it to his lips in a gallant gesture redolent of Old World charm. When she noticed his full clan dress but that no Scottish brogue enhanced his deep voice, she knew this must be the man so many spoke of at the festival. The "heir." Her gaze moved from his well-muscled thighs below the kilt up to his face and then his eyes. Ah, this must be the color they called "MacKendimen blue." How charming, she thought, feeling herself respond almost unconsciously to the warmth of his rakish smile and the appreciative glint in his eye.

Horrified at her response, she jerked her hand from his as memories of Don's empty charm rushed through her mind. "I'm afraid you're mistaken. I am not one of your 'lovely Scottish cousins,' as you put it." Maggie rubbed her hand on her skirt, anxious to remove the feel of his mouth from it. The last thing she needed or would allow was another charmer in her life.

"You don't sound Scottish." He sounded confused as he pointed out the obvious to her. His forehead creased and he tilted his head to one side, studying her closely as though he found her intriguing. His voice was deep and purely masculine. She tried to ignore the almost instant physical reaction she was having to him.

"Neither do you." Maggie realized her voice bordered on offensive. "I mean, I don't because I'm not—Scottish, that is.'' She forced a neutral tone into her words. He had not really done anything but remind her momentarily—and painfully—of Don. She told herself to be more pleasant, since it wasn't his fault that he raised difficult memories. Determined to make up for her rudeness, she offered him a tentative smile.

He took a step back from her and held out his hand in a more recognizable gesture. She hesitated for a moment and then shook it—American-style.

''I am Scottish but, as you can tell, I'm not from here. I'm Alex MacKendimen, from the States.''

''That answers my question of the day.''

''What question?''

''What the real heir of the clan looks like. It's the topic of the gathering.''

He blushed. She didn't remember seeing a man blush before, but it looked so darn attractive, she hoped to see it again. The blush made his blue eyes look a shade lighter than they were. Ruggedly handsome features stood out on his tanned face. He wore his hair, a shade of dark auburn with red highlights that flashed in the strong sunlight, in a conservative cut above his ears and short all around. And the blush spread to the tips of his ears.

''I'm sorry,'' she said, ''I didn't mean to embarrass you.''

''I really don't like being the center of conversation. But it's not your fault at all.''

''Then whose is it?''

''Well, mine, I guess. I brought my aunt here for this reunion without knowing all the details.''

''Details such as you're the lost heir of the clan?''

''No, not lost. They knew where I was all along.''

She let herself join his laughter at his words, and Maggie realized she hadn't introduced herself.

''I'm Maggie Hobbs,'' she smiled as she said it, ''also from the States.''

"Nice to meet you, Maggie. From where in the States?"

"New Jersey."

"New Jersey? Really?"

"Yes, the good old Garden State."

"I don't believe it! Me too!"

"Really?" she asked, "Where?"

"I live in Haddonfield."

Maggie sat back down on the wall. "I live in Winslow. Can you believe it? We're almost neighbors and have to travel more than a thousand miles to meet." She shook her head at the irony of coming all the way to Scotland and meeting someone who lived close by.

"How did you turn up here?" Alex asked.

"I'm a teacher, and this is the first summer *I'm* not going to school. So, I came here for the history. And," she added in a low, conspiring tone, "I've wanted to visit here ever since I read my first Scottish romance novel. And you?"

"As I mentioned, I brought my aunt Jean back to attend the gathering. You know, she played on my sympathies to come with her, but I think she had this 'rightful heir' thing planned all along."

"Are you?" Maggie raised her eyebrows in question.

"The rightful heir?" At her nod, he continued, "Apparently. My father was the eldest son and would have inherited. But he refused his inheritance and moved to the States in search of the woman of his dreams."

"That sounds romantic. Did he find her?"

"Yes, he did. He married my mother a year after arriving. Anyway, I guess if he had stayed, I would be the heir of the clan. But . . ."

"Does the real, I mean, the proclaimed heir know that you're not going to challenge him?"

"I think Uncle Calum realizes I'm no threat to him. I am here to enjoy the gathering and meet the clan. But I am definitely not enjoying the dress.'' He must have noticed her gaping at his legs again. How embarassing!

''Dress?'' she asked, forcing her eyes back up to his face. ''Don't you call it a plaid?''

''They can call it anything they want to, but I call it too short and too damned drafty.'' He twisted the kilt at his waist and resettled his belt. He turned away from her and adjusted the long scabbard that hung from his belt and contained a sword. After another moment, he shifted again and pulled the sword from its cover. Alex placed it point down along his leg, resting it on his boot and holding onto its jewel-encrusted hilt. Then he sat on the wall next to her. ''So, how long are you going to be here in Scotland?''

Maggie pushed her hair over her shoulders and sighed. ''I'm nearly done. I have three more days in the Trossachs and Glasgow, four days in England, and then home. How about you?''

''We leave here at the end of the week and are spending a few days in Inverness. After that Edinburgh, and then home. By the way, do you have plans for dinner?'' He extended the invitation without a moment's hesitation.

''Well, actually I do. My tour bus will pick me up, and I'll have dinner with the group.'' Not wanting to be rude and realizing that they would both be going back to the same area in New Jersey, she added, ''Maybe we could get together when we're back home?''

''That sounds great. I just wish we had more time here.'' Sincere regret filled his voice. She heard it, *felt it,* and found herself hoping for the first time in their conversation that they would see each other again.

''Time?'' A scratchy voice interrupted their conversation. Maggie never saw or heard Mairi's approach. Now, she stood directly in front of them, so close that they couldn't get up from the wall. Maggie felt the vibrations under and around her grow stronger. A buzzing sound, like a swarm of bees attacking a hive's enemy, surrounded them.

"Mairi, you startled me." Looking at Alex, she said, "Do you feel that?" She placed his hand under hers on the stones between their bodies. Even the stone wall beneath them carried the vibrations now.

"Feel what?" He frowned, obviously not feeling or hearing what she could.

"That pulsing and heat coming from the stones."

"I don't feel anything, Maggie." Alex looked back at Mairi. "Who are you?"

Before the old woman answered him, she placed one hand on both of them, on their shoulders.

"Time? Ye can have all the time ye need, lad. Remember, time will prove if a love be true."

Then, with a force completely at odds with the frailty of her figure, Mairi pushed them backward, through the arch.

Chapter 3

I'M BLIND! BLINKING against the complete darkness and fighting against the terror overwhelming her, Maggie's chest tightened. Unable to breathe, she reached up to rub her eyes, but her hands refused her mind's command to move. *Oh, God, blind and paralyzed. But how?* A few . . . moments? minutes? hours? ago, she was sitting on that wall, talking to Alex. And now? Had she fallen and hit her head and done this to herself?

Just before utter and uncontrollable panic took over, she heard a voice: Mairi, the old fortune-teller from the festival. She struggled to call out to the woman, but her voice also failed her. She must have really banged her head hard because her hearing wasn't working well, either. Mairi's words weren't clear at all. She seemed to be mumbling about time. Time would prove . . . Time would prove what? A blinding flash of light roared through her darkness, and she could move once again.

''If love be true.'' Alex repeated aloud the words he just heard in that all-encompassing darkness. Finally able to move, he shielded his eyes against the brightness. Squinting, he raised his head and saw that he and Maggie were lying in a field. Scrambling to his feet, he reached down to help her stand.

"Are ye weel?"

"What did you say?" she asked. Her voice trembled as she accepted his help to stand.

"I said, 'Are ye weel?' "

He watched as her face scrunched up in an expression of complete confusion. Well, he wasn't feeling quite clear about this, either.

"Why are you talking like that?" she asked.

"Speaking how? I dinna ken yer meaning."

Her mouth hung open now, gaping in . . . surprise? Shock? What was her problem now? First, she seemed offended by his greeting when they first met and now . . . *what?*

"What is the problem?" he asked as he straightened, yet again, the damned plaid at his waist.

"Was it just an act? A line to pick up women?"

"A line? What are ye blabbering aboot?" He scratched his head. Obviously, their fall backward must have shaken them both. Maggie was making no sense at all.

"The one about being the missing heir of the clan? You are obviously Scottish, from *here* not *America*. I mean, you have such a strong brogue that I can hardly understand you!" She took a few steps away from him and crossed her arms over her chest, chin out in challenge.

"Are ye daft, woman? I told you, I am from New Jersey, just as ye are." He crossed his arms in a matching gesture.

"Look, no one I know in any part of New Jersey sounds like you do. If this is a game—try out an American accent and meet women—well, you can play by yourself." She grabbed her backpack off the ground, flung it over her left shoulder, and turned away from him.

That's when he noticed.

It was at that moment he realized that everything was gone. The ruins, the tents from the festival, and all of the people. The only sounds in the air were the singing of some birds and rustling of the wind through the branches of the nearby trees. He spun around, looking up, down, through the trees, and off in the distance where the meadow seemed to end. Nothing. They were alone.

Maggie apparently noticed it at the same time because, as she turned back to him, all of the color drained from her face and she swayed slightly. Alex grabbed for her and helped her to sit down in the grass; then he joined her on the ground.

"I don't think I understand what's going on here, Alex."

"Well, I amna sure I ken anything more than ye do, but let's try to figure out what's going on."

Maggie reached into her backpack and pulled out a small bottle of water. After taking a swallow of it, she offered it to him. "Are you really from here? Is your accent real?" she whispered as he took the bottle from her grasp.

"Please believe me, Maggie. If ye are saying that I hae a brogue, I dinna understaun. I canna hear it. I am hearing my words in the English I hae always spoken."

"Alex, you now have an accent as thick as the seer woman at the festival. You really can't hear it?"

"Nay, Maggie. 'Tis clearly English to me," he pointed to his ear and head with his free hand, "in here. I swear to ye—'tis no line to pick up women. What seer woman do ye mean?"

"Mairi, from the festival. She said she has the sight."

"The old woman who was wi' us in the ruins?"

Maggie just shook her head and looked around at the empty field. "Where is she? Where is . . . everything?"

After he took a swig from the bottle and handed it back to her, tapping her on the shoulder with the bottle to gain her attention, he said, "We should probably move closer to the woods. We're out in the open here, and I dinna hae any idea of what's going on. Let's get under some cover and then we can talk. Can ye walk over to those trees?''

At her nod, he helped Maggie back to her feet. His legs still felt wobbly, and his head was still spinning slightly. After standing for a few moments, he guided her to the edge of the field where the woods began. They used some large boulders as seats as they both surveyed the area.

''So, what's the last thing you remember?'' she asked. The color was finally returning to her cheeks and she didn't look ready to faint anymore. Thank God. He was a wimp when it came to crying or fainting women.

'' 'Tis as I said before, I remember talking to that old woman while we were sitting on the wall. She was rambling on aboot something.'' He rubbed his forehead with the back of his hand and tried to clear his memory. ''Time. She was saying something aboot the power of time. Does that make any sense to ye?''

''I remember sitting and talking to you. And I remember Mairi, too. Did she put her hand on your shoulder? I can kind of see her resting her hand on my shoulder . . . and pushing me backward? This doesn't make any sense at all.'' Maggie shook her head in confusion.

''She did push me backward!'' Alex jumped up and started to pace. He always felt better if he could pace. ''I remember losing my balance and grabbing for the sword to steady myself. The sword . . . Hae ye seen it?'' With a hand on his forehead to shield his eyes, he scanned the field where they had been, looking for the laird's sword. The sunlight would reflect off the polished metal, making it easy to spot. ''I dinna see it.''

Alex ran out onto the field and looked for the claymore.

''I flung it back o'er my head as I fell,'' he called out to Maggie as he walked quickly back to her. ''I can remember thinking that I hoped no one was close by as I released my grip on it.'' He touched the empty scabbard on his belt.

''Okay,'' Maggie started, ''we were sitting on the wall, Mairi pushed us backward, and we fell, landing where?''

''I dinna hae any idea where. What do ye remember aboot the fall? Did ye hear or feel anything?'' Alex probed, trying to come up with some plausible explanation of what had happened.

''I thought that I was blind—the darkness was that complete. I tried to move, and I couldn't. Breathing was even difficult, but that might have been because I was terrified.'' She shivered and blushed a little at her admission. ''I tried to scream, but nothing came out. I heard Mairi, but her words weren't clear. Something like 'Time will prove.' How does that compare with your experience?''

''Ye hae pretty much described what I went through, too,'' Alex agreed. ''And I heard, 'If love be true.' Now what can 'Time will prove if love be true' mean? 'Tis nonsense to me, how aboot ye?''

''It sounds like a proverb or old saying. Well, any suggestions about what we do now?'' Maggie asked, still eyeing him suspiciously. He wished he could hear the accent she was hearing. Maybe then he could understand her misgivings.

''I guess, if ye are feeling up to it, we could try finding someone. Head in a direction and look for signs of civilization?''

''Sounds fine to me,'' Maggie said. ''Maybe we can find someone who can explain what's going on and how we got to wherever this is.''

Alex grabbed her hand and then paused to look at the sun. '' 'Tis the east. Let's head in that direction for a bit and see where it leads us.''

Maggie took advantage of Alex's leading to try to collect her very scrambled thoughts. She knew that Mairi had said some strange things to her both during her ''reading'' and before they fell off the wall. She smiled to herself and hoped Alex didn't see it. This strange situation was no laughing matter, but *falling off the wall* just struck her in a funny way. What had happened to them? And, more importantly, what about him? Was he telling the truth about being from America? The accent sounded as authentic as any she'd head on her tour. None of this made sense.

Well, until they met up with people, she'd have no way of even guessing where they were and how they got there. But, at least, she wasn't alone. Although they had just met and she'd not liked some of his mannerisms, she felt very comfortable with Alex. Even holding his hand while they walked felt somehow familiar and reassuring. She realized that they were slowing, and she looked around.

"Why are we stopping? We couldn't have walked more than a half mile."

"Maggie, sshhhh. Dinna ye hear it?" Alex whispered.

At first, the only sound she could hear was their breathing. That's when she noticed that the birds had stopped singing around them. She tilted her head back slightly and listened intently. Rumbles of thunder came from off in the distance, growing louder and closer.

"Thunder? A storm is coming this way?"

"No, Maggie, 'tis no' a storm. It sounds like a stampeding herd."

Maggie swallowed convulsively, her throat beginning to tighten as the fear built in her blood. "A stampede? But where is it coming from?"

Vibrations swelled and pulsed in the ground under her feet and her heart pounded to the same beat. She and Alex both turned to try to get a bearing on the direction of the sound when a flock of birds scattered into the air, frightened from the trees in the distance, off to their left.

The tension and terror and thunder in the air made it impossible for her to make her feet move. She looked over at Alex and watched as he tried to draw his missing sword against whatever was coming at them. The sounds grew louder and more terrifying until she fought to release the screams trapped inside of her. And then she could see, rampaging toward them, unbelievable images straight out of Scotland's past. The far past!

Chapter 4

NOTHING THAT SHE'D ever read or seen could have prepared Maggie for what she saw now. Coming through the trees, racing toward them were huge, hairy, dirty warriors on huge, menacing, snorting horses. Enormous swords and knives were drawn, gleaming dangerously in the bright afternoon sun. The line of horses stopped for an instant after breaking through the trees, and then ominously moved forward until Maggie could feel the hot, moist breath of the horses on her face. In no way did they resemble the romantic images she'd produced in her mind when reading about the ancient and daring Scots.

Maggie stood as still as stone, not even daring to take too deep a breath. Using their legs to exert control on the horses, the entire group of men sat, weapons ready, while they examined the two outsiders. The expressions on their faces remained unchanged while they completely perused Maggie and Alex from head to toe and then back again.

Alex finally broke the stalemate with a question. At least it sounded like a question. Maggie turned quickly, surprised at the unfamiliar language that came out of Alex's mouth. Now, in addition to the deeper, fuller, brogue, he was speaking in a different language!

Unfortunately, in her surprise, she turned too quickly and the gigantic black stallion in front of her nudged her shoulder in response. She lost her balance and ended up sprawled in the dirt with her skirts up around her thighs. Without moving from their stonelike poses, the warriors leered at her exposed legs and snickered.

Alex didn't look over at her. He continued staring at the man who seemed to be the leader of the group. Alex stood straighter, looked more menacing than before, and, with even angrier words, made another demand to the men's leader.

The large, red-haired ruffian yelled out again, jumped off his mount, and swaggered over to Alex, placing his large dirk back into its scabbard as he walked. She still couldn't understand the words as he grabbed Alex by the shoulders and turned him back and forth, as if trying to get a closer look at his features.

"Brodie," the man said and then continued again in what she was pretty sure now was Gaelic. Finally, a word she understood: a name. Alex choked out a response, definitely not a good sign. Her stomach tightened and her discomfort grew. Why didn't Alex speak in English? Why did he continue to carry on this conversation with these . . . men?

Unless.

Unless he was part of whatever was going on? Damn him! He swore he didn't know any more than she did. What was she supposed to believe now? What *was* going on?

The leader of the group had paused in the conversation and spit in the dirt as though the talk had turned distasteful. She watched, still frozen on the ground, truly fearful to move, as Alex pulled free of the big man's hold. Striding over to Maggie, he offered her a hand. In one smooth motion, he pulled her up to stand next to him. She brushed the dirt off her skirt and straightened her blouse and bodice.

Alex ran both hands through his hair and looked thoroughly confused. She turned to him and whispered, "Alex, tell me what is going on. I thought you said you weren't part of this."

"Give me a moment more, Maggie. Even I am trying to figure this out."

Maggie was no longer willing to wait while men made decisions for her, so she called to the men in front of her.

"Who are you men, and why have you stopped us?"

Although he seemed to be completely ignoring her, Brodie squinted at Alex and then at her before responding. Her words were greeted by the others first with silence, and then whispered words that drifted through the still air to her.

Sassenach . . . Sassenach whore.

Sassenach? They thought she was English. But, *whore?*

"And, who is *this*?" His words were in a heavily accented English as he grabbed Maggie's arm and turned her around. His eyes roamed her body, stopping at her breasts, her hips, and her thighs. The gleam in his eyes and the way he licked his lips told Maggie that this man thought he knew *what* she was.

"You havna gone and promised anything to this wench, hiv ye?"

Much to Maggie's dismay, she wasn't sure if she liked knowing what was being said, after all. She watched as Alex's face flushed red.

"Nay, I havna promised her anything but that she could come wi' me."

How could he so effortlessly pretend the warm tones that his voice now carried? How could he suddenly be speaking in this mix of Scots English and . . . Gaelic? And, damn it, what was this all about?

"Weel," Brodie said with a husky laugh, "Anice will

be pleased to hear that.'' The rest of the men joined him in a hearty laugh. Brodie dropped her arm and walked over to Alex and roughly put his arm around Alex's shoulder. Leaning over close to Alex's ear and whispering loud enough for anyone within miles to hear, Brodie stared at Maggie as he continued, ''Yer betrothed might no' be verra understanding about ye bringing' yer leman from England, though.''

Maggie stared in shock as Brodie smacked Alex on the back in a blatant display of masculine approval and Alex hesitantly joined in with the laughter. These men were barbarians, that much was clear. But what was Alex's part in this?

Aggravated beyond control and probably past good judgment, Maggie walked away from the men and over to the pile of belongings she had dropped in panic only minutes ago. She picked up her bag and searched through it, making sure nothing was missing. She walked over to a nearby rock to sit and try to figure out what was happening.

This was getting stranger and stranger by the minute. Wait a minute—maybe this was one of those reenactment groups? That would make sense. Was Alex part of this, had he brought her in as part of their game? Or was he telling the truth when he said he was as foreign to this as she was? He had sounded sincere when he'd told her he didn't understand any of this. He kept giving her pleading glances over his shoulder from where he stood with the other men. Pleading for what? Her silence? For her to play along?

Maggie grabbed a length of ribbon from her bag and quickly pulled her wild hair into a ponytail. Then she realized it was too quiet. Looking over toward the horses, she saw that the men had all dismounted and were standing around Alex, but they were staring at her. Quickly, she tied her backpack and threw it over her shoulder. Then she met the louts' stares with one of her own—one perfected by years of practice as an elementary schoolteacher . . . and the most glaring look she could muster.

The man called Brodie loudly cleared his throat, getting the group's attention. "If Anice willna let ye keep her, I'll take her off yer hands, Alex. I like a woman wi' a little fire in her eyes." And then, the rest of the men laughed at his comment like a band of hyenas. Turning their back to her, they continued talking and laughing with Alex.

Leman? Brodie had called her a whore, that's what a leman was after all. Is that what they thought her part was? She should play Alex's mistress? She now had several things to straighten out with Alex as soon as she got him alone!

Her chance with Alex came a few minutes later when some of the group left. Alex approached her as she was searching through her bag.

"Maggie?" His voice, whisper soft, was almost without the new accent.

"What do you want?"

"Some of the men are riding ahead to tell the laird of our arrival. I think we'd better talk."

"The laird? Who would that be?" He opened his mouth to answer, but she interrupted first. "He called me your whore. Did you at least tell him that I will not even playact that role for any man?" Leman or whore, it wasn't nice to be called by either name, but she knew that the names were not quite the personal insult in times past as they were in her own time. This must be a game; there could not be any other explanation. Could there?

"No, I didna tell them. The laird is waiting for us in his castle. Apparently, I am the spitting image of the laird's son, whose name also happens to be Alesander. And, just as apparent to them, the laird's son is engaged to someone named Anice. The men jumped to their own conclusions aboot yer role in this."

"So, this is a reenactment group? You told me you didn't know what was going on."

"A reenactment group? What are ye speaking of now? I tell ye yet again that I amna part of this! I hae no' met these men before and don't know what they are speaking of, either." He dragged his hands through his hair again, shaking his head. For a moment, she saw a glimmer of vulnerability in his eyes, making her doubt her assessment of this situation and him.

Maggie knew that the complete craziness of this whole situation was getting to her. She shook her head in disbelief at this turn of events. From the look of things, and people, they were in a different time in history. If they were acting, they were good; these men didn't break character at all. They even smelled like warriors who spent too much time with horses and not enough time with soap and water. But she wasn't ready yet to accept any other possibility. After all, how else could this be explained?

"Alex, are you, are we, part of a reenactment here?"

"Maggie, I swear to ye, agin, I amna part of anything. 'Tis as I told ye when we met at the ruins, I came here for my clan's gathering. I hae never met any of these men afore this moment."

"And never spoken Gaelic, either?" She watched for his reaction.

"Nay, never that, either." God, he sounded sincere again. His eyes darkened as he stared at her, waiting for her reaction—her belief or disbelief. "I dinna hiv the Gaelic before I came here. I dinna know it was going to come out until I opened my mouth."

He took her hand and pulled her closer. "We are in this together, ye and me. I dinna want to say what I think haes happened to us or you will give me e'en stranger glances than the ones ye give me now."

"Tell me. Tell me what you think is going on here, because I am completely lost."

"I think ye should be asking me *when* is this happening."

"When? *When?* We already know the date. It's July 30, 1998."

"Do ye really think so, Maggie? Take a closer look around ye and at those men. They are no' players in a game. I fear they are real."

"Real? But that would mean . . ." Her hands started shaking and she couldn't take a breath. Oh God, she couldn't panic now. "Are you lying to me, Alex? Please, tell me the truth."

"There's no' a lot aboot this whole situation that I do understaun. All I ken is that we're hundreds of years in the past—I dinna ken when exactly." He put his arm around her shoulders and held her tightly. She didn't resist. She needed to be in his arms, she felt safer in his arms.

Before she could say any more, Alex continued, "But we should probably play along until we find out the truth of the matter. Let's get our story straight now. They believe, or hae given me the opening to be the laird's son returned from England. Evidently he's been there for the last several years, so no one here haes seen him for a while." He paused and took a deep breath and let it out. "Maggie, until we can figure this out, I think we need to play along and keep up the pretense of ye being my leman. The truth will come out soon enough."

Shocked into silence, Maggie's mouth dropped open. Of all of the suggestions she thought Alex would make, this never entered her mind.

"Come on, think! I am afraid they are no' playing here. I think we may be in a verra dangerous situation . . . for real." He whispered harshly as he shook her by the shoulders. "If this *is* real, then they maun believe ye are my mistress so that none of the men will try to harm ye. Ye be under my protection. And this Anice willna even want to acknowledge yer presence here. 'Tis the safest way for us, for ye, until we can find out where and when this is."

"I must be crazier than you because I think . . ." she paused before uttering the words even she thought were outrageous, "you may be right. So, how do we explain how we met? How did our relationship happen? How did we get here?" She must be under stress—she was whining, she could hear it in her own voice. There were so many questions they still had no answers for.

"We can tell them that we met when I stayed wi' the king, 'tho which king, I dinna ken; it was in England and ye sound English. I was sick before I started for home and ye accompanied me. We were ambushed a few days ago and our horses and bags were stolen by the bandits. How does that sound to ye?"

Maggie stared into his clear blue eyes, completely amazed. The story was good. If this was a reenactment, the story would fit right in. And if it wasn't one, well, it might even work. Alex's voice took on more and more of a Scottish brogue and he seemed to be getting into the roles they were to play. Since medieval studies were part of her education, she knew he was right. As a leman to a laird's son, she was an unperson. If this was really happening, she'd have a good deal of freedom and could look for clues about what had happened to them. She wouldn't be his mistress, she'd just play at it. And, if it was an act, she . . . they would know soon enough.

Maggie grinned recklessly. In for penny, in for pound was what her grandmother would say. Playing it to the hilt, she tossed her long ponytail back over her shoulder and adjusted her bodice and breasts in a provocative move that caught the attention of all of the men still nearby.

"Well, sir, I think you're right about this leman thing," she whispered, in a low, husky voice. "You now have a mistress. Do with me what you will."

To add authenticity to the scene, she threw herself against him and pulled his face down to hers. With her mouth open, she gave him a kiss that left them both breathless and left their observers cheering. They parted, and Alex turned toward the warriors now mounting their horses. Before she could move away, Alex grabbed her by the wrist and pulled her up against his body. As she started to squirm, she felt his rock-hard arousal between them. He locked his arms around her waist.

"Two can play at this game, ye ken. 'Twill be like Richard Gere in that movie, having a woman at my beck and call." He wrapped her hair around his fist several times and forced her face to his. Mimicking the hot kiss she had given him, he molded her curves to his hardness. Their tongues touched and tasted until she heard them both moan. Her hands crept up his back and grabbed at the plaid tossed over his shoulder. Maggie stopped breathing. Unanticipated fire pulsed through her body. The heat inside expanded until she found herself lost in the unexpected passion and power of his kiss.

When the raucous shouts and cheers finally broke through the barrier made of their increasing desire, Alex released her abruptly. Trembling, she turned away and tried to put some distance between them. Laughing, he swatted her on her backside as she walked away.

"Remember, you're at my beck and call, wench!" The men clapped him on the back as he reached the group and made some remarks in Gaelic that were recognizable in any language.

She raised her hand to her cheek and felt the heat there. Caught and embarrassed by her own game, she walked briskly back to her bag to get ready to leave for the village. If he knew Gaelic, then he'd better teach her. Maybe that's how they could spend their nights, since nothing else would be going on between them. She felt the heat rise again in her face as she remembered the passion-filled kiss they had just shared. Well, learning Gaelic would be safer than kissing this Alex MacKendimen.

Chapter 5

THEIR NEXT BIG challenge came a few minutes later from Brodie. He led forward a huge, gray and white stallion and motioned to Alex and Maggie.

"I sent Malcolm on ahead wi' news of yer arrival. Ye two can share this mount." Brodie gave the reins over to Alex, who was staring at the horse's back. It was taller than his own shoulders. Brodie called out some commands, and the rest of the group mounted up and gathered near them.

Maggie was stunned into silence. She had never ridden a horse in her life, and she had no idea if Alex could even get up on one. They had explained away many of the details, but this would be impossible. Chances were, if these men were warriors, they had learned to ride at almost the same time they learned to walk. Her mind was empty of any plausible excuses.

All at once, Alex grabbed the horn of the leather saddle and pulled himself up. Grinning a wicked smile, he leaned down and reached out a hand to her. He laughed out loud at the disbelief that must surely be showing on her face.

As he directed her, Maggie placed her foot on his and mounted behind him, unsuccessfully trying to keep her legs covered as she did. A few whistles and rumbles of laughter passed through the group as she finally got settled on the horse's back.

"Oh, ye of little faith," Alex said, as Brodie gave the signal to head for the village.

"Did you learn to ride a horse the same time you learned to speak another language?" Maggie asked sarcastically. The unknowns of this situation were wearing heavily on her mood. She didn't respond well to surprises, and it showed in the bitchiness in her voice.

"I dinna think ye should use that tone of voice wi' me. I am yer lord and master now." Alex's voice reeked of his enjoyment of her uneasiness. "And, no, I learned to ride horses at my sister's farm in Swedesboro. I still havna figured out where the Gaelic comes from."

As Alex urged the horse forward, Maggie suddenly swayed and screamed. Alex pulled up on the reins to slow the horse's gait, and Maggie reached around his waist and locked her hands together. With her body pressed closely against his, she decided to drop the sarcasm for now. She needed more information about the place and time.

"So how far is this village we're traveling to? Do you know the name of it?" She spoke softly so that she couldn't be overheard by the men around them. Before he answered, she noticed that he somehow increased the horse's speed and they were moving more swiftly than before.

"It's called Dunnedin, and it's only about a mile away. Brodie said the laird is in the process of enlarging the keep wall and refortifying it." He spoke over his shoulder, keeping his eyes on the path ahead.

"Wait a minute. The ruins near the festival were called Dunnedin. Are these the same?"

"Their village might be near the ruins. This will be the thing that tells us if we've done the impossible . . . the unthinkable. If this is just a 'medieval day,' the village they speak of will be but a temporary gathering. If we arrive at a working castle, we will ken how deep in trouble we are.''

''And they think that you're the son of this current laird? What did they say the laird's name is?''

''Struan. My mother was Edana and my . . .'' he paused and cleared his throat, ''my betrothed is Anice MacNab.''

''Whatever will your dearly beloved say about you bringing your mistress home to stay?'' Damn, but the sarcasm came back so easily.

''Jealousy doesna become ye, Maggie.'' He chuckled at her and her anger grew. At her angry gasp, he continued, ''Besides, Brodie told me she's just turned fifteen.''

''I'm not jealous, and could you slow down just a bit? I'm having trouble staying on this horse.'' She didn't know how he managed it, but the horse slowed a bit. ''Did you say she's only fifteen?''

''And apparently she's been languishing at 'my' family's keep, waiting for my return from England. Brodie assures me that she'll want the wedding scheduled as soon as she meets you!'' He laughed heartily at his own humor.

Maggie didn't react to his comment. From the few observations made and facts gathered, a part of her was now facing the possibility that they were indeed in medieval Scotland. Another part of her couldn't believe that she was considering the situation rationally. That she and Alex could have traveled through time to Scotland's past!

She tried to think back to the medieval history courses. If Anice was fifteen and unmarried, she was probably not happy about it. And Alex bringing Maggie home with him, even if it was his right to do so, would make them instant enemies. She shifted her position, trying to make her inexperienced bottom more comfortable.

''Alex, we're going to have to watch our step. Do we have to get any other details straightened out between us before we get to the village and 'your father'? I'm getting very, very scared that this is real."

"I am also afraid that ye are right, Maggie, as impossible as it sounds. Do ye have any idea which king it would be in England? I canna remember anything my aunt has told me aboot the clan history, and I amna sure I can bluff about that."

"I would just refer to him as 'the king' and avoid specifics as much as possible. If I remember anything about Scottish history, it's that the few Scottish kings who went to England did not go of their own free choice. Brodie spoke of Anice languishing?"

"Aye. What has that got to do wi' anything?" His voice shook, and Maggie realized that he might be a tad nervous about this, after all.

"That means you have, I mean the real Alex has, been away for awhile. Some unfamiliarity will be expected. Just play along with everything. I'll try to feed you any information I get as we go. Do you have a watch on?" Alex raised his arm and started to reveal the watch on his wrist. She laid her hand on his arm before he could pull up his sleeve.

"No, don't uncover it. We'll have to keep anything that looks not of this time or place out of sight. I'll have to find a safe place to stash my bag. One other question, Alex."

"What?"

"Are you wearing underwear?" The horse came to an abrupt stop and Maggie tightened her hold. If a horse had brakes, they would have squealed.

"What the hell kind of question is that?" Alex asked, forcing the words through his clenched teeth.

"It's just . . . well, I don't think the people here wear underwear as we know it. If anyone sees your boxers . . ." she paused at his upraised eyebrows. "Okay, if anyone sees your briefs, they'll know something is wrong. Get rid of them as soon as possible."

"I canna believe that I am sitting on a horse somewhere in godforsaken Scotland listening to a woman tell *me* to get rid of *my* underwear."

"I'm only trying to help," Maggie explained as she tried not to laugh at his discomfort. "I'm trying to cover all the details I can think of, since we agree that this might be real."

"I ken. This whole thing is just too much for my brain to handle." Alex shook his head and urged his mount into action again, catching up easily with the group.

"It'll work out, Alex, just hang in there." Maggie tried to sound soothing, but she was just as confused and worried. Then she realized what she had asked someone she had met only hours before. *Was he wearing underwear?* Luckily, his attention was back on the horse and the path, so he couldn't see the blush that once more must surely color her cheeks.

"Look, we come to the village." Alex pointed as they passed through the last edges of the thick forest and into a clearing, the point of no return for them. Maggie leaned carefully to one side and peered ahead.

Looking like a picture out of a medieval storybook, closest to her were clusters of small cottages with thatched roofs. She could see smoke and hear the telltale sounds of a smithy in the distance. Farther up the hill, a dark gray stone keep with a high wall grabbed her attention. It wasn't the make-believe village she had hoped to find. It was larger than she'd expected, and it looked solid and defensible . . . and dirty! The squawking of geese, the barking of dogs, the snorting of pigs, and the obvious odors of their refuse hit her like a brick wall as they approached the village border. She grimaced at the earthy smells.

"I wonder where they're keeping the infamous Scottish sheep?" Maggie asked under her breath. Alex chuckled but didn't respond.

As people began to gather along the sides of the road

leading through the cottages, Maggie saw the gap-toothed smiles, the well-weathered skin, and the premature aging that were shared by the inhabitants. Living in this time was so hard that it made the people old before their time. But, without fail, each man, woman, and child raised their hand in greeting to Alex and her.

The warriors urged their mounts into a gallop as they approached the wall of the keep. Alex kept their horse to an even pace, and they were soon passing through the gates into an-all-too-real Scottish medieval keep.

"I'm afraid we're not in Kansas anymore, Toto," Maggie uttered as she faced the unbelievable situation.

"I'm afraid yer right, Maggie. Verra afraid."

Chapter 6

MAGGIE RESISTED THE urge to clap her hands over her ears when the warriors began to shriek their battle cry, but instead, she clutched Alex's waist even tighter. The doors to the keep swung open wide and an older man and a girl took their places on the steps leading up to it. The man raised his arm in greeting, and a broad smile brightened his life-toughened face. Alex drew in the reins and brought the horse to a stop at the landing. Brodie ran up to them and pulled Maggie from the horse's back. Alex then dismounted. She tried to keep up with him, but Brodie's unyielding grip on her upper arm kept her a few steps behind. Frowning, she looked at him and struggled to get free. Brodie just shook his head and held her tighter. To avoid any more pain, she ceased struggling and turned her attention to the top of the steps.

"Is that Struan?" she whispered.

"Aye, that's the laird, Alex's faither," Brodie answered quietly.

Nodding her head in the direction of the girl standing off to the laird's side, she raised her eyebrows in question.

"Aye, that is his betrothed, Anice MacNab, a fine Scottish lass, if ye ask me." Brodie smirked as the insult sank in.

Maggie yanked her arm unsuccessfully one more time, then watched the scene unfolding in front of them. Alex had reached the top and paused in front of the man. Even if not true father and son, the resemblance was strong between them. Alex knelt on one knee and bent his head. She could barely hear his words when he finally spoke.

"I'm home, sir." Alex spoke in that accented English she was beginning to like.

"I can see that much. I dinna expect ye home wi'oot the king. How is it that yer here and he isna returned to Scotland?" The man's gruff voice could be heard clearly by the crowd that had gathered. Alex raised his head and looked around. Everyone was waiting for his answer. Before he could offer one, the laird pulled him up by his shoulders and embraced him. "Weel, no matter. 'Tis good to hiv ye back any time. Ye can tell me more inside after some food." Turning to the crowd, he called out, "Ye can all greet my son after our evening meal. Now, go back aboot yer work."

The crowd started to disperse, and Maggie tried to follow Alex. Brodie again held her in place. She looked up and saw the laird motion to Alex and nodding, Alex stepped over to the girl standing behind Struan. Anice was dressed plainly but well. Wearing a plaid skirt and bodice with a white blouse under it and a plaid shawl over it, she looked like a typical Highland lass. Anice had obviously prepared herself for Alex's arrival; she looked freshly scrubbed and young. Her long, red hair was bound back with only a ribbon and her face was glowing when Alex finally approached her. She dropped into a perfect curtsy and lowered her head and eyes demurely. It was at that moment she looked directly into Maggie's eyes.

Maggie instinctively stepped back when she saw the hatred in Anice's glance. For once, Brodie's rock-hard body behind her was to her advantage. Maggie regained her balance and waited for the rest of the scene to unfold.

Alex reached out to Anice and assisted her in rising. He leaned over and kissed her hand briefly. Struan burst out laughing at the sight. He smacked Alex on the back and warned him, "Ye been wi' the English too long, Alex. Yer acting like a damned courtier instead of the good Scottish lad ye are. Kiss her, by God, she's been waiting long enough for ye."

Alex hesitated briefly and then drew Anice into an embrace and kissed her on the mouth. It seemed to last an indecent length of time, but Maggie knew it was only a few moments in reality. Brodie must have felt her tension because he again whispered in her ear, "Ye better get used to it. That's the woman that'll bear his name and his bairns. And, believe me, she'll not be liking ye any more than ye like her."

Maggie gasped in outrage and stomped on his foot. Brodie laughed loudly, drawing attention. Alex and Anice looked down at them briefly before Struan urged them inside the keep. Alex looked from Anice to Maggie and saw the anger in both women's eyes.

"Brodie. See to her?" Alex called down to them.

"Aye, Alex, I'll see her settled." Brodie nodded.

Instead of following Alex and the others into the hall, Brodie directed her around the building to the back. His grip had loosened a bit, but Maggie felt a band of bruises already forming around her upper arm from his grasp. He walked briskly through the dusty courtyard, pulling her along, until they reached a busy door in the back.

"This is the kitchen. Ye can find food and drink in here. Then I'll take ye to the laird."

Maggie swallowed slowly. "The laird? Why are you taking me to him?" He shook his head at her, and she knew she was missing something.

"The laird will decide what yer duties will be when yer not servicing his son."

She was so angry at his crude comment that, without thought, she wrenched her arm from his hand and back-handed him across the face. Brodie stepped back, not from the force of her blow but in complete surprise. She could tell the exact moment when the shock turned to anger. His freckled face flushed a bright red and then he stepped menacingly closer to her.

Without hesitation, he grabbed her hair in one hand and her neck in the other. Forced to stand on her toes because of his height, she wobbled, off balance. Choking and fighting for breath, she clawed at his hand, trying unsuccessfully to break his hold.

''Now, I'll let ye get away wi' that once, seeing that yer not one of us. But be warned,'' he shook her head to emphasize his words, ''I dinna want to hit a woman. But do that again, and I'll see ye laid flat in the dirt wi' the back of my hand. Do ye ken?'' He waited for her to respond, and Maggie forced her head up and down. She could hardly breathe in her position.

''If yer going to be staying wi' Alex for awhile, ye better learn yer place. The laird will find ye duties that will keep ye out of Anice's sight. The less she sees ye around the keep, the better for all concerned. Now''—Brodie let go of her and Maggie slid down the wall at her back, gasping for breath—''let's go inside.''

''Brodie, ye should be ashamed of yerself. Picking on a lass half yer size.''

Maggie, still taking in huge gulps of air through her injured throat, watched as the giant who just manhandled her turned into a huge, cuddly bear. She looked up to the source of the voice to see who had caused this metamorphosis. A petite girl with bright blue eyes stood at the door to the kitchen. A few wisps of pale blond hair escaped the kerchief that held the rest of it back. She smiled at Brodie and he just seemed to shrink. Turning to Maggie, she reached out a hand to help her up.

''Sometimes Brodie doesna even ken his own strength.

Ye must be Alex's le— Begging yer pardon, but I dinna ken yer name.'' The girl blushed as she realized what she had almost said.

''Maggie. My name is Maggie Hobbs. And you are?''

''Rachelle. I work in the kitchen. The laird said to get ye some food and let ye rest while he's talking wi' Alex. Come wi' me.'' Rachelle led her into the busy kitchen, past the gawking workers, to a small wooden table in an alcove. ''Sit here, and I'll see to yer food.''

Rachelle had barely moved away when Brodie took a seat across from her. She looked directly at him, and to her surprise, he had the good grace to blush. Deciding that the best defense is a good offense, Maggie made her move.

''So, should I tell Rachelle that you've offered to take me off of Alex's hands when he's done with me?'' Maggie couldn't help smirking at Brodie's obvious distress.

''I was only having a bit of fun wi' ye and Alex. Ye shouldna be taking everything I say to heart.''

''Should I take your threat seriously?''

''Oh, aye. I meant that. But ye hiv a good backhand for a Sassenach.'' Brodie smiled as he rubbed the redness on his face where her blow had landed.

''Should I take that as a compliment?'' Maggie asked.

''Aye, that's how it was meant.'' Brodie leaned back a bit and looked her up and down. ''Can we cry peace afore Rachelle gets back and blisters my ears aboot what I did to ye?''

Affecting an accent that came close to his, Maggie answered, ''Oh, aye, Brodie, peace.'' She offered her hand to him, and he accepted it in a strong grasp.

''Peace, then.''

''Weel, that's a better sight to see than the one that greeted me outside the door.'' Rachelle approached the table with a large tray of food. Brodie reached up as she got closer and helped her ease the tray onto the table.

He received a warm smile in thanks from the woman who obviously returned his feelings.

Maggie looked over the selection of food and saw a chunk of hard cheese, a small loaf of bread, and two bowls filled with some kind of stew. She sniffed the hot concoction, and it smelled reasonably appetizing. She waited for Brodie to start.

It didn't take long for him to begin. First he brought out a dagger from his belt and cut off two pieces of the yellow cheese. Then he broke the loaf into two pieces and offered her a piece. He took one of the bowls and used the bread to scoop up the stew. Enjoying the food, Brodie soon disregarded her presence and attacked his meal with gusto.

"Would ye be wanting to use a spoon for yer stew?" Rachelle asked. "I put one on the tray for ye." She moved the remaining items on the tray and found it. "Brodie doesna let a spoon slow him down."

Maggie laughed as Brodie lifted his gaze to Rachelle and grunted his response. Rachelle left for a few moments and came back carrying two leather mugs, which she placed in front of them. Brodie again wasted no time sampling his, and Maggie could smell a beerlike aroma as he drank from his mug. Maggie wrinkled her nose and slowly reached for her mug.

"Dinna worry, I brung ye water to drink. I wasna sure if ye like ale or milk."

"Thank you for all of this," Maggie said, gesturing at the tray. "I didn't realize how hungry I was." Rachelle nodded and went off on another errand. There wasn't any conversation between her and Brodie as they finished the food before them.

Maggie's attention to her food was interrupted by the loud clearing of Rachelle's throat. Subtlety was not something indigenous to the Highlands, Maggie thought.

"Brodie, I think Rachelle wants to talk to you."

"Thank ye, I hadna noticed." Brodie wiped his hands on his plaid, drank down the last of the ale in his mug, and pushed back from the table. Rachelle grabbed him and pulled him over to her so that no one could hear their exchange. From the finger-pointing and angry whispering, Maggie gathered that Brodie was in trouble for something. It was amusing to watch this giant of a man be put in his place by a petite, soft-spoken lass. He didn't stand a chance.

After watching them discreetly for a few minutes, Maggie looked around the kitchen for the first time. The table she sat at was near the storage area. One whole wall of the room consisted of three hearths, all equipped with black, metal pothooks or spits suspended over the fires. Those fires were being fed constantly as the various cooks and assistants prepared for the evening meal. Small boys carried pots, turned the roasts on the spits, or added wood to the fires to keep them roaring.

A dozen women of varying ages and sizes worked chopping vegetables or making dough. They laughed and joked in what sounded like Gaelic to her as they prepared different dishes for the meal. They were industrious workers. Maggie noticed that their fingers and hands moved as fast as their tongues did. Every so often, they would glance over at her and then comment under their breath. God, she wished she understood Gaelic!

Before she could investigate any further, Rachelle and Brodie sat down on the bench across from her. She looked from one to the other, waiting for someone to break the silence.

"Maggie," Rachelle began, "Brodie has something he wants to say to ye. Brodie?" Rachelle's voice deepened into a threatening tone, and Brodie was clearly uncomfortable.

"I beg pardon for handling ye so rough-like outside. I dinna realize that ye would take offense at my words aboot yer . . . er . . . position here in the village."

''What do you mean by 'my position'?'' Maggie watched as Brodie's face turned a bright red. He looked to Rachelle, who finally took pity on him. She reached over and took Maggie's hand in hers.

''Maggie, I dinna ken how things like this are done in England, but yer presence here is not out of the ordinary run of things. Lemans are just part of a clan's life. The laird's son is expected to marry for clan alliances, not love nor comfort. The only real surprise is that Alex chose an English woman and, if ye dinna mind me sayin', an older one, at that, as his leman.'' Maggie tried not to take offense at being called an old woman. She knew she was one, for this time and place.

Brodie began shifting around on his seat as though it was the hottest surface on the face of the earth. Obviously, this talk of lemans and wives made him extremely uncomfortable.

''Brodie, why don't ye go check in on the laird and Alex? Mayhap, they need ye for something,'' Rachelle finally said.

Rachelle winked at Maggie as Brodie moved off the bench and into the main hall as fast as his legs would carry him. Maggie looked at Rachelle, and they broke out in laughter. When she could finally get her breath, Maggie had questions to ask.

''Are you married to him?''

''Not yet, be we will be verra soon.'' Rachelle answered like a woman who knew what she was after.

''Does he know that yet?'' Maggie almost felt sorry for Brodie. Almost.

''Are ye planning on setting yer sights on him?'' Rachelle asked quietly. ''I dinna think I could offer him what ye do, after all, yer so expairienced.''

''Rachelle, you heard about his offer to Alex, didn't you?'' Maggie was disappointed that Rachelle would feel threatened by her, especially seeing how Rachelle felt about the big lummox. Rachelle nodded, her blue eyes wide and serious.

"It was said in jest, to goad Alex, Rachelle. I am here for Alex only, and if this doesn't work out between us, I'm going back to . . . England. I have family there." Rachelle released a deep breath, obviously relieved by Maggie's declaration.

"I believe ye, and I am pleased. I canna fight yer fair looks and yer expairience, too. I feared losing Brodie if ye set yer mind to catching him."

First she was old and now she was coming off as a loose woman who would steal another's man! This conversation was doing wonders for her self-esteem, Maggie thought.

"I am not after Brodie. Brodie is yours, and I have no interest in him. Okay?"

"I dinna ken what 'okay' means. Is it an English word that we dinna have in Scots?"

Maggie slapped her hands over her mouth as she realized what she had said. American slang words, especially modern ones, would be inappropriate here.

"Yes, it's an English word that doesn't have a word in Scots. It kind of means 'Is that acceptable?' "

"Aye, he's mine. An I'll say no more aboot it to ye or anyone else."

Brodie's loud footsteps approaching drew both of their attentions. He pointed at Maggie and motioned for her to follow him. Maggie felt the color drain from her face and her hands shook nervously. The laird had complete control over this whole village and everyone in it. His word meant life or death to all in the clan. And now, without knowing what Alex had said or done, she had to face him.

She stood up slowly and took a deep breath. It was then that she felt Rachelle grabbing her hand.

"The laird's a fair mon, Maggie. Ye hiv nothing to fear from him."

"But what about Anice?"

''Anice has her place, and ye have yers. The laird kens that Alex wants ye. Now, show yer grit, Sassenach.'' With a grin on her face, Rachelle pushed Maggie toward Brodie.

Chapter 7

ALEX WATCHED, SEATED at the table on the raised dais at one end of the hall, as Maggie was led in by Brodie. Her face was lacking all color, except where a dirty handprint was visible on her neck. He closed his eyes, leaned his head back, and tried to imagine what kind of trouble she had gotten herself into while they were separated. He opened his eyes at her gasp. She hadn't been able to keep up with Brodie's long, purposeful strides and had stumbled. Alex motioned to Brodie to slow down, waving his hand at the burly clansman.

The pair finally reached the steps and paused at the bottom. He saw Maggie's chest and shoulders heaving as she tried to catch her breath. She rubbed her upper arm where Brodie had held her. Alex started before the laird could say anything.

"Maggie, what haes happened to ye?" Alex pointed at her neck.

Maggie looked at him first, then Brodie, and then Struan. Before she could answer, Brodie interrupted.

" 'Twas a bit of a misunderstauning, Alex. The lass is fine."

"Are ye, Maggie?" Alex watched her as she paused before answering. Then, he noticed Brodie's face getting redder and redder with each moment Maggie delayed.

"Yes, Alex. I am fine." The words came out as an exhausted whisper. Alex turned back to Struan and waited.

"My son tells me that ye aided his return home. I am grateful to ye for yer help." Struan called out from his seat at the center of the table. He pushed his chair back and stood up, watching her the entire time he walked around to the top of the steps. Maggie nodded her head in acknowledgment but said nothing.

"But I am telling ye straight out that his bringing ye here will cause some problems. Anice isna pleased."

"Faither . . ." Alex began.

"Nay, Alex, ye willna get a battle from me aboot keeping her, but ye need to see the problems ahead." Struan stopped Alex's protest with a wave of his hand. "The woman has a place here wi' ye, but it might go a wee bit easier if she dinna stay at the keep until after yer wedding. She could stay in one of the cottages in the village, out of Anice's sight."

"But she kens no one else here but me. I want her at the keep." Alex prayed that the laird would relent. He and Maggie had to stay together to figure out the mess they were in. If the laird tried to remove Maggie from the village or send her back to England, all hell could break loose!

Struan extended his hand to Maggie, and Brodie pushed her to go up the steps. The laird led her over to Alex, looking her over with the eyes of a very experienced man. Alex stood up as Maggie reached him.

"Weel, I can see why ye want her close by to ye. She looks woman enough to keep yer bed and body verra warm at night." Struan chuckled as he focused on her breasts and then her hair. He grasped a handful of hair and ran his fingers through it, laughing at her disgruntled look. Alex prayed she would stay calm.

"Weel, lass, I will offer ye my protection if Alex has no more need of ye after his wedding wi' Anice. I think ye would be able to help me work the stiffness out of my bones." Struan looked at Alex, then Brodie, and winked at Maggie.

"And a lot of other places too, laird," shouted Brodie, and everyone present in the hall joined in the laughter. Except Maggie and Alex.

Alex looked at Maggie and saw tears gathering in her cobalt blue eyes. Her face, chin, and neck were smudged with dirt, and her hair tumbled loose from the ponytail she had made a short time ago. Even without the added stress of playing a part, he could see that she was tired and almost at the end of her endurance. When he saw her lower lip begin to tremble, he knew he'd better do something.

"Faither," he said quietly, "she's haid a verra difficult journey here and doesna ken our ways. Wi' yer permission, I will take her to my room and let her rest awhile."

Struan approached them and patted Alex on the back. Then he waved to a serving girl standing near the doors to the kitchen.

"The lass does look near to fainting, Alex. Take her to yer room and come down for the evening meal. Jean will show ye the way to yer new room and get ye some water for washing." At his order, the girl nodded. "The lass can start her work in the kitchen on the morrow." Struan strode down the steps and through the great hall with Brodie close behind him.

Alex took Maggie's hand and pulled her close to him. Lowering his voice so no one would hear, he whispered to her, "Just hold on a few more minutes, Maggie. We can talk when we get to my room." Maggie nodded mutely, and they followed Jean through the room and up the steps to the second floor in one of the towers where his room must be located.

Alex led Maggie to the bed and helped her sit down. He closed the wide door to the chamber, and paced around the room. The soft crunching of what looked to be dried grass or hay on the floor echoed through the still room. When Maggie started to speak, he motioned with his finger to quiet her conversation.

"Wait until after the girl leaves. I hiv much to tell ye, also."

Maggie nodded, dropped her backpack on the floor, and fell back on the rough covers of the bed. Near sleep, she sat up when she heard the soft knock at the door. Alex opened it and the serving girl entered with a pail of hot water in each hand and some linens over her shoulder. She placed the buckets on a small table and the linens next to them and looked at Alex.

"That is fine, Jean. We thank ye."

Jean nodded her head and left the room, pulling the door closed behind her. Alex paused and then checked out the hallway. He closed the door securely and turned to face Maggie.

"I think we can talk now, no one is near. But keep yer voice down." He crossed the room and sat next to her on the bed. The ropes squeaked under his weight.

"Now, what really happened to yer neck? 'Tis covered wi' dirt and shows a man's handprint. Are ye weel?" He reached to touch the marks, but she pulled away.

"I had a bit of a run-in with the big one—Brodie. We didn't agree on my proper place here in the castle hierarchy."

She felt her neck, rubbing some of the bruises that were already visible beneath the dirt on her throat. At his questioning glance, she continued.

"When Brodie insulted me, I hit him."

"Ye hit a man twice yer size? Are ye daft?"

"He said I had a good swing for a Sassenach."

"But how did ye get the bruises?"

"Well, he responded to my punch by grabbing my throat and shaking me. I guess I should've expected something like that from a Highland warrior."

"Please, I beg ye, Maggie, step carefully around here. Yer verra life is at stake, I'm afraid."

"Okay, I'll be careful. Do you have any idea of 'when' we are?"

"I dinna ken until we got to the keep that this really is still the MacKendimen clan that we are dealing wi'. I should hiv recognized the name 'Struan' from my aunt Jean's stories, but I think I was in shock."

"I think we both are. You know, you are sounding more Scottish now than even a little while ago." He shrugged at her comment. "What else do you remember about this part of your family history?"

"Not much. I ken that the laird's son was sent to England wi' King David, Robert the Bruce's son. And that he remained there and was rather notorious wi' David. Unfortunately, I canna remember what that was or when it happened." He shook his head.

"Well, it obviously hasn't happened yet or your look-alike relative would be here, too." Maggie slid to the edge of the bed and stood up. "Maybe I'll feel better if I wash up a bit. Tell me what else you've found out."

"Anice is verra pleased to hiv me back. Struan wants to set the wedding date as soon as possible." At Maggie's raised eyebrows, Alex laughed. "I canna help it—I'm irresistible."

"What does he have planned for me? Did I hear him say kitchen work?"

"Aye, he wants to keep you from Anice's path. He thinks the kitchen is the safest place for ye—out of sight, out of mind. Anice was all sweetness until the laird started to ask aboot ye. Then she stiffened up and got a strange look on her face. The laird *dismissed* her so we could talk man to man."

"What did you both expect? She's fifteen and has been living with her betrothed's family for years without him. Then he returns, *you* return, dragging along a foreign woman with whom you are intimately involved and one you plan to keep with you. You and I are both lucky that she hasn't come after us with knives yet."

"Weel, now that ye put it that way, I can see why she'd be angry. Go ahead and wash up first. Ye look like ye need it more than I do."

Maggie poured some of the water into a basin she found and splashed her face and neck with the warm water. Using a small cloth to wipe and dry her face, she finished washing quickly. Alex watched as she grabbed her bag, searched around in it, and came out with her brush. As she sat on the bed and started to pull the brush through her long curls, Alex felt his body react. Raising her arms to reach behind her head brought her breasts up higher, pressing them against the thin blouse she wore. He could see that her nipples had hardened into enticing points and his mouth began to water. Her long, shapely legs were bared to his sight as she sat cross-legged on the bed.

He felt himself grow hard in response to the sight before him and then realized that an erection wasn't as uncomfortable in a kilt as it was in jeans. Maybe he would like this plaid thing after all! Then he felt his underwear being stretched across his groin and remembered what Maggie had said about them being seen. Since she was turned away from him, he reached under the kilt and pulled off his briefs. The rush of damp, cool air under the plaid helped to cool his body's reaction.

"I dinna think I will get used to this damn skirt verra quickly." His voice was gruff as he walked to the bed carrying his underwear. "Where do ye suggest I put these?" He held out his hand, catching her off guard.

"Put what? Oh! Well, I don't want them. Put them in one of the trunks over there." Maggie pointed to the trunks that lined the wall of the chamber. She had finished brushing and braiding her hair and turned to face him.

"You know, I don't think I've ever had a day that can compare to this one in my life. First, we arrive here, wherever and whenever this is. Then we are almost run over by a herd of barbarians and brought to this village. Next, because I'm said to be your mistress, I am propositioned by your best friend and your father. Add to that your fiancée, who would rather see me dead than alive, and being told that I can work in the kitchens when I'm not 'servicing' the heir of the laird, and you can see the kind of day it's been for me. I can't imagine what could happen tomorrow to make it more memorable than today!"

Alex could hear the fear and exhaustion in Maggie's voice. He pulled her into his embrace and held her quietly. Rubbing her back to soothe her, he whispered to her, "Maggie, we will figure out what is happening here and we will get back to where and when we should be. Something sent us or brought us here, and that same something can send us back. We will just bide our time and look fer clues."

He felt a moment of regret as she stepped back out of his embrace. Her body leaning against his had felt so right. He let her go and walked over to the trunks. Sitting down on one, he took his first real look around the chamber.

The large bed was pushed against the wall, and a small table with several candles stood next to it. Some wooden shelves lined the wall on either side of a small window that was covered with leather and fur. He walked to the opening and pulled the covering back. After a moment of looking out over the courtyard where they had entered, he turned back to the room.

He noticed three large trunks, including the one he had

been sitting on. He opened the closest one slightly and stuffed his briefs into it, making a mental note to investigate them thoroughly tonight. Finally, he looked at the fireplace in the corner of the room. Since it was obviously still summer here, no fire had been lit. But the dampness of the chamber made him realize that one would be necessary later to drive away the chill. Sniffing, he noticed a smell emanating from the floor that was not unpleasant.

"Herbs," Maggie said, she must have noticed him wrinkling his nose. "They put herbs in the rushes to cover the odors. These are obviously pretty fresh since you can still smell the herbs."

"Rushes? Oh, the grass on the floor."

Maggie laughed at Alex's comment. "Well, yes, they are a kind of grass. Sometimes they were woven, but mostly they are just spread around to catch all of the dust and dirt. If they're left too long, the odors will get very strong. Fresh rushes in your room are a big treat."

"How do ye ken all of these details, Maggie?"

"I read a lot," she replied, "and I've taken a number of history courses in college and after." *And read many, many romance novels set in medieval Scotland,* she thought. "I guess Anice ordered them before she knew about me. By the way, there was something funny that happened with Brodie in the kitchen."

Alex remained by the wall, facing her. "What was that?"

"Rachelle came to my rescue."

"Who is Rachelle?"

"Rachelle is this little bit of a girl that Brodie loves. She works in the kitchen and has him wrapped around her little finger." Maggie smiled as she remembered Brodie and Rachelle together. "It was quite a sight."

"Struan told me that I need to train wi' the men to rebuild my strength. He said I look pitiful fer a warrior of the MacKendimen clan. So, whilst yer in the kitchen, I will be in the training yard."

Maggie looked his body over more closely than before. His arms and shoulders were well-developed. His thighs looked strong, too. At least what she could see of his thighs under the kilt. She remembered how it felt to press up against his back while they were riding the horse. His stomach was flat and hard under her hands, and his—Maggie shook herself to stop this train of thought. It was going to be difficult enough living in the same room with a perfect stranger. Adding sexual attraction to the mix would be downright dangerous. She cleared her throat.

"Do you have any experience with weapons training?"

"Nay, not with swords. I do hiv some expairience with martial arts. At least I amna in bad shape to start this training."

"The laird obviously thinks you've been lying on your behind while you've been in England. That will help explain your lack of stamina." Maggie laughed at his affronted expression.

"If yer done insulting me, I think I will hiv a look around the keep. Why dinna ye get some rest? I will come back to get ye afore going to the evening meal."

Maggie moved her bag aside and lay back on the lumpy but inviting surface. She couldn't control the loud yawn that sounded and felt like it had started at her feet and moved through her whole body. Her eyes were fighting her best efforts to keep them open.

"Alex? Try not to get into trouble, okay? I don't think I could handle anything more right now."

He smiled, winked at her, and left the room, closing the door soundlessly behind him. Maggie fell asleep almost instantly.

Chapter 8

"MAGGIE, WAKE UP."

Instead of waking up as he told her, Maggie rolled over and curled into a tight ball on her side. Not to be ignored, Alex climbed onto the wide bed and shook her again.

"It's time for the evening meal, Maggie. *Wake up.*" This time, he accompanied his call with a stronger shake. Damn but the woman could sleep soundly!

"Come on, Don. Fifteen more minutes, just fifteen more." Her words were muffled, but he clearly heard the man's name: Don. Who was Don?

"I'm not Don, and this is yer last warning." Alex's voice came out a bit louder than he planned, and Maggie reacted swiftly. Her body snapped into a sitting position, eyes and mouth wide. Alex moved off the bed.

"I'm awake." Maggie tossed the hair that had come free of her braid over her shoulders and rubbed her eyes. After she looked around the room, dark except for the light shining in from the hallway, she rubbed her eyes again.

"We're still here. It wasna a bad dream, Maggie."

She slid to the edge of the bed and let her legs dangle off the side. Alex went to the basin, wet a piece of linen, and handed it to her. "Here, wipe yer face. We need to get to the hall quickly."

Maggie washed her face and straightened her clothes and her hair. Alex grabbed her bag when she finished with her ablutions and shoved it into the same trunk where he had stored his briefs earlier. He reached out for her hand and pulled her behind him into the hall. "Let's go."

The passageway was empty of people and lit by torches set high in the walls every few paces. They only had a few more moments of privacy, so Alex told her what he had found out so far.

"The entire village knows about 'my' return from England and about you, too. They are all waiting to see what kind of explosion will happen between ye and Anice."

"Explosion?"

"Anice's temper is legendary in the village. The people see her as verra capable of bein' the next laird's wife, but they stay out of her way when she's been angered."

"Oh, great. Now, not only do I have to worry about being propositioned by the men, but I also have to watch out for a vengeful fifteen-year-old girl." Maggie pulled his hand to make him stop. They had reached the top of the stairway and the sounds of the hall muffled their conversation.

"I found out more, but ye need to ken that right away. I hiv to sit at the high table for the meal, so I will see ye back in the room tonight. Brodie said ye can sit wi' them. He will keep ye far from Anice." Alex squeezed her hand, and they started down the steps to the great hall. When they reached the entranceway, the hall quieted as the people inside caught sight of them. Alex dropped Maggie's hand and pushed her in the direction of Brodie, who stood off to the side. At Brodie's nod, he walked toward the dais.

The path to the front of the hall was filled with men,

women, and children, anxious to greet and speak to him. He decided it was safe just to stay with general comments and not ask questions as he made his way through the crowded aisles. He promised to visit some and to talk with others later. Finally, he took a deep breath as he approached the steps leading to the high table.

Struan stood up and held out his hand, gesturing to the empty seat next to him. Alex made his way around the table, stopping to greet Anice, who sat to the other side of the laird. He took her hand, trying to imitate the action of every courtier in every period movie he had ever seen. He leaned over and placed a light kiss on her knuckles. Anice blushed and smiled and nodded her head at him so he felt pretty good about the move. He was on a roll now, so he thought he'd better compliment her dress. Women, even those in the Middle Ages, always liked to be complimented.

"Anice, 'tis a lovely dress yer wearing. And ye have my thanks fer preparing my room for my return. 'Tis quite comfortable."

Anice looked too surprised to respond. She bowed her head and stammered out, "Yer welcome, my lord."

"Alex. Ye can use my name when ye speak to me, Anice."

"Alex," she repeated. Anice blushed more deeply and raised her head, giving him a glimpse of a slight smile.

Alex released her hand and moved to the stool next to the laird. As soon as he was seated, servants placed huge platters of food on the tables. Others poured beverages into metal goblets at each place. He lifted his to his mouth and smelled it before drinking it. He inhaled the aroma of yeast, so it must be medieval beer or ale. He cautiously sipped before swallowing a mouthful. The sweetness of it surprised him, and he took another drink.

"Dinna drink all the mead afore ye eat, Alex. Anice assures me this is a strong batch." Struan look pointedly at Alex, then at Anice.

"Ye brewed this, Anice?" Alex leaned forward to see Anice across the barrel chest of the laird.

"Aye . . . Alex. I brought the recipe wi' me when I came. This honey mead is an old MacNab clan blend. Do ye favor it?"

Alex was about to answer when he noticed that Anice's eyelashes were fluttering as she looked at him from beneath them. Damn, this fifteen-year-old child was flirting with him! He had better watch his step. Fifteen was far too young for his tastes, even if it was acceptable in the Middle Ages.

"It is good." Alex took a small sip and put the cup down. The serving boy behind him stepped forward and refilled it. Alex decided to stay away from any liquor until he knew what was really going on. He pulled the plate in front of him nearer, and then realized it wasn't a plate after all. It looked like a hardened pizza crust. He looked around and saw that everyone was putting food from the platters on the crust, so he followed their example. Alex wasn't sure what the foods were, but everything smelled appealing. His stomach grumbled loudly, so he piled food onto the plate. Everyone else around him was eating heartily, so he joined in.

From her place near the back of the hall, Maggie watched the diners at the high table. Anice may have looked like a Highland lass this afternoon, but she'd had all day to get ready for this appearance. With her pale green flowing gown and its matching over-tunic of deeper green, she looked like the noblewoman she was. With her hair braided and held over her ears in a lace crispinette, she looked much older than her fifteen years. And when she was involved in conversation with Alex, she looked every inch the young woman in love.

Maggie sighed as she watched Anice bask in the brief light of Alex's attention. She pushed her trencher away and took a deep swallow from the mug of cold water.

This, she realized, was going to be difficult, if not downright dangerous. She knew that her background on this period and place was extremely limited. They would have to be very careful not to look or sound or act out of place . . . or time!

The hall quieted and Maggie noticed that Struan had stood up and started talking.

"Most of ye have had yer chance to welcome Alex back to the clan." He rapped Alex on the back and laughed heartily. "As ye ken, Anice and Alex were betrothed years ago by King David himself after he raised Anice's faither, the MacNab, to the rank of baron. This marriage will join our clans and strengthen us both." Struan reached over, took Anice's hand in his, and pulled her up to stand at his side. He did the same to Alex, who Maggie could tell, even from her distance, looked vaguely uncomfortable with where this announcement was going.

Struan placed their hands palm to palm and wrapped his around the two. "I have sent word to the MacNab announcing Alex's return and the impending marriage. The wedding ceremony will take place in one month, here. Dougal," Struan nodded at his steward, who was seated at the end of the high table, "prepare a wedding feast to mark the occasion of the joining of the MacKendimen and MacNab clans." Dougal, straight-faced and stiff-spined, bowed his head in acceptance of the command from his laird. Laughter entered his voice as the laird continued, "And Dougal, make it a feast befitting my son and heir."

The hall erupted with cheering and clapping. Even Rachelle and Brodie had joined in the celebration of the news. Maggie sat quietly in the midst of the revelry and waited for it to calm down. The laird stepped aside and allowed Alex to sit in his chair next to Anice. At Struan's signal, servants entered the hall with pitchers of wine. They made their way quickly through the crowds, pouring and filling drinking vessels throughout the hall. Maggie immediately recognized the importance of the gesture since wine was not served every day or even at all to most common people. Surprisingly, or maybe not, her mug was passed by.

"And so, to the joining of our clans and the *fruitfulness* of Alex and Anice."

Struan raised his pewter goblet to Alex and Anice and then to the hall and then drank the wine down effortlessly. The crowd roared its approval again and imbibed their drinks. Maggie took advantage of the noise and left the table to stand at the back of the hall. Looking over the people who filled the room, Maggie wished this was just playacting. At least then she could join in the camaraderie and enjoy the moment. But she and Alex were truly outlanders and needed to proceed with caution.

She knew that some of the people were watching her as she left, believing that Alex's mistress would be uncomfortable staying and celebrating his upcoming marriage. Alex's mistress? No. Uncomfortable staying? Yes. There was just something about all of this that gave Maggie a sinking feeling in her stomach. The hair on the back of her neck tingled in warning that the worst was yet to come.

In the hopes that she was experiencing a kind of time travel sickness or time lag, Maggie trudged up the stairs and followed the hall back to Alex's room. Now was as good a time as any to sort through her belongings and inventory the things of the future that had traveled with them to the past.

Chapter 9

ALEX WATCHED THROUGH the smokiness of the room as Maggie wove her way through the people and stood at the very back of the hall, near the door. He saw her pause briefly, shake her head, and leave. Thankfully, she walked in the direction of the stairwell, or he would've had to follow her. That, of course, would gain him the attention of everyone, which was probably not a good idea at this moment, especially when his father had just announced his upcoming marriage and Anice was still making cow eyes at him. No, he had to wait for the right time to leave and find Maggie.

"So, Alex, ye need to spend some time wi' Anice afore the wedding day. Ye hiv been separated fer a long time."

Struan's words brought his attention back to the head table. Anice sat, beaming, next to Struan. Young, damn it, she looked so young! Well, fifteen was too young for him, even if everyone around here accepted it. He forced a smile to his face and sat back on his seat. A serving woman stepped forward and offered him more wine. He shook his head. The last thing he needed was to overindulge and lose his wits. He swallowed the last mouthful in the goblet.

Well, maybe he had already lost what wits he had. How could this be happening? A few hours ago he was touring his family's ancestral property and now he was, according to what his eyes and ears told him, feasting with his ancestors.

Struan elbowed his side. In a very loud stage whisper, he advised Alex.

"Mayhap, ye want to take yer lassie fer a long walk? The night is fair and the moon no' so bright to shed too much light on yer . . . activities." Before Alex could reply, Struan directed his comments to Anice.

"Anice, why dinna ye show Alex where ye placed the new gardens? He will be pleased to ken that ye honored his maither's wishes." Struan pulled Anice gently to her feet and then eased them both toward the door out of the hall. "Go ahead, lass, ye need to learn yer mon."

As Alex watched, Anice nodded at Struan's suggestions and then faced him.

"Come, Alex, I will also show ye where we placed yer maither's favorite roses. I hiv managed to keep them alive for ye to see on yer return to us." She slipped her arm under his and guided him toward the door. He didn't resist. As they reached the exit, Alex thought he saw Anice smile back at Struan, but he couldn't be sure. But, by the way the hairs on the back of his neck were tingling, he felt as if he was being set up.

Maggie reached the room and closed the door firmly. She couldn't take any chances that the contents of her backpack would be seen. Hopefully, no one would breach the relative security of Alex's room. The room was too dark by her standards, so she lit a few more of the short, fat candles and placed them around the room. Satisfied that she'd be able to see now, Maggie opened the trunk and dug to the bottom for her bag. Grasping the handles, she pulled it out and walked to sit on the bed.

Holding the bottom and shaking it vigorously, she emptied the bag's contents on the bed. Containers, bags, brochures, and more ended in a pile. She slid her sleeve up and removed her watch and added it to the collection. A scraping noise in the hall grabbed her attention. Maggie leaped from the bed and ran to the door. After a few moments of listening with her ear against the door, she opened it and peered out in the hallway. She could see no one nearby, but she couldn't take any chances. Maggie stepped back into the room, closed the door tightly, and then pulled the nearest trunk over in front of the door. *That should keep everyone out,* she thought as she crawled onto the bed.

Making smaller piles from the large one, Maggie sorted through her belongings. Into one heap she tossed any papers she had collected through her tour. The brochures from England and Scotland showed a very different landscape than the one that existed now. Several vials of pills made up another pile. Maggie examined the two bottles of antibiotic tablets she carried. Her physician had warned her to carry them in case her recurrent ear infection should flare up while she was traveling. She threw those and another container filled with various headache relievers into a small pouch.

Tucking her electronic calendar, address book, her wristwatch, and her camera into various pockets inside the bag, she then sorted through her more personal toiletry items. Her brush and comb and toothbrush were all made of very modern plastic, so they couldn't be left out in plain view. Some hair ties and ponytail loops of material would pass, so she left them on the bed. Following the same rationale, Maggie sorted and separated everything in the bag. She was nearly finished when the sound of footsteps approaching the room startled her. The person stopped and pushed on the door.

"Maggie? Are ye in there?" Alex's deep whisper relieved her fears. She climbed off the bed, shoved the trunk aside, and pulled the door open to allow him to enter.

"This isna good, lass. Locking me out of my own room is not a good sign." His eyes twinkled in merriment.

"You shouldn't tease me. I heard a noise earlier and thought someone was trying to get in."

Alex reached out and rubbed her shoulders and upper arms. "It will be all right, Maggie. We will figure this whole thing out." His touch was very soothing, but she couldn't let herself relax yet. There was still too much she didn't know . . . about Alex, about this time and place . . . and their fate.

He glanced past her to the bag on the bed. Maggie turned and followed him over to it.

"Yer treasures?"

"Treasures? I don't think I've ever thought of them as treasures before."

"I'm certain the locals would be dazzled by most of the things in yer bag. What do ye hae?" Alex sat on the edge of the trunk.

"Well, I carry the same things that most . . . er . . . women carry. Hair things, calendar, makeup, and camera. Unfortunately"—she held out her calendar, which was also a minicalculator and electronic memo—"even my normal stuff won't be explainable here and now. And, by the way, you should take your watch off, too. Anything else?"

Nodding his head, Alex removed it and handed it to her. Then he reached inside his sporran and pulled out his cellular phone. He clicked the power button one more time and got no response. Shaking his head, he passed it to her.

"So, where do ye think we can hide yer bag? I dinna think the trunks in here will be verra secure wi'oot a lock once the servants start coming in to clean."

"You're right. Any suggestions?" She pulled the ties tight and knotted them.

"I'll try to find a lock for now. But that might draw more attention to it. Mayhap, in the corner under the bed until we find better?" Alex paused and looked around the room. Maggie could tell he was studying the size and location of the furniture.

"Speaking of the bed, I think we can both share it, Alex. I won't ask you to sleep on this floor," she wrinkled her nose. "It may look and smell fresh, but the herbs may not have killed all the creatures."

Alex jumped up and stared at the rushes on the floor. "Creatures?"

"Lice, fleas, ticks. Maybe even other insects I can't think of." She fought off a smile at his reaction to the mention of bugs. "Anyway, I think we can both fit in the one bed. And, since I'm very tired," her yawn interrupted her words, "I'm going to sleep. I'm sure they get started at the crack of dawn around here."

"Yer right. Struan said he would send Rachelle to fetch ye in the morning. We better get to bed . . . er . . . sleep." He looked around and then unfastened his belt. The kilt that had stayed in place through everything so far fell in a pile around him. Maggie's gaze was drawn inexorably to his legs, which were now visible below the end of the linen shirt he wore. *Nice legs,* she thought, experiencing another unwanted tug of attraction to Alex. *Very nice legs.* And his shirt didn't fall low enough to cover all of his . . .

"Do I meet yer standards?"

Maggie felt her cheeks heat up as Alex cleared his throat and turned away. She was standing there, examining him from head to toe and every place in between, and never realized that he was watching her. Well, she couldn't help it. She had a weakness for looking at men with nice legs. Pat had teased her about it constantly.

"I'm sorry, Alex. I haven't had a man undress in front of me for a while. I didn't mean to be rude."

Alex tugged the covers down, exposing several pillows, before he answered. "I know, Maggie. I had no idea that the plaid would just fall like that." He pulled the linen shirt down before climbing into the bed and adjusting the covers.

Maggie realized she was standing in the middle of the room and Alex was ensconced in the bed already! How was she to undress?

"Dinna worry, Maggie, I willna watch. I promise," he said, as if he had read her mind. But she could hear the huskiness in his voice that told her his body was responding against his mind's direction.

Maggie made her way around the room, blowing out the candles. Delaying her climb into the bed with him, she picked up and folded his plaid. Then she rearranged the position of the trunk out of her path to the door. Soon, it was obvious to her and Alex that she was stalling.

"I amna quite ready to sleep yet. Just get in bed. I gave ye my word, dinna ye trust me?"

She looked at him and realized that she did trust his word. Silently, she took off the skirt and bodice of her outfit and climbed into bed in just her chemise. It actually covered more than most of her nightgowns did. He held up the covers and she settled down between him and the wall.

"There now. That wasna so bad, was it?"

"No, Alex, it wasn't."

When he took her hand in his and entwined his fingers around hers, she felt only comfort from the gesture.

"What is this all about, Alex?"

"I dinna ken, lass. We maun wait and watch for signs and clues aboot what happened to us. Mayhap someone here can aid us." He squeezed her hand before letting go of it.

"I just don't understand. This can't be real. It can't really be happening to us." Tears welled and burned in her eyes and throat. She fought their release. "This can't be what I'm thinking—traveling through time? How? Why us?''

''I dinna ken. But try to stay calm aboot it. Get some sleep. Morning will be here afore ye ken it.''

''Are you worried, Alex?''

''Aye, I am, but I'm trying to control it for now. We hae to give it a few days and see what comes to us. Good night, Maggie.''

She turned over on her side and still fought the tears that threatened to fall. In a whisper, she said, ''I'll try not to worry, either, Alex. Maybe we'll wake in the morning and find that this is all just a bad dream. Good night.''

Sleep eluded her for a long time that night.

Chapter 10

"IF YE DINNA raise yer sword, yer a dead mon, Alex MacKendimen."

"Go ahead. Put an end to it." For a split second, a part of him hoped Brodie would take his head and end his suffering. Already bloodied and bruised by the swordplay of this day, Alex was sure a few of his ribs were broken.

"Nay, I canna. The laird said to work ye, not kill ye."

"I think yer nearer to killin' than ye ken, Brodie."

Brodie guffawed, and the men watching the pair fight joined in. Alex just stood, bent over at the waist, with his hands on his knees. His breath was coming in deep gasps, which pained his screaming ribs. And he thought he was in relatively good shape. From the cuts and bumps spread over his body, *relatively* was a relative term! One of the younger boys came forward with a bucket and offered Alex a dipper of water. Sitting on the hard ground, he took the first one and poured it over his head and face. Pushing his sopping hair out of his eyes, he accepted the second one to drink.

"Are we no' done yet, Brodie?"

"Nay, Alex. Ye still hiv a wee bit of fight left in ye to work out." Brodie reached for his hand and pulled him to his feet. "It's yer turn to attack me now." He handed Alex the sword he had dropped, a practice sword that was well broken-in.

"I dinna think I can raise my arm above my head."

"Ye wee puir bairn. Weel, ye better lift that arm now!"

With that brief warning, Brodie charged him from a short distance away. From the fierce frown Brodie wore, it was hard to tell this was only practice. From the intensity of the blow he dropped on Alex's blade and weakened sword arm, it definitely did not feel like practice. Alex managed to maneuver out from under most of the force and jump to his feet, but his arm and hand were shaking from the power of Brodie's blow.

His true level of pain and weariness must have been apparent to Brodie, because after the one nearly devastating strike, Brodie stopped and smiled.

"That's enough for this day. We must leave you some strength in yer body to take care of yer lovely Maggie."

"Surely she will thank ye fer that," Alex retorted.

"Well, if ye canna take care of her, ye can always call on me."

"Or me," added another voice.

"Or me," chimed in a third voice from the group of men and boys that had been observing the training.

"I thank ye all fer yer kind offers of assistance, but I can take care of my woman." He made eye contact with a number of the men who were now grinning and obviously lusting after Maggie. "And make no mistake; she is mine."

The men nodded in agreement, acknowledging Alex's ownership of the woman in question, and then broke up. *Hopefully, that will keep her problems with being accosted by unwanted attentions to a minimum,* he thought.

"Let's go to the loch. The cool water will clear yer head and lessen the heat." Brodie trotted off through the gate and into the woods on one side of the road leading into the village. Alex dragged himself to stand and handed his weapon to the boy who stood waiting nearby. He watched him run off to take the sword back and wondered briefly where he would get the strength to get to the loch. He took in a deep breath that stretched his aching ribs and walked slowly in pursuit of Brodie and the promised relief.

Brodie was waiting for him on the path, and Alex caught up with him.

"I feared I left ye in the dirt of the yard."

"Yer concern fer me is heartwarming, Brodie. It took but a bit of time and effort to get this body moving."

Brodie slapped him on the chest. Alex gasped at the waves of pain that shot through the body under discussion.

"Dinna worry, Alex. The first day is the worst. And, I promise, the loch will revive yer puir beaten body." Brodie laughed in his frowning face and took off again. This time, when Alex caught up with him, Brodie was standing naked next to a shiny, blue lake. A second later, Brodie took a flying leap into the water and disappeared below the calm surface.

As he spied Brodie emerging from the water, Alex took off the heavy belt around his waist and let the plaid fall. He had worn only the plaid and the breezes reaching his skin were a godsend. He walked to the spot where Brodie had jumped and dove into the water. He wasn't sure if it was the icy temperature of the water or the force of his dive that stopped his breathing. He touched bottom and turned his body upward. His scream began before he broke the surface and tore out of the water as he did.

"Bloody hell! Ye are trying to kill me." He found Brodie floating on the water a few feet away, a knowing smile on his face.

"Did ye forget that this loch never warms? From the

look on yer face and the bumps on yer skin, I think ye did forget."

"Or never knew," Alex muttered under his breath. He sank back into the frigid water and washed the blood and dirt from his body. Taking a breath, he sank again into the water and swam away from Brodie. After a few strokes, he turned and floated on the calm surface. Now, this he could learn to like. He had hesitated for the briefest moment before dropping his plaid and swimming naked. But, in this time, bathing suits did not exist. He had swum nude as a kid at the small pond on his parents' farm and enjoyed the freedom of it, freedom he had rejected over the last few years. Instead, he had placed all kinds of limits and restrictions on himself: organized, not restricted, he tried to tell himself. Goals, not limits. Somehow, the importance he placed on those plans seemed to fade away as he faced the first truly unexpected and unanticipated turn of his adult life.

The need to be the youngest partner in the history of the accounting firm he worked for paled beside his current need to survive in this foreign world—and the need to find his . . . *their* . . . way out of this. His job-oriented priorities looked very out of line here in this primitive place and time. And, thinking about survival . . .

He stood as he reached the shallow part of the water and walked out of the lake. Brodie followed him to the pile of clothes. Mimicking Brodie's actions of using the material to dry off his skin and Brodie's example of how to rewind the length of plaid around his waist, he dried and dressed.

"At least ye look presentable to yer woman now. Bein' a Sassenach, she may have fainted if she saw ye covered in blood."

"I think Maggie has almost as much grit as a Scottish lass. She stood up to ye, dinna she?"

Alex watched the red flush move up Brodie's neck and face and even his ears.

''So, she told ye.''

''Weel, I knew something was wrong when I saw yer handprints on her neck yesterday. But, aye, she told me.''

''She has a good backhand, ye ken. Fer a woman and a Sassenach.''

Although he could hear the respect in the man's voice, Alex knew Brodie was waiting for his response. And he didn't keep him waiting. He drew back and punched Brodie in the face, hitting the lower edge of his jaw. Brodie barely flinched from the blow—he just rubbed his face and laughed.

''I think she has a better blow than ye, Alex. Mayhap she can teach ye how to hit a mon.''

Alex laughed with him and shook out his throbbing fist. Remembering that Maggie was indeed a teacher, he answered, ''Aye, Brodie, I have a feeling that Maggie will teach me many things. Weel, we'd best be getting back to the keep.''

''It's a good thing I'm used to dealing with children,'' she muttered under her breath. ''A good thing indeed.''

Looking around the huge room, it was hard to believe she was dealing with any adults at all. The women were cleaning the room, but their attention focused on her. Elbowing and shoving, they moved closer to her work area, each one pushing a bit harder to get the best position. To do what, she wasn't sure. It seemed as if they had never seen a woman from outside of their village before. She shook her head and went back to scrubbing the worn tabletop.

''Ye will all get more of yer own work done if ye leave the Sassenach be.'' The steward's loud voice filled the cavernous room.

Their reaction was comical. Maggie watched as the group went completely still for a moment and then ran off in different directions. She tilted her head down to cover her smile. Children, just like children caught doing something they know they shouldn't be doing.

"Ye will hiv to pardon us." Rachelle approached the table, carrying a pail of water. Lifting the bucket onto the tabletop and pouring it slowly on the surface, she continued, "We dinna see many Sassenach women here."

Maggie used her brush to spread the water and leaned over and scrubbed another area of dirt on the table before replying.

"Really?" She batted her eyelashes at Rachelle. "And do I have the three eyes and horns on my head that you all expected?"

"Actually, it's no' yer appearance that is a surprise. They heard aboot yer run-in wi' my Brodie and canna believe ye live to tell." Rachelle winked at her.

Both women laughed and then bent over their task. Maggie knew she liked Rachelle. She was quiet, almost to a fault, but when she spoke, it was worth listening to. She was also deeply in love with the barbarian Brodie, and Maggie had learned that they would indeed be getting married. The laird recently granted Brodie permission to build a cottage and gifted him with the land to do it. Rachelle told her earlier this morning that, as soon as the new section of wall around the keep was completed, the builders would begin on their new home. Rachelle's comments had ended with a blush as she mentioned the wedding.

After the table had been scrubbed, they signaled to two of the men, who would lift and carry it to a place nearer to the wall. Maggie watched the men's approach with suspicion. Each time they moved a clean table, they pinched or fondled her in some way. From the smirks on their faces and the whispered exchange of comments, she knew they planned more of the same. Rachelle moved on to the next table, but Maggie's path was blocked by the two approaching men. As she tried to pass between them, she found herself sandwiched between them.

"We been watching ye work, lass, and we like what

we see, eh, Farlan.'' The smell of unwashed bodies and new sweat poured from them. Maggie shuddered, sickened by the stench. Unfortunately, they interpreted it as fear and it egged them on. They stepped closer to her, if that was possible, and the man behind her put his hands on her waist. When she started to struggle, the man in front took her wrists in a stinging hold.

''We ken a place where we can hae a wee taste of what a Sassenach whore gives out. Farlan, let's go there now.''

Maggie froze in shock, the insult cut her so deep she couldn't take a breath. It was absolutely unbelievable that these two thought they could just take her out of the hall and that no one would stop them. And yet, they were trying to do just that. Farlan wrapped his arm around her waist and dragged her, as his friend, a man called Innes led the way. Maggie realized she was the only person who was going to save herself. Even Rachelle stood watching the scene mutely from nearby, her eyes wide and questioning.

They were nearly to the doorway when she jammed her elbow into Farlan's stomach and stomped on his foot at the same time. His arms loosened enough for her to break free. When Innes turned to look, Maggie drove her knee into his groin. The very large man crumpled to the floor like a wilting flower. Maggie began to run away from the two when another pair of arms grabbed her.

''Dinna fight me, lass. It's Alex.''

''Alex. I'm glad to see you. Those two men . . .'' Maggie sputtered.

''The twa willna bother ye agin from the looks of it.''

When faced with the stone-cold anger of their laird's son, the culprits were quick to get up and back away. Maggie wasn't sure if it was her quick moves or Alex's proprietary embrace that spoke more clearly to the men.

Alex glanced around the room and called out, ''Maggie is under my protection while she lives here. Make no mistake—anyone who abuses her will answer to me.''

"So much for women's liberation," she whispered to him.

Still in his embrace, Maggie looked up at him. His hair was wet and he was wearing only the plaid. His shirt was tossed over his shoulder. His chest was covered with pale red hair that curled enticingly under her hand. Her hand! She tried to move out of his arms, but he tightened his hold.

"Weel, lass, in for penny, in for pound."

Without warning, Alex dipped his head to hers and took her mouth in a kiss. It was possessive, meant to show everyone present his ownership of her. His lips opened and he plunged his tongue into her mouth as she opened it in surprise. Her body reacted before she could stop herself. She leaned into his embrace more fully, stepping between his legs, and wrapped her arms around his body. His plaid and her thin skirt did little to disguise his arousal. His erection pressed against her belly, unmistakable in its length and hardness. She arched against it as he rubbed his mouth on hers and explored deeper with his tongue. His hands roamed over and down her back and reached her buttocks when the noise of their spectators finally broke through the oblivion that the kiss had created.

He lifted his mouth from hers and loosened his hold on her. Smiling a predatory-male smile, he whispered back to her, "Women's liberation be damned. It hasna happened here . . . yet."

His wink was the only thing that stopped her from arguing with his actions. Looking around, she noticed that the people were going back to their tasks and Farlan and Innes were carrying the cleaned table to its new position. They were moving a bit gingerly though, thanks to the self-defense moves she had employed.

She stepped back and straightened her bodice and skirt. Tugging it back into place, she noticed Alex watching her movements with a glint in his eyes. Then he called out to the steward who sat working at his tasks at the head table.

"Dougal!"

The older man hurried down from the dais and reached Alex's side in a few moments.

"Aye, Alex?"

"Dougal, hiv ye a dagger?"

Dougal looked from Alex to her and she saw the man's Adam's apple bob as he swallowed deeply. He frowned as he considered Alex's question.

"Mayhap if ye tell me what ye need it for, I can help ye?" Dougal now shifted nervously from one foot to the other, his plaid swaying to his movements.

"A small dagger, for Maggie. 'Tis clear she needs one . . . a dagger for eating and for anyone who bothers her again." His voice raised at the end of the sentence.

"Alex," she began to protest. Backing away, she shook her head. She didn't want to carry a weapon. Not in her time and not in this time, either.

"Lass, ye need one to eat and ye maun hiv lost yers in the fight wi' those damned men who robbed us." Alex nodded to her, leading her along.

As much as she feared carrying one, it was customary to have at least a small dagger to spear meat and food during meals. She had seen it at dinner the night before. Alex apparently wanted her armed, so she smiled at him and nodded at Dougal in agreement.

"Oh." Dougal let out his breath. Maggie wondered if Dougal thought she planned on using the daggers on the two men who had just accosted her . . . or against him.

"I will find one for . . . er, yer . . ."

"Maggie. My name is Maggie." She smiled at him as she enjoyed his brief moment of embarrassment. Evidently, he was comfortable calling her "the Sassenach whore" behind her back but not to her face.

Dougal nodded to Alex and walked quickly away, up the steps of the dais and to the table. Alex led Maggie to a quieter part of the room.

"Are ye all right, Maggie?"

She smiled at the concern she heard in his voice.

"Yes, Alex, I'm fine. I never thought . . . I had hoped . . . that I wouldn't have to use the self-defense training I received. But," she smiled at him, "it's come in very handy."

"I hope ye dinna use that against me." Alex laughed and then rubbed his hand over his rib cage, wincing.

"What have you done to yourself?" Maggie looked at his chest . . . again, searching for signs of damage. Some scrapes were obvious but no bruises.

"Weel, I had my own run-in wi' Brodie today."

She reached up and touched the still-sore marks on her neck. If Brodie had done that to her, what had he inflicted on Alex? Her dark thoughts must have shown on her face because Alex started laughing.

"Nay, Maggie. He was my sparring partner today, assigned by the laird to give me a workout. And, what a workout he gave!" His hand moved back to his ribs.

"Did you break anything, Alex? You know, you need to be careful here. They really think you are a warrior already and up to this."

Alex snorted at her comment. "I was being careful and you may be surprised to learn that I held my own against him."

She laid her hand on his arm, trying to ease the pride that was now more bruised than his body. He seemed to take her concern too seriously.

"Alex, there is still so much, too much, that we don't know about this time and place. Try to stay in one piece, okay?"

"I'll be careful, Maggie. And you be careful, too." He nodded in the direction of her two admirers. "I meant to ask ye . . . are they being cruel to ye?" He lowered his voice as he asked.

"No, Alex, it's okay. I'm just a novelty and they're

curious. Rachelle said it's really because of my encounter with Brodie."

"Ha!" Alex laughed loudly, drawing the attention of the workers. He kissed her again and whispered, "I willna see ye until after the evening meal. Struan 'suggested' that I spend time wi' Anice this afternoon." Maggie stepped back and he strode out the nearby door to the yard.

As she watched his progress through the courtyard, Maggie realized that, other than knowing he was from the same area as she was, she knew nothing about this man. She sighed, letting out some of the tension his kisses had caused in her body. She had better get to know this man, now that she was trapped with him in the past.

"Aye, he is a most handsome mon."

Maggie whirled around to face Rachelle.

"What?"

"Ye were sighing, loud enough for the horses in the stable to hear. Yer Alex hiv grown to be a fine looking mon."

"Did you know him before? Before he left for England?" Maggie thought this might be a chance to learn about the real Alex.

"I knew him." Rachelle's voice lowered to almost a whisper.

"Rachelle, what's the matter?" Maggie saw the woman's hesitation—fear, if Maggie didn't know better.

"Let's just say that the laird's son thought he should hiv whatever . . . whoever he wanted. He wasna an easy mon to thwart."

"Alex made a pass at you?" She tried to keep her curiosity under control. This woman was *not* talking about the Alex she knew, but one who was even more a stranger.

"A pass? Is that another English word of yers?" Rachelle took advantage of a moment of silence and started walking toward the tables. Maggie caught up with her and stopped her with a hand on her shoulder. Rachelle had regained some of her color.

"I willna tell tales, Maggie, but I am glad that Alex brought ye wi' him. Mayhap things will be peaceful between he and Brodie."

"But I thought they were the best of friends."

"They were when they were but lads, but not when Alex left wi' David fer England. He and Brodie didna part on good terms."

And Rachelle was the reason. Unspoken, it rang out loud and clear to her. Alex, the real one, had been making moves on Rachelle, who felt pressured not to resist because he was the laird's son. Brodie, his cousin, apparently already enamored of Rachelle, couldn't have been happy. Most likely, Struan chose Alex to go to keep things peaceful in his clan and castle.

Rachelle, clearly uncomfortable with this conversation, had turned back to her work. Maggie walked to the dirty table and picked up a brush, lathering the surface and scrubbing the patches of dried food. Without looking at Rachelle, Maggie asked, "Were you the 'whoever' that Alex wanted?"

"Aye." The reply came out as a soft whisper.

"And now?" Maggie pressed for more.

"I hope he haes given up being a spoiled child who expects to get what he wants."

Maggie reached across the table and took Rachelle's hand, trying to comfort her. "I think that Alex will be too busy with me and Anice to even think about you."

Rachelle offered a slight smile at Maggie's attempt at humor. They finished the last of their tables and walked to the kitchen for their next assignment. At least now she had some information to share with Alex when she saw him next.

Chapter 11

"GOD SAVE ME from overdeveloped teenagers!"

He slammed the door behind him, finally feeling safe from Anice's advances. He glanced around the room and noticed that only two candles were burning to light the darkness. The faint light thrown by the candles showed an outline under the covers of the bed. He moved closer and saw that Maggie had beaten him to sleep. A tray sitting on one of the clothes trunks explained why he had not seen her at the evening meal.

He walked, quietly he hoped, over to the trunks and sat on one. His body was beginning to tell him very clearly how much he needed rest. Reaching down, he pulled off one boot and then the other. The pain in his ribs and chest was lessening, he thought. Breathing didn't hurt as much as it had earlier in the day. His arms and shoulders were very sore, though. Swordplay was a misnomer—it wasn't even close to play.

Alex unfastened the large broach that held his plaid in place over his shoulder and placed it on the nearby shelf. Stretching his arms over his head, he pulled off the linen shirt and tossed it on the trunk. Then, loosening his belt, he dropped the plaid to the floor.

As he approached the beckoning bed, he realized that he could not get in bed naked. He and Maggie were complete strangers, though at times he felt as if he'd always known her. But what could he wear? He walked back to the trunks and searched through one and then another. They must have something comfortable he could use for sleeping in this time. He was reaching for the third when Maggie called out to him.

"What are you doing, Alex?"

"I am looking for something suitable to wear to bed. Do ye hiv any ideas?" Only when he watched her eyes move, scanning down his body and up again, did he realize that he faced her, completely naked. So much for not offending her sensibilities!

Alex turned back to the piles of clothes and pulled out another clean shirt and tugged it on. When the length fell around his thighs, he turned back to face the woman in the bed. Maggie dropped the covers she held up to her neck as he walked closer.

"Look," she held her arms up, "we match now."

He saw that she was also wearing one of his shirts. The room wasn't so dark that he couldn't also see that she was wearing nothing under it; the curves of her breasts were clear through the material. It looked much better on her!

"Sorry, I dinna mean to wake ye, Maggie."

She patted the empty part of the bed. He sat next to her.

"I didn't think I would fall asleep that fast. But, the bed is comfortable and warm and I couldn't fight it any longer."

"Hiv ye been here long?" The room was straightened, well, except for the clothes he had just thrown around from the trunks.

"No, I just climbed into bed a few minutes ago. If I had been truly asleep, you would never have roused me."

He remembered trying to wake her the afternoon before and the difficulty of it. And, he remembered she had spoken a man's name.

"Who is Don?" he asked abruptly.

"Don? How do you know Don?"

"You called out his name in yer sleep."

"I did? What else did I say?" She sat up straighter as she eyed him suspiciously. He thought for a moment about teasing her, but if her day had been half as trying as his, she'd probably hit him.

"Nothing else, Maggie, just his name. Is he yer . . . boyfriend?" She hesitated, and dropped her gaze from his. She twisted some strands of hair around and around her fingers, pulling them, as she decided how to answer his question.

"He was my boyfriend. We broke up a few months ago."

"Did ye date for long?"

"We were together for over two years."

"Ye seem a bit hesitant to answer my questions. Would ye prefer if I dinna ask?"

She put her hand on his before answering. His body reacted to the heat that traveled from her touch.

"I don't mind at all, Alex. Since we don't know how or what happened to us and don't know when we'll get out of here, I think it would be good to get to know each other better."

"We just need to be certain that we dinna mix the facts wi' the fiction we're living here," he added, nodding his head at her questioning glance.

"I agree, we need to keep our stories straight and separate."

"So, if ye dinna want to talk about Don, tell me aboot teaching." He thought to steer the subject to something less personal.

A wide smile brightened her whole face. "I've been teaching for six years now. I love it. You can have such an effect on children, really influence the rest of their lives with what you do as a teacher.''

He watched as her eyes grew wide and her love of teaching and children just poured out. The enthusiasm was so clear that he thought any of her students would have no choice but to excel. When had he lost that kind of enthusiasm for his job . . . for his life . . . for love? When had he ever had it?

Maggie had continued for a few minutes before he realized that his thoughts had strayed to his own life. As he focused his full attention back on her, she stopped and blushed. And she did it so attractively, too!

''I'm sorry. My friend Pat says that when I start talking about teaching and my kids, I'm harder to shut up than a used car salesman.''

''It's all right, I did ask the question. It's great to see someone who still loves their job.''

''Oh, Alex, I have never thought of teaching as a job. It's my life.'' Still idealistic, still enthusiastic, still committed. And all he felt now that he was involved in his quest for partnership was frustration, disillusion and stagnation.

He noticed that she had thrown her braid over her shoulder when she started speaking about her life . . . not nervous anymore. He could see more of her body again since they sat so close together. His body betrayed him as he noticed her breasts pressing against the linen shirt. Her nipples hardened to points. He hardened, too.

How in God's name would he be able to sleep in the same room with her if he reacted this quickly and vigorously to this slight temptation? Trying to put some distance between them so that his body could cool a bit, Alex stood up and walked to the window. The shirt was longer than the one he wore yesterday, so at least his ass didn't hang out when he walked.

''Tell me aboot yer day. Did they leave ye be?''

''Farland and Innes?''

He nodded.

"They didn't bother me after you left. Innes never even got close—never within a leg's reach!"

"I ken that ye were offended by my actions in announcing that ye are mine, but I think it will ease yer problems wi' the other men." She started shaking her head at him, disagreeing.

"I wasn't offended, Alex. I'm just not used to being owned by a man. I've worked, loved, played, and slept with a man. But I've never been owned by one before."

Alex couldn't say anything, he was still thinking about the "loved, played and slept with" part of Maggie's answer. His body was still thinking about it, too. No, his body just said, "To hell with it," and rose to the occasion! He grimaced. So much for his efforts to cool off.

"I don't think that came out the way I intended, Alex." She smiled at him and he knew that the next days or weeks or months would be hell on earth for him and his body. He was destined to be beaten to a pulp by the men and constantly aroused by this woman.

"And the rest of yer day?" There . . . that was a good change of subject.

"Well, I did find out something interesting about you. Or really about your counterpart, the real Alex."

"Ye did?"

"He *is* in England with King *David* who *is* Robert the Bruce's son. He's been there for almost five years and was a spoiled, overbearing brat when he left!"

"I dinna like the sound of that."

"You shouldn't. From the comments I've heard and overheard today, the real Alex was not well-liked. You are a pleasant surprise to the clan, so far. But they're waiting to see how you handle the Anice versus the 'Sassenach whore' situation."

"What? Is that what they called you?"

Maggie climbed off the bed and walked to where he stood. The shirt definitely looked better on her. Her legs were long and shapely. He swallowed convulsively at the thoughts that entered his brain about what he would like to do with those legs.

"They didn't call me that to my face. But the words were used several times behind my back and to Rachelle."

"Rachelle, that's Brodie's woman?"

"Yes, and apparently a past attempted conquest for the real Alex."

Alex was shocked. "Really?"

"And apparently, the real Alex was not so gracious when she refused his advances. The laird sent him to accompany David to avoid more problems within the clan."

"More problems?" He was intrigued now, wondering what his counterpart was like.

"He and Brodie had come to blows several times over the matter. And Brodie's father, Struan's brother, was pressuring Struan to control Alex."

Alex let out a slow whistle. "So, Struan allowed his son to go into captivity wi' David to restore peace to the clan?"

"You got it. So far, the comments I've heard have been favorable to you, the new and improved Alex. The ones who spoke said that it appeared that you had grown up and might be ready to take your place in the clan hierarchy."

"Except that ye and Anice now threaten more unrest." He watched anger flare in her expressive eyes. "Weel, I amna saying that ye are the cause of this situation. But, we hiv dropped into the middle of something bigger than both of us."

He watched her hips sway as she walked back across the room to the bed. Even covering her from head to toe with some heavy canvas would never hide that walk. Finally, and moments too late for his own peace of mind, she sat on the edge of the bed.

"Speaking of Anice, how did your afternoon and evening go with her?"

Anice's antics came flooding back into his thoughts. She sat as close as she could to him on the stone bench in the garden. She rubbed her barely covered breasts against his arm and her thigh against his leg as he escorted her through the castle grounds! And, her attempts to kiss him! She was certainly aggressive. He shook his head and then ran his hands through his hair. There was no need to mention all of that to Maggie now. Her dislike of Anice was becoming clearer each time the name was mentioned. Before answering, he started to walk the length of the room.

" 'Tis difficult to believe that she is only fifteen. I hiv never met a more 'knowing' fifteen-year-old girl."

She gifted him with a brief smile. "In our day, there are plenty of 'knowing' fifteen-year-olds. I see them in the high school. But, Alex, we're in her time now."

"Ye really think she has been waiting for me here?"

"Yes, in this time she would have been sent here for training, fostered under the care of the laird and lady. She is destined to become lady here when the real Alex assumes the position of laird."

"It's obvious that she's learned weel."

"One other thing you should keep in mind, Alex." He thought he heard a cautioning tone enter her voice. He walked closer to hear her warning. "A betrothal was considered by most as just as good as married. It was not unusual for a betrothed couple to . . ."

"To . . . ?"

"Let's just say, explore the physical side of their relationship."

He could not help it. His mouth dropped open. Sex? Sex with a fifteen-year-old . . . *girl*? "Ye are joking, are ye no'?"

"No, Alex, I am very serious. And, knowing the temperament of the Scots, most betrothed couples do. Actually, if you avoid her too much, it will seem very out of place.''

''Great, just great. So now I maun accept her advances?''

Maggie laughed. If it wasn't himself in this predicament, he might find it humorous, too.

''Weel, I canna say that I like this, but I thank ye for yer warning.'' He paused and thought about the warning he needed to give her.

''And I hiv a warning for ye.'' He sat next to her at the edge of the bed before continuing his words. He turned to face her and saw the worried look that marred her brow.

''Ye need to watch out fer not only the lady Anice but her maids and companions as well. They are all verra displeased aboot yer presence here.''

''I haven't seen any of them. Who are they?''

''They hiv seen ye. Each one took her turn when I visited the solar today. Even 'my' aunt Gunna shared her displeasure wi' me aboot ye.''

''How many are there?'' She was twisting her hair again. Nervous again. Well, with what he heard today, she had reason to be nervous.

''Anice has a maid, Firtha, and a companion, Wynda. Both are much older than she . . . and both are much bigger, too. Aunt Gunna also spends her time wi' them. Just try to stay clear of them.'' She had realized the seriousness of it because her eyes widened and she nodded her head, not arguing.

''Now, we haid better get some rest or we willna make it through another day here.'' He paced the room once more, putting out the candles as Maggie climbed over to the side of the bed near the wall. He watched as she settled under the cover, facing the wall.

As he was drifting off to sleep, he heard her ask, ''It isn't really a bad dream, is it, Alex? This is real?''

He searched for a comforting answer, but there was

none he could think of to give her. "I'm afraid 'tis real, lass. Just keep yer eyes and ears open, and I'm sure we'll figure out what's going on here."

"Good night, Alex."

"Good night, Maggie." He placed his hand lightly on her shoulder. "We'll get through this."

She shrugged but didn't answer. He sensed that she was fighting for control of her fear. He didn't move his hand until he felt the rhythmic rise and fall that told him she was asleep. His hand dropped down to her waist and, since it felt so comfortable, he let it stay there. In a few moments, he was snoring.

Chapter 12

THE CALL DRAGGED her again from sleep. Resisting it was futile; it would not stop until she answered. Now, sitting back on her heels, Moira waited for the smoke to fill the daub and wattle cottage. She knew that after the thick haze blew off the hot fire, she would see. It took but a few moments and the room was hazy, the fire hot and blazing. She leaned closer, closed her eyes, and waited for the wisdom.

As in the countless times before, she opened her eyes as the visions appeared in the flames. A young woman in a strange place and time, a young man who looked to one and all like the young heir, the newly built arch in the laird's new wall.

The arch! It called to her in the night and in the daylight. She saw visions there, too, and that was different from the other times. Never had she seen things anywhere but in the flames. Now, the archway cast scenes in its shadows for her to view. Damn that stonecutter for not watching his empty-headed son! Look what had come from his stupidity.

But, the arch she looked at in the flames was ancient, broken, filled in partway with mortar and stones. As she watched, the young man and woman approached it and sat within its power. They couldn't see the power building around them, but she could. Flashes of light, bands of colors and heat came from the curving structure. She reached toward the scene to warn them, but before she could call out, another was there. The flashes of light and heat grew more intense around them, and then they passed through the arch.

Moira sat back, stunned at what the vision had revealed to her. They were here, now! The man living in the keep was an impostor, but he was the one she waited for, had seen many times in the flames and in the arch. The young woman, not really his leman . . . *yet,* sent to teach him. This man had tempted the fates in some way unknown to her, and they had sent him to learn a lesson. The arch was the tool used to bring him to this reckoning.

Since the knowledge had been sent to her, Moira knew she would be part of this lesson. It had happened before and would again. She lifted a hand up to her face, pushed her loosened hair back, and rubbed her weary eyes. The room began to clear of smoke, leaving only the familiar odor and haze of her peat fire. A loud snore broke into her reverie. Looking toward the straw pallet in one corner, she smiled. The brawny, good-hearted blacksmith still slept. It would be hours before the sun rose in the sky, so Moira crept back onto the pallet and into her lover's protective embrace. A fortnight or more before her part in this lesson began. There would be no time for peace and protection when the fates moved forward with their plan. She had much to prepare.

Chapter 13

"YE LAZY SLATTERN!"

Maggie gasped at the hostility aimed with as much force as a physical blow. She rolled over on the bed and sat up to face her adversary. Another gasp was torn from her throat as she beheld one of the largest women she had ever seen. With a face that could have been carved from granite, the woman stood almost as tall as the doorway. Her body was proportioned to her height, and Maggie swore that this giantess could give even Brodie a run for his money.

Hoping that this intruder had not spied her hiding her backpack under the bed, Maggie slid to the edge, stood, and took a few steps away from it. It was then that she noticed the pile of clothes held in the woman's arms.

Raising her chin and putting forth a brave face that she didn't particularly feel, Maggie asked, "Are you looking for Alex?"

The woman glared at her with an icy look and snorted in answer. She looked around the room and began walking toward one of the trunks against the far wall. Without thought, Maggie placed her hand on the woman's forearm to stop her progress. The woman pushed Maggie out of her way and continued. "This is Alex's room, and you cannot just come in here whenever you like. And, who are you?"

"I dinna usually converse wi' yer kind, whore, but I am the Lady Anice's maid. Now, get out of my way while I carry out her wishes."

In shock from the harshness shouted at her, Maggie released her weak hold, backed away, and watched the maid open the trunk and put the garments inside. The woman straightened and walked wordlessly from the room, without sparing Maggie another glance.

Maggie let out the breath she didn't know she'd been holding and slammed the door. She raced the few steps to the trunk and opened the lid. Searching through the pile, Maggie found three shirts, two pairs of tight pants, stockings unlike any she had ever seen before, and two more lengths of plaid cloth. So, the Lady Anice was providing Alex with more clothes. Well, that meant that their story of being robbed was accepted.

Closing the lid, Maggie looked at her wrist instinctively. She was so accustomed to wearing a watch and being on a schedule that she continued to try to check the time. She made a mental note to tell Alex about their watches. They were both ticking, but neither one was advancing. They stopped at 1:23 P.M., the time she and Alex first sat on the wall inside that old arch. Another part of this growing mystery.

It was nearly time for the noon meal, she thought, as she made her way out of the room and back to the kitchen. Passing through the doorway to the great hall, she paused and surveyed the crowded room. A hazy, dizzy feeling washed over her, forcing her to grab onto the stone entranceway. She closed her eyes, waiting for the room to stop spinning. After a few moments, she forced her eyes to open. The strange feeling was gone as quickly as it came, but she was still suffering its confusing effects when a booming voice grabbed her attention.

''Mistress Hobbs!''

It couldn't be . . . it just couldn't. She turned toward the kitchen, but he would not be ignored.

''Mistress Hobbs, bring yerself up here.'' The laird's tone was clear; he would brook no defiance, especially not in his hall.

Maggie's throat and chest tightened, her palms grew sweaty, and she fought to remain calm. As she took her first step toward the dais, she let her gaze sweep over the room. No Alex. No Anice. No Rachelle. Just Struan and his steward.

Her second and third steps were just as difficult as the first. She focused on her breathing, forcing air in and out of her rebellious chest. Although the room had quieted, most were going about their own tasks. She took one more look around as she reached the bottom step. The whispered voices of Struan and Dougal cut through her concentration.

''Ye canna think to do it, Struan.''

''Ye dare to question me?''

''Ye ken what she is? How can ye seat her at yer table?'' Dougal's voice became an exasperated whine as he huffed out his complaint to the laird.

''Because I am the laird here, Dougal. Ye willna naysay me in my own hall. If ye are bothered by the wench, ye hiv my permission to leave.''

Maggie stopped and waited. Struan wanted her seated at his table and Dougal objected, strongly. Struan motioned her forward and pointed to a stool near his chair. ''Sit there, lass. Dougal, tell Odara I am ready to eat.''

Looking as if he had smelled something very rotten, Dougal gave a slight bow to Struan. His lips were closed tightly, a thin line of disapproval in an overall expression of his distaste. He left before Maggie could climb the steps to the table.

* * *

Fear was clear on her lovely face, but he could see she was fighting it. His son's leman reminded him of his beloved Edana in many ways. Her hair was the same color, her eyes nearly the same hue. But it was the strength and backbone she displayed in this unfamiliar place that made him smile. Edana was forced here against her wishes by her clan. Their marriage was arranged to unite two warring factions, and she had not agreed to it. Well, at first. It took but moments in the same room for them both to realize that they should be together. A love match from an arranged marriage, no one had thought it possible.

His eyes burned with unreleased tears as his lifetime of memories with her flew through his mind. He shook his head; this was not the time or place to sink into reverie. The woman stepped back at his gesture and waited.

''Take yer seat, Mistress Hobbs. I hiv matters to discuss wi' ye.''

She nodded at him and walked up the steps before him. He examined her from head to toe and everywhere in between as she made her way to the stool next to him. Her eyes widened as she stood next to him.

''I may be hungry, but I promise not to bite ye. Join me,'' he pulled the stool closer to him, ''for the noon meal.''

Odara and some serving maids crossed from the kitchen, carrying platters to the dais. At her direction, the girls began to place trenchers of day-old bread in front of them. Platters of another meat stew, boiled peas and beans, and assorted cheeses were presented. Grunting his satisfaction, he piled both trenchers with a selection of foods. At his nod, the trays were placed behind them on a smaller table to await their call for more. A young boy filled their goblets and then moved away. Struan winked at young Kenneth, who hadn't spilled a drop over the rims of the goblets. The lad was learning quickly.

''So, lass, tell me how ye came to meet my Alex?'' He pushed the trencher of food toward her and watched as she drew a small dagger from her apron pocket and cut the larger chunks of cheese. He dug in with his own, awaiting her answer.

"As I told Brodie, we met in England . . . where he was . . ."

"Whoring and gambling wi' the king?" His reports were as close to the facts as anyone's, he knew what his son and heir spent his time doing in Londontown.

"Ah, Laird, er . . . my lord . . ."

"Ye can call me Struan, or Laird if ye be not comfortable wi' that. Now, 'tis the truth of it and I ken it, lass. Young David and my Alex hiv plowed their way through the women of Edward's court and hiv now set their sights on those least able to say no."

He watched as a blush moved up from her neck to her face. She stammered even more as she tried to speak. Her long braid had fallen over her shoulder and she began twisting the end of it around her fingers. Edana had been bashful, too, but it had not lasted long. He had a feeling that it would not last with this lass much longer.

"Were ye still a maiden when Alex found ye?" He purposely provoked her in order to learn more about this Sassenach who had enough grit to stand up to Brodie and to others who tried to accost her. He almost smiled as she faced him straight on for the first time.

"No, Laird, I was not a maiden when I met Alex." The blush deepened in her cheeks.

"Did he promise ye anything to get ye into his bed?"

"Well, Laird," she began quietly, "he did promise me a good time in his arms and in his bed." He saw her eyes twinkle as she spoke.

"And, lass, did he fulfill his promise to ye?"

"Aye, Laird, he did." And she winked at him!

He roared out his enjoyment of bantering with this lively foreigner who belonged to his son. Laughing loudly, he watched her hesitate and then join in with him.

Her laugh was light and without false pride. He liked this girl!

"Come, Mistress Hobbs, eat yer fill. Ye maun need yer strength to keep up all yer tasks."

He gave himself and the girl some time to fill their bellies before beginning anew to question her. The reports he received on his son's escapades only went so far, and none had mentioned a Mistress Maggie Hobbs.

After sampling all of Odara's fare, he pushed his chair back from the table's edge and looked over at Maggie. She dropped her hands to her lap and lowered her eyes to avoid his.

"Nay, lass, eat more if yer hungry."

"Thank you, Laird. Odara's bread is very good." She tore another piece off the loaf and wiped up the gravy from the stew. She washed her food down with a large swallow of water and sat back. Without warning, she stood quickly. "I should get back to my duties. If you would excuse me?"

Struan grabbed her hand and tugged her back on her stool. Dougal, the old fool, saw it as he came up the steps and approached the table. "Ye are no' excused, Mistress. Sit." She was trying to slip away before he got what he wanted. "What is it, Dougal?"

"I wanted to inform ye that the messengers hiv been sent as ye ordered."

"Messengers?" He knew the answer, he waited to see her response.

"Aye, messengers to the MacNab. They left early this morn to bring news of the marriage to the Lady Anice's family."

She paled a bit, but he couldn't see any other reaction to the news that her protector and lover was marrying soon. "Thank ye, Dougal. Ye may go now."

He could see the indignation rise on Dougal's face. His loyal steward was not used to being pushed out of the way and was not used to having his advice ignored. Dougal straightened his back and held his head high and, with a loud *hmmpff,* he stormed out of the hall. He would survive the insult.

"So, Mistress, how is yer work in the kitchens? Are ye able to keep up wi' it?"

She stood at his side again and tried to leave. "Aye, Laird, I am familiar with kitchen work. I can do the work you've assigned." Taking a small step backward, she continued, "I'm sure Odara is waiting for me to return now. If you'll excuse me?"

He would have his answers, but he wouldn't have them this day. She was too new to this place to answer him yet. But she would one day. He was Laird, by God, and she would speak the truth to him when he demanded it of her. But he would give her time.

She hesitated before leaving the table, waiting for his permission. A brief nod of his head and she sped off down the stairs to the kitchens.

Somehow, the story of Alex and the wench's return to the clan didn't sound right. Something about it raised his hackles. He would get to the bottom of this and find out what neither his son nor his son's woman would say aloud.

Chapter 14

"WE HIV SOME time afore we are needed again. Would ye like to walk?"

Stretching shoulders and arms sore from too much kneading, Maggie nodded her answer. Fresh air would feel good, and a walk would give her a chance to check out their surroundings.

"Lead on, Rachelle." With a sweep of her hand, she motioned to Rachelle to go ahead.

Rachelle led her through the doorway into the bailey and past the exercise yards. The sounds of men yelling and metal against metal and wood against wood became louder. Then, after a huge roar, disappeared. If she was in her own time, she could have sworn she was listening to the crowd at a baseball or football game.

" 'Tis the men in the yard. The laird ordered their practice."

"Does he expect trouble?" It would be their luck to end up in the middle of a clan war!

"I dinna think so, but he takes no chances wi' the clan's safety. Besides, ye never ken what our neighbors, the MacArthurs, will do since David is still held in England.''

Rachelle waved Maggie closer. ''Come, there's a place I want to show ye nearby.''

Maggie ran to catch up with her, and a few minutes later, they broke through a line of trees into a clearing. They stood at the edge of a huge lake. The surface, moved by deeper waves, reflected back the bright blue of the sky. A breeze, traveling over the water, wafted over her and cooled her sweaty face. Rachelle sat on a rock and pulled off her shoes and stockings.

''Come. The waters will refresh ye.''

She removed her shoes and stockings and followed Rachelle's steps into the lake. She couldn't control the squeal that broke free.

''By God, this is cold!'' She wiggled her toes in the water. They felt numb already and fought her attempts to move them. She jumped out of the water and onto the sand surrounding the lake.

''This loch never gets warm. The waters come from the Ben Nevis's snows.'' Maggie followed Rachelle's gesture to the north. ''They feed the loch all year. But, we dinna mind it here.''

''Well, it's too cold for this Sassenach to go swimming.'' She shivered from head to toe as she touched the water again.

''Come, let's sit in the shade.'' Rachelle walked over to a part of the shore where the trees hung low over the water's edge. Maggie walked over and sat next to her, enjoying the clean, crisp air.

The air was one big difference that she had noticed almost immediately upon arriving here. You could actually smell the surrounding trees and plants here. Smells and odors were carried by a background air that had no fluorocarbons to dull their scents. They had not learned the basics of how to keep the air in the kitchen moving, but outside was pristine and cool.

And, it was quiet here, she thought, looking at the lake and cocking her head to one side. Well, not in the castle during most of the day, but out here and at night. The sounds of birds calling to their mates in the forest traveled far in the tranquil surroundings.

"This is very nice, Rachelle. Thank you for bringing me here."

"Weel, if we wait a few moments more, it will be e'en nicer." Rachelle winked at her and held her finger in front of her lips.

The sound of voices started out low, then gained in volume and strength. Maggie waited quietly as they came closer. Rachelle pointed to a spot down the shoreline and she watched as two men burst through the trees, laughing and yelling as they plunged into the water.

It was Alex and Brodie . . . naked as newborn babes and just as loud!

"You are a wicked woman, Rachelle. They're naked!"

"Weel, how do ye expect them to wash? Wi' their plaids on? Now, hush afore they hear ye!"

The men broke the surface of the lake, and Alex's curse split the air. Brodie's laughing answered Alex, and then they both began walking from the water. Maggie turned to see Rachelle's reaction to the sight of the two, very well-endowed warriors who stood drying themselves not twenty feet away. Rachelle's face glowed with love as she watched Brodie. She smiled when he did and blushed as he and Alex made disparaging remarks about each other's physical attributes.

Maggie took advantage of the opportunity to study Alex in the daylight. She had watched him when he searched for a nightshirt in the trunk, but she had seen mostly his backside that night. Although he was more distant from her now, the sunlight made it easier to see more. He was not as big in bulk as Brodie, but his body was nicely proportioned: wide shoulders, narrow waist and hips, strong thighs. The furry pelt of hair on his chest was more red than the hair on his head and thinned as it went below his waist. Her face began to burn and her breathing increased as she gazed at the area below his waist. Though his body was obviously affected by the coldness of the water, she was nonetheless impressed.

It was Rachelle's laughter that roused her from her close inspection. As her glance traveled back up to Alex's face, she realized that they had locked gazes.

"Weel, Maggie, do I still meet yer approval?" He called out.

She looked him straight in the eye as she answered. "Oh, yes, Alex, I do approve."

All four burst out in laughter at her answer, and the two groups walked toward each other. Rachelle ran into Brodie's spread arms and he twirled her around in his embrace. By the time they came to a stop, Brodie was kissing her passionately.

Maggie looked at Alex, and he nodded and reached for her. With an arm around her shoulders, he drew her close and leaned down to kiss her mouth. Maggie sighed helplessly as his warm lips caresed hers. A throbbing sensation began low in her belly. What started out for show turned into something quite real in just a few seconds. The sight of his naked body had aroused her, and she fed the fire by responding recklessly to his kiss.

His skin was cold, but her heat was warming him quickly to the core. He wrapped his arms more tightly around her and spread his legs, urging her to come in closer. She did. He plunged his tongue deeper into her mouth and heard her moan in response. He moved one of his hands behind her head and slipped his fingers into her hair. Slanting his head, he tasted her again and again until her tongue joined his in play. Her hands moved over his skin, and he felt her fingers in the hair on his chest.

"Alex," she sighed as they finally parted, and she lifted her mouth to his for more. A quick glance told him they were alone, Brodie had taken Rachelle off for some privacy. He opened his mouth and let her tongue move into his, enjoying the tickling, tingling feeling as she tasted him. He was also enjoying the movements of her hands, sweeping over his back and down to his waist and hips. He pushed his arousal toward her and rubbed against her hips, the friction and the heat making him harder than before.

Her questing hands reached his backside and they stopped. Maggie pulled from their kiss and looked at him with passion-glazed eyes.

"Alex, you're naked!"

"Aye, lass, I am that."

"What are we doing?" Maggie turned her glance to the trees over his shoulders.

"Weel, we call it preein' the lips o' here, but I think they call it kissing in England." She slapped at his shoulder and pulled away. He watched as she took deep gulps of air and forced them out loudly.

"I know what it's called, Alex. But, have you lost your mind?" Their gazes locked and never wavered, even as he leaned down and picked up the length of plaid lying nearby on the ground.

"Was there something wrong in what we did?" He began to wrap the plaid around his waist as Brodie had shown him and threw the excess over his shoulder.

"I'm afraid, Alex." Her voice lowered to a mere whisper, her eyes were wide. He moved closer to hear her concerns. "It felt real, Alex, it didn't feel like we were acting."

"Is that wrong? I saw the way ye looked at me. Ye were just as hot for me as I was for ye."

"I'm not blaming you, Alex. I got caught off guard by Rachelle. I didn't expect to see you standing by the lake in nothing but your birthday suit." She shook her head as she continued. "There's too much for us to worry about here, Alex. We can't allow ourselves to become, you know, involved. We have to find out what's going on.''

He took a deep breath and ran his hand through his dripping wet hair. He walked down to the edge of the lake and tried to straighten out his thoughts. She was right; they shouldn't even think about getting involved with each other. The safest thing was to keep themselves from believing in the relationship the others thought they had. But he had seen the hunger and fire in her eyes when she watched him leave the water. And, he'd felt the passion in her kisses and the welcome in her embrace.

Yes, she *was* right, he would need to control himself around her. That shouldn't be a problem, but it was. He turned to look at her. What was happening to him here? At home, he'd kept his life with Nancy in a separate compartment, and it had never intruded on his work or his pursuit of a partnership.

But, here and now, every time he forced this beautiful stranger out of his thoughts, she crept back in. He had to focus on finding a way back to their time and this sexual attraction would hinder that. Taking a deep breath, he mentally resolved that theirs had to be nothing more than a business arrangement: finding a way home. Anything, everything else could wait.

''Maggie, I'm sorry. Yer right, we maun focus our efforts on finding a way home. I will try not to surprise ye anymore and will try to keep the kissing for times when we need to put on our show.''

''Alex, it was just as much my fault as yours. I will try to behave myself, too. Okay?''

''Fine. Now, I think we should make our way back to the keep.'' He could do anything he set his mind to; he knew it.

''Maybe you'd better go ahead by yourself? If Anice is watching, she won't be happy that we've spent time together.''

''Yer right, Maggie. I will go on ahead of ye then.''

He turned back to her before leaving. ''Be careful.'' At her nod, he took off running through the trees. The exercise would do him good. Another dip in the cold loch before bed would do him even better.

Chapter 15

THEY BOTH JUMPED when the loud knock hit the door. He and Maggie exchanged worried glances, and he nodded at the bed. She ran to it and climbed quickly under the covers.

"Wheesht! Who is knocking at this time o' night?"

" 'Tis I, Alex, open yer door," Struan ordered.

Alex did not hesitate to respond.

"Coming, Faither, coming," he yelled at the door. Lowering his voice, he whispered, "Quickly, Maggie, take off yer shirt. Loosen yer hair."

He pulled his shirt off and walked to the door. After glancing at her to check and seeing her shocked look, he explained his strange order. "They all sleep naked here. It would look strange for us to be lovers and go to bed covered." At her nod, he gave her a moment and then shoved the trunk out of the way with his foot and opened the door.

"Weel, Faither, do ye want to come in? Should I dress?"

Struan entered, walking past Alex and stopping at the foot of the bed.

"Nay, dinna dress, I amna staying. But close the door for now."

Alex obeyed and waited to discover what caused this midnight visit.

"Hiv ye heard that I haid words wi' yer woman at the noon meal?" Alex hadn't heard. "Dougal wasna verra happy wi' me since I invited her to join me at the meal."

"Ye haid her sit wi' ye at the table?"

Struan nodded. Alex *was* surprised. The separation between the clan and strangers, the noble and the common people was very clear to him. And a man's leman did not join the man's father at the table, especially if the man's father was laird of the clan. He looked from his father to Maggie and back again.

"Are ye trying to take her from me, Faither?"

The implications of this were staggering. He couldn't stop Struan if he laid claim to Maggie. He heard Maggie move behind him on the bed and prayed she would keep silent.

"Nay, Alex, I amna. I tell ye this because I was trying to find out more aboot the woman who ye would bring into yer home and before yer betrothed."

"Did ye find what ye were looking for?"

"Aye, I did. She reminds me much of yer own maither. She has the same strength as Edana when she first arrived here. And, of course, she is a beautiful woman, much like Edana in her coloring."

From the tightness about the man's lips and his tightly clenched fists, Alex sensed that Struan was holding something back.

"Ye hiv more to say than aboot the looks of the woman I sleep wi', Faither. Just say it."

"I sent ye away five years ago to keep peace wi'in the clan. It was the hardest thing I ever haid to do and yer maither, God rest her soul, fought me every step of the way. She wasna pleased wi' me and 'twas weeks afore she spoke to me after ye left." He paused and looked at

Maggie. "Now ye are back, and the woman ye brought wi' ye threatens the peace of the clan once more."

Maggie gasped at his comment and started to answer his words, but Struan shook his head at her.

"It isna something ye hiv done, Mistress Hobbs, 'tis yer verra presence here that is creating upheaval. I ken and agree that as my heir and the future laird of this clan, Alex haes the right to choose a woman as his leman. This may just not be the time for it."

"What are ye saying?" Alex prayed silently that Struan was not planning to send Maggie away.

"I like this lass, Alex, and I can see why ye want her in yer bed. And she can stay here for now. But if there is any trouble, she willna remain."

"What?" His voice was louder than it should have been, and Struan's eyes flared with anger at Alex's inadvertent challenge.

"If there is trouble, any trouble in the clan because of this woman," he pointed at Maggie without looking at her, "she willna remain in this keep and mayhap not e'en in Dunnedin."

"But, Faither, she saved my life. I owe her."

"Aye, ye do and I do as well. If she wishes to remain here, she maun stay out of Anice's way. And, that includes her companions as well as her servants. Do ye understaun, lass?"

"I understand, Laird." Maggie's voice was just a whisper.

"If Anice continues to take exception to ye, I will arrange for yer return to England or find a mon here to wed wi' ye. It will be easier that way. And it will keep the peace in the clan."

Struan looked at both of them before walking to the door. Without another word, he pulled the door closed behind him.

* * *

Maggie searched under the covers for the shirt she had stuffed there at Struan's appearance. Shaking it out and pulling it over her head, she tried to still her trembling hands, her racing heart, and her heaving breaths. This was not good. Not good at all. She waited for Alex to finish securing the door.

He turned back to the bed and grabbed his shirt from the floor and put it back on. Then he started pacing. She watched as he walked back and forth in front of the hearth.

"I never thought we would hiv this problem. Ye ken the need to stay out of Anice's path. What happened?"

She didn't particularly like his tone, accusing her of something.

"Nothing happened."

"Something maun hiv happened for Struan to disturb us in the night. I warned ye of Anice's women."

"Yes, you did," she answered him, her voice cold with anger. "I had no idea that one of them would show up here while I was hiding my backpack."

"And?"

"And? And, she called me some filthy names and brought you more clothes to wear. Then she left." At his upraised eyebrow, she snorted. "That is what happened. She must have gone right back to Anice to tell her I was in your room during the day."

"I'm sorry, Maggie, that was uncalled for. I dinna think yer starting the trouble. We maun watch our step until we find our way back home."

"It's just hard, Alex, really, really hard. I've done what I've been told to do and followed all the customs I know about. I am trying to fit in. At least you have the easier part of it."

"I do?"

"Yes, you get to play around with the men and romance Anice and everyone thinks you're the clan darling returned home. I have to put up with the insults and sly comments behind my back. And the fear. I am so afraid of so many things here, and I don't like living in fear."

"I can tell ye that my part isna any easier than yers, Maggie. Did ye say 'play around wi' the men'? Believe me, they are no' playing with those weapons! And, I hiv to keep up the same pretenses as ye. Pretending that I ken everyone here, and that I am willing and even eager to marry Anice. 'Tis hard for me, too, lass."

Alex had put out the candles and was now standing next to the bed. She pulled the covers back and patted the mattress.

"Come to bed, Alex. I think we have both been pushed to our limits today."

He settled under the covers and folded his hands under his head. He was silent for so long she thought him asleep. His voice in the dimness startled her.

"Share yer fears wi' me, Maggie. Mayhap it will help."

She turned on her side and propped her head up on her hand. "The thing that makes me most uncomfortable here is the physicalness of this time."

"What do ye mean?" She felt him turn toward her in the bed as he waited for her answer.

"Well, you kind of mentioned it yourself. Everything here is settled with force, or maybe strength is a better word. I saw one of the servants in the kitchen get hit today for not doing something fast enough. And those two who bothered me in the hall? It was all about them being bigger and stronger. In our time, I teach kids how to settle problems without force or violence. Here, it's the way of life." Gosh, it felt good to talk about the feelings that had haunted her the last few days.

"I ken what ye mean, Maggie. I'm used to making my way in the world wi' a laptop, a calculator, and a cell phone. Here, I'm using a sword, a staff, and my fists. I pride myself on my restraint and self-control, but in this world, I'll survive better wi'oot it."

She nodded, understanding well what he meant, too. "All our rules are gone, and it's tough to learn how to play the game."

"The rules are gone and my cell phone! I amna sure which I miss more."

She chuckled at his attempt at humor.

"Weel, lass, we haid better get some rest. Each day here is more a challenge than the last one, and we need to be strong and well-rested to face them."

"Good night, Alex, and thank you for listening."

"Good night, Maggie, and, thank ye as weel."

She rolled over to her other side, rearranging the covers and getting comfortable. Thinking about the coming day, she decided to take a tour of the area surrounding the keep, if she got the chance. She needed to get a look at the village one day soon, too. She could feel sleep pulling her into its control as she made her plans. Another day here, and the unbelievable nightmare continued.

Chapter 16

SHE HAPPENED UPON it completely by accident. A few days after Struan's midnight visit, Maggie took a wrong turn on her way from the gardens. Instead of leading back to the main gate of the keep, the path she chose led her to the perimeter of the outer wall that was being expanded. When the basket grew too heavy, she rested in the shade of the wall for a few minutes.

She swatted at the air around her when she first heard the noise. A bee? A fly? She couldn't see an insect, but she could hear it. Brushing the loose strands of hair from her face, she picked up her basket to leave. The noise got louder: buzzing and fading, buzzing and fading.

She walked through the stone archways and cocked her head to listen. It was getting stronger, pulsing its signal to her. The air around her felt electrified, and the hairs on the back of her neck stood. She felt dizzy, the scenery before her spinning in front of her eyes. She tried to slow her breathing, tried to get control over the myriad sensations passing through her. Stumbling, she reached out, resting her hand on the arch in front of her to get her balance, and was taken aback by the vibrations.

The archway! It must be the same one! But, this was new, freshly built, hardly finished. She tested it again, using her palm. The noise grew louder and she could feel waves of heat coming from the stones. Dropping the basket to the ground, she stepped closer without entering the arch.

Looking around the site, she saw workers carrying stones, buckets of mortar, and tools, but no one was near this arch, and they didn't see her. The other arches were the same size and shape, but they were in a different color stone. It wasn't much different, yet it stood out in the bright sunshine. The boulders were an odd shape, smoothed in a manner and texture that the others were not. Running her hand over their surface was not unpleasant, not after the initial contact. And it was just like when she and Alex had sat beneath it at the festival.

She had to tell him! Looking up at the sun's position, she decided it was about an hour till the noon meal. Alex would be working in the yard with Brodie. She had to get to him. This was their way home. Turning away from the arch, Maggie ran in the opposite direction. She couldn't take the chance of walking through it without Alex at her side. Taking a deep breath, she ran faster.

Weaving through the workers, she found the main gate and hurried inside. The stitch in her side grew stronger, but she tried to ignore it. Holding her hand against her side, she headed for the exercise yard. Brodie's form and voice was unmistakable. She paid no heed to the gasps of the warriors as she entered the area. She had to find Alex.

"Brodie," she yelled, still gasping for air, "where is he?"

"He left for the village, lass. Can I help ye wi' anything?"

She saw the twinkle in his eyes and finally realized that this was Brodie's natural state—a born flirt. He meant no harm or insult to her. Besides, Rachelle would kill him if he did anything more than flirt.

"I need to talk to Alex, Brodie. I'll find him in the village." She had nearly caught her breath when she took off running again, back toward the gate again.

"Wait, Maggie. He's. . . ." Brodie hesitated in his answer.

"Thank you, Brodie," she yelled, not looking back.

She raced down the path to the village, slowing only around some cumbersome carts making their way up to the gate. Looking up as she approached the first group of crofts, she could see Alex's head in the crowd. Holding her side against the pain pulsing in it, she made her way over to him. When she broke through the villagers, she could only gasp for air again. She finally forced out the words.

"Alex, I've found it." She waited for his response. Silence greeted her announcement. "Didn't you hear me, Alex? I found it."

She finally caught her breath and looked at him. His eyes were wide and the shaking of his head was barely noticeable. But she saw it and then heard a loud gasp from somewhere near Alex. The crowd parted to reveal Anice and her companion, both gaping at her.

"Alex, what is she doing here?" Anice's voice was sugary sweet as she spoke to him. She walked over to him and placed her hand on his arm. "She should be in the kitchens carrying out her duties." Anice's eyes flared with anger and it was directed at her. "*Servants* canna simply take off to wherever they like, whenever they like." Her point was well made, her insult on target.

"I will handle this, Anice." His voice was pitched low and bland, even to her ears.

"Wynda, go back to Odara and tell her I will deal wi' this one when I return." Anice pressed the issue. She smiled at Maggie, like a cat breathing down the neck of a canary. Maggie shivered at the malice in that smile.

Alex turned to Anice and raised his voice, ''I said that I will handle this, Anice. Wynda, stay with yer lady.'' Wynda nodded at Alex and moved closer to Anice.

''Maggie, go back to yer duties,'' he paused, then shouted, ''Now.''

His voice was stronger and louder now, and he was angry. She was paralyzed for a moment before nodding in reply and turning away.

Walking back to the keep, she wondered at his tone. She had only one thought in her mind: to share with him the news about finding the arch. Their way back home! She had not even thought about what he was doing or who he was with. Now she understood the hesitation in Brodie's voice. He had known! And she had not stopped to listen. She reached the main gate and was about to pass through it when she thought of the task assigned by Odara.

The basket! Damn! She remembered dropping it when she found the arch. Just great! Now she would have to get it and get back to Odara before news of her confrontation reached the castle. Hurrying her pace, she retrieved the basket of herbs without getting close to the arch and made her way to the kitchen. She paused to straighten her hair and replace her scarf before entering. It was then she heard the voices, conveniently in heavily accented English.

''Just as proud as can be, she went right up to him in front of the lady Anice.''

''Can ye imagine? As if she haes a right to his time and attention, outside of his bed, that is!'' Those inside laughed at the comment.

''Weel, she is a Sassenach, ye ken.''

''We ken she's a Sassenach, Gertie. What haes that to do wi' anything?''

''Mayhap she dinna ken the way we do things here?''

''Weel, from the look on the lady's face, she'll learn right quick. Anice wasna pleased. No' pleased at all.''

She peeked around the doorway and saw that they were all shaking their heads over the last comment. Unease crept up like icy fingers on her back at their expressions. It seemed as if they were all thinking about the lady Anice's displeasure. Maggie entered the kitchen with the basket on her arm. Odara broke the uncomfortable silence.

"Come, lass, give me those. I hiv been waiting for ye."

"I am sorry for the delay." She tried to sound apologetic. Odara had treated her fairly since her arrival into the hierarchy of the kitchen. She never insulted her or allowed the others to when she was present. Maggie walked over to the place where she usually worked and lifted a large lump of dough from a covered basket. Spreading some coarse flour over the table's surface, she began to kneed the dough for the noon meal's bread. The usual kitchen chatter started after a few minutes, and since it was now in Gaelic, she knew she was the topic of conversation.

She was lost in thought about the arch when she noticed that the kitchen was silent and the workers stood watching her. Alex stood at the door, his face reddened and angry.

"Maggie, come wi' me now." His tone made everyone present cringe at its severity.

She wiped her hands on a towel and followed him from the room. He preceded her into the great hall and reached back to grab her wrist before they were halfway through the room. She had to jog to keep up with his long, fast strides. At the landing to the stairs, they passed Anice's maid. Her expression, gloating and smirking, made Maggie want to slap her. She resisted since she could tell there was trouble afoot already.

Alex pushed open the door to their room and pulled her inside. He slammed the door closed behind them.

"Get on the bed." She stood in front of him, rubbing her wrist when he began to remove his belt. This had better work, he thought. If Anice and her insulted pride was not satisfied, they were in deep trouble.

When he doubled his belt, all color drained from her face. She started shaking her head at him and backed away a few steps. He followed her movements and pointed at the bed with the belt he held. Knowing that there were people outside their door ready to report back to Anice, he raised his voice.

"I told ye to get on the bed, now!" She jumped at his harshness but climbed up on the bed as he had commanded.

"Ye will ken yer place from now on." Alex raised his arm and struck the bed with the heavy leather belt. Maggie screamed in fear before she realized where the blow was aimed. Perfect.

"Ye hiv no right to approach the lady Anice or to speak to her wi'oot her permission." His voice got louder and he struck again. Maggie swayed on the bed and moaned loudly.

"Ye are here to serve me, and ye will not put on false airs around others." He hoped the bedcover wouldn't tear. Maggie screamed a moment after the blow landed.

"Dinna move from this room until I give ye the word. Ye will learn." He held a finger to his lips and moved to the door. "I'll be back later. Stay here," he whispered.

He pulled the door open and several women scattered down the hall. He stepped out of the room and slammed the door closed. Muttering under his breath, he made a big show of putting his belt back on. Hopefully, their little act would satisfy everyone's hurt pride, and things would quiet back down. He hoped.

Chapter 17

"MY GOD, MAGGIE, what could ye hiv been thinking of?"

Searching through her backpack with her back to the door, she hadn't heard him come in. She jumped at his words and turned toward him. Which Alex would this be—the sensitive man who comforted her at night or the angry warrior who had shown his face today?

"*What could I hiv been thinkin' of?* Maybe just the way for us to get home. How's that?" Sarcasm, her best weapon.

"The way home? Really? What did ye find?"

He took her by the shoulders and pulled her close to him. She couldn't help the fear that entered her eyes, and she knew he saw it. He took a step back from her and released his tight grip on her arms.

"Are ye all right?" He perused her face and eyes. "I mean, after this afternoon? I maun hiv frightened ye when I dragged ye in here and took off my belt?"

"Yes, you did, Alex. And I don't know what to expect now." Maggie rubbed her upper arms as she walked over to the small window to await his response. It would tell her more about their predicament than anything else that came later.

"Maggie, I am struggling, too, to find my way through this world. When ye burst into the village screaming my name, I could see the shock on the villagers' faces who heard ye. They can blame much on yer being an outlander, but today ye crossed even that line."

"But, Alex . . ."

"No, Maggie, no buts. We canna get home if we're killed or maimed here. We maun watch our step even more closely. Ye maun behave inside the role ye play."

"Is that why you dragged me up here and pretended to beat me?"

He walked closer to her and raised his hand to her cheek. She tried not to flinch or pull away, but his violent explosion earlier had deeply frightened her. He touched her face gently with his fingertips.

"I had to show that I could control ye, Maggie. The clan needed to see a demonstration of that, and I gave them one. But, Maggie," he paused, "I am sorry that I made ye fear me."

"I'll be okay. You really surprised me, that's all."

He pulled her over to the bed and sat beside her. "So, tell me now what ye found."

"The arch, Alex, I found the arch!"

"Where is it? How did ye find it?"

"It's here, It's part of the new section of wall that Struan is building. I was getting some herbs from the far gardens for Odara and I felt it."

"Ye felt it. What do ye mean?"

"First, I heard it. I heard a buzzing noise that got louder and louder as I walked closer. Then, when I raised my hand to the stones, I experienced the same shock I felt at the festival."

"I dinna feel anything from the stones. When did ye notice it?"

"I touched the arch when I found it. I've been doing that all over Scotland and England—touching ancient walls and buildings. Anyway, I felt a pulsing in the arch that day, almost like an electrical current in the stones."

"Did it hurt ye?" He was watching her closely.

"No, it didn't hurt or feel bad at first. When you sat next to me on the wall, the pulsing became stronger, hotter. Then, well, you know what happened."

"And this arch, ye felt it here, too?"

"Yes, I did." She pulled her legs under her skirt and sat facing him on the bed. "It was stronger and louder here, maybe because the arch is new? I touched it and felt the same sensations again, only much more this time."

"Did ye try to go through? Did ye try to see if it worked?"

She *had* thought about trying it. For a moment, she had thought of nothing but escaping and getting home. But after that instant of self-preservation passed, Alex had entered her thoughts. They had come here together for some reason and they had to get home together. She knew that, *felt that,* deep inside. They were joined by fate in whatever was going on and, until they both left, neither one would be able to alone.

"No," she shook her head, "I didn't. I wanted to tell you about it first."

"I thank ye for no' leaving me behind." He leaned over and kissed her lightly on her forehead.

"I can take you there now that it's dark out. Come on." She slid from the bed and took his hand. Dropping his hand, she walked over to the door and opened it.

"Wait, Maggie. We canna go yet." He reached over her head to push the door closed again.

"Why not?"

"Because the hall is still filled. We maun wait a bit more unless we want witnesses or even companions."

"You're right, Alex. We'd better wait." She watched him begin to pace over to the window and back again.

Smiling at his unconscious habit, she sat on the bed. ''Is there something you'd like to talk about? Something worrying you?''

''Nay. Do ye hiv something ye wish to speak aboot?''

He had changed, just a bit, but enough for her to notice, since he had arrived. First, the Gaelic, and now, his use of physical means to solve a problem. This might be her chance to learn about him before he changed even more.

''You never mentioned what you did, back home, I mean.''

He paused and looked at her for a few moments before answering. Almost as if he'd forgotten already!

''I was . . . am an accountant, soon to be a partner in Friedman, Thompson and Bansch, a CPA firm.''

''You're an accountant?'' Her mouth dropped in surprise.

''Aye. Why are ye giving me such a look? Don't I look like an accountant?''

She couldn't help it; she broke out in laughter, right in his surprised face. He glanced down at his clothes and then looked around the room. When he realized what she was laughing at, he joined her.

''Yer right, lass, right now, I dinna look much like an accountant. But I am one, a damn good one.''

''Now I understand some of your discomfort being in this situation.''

''Ye do?''

Maggie joined him where he had stopped in his pacing. She touched his forearm when she was close enough.

''You are used to order in your work, not chaos. Things in straight lines and numbers that always behave the way they should. I'll bet you run your life that way, too?'' At his nod, she continued, ''Oh, Alex, how difficult it must be now that we've been thrown into a world so different from ours. Nothing where or as it should be. Nothing orderly. No one behaving civilly. No one following the rules. You must be lost.''

She couldn't help herself. She reached up, slipped her arms under his, and wrapped them around him. At first, he held himself rigidly in her embrace. Then she felt him relax.

"But, you're enjoying this, aren't you? This time and this place have given you freedom, a chance to be a different man than the one behind the desk. The question for you is, how will you go back to being that Alex?" Maggie raised her face to look at him and was startled by the intent gaze that met hers.

"Is that why yer such a good teacher? Ye ken what yer bairns are troubled by even afore they understaun themselves?"

He never gave her a chance to reply. She couldn't speak even if she wanted to because his mouth covered hers an instant after he'd asked his question.

While she could still think coherently, she realized that this kiss was different than the others they had shared. Some had been blatant, to show Alex's ownership, and the one by the lake had turned into something very sexual. This kiss was somehow deeper, more caring.

Although nearly a stranger to him, she had been to able to see his troubled emotions and confusion. He touched her lips gently at first, rubbing his over and over hers. When she opened to take a breath, he slipped his tongue inside and tasted her mouth. He moved his arm to her waist and pulled her closer. He held her tightly in his embrace and continued to touch and taste her with his mouth. His body reacted to her softness, but not with the blinding wave of lust he had experienced by the lake. He just wanted to hold her, keep her touching him with her words and her body. This kiss gave him comfort, and he luxuriated in the warmth of her spirit as well as her body. Her concern and caring were clear in her acceptance of this touching. He lifted his head back and took a breath.

Her eyes were closed, so he waited for her to open them and look at him.

"I hiv been tortured by the same thoughts since before this happened. Could I survive as the man I haid become? I had a chance here to be something, someone different. In spite of the uncertainty and some fear, I do feel as though I've been set free. But which one is the real person, Maggie? Which one will I be if we get back home?"

She wrapped her arms around him and hugged him strongly before she answered.

"First of all, it's *when* we get back home. And, second, I think you're just seeing a different part of your personality. I think the barbarian, warrior Alex has been there, but you use the controlled, organized Alex to restrain him." She reached up and caressed his face. "Since we're here *for now,* you may as well look the part. With this beard you're growing and the wild hair, you do look like the barbarian Scot."

His heart contracted at the tone of her voice and her soothing touch on his face. He didn't understand his feelings toward her or himself. Oh, he recognized the sexual attraction, that was the clearest and most unmistakable of everything he felt. It was the rest of the feelings that caused him restless nights and preoccupied days. *Escape,* his mind whispered, *escape.*

"I'll be right back. I will check to see if we can go undetected." He stepped out of her arms and went to the door. "You may want to gather yer things. If this works, we will be going home." He waited for her acknowledgment and left, pulling the door closed behind him. He paused, leaning back on the frame of the door, and listened to Maggie's movements in the room. "Home," he had told her. *Home?* The word and thoughts of that place did not give him the same sense of comfort that being held in her arms did.

Pushing away from the doorway, he strode down the hall toward the stairway to the great room. The sound of a few voices traveled to him, but the place was definitely quieting down for the night. Luckily for them, late-night television had not been invented yet. Alex walked back to his room and knocked on the door.

"Come, Maggie, 'tis time."

Chapter 18

"OUCH!"

"Haud yer wheesht, Maggie. Keep yer voice down."

"I'm sorry, Alex," she answered in a loud whisper, "but I can't see the ground, and I just rammed my toe into a rock."

He slowed his stride and grabbed her hand, pulling her close. "The moon is favoring us by not being full, but I ken it's difficult to see the ground. Let's take it a wee bit slower."

She nodded at his comment and pointed off in one direction. "It's over that way, Alex. I'm sure of it." But she wasn't sure of it. They had searched for nearly an hour for the right construction area, but the dark of the moon that covered their steps also made that search difficult.

"All right, lass, let's try that direction for a bit." She let him lead the way while she concentrated on not injuring her swelling toe again. After a few minutes of walking, she pulled him to a stop. A shiver ran through her body and the hairs on her neck stood on end.

"Do you feel that, Alex?" Her skin puckered into thousands of goose bumps and her breath caught in her throat.

"I dinna feel anything but yer trembling, Maggie." He turned to face her. "Are we close?"

"We must be. The sensations are much stronger now than this afternoon." She rubbed her arms to try to get rid of the tingling in her skin. It didn't help.

Alex put his arm around her shoulder and moved them forward. They rounded a corner of the new wall, and Maggie stopped dead in her tracks.

"There it is, Alex. The arch."

She heard him expel a loud breath and felt his arm slip from her shoulders. The tension within her grew, coiling in her stomach and chest. The loud buzzing invaded her ears and made her head spin. Fearing she would fall over, she grabbed at Alex and took hold of his arm.

"Maggie? Are ye sick? I can feel yer shaking. Take a deep breath, now." He guided her over to the wall and leaned her against it for support. Her body would not respond to his command, and her breath came in shallow pants. The power emanating from the arch was too strong.

"It's the arch. Can't you hear that sound? Can't you feel the vibrations?" She couldn't believe that he was oblivious to all of the effects that were pulsing through her.

"I'm sorry, lass, ye are the only one being affected by it. I feel fine." He looked over at the arch and then back at her. "Stay here while I look closer."

She watched as he approached the stone structure. She tensed, waiting to feel what Alex's nearness to the arch did to the vibrations. Her lungs hurt from the need to take a deep breath and her eyes teared from the pain inside her head. She clenched her teeth, preparing for more pain, but it didn't come. Alex's presence caused no change in the pulsing power surrounding her.

She squinted in the shadows, trying to see his movements. It was just too damn dark to see much. Maggie slumped against the wall, gathering her strength. His reappearance at her side startled her.

"Sorry, lass, I dinna mean to frighten ye even more."

"Well?"

"Weel what?"

"Did you see or feel anything over there?"

"Nay, Maggie. I couldna feel anything different aboot that arch. Are ye sure it's the one?"

"Oh, yes, Alex, I'm sure."

"Shall we give it a try then?" She nodded at him. "Weel, take my arm and I will help ye over there. Is yer head still aching?"

"Yes, Alex. It hurts from this." She waved at the arch.

"Can I carry yer pack for ye?"

"No, thank you. I'd better carry it since I brought it through the first time."

Thankfully, the noise and pulsations did not increase as they neared the arch. They approached slowly, with Maggie leaning on Alex's arm for support. The dizziness moved through her in waves, and she fought to keep her eyes focused on their way home.

"How should we do this, Maggie?"

"I'm not sure. From what I remember of the other ruins, I think we came in from this side." Maggie pointed to the near side of the opening. "We were sitting on a wall, and fell that way." She gestured from right to left. "Does that match what you remember?"

"Aye, it does. Weel, shall we?"

She wrapped her arms around his one, closed her eyes tightly, and murmured a brief prayer as they advanced on the stone gateway. They paused and simultaneously held their breath. Then together, they entered the overhead curve of stone.

"Bloody hell!"

"Alex?"

"Open yer eyes, Maggie. We are still here." He watched as she opened her eyes a scant sliver and closed them again. Her trembling had lessened. "Do ye still feel anything?"

"Yes. The same." Her voice was barely a whisper, so weak.

"It dinna work, Maggie. Any suggestions?" He ran his free hand through his hair.

"Let's try going back through, in the other direction."

He turned and led her to the edge of the structure. He could still feel nothing like what she described. No pulsations, no vibrations, no noise. "Ready?" At her nod, he took a step forward.

Two more steps took them through and out the other side.

He let out the breath he was holding. "God damn it!"

Before he could utter another curse, he felt Maggie sag at his side. He caught her and lifted her gently in his arms, walking away from the damned arch. She tried to struggle, but her feeble protests never slowed his pace.

"How is yer head?"

"Better now, Alex, this is far enough away."

He stopped and put her feet back on the ground. He kept a strong hold on her waist until she stopped swaying.

"The noise, the vibrations? Hiv they stopped?"

"They have lessened, almost gone. But, Alex . . ."

"I ken, lass. It dinna work for us. What do ye think we did wrong?"

"Right now, I can't think. I feel really sick, and my head is pounding. Can you take me back to our room?"

"Aye, lass. Ye look more than a bit peaked. Let me carry you." Before she could protest, he lifted her into his arms again and started back toward the castle itself.

"I didn't mean this way, Alex." If it had been brighter outside, he knew he would see her blush.

"I ken, Maggie. Rest yer head against me and let me do this for ye. We will be back in our room in but a few minutes.'' She nestled her head into his shoulder and sighed deeply. She was exhausted and dozed off on the way back.

Maggie never woke as he took off her skirt and bodice, shoes and stockings. He untied and loosened her hair and pulled the covers over her sleeping form.

He was too awake to get into bed. He walked over to the window and stared out into the darkness. They had found the doorway home, but it didn't work for them. What had they done wrong? What had they missed? Why didn't it work?

Chapter 19

SHE WAITED IN the shadows until they passed her by. They were so wrapped up in their confusion and disappointment they never noticed her standing nearby.

The arch drew her. Its powerful call had broken once more into her sleep and demanded her presence here, now. She walked over and placed her hand on the boulders. The heat grew stronger and spread into and through her body. The sacred stones, stolen and put in this wall, called to her.

As she had done before the fire, she closed her eyes and waited for the wisdom to come to her. It was quick in coming. Moira opened her eyes and saw images of the couple in a passionate embrace, bodies entwined.

"Ah, lovers first."

Pictures flashed before her eyes, scenes moving quickly, the man and woman together, working, arguing, bathing together. Anice, her eyes flashing anger and humiliation, appeared. Pain, dear God, the pain. Moira clutched at her back as the pain struck. Blood, death. No, almost death, but saved. This Alex soothing the hurts of the woman.

''Then love.''

She drew in a breath and forced it out. The pain was not hers and was gone. The place beneath the curve cleared, and the stones grew cold. Moira lifted her hand and took a few steps away from the special arch.

''So, they ken the door is here but havna found the key. How long, I wonder, until they ken the true power that controls the archway?'' she whispered. ''And how will they make their way here until they find it?''

With a certainty that was rooted deep inside her being, Moira knew that it was her place to show them the way, her task to guide them to love and to their home.

Weel, she thought, *I dearly hope I am up to the task.*

Chapter 20

SHE COULDN'T OPEN her eyes. Trying to force her lids to lift, Maggie raised her hand against the glare coming through the small window. The pounding pain returned as she tilted her head off the pillow.

"Arrggghh."

Laying her head back down slowly, she pushed the loose strands of hair out of her face and rolled to her side. Alex was gone. Sliding her hand along the surface of the bed, she knew by the coldness that he had left some time ago. Pushing up on her arms, Maggie forced her head upright and clenched her teeth against the throbbing spasm. The strength of it made her stomach roll and bile surge into her throat. Without a second to spare, Maggie slid off the bed and dove for the chamber pot. She was wiping her mouth when the door slammed open into the wall. Anice's Amazonian maid entered, again without notice or permission.

Firtha paused at the doorway and then swept in, carrying another pile of clothes. Casting her a look of pure revulsion, the maid traversed the room in three strides and placed the bundle on Alex's trunk. Turning quickly, she strode to the door to leave when she paused and pivoted back to Maggie. A new expression filled her face.

"What do you want, Firtha?"

"The day is half o'er, whore. Will ye do nothing more than spread yerself for him and lay aboot the rest of the time?"

"Firtha . . ." Maggie growled the maid's name in warning.

"Ye dinna look good. This is more than the beating he gave ye and the bed sport he demands from ye." Firtha's glance fell on the nearby chamber pot. Her eyebrows raised and her eyes bulged. "Ye filthy slut! Are ye breeding his bastard?"

"Bastard?" Maggie looked at the maid and then realized what this must look like to Firtha: her illness, the chamber pot, the unmistakable odor of vomiting. "No, Firtha, I am not . . . with child."

"I dinna believe ye. My lady willna be glad of this news."

Maggie jumped to her feet and grabbed at Firtha's wrist. It took all of her meager strength just to remain upright. "Firtha, don't make things worse by spreading lies to Anice. Alex will not be pleased if you start trouble."

"I serve my lady above all others, and she will decide what to do with this turn." Firtha shook free of her hold with little effort. "Yer mistake will be seen by all in a little time, whore. Then ye can tell me who is lying when the laird throws yer worthless body out of the keep and into the dirt where ye belong." The maid left the room without closing the door.

Maggie dragged herself over to the bed and collapsed on it, her legs still dangling over the side. Could this get any worse? What would Struan do when word of this got back to him? She closed her eyes and imagined she could hear Anice's screaming when her maid shared the news with her. Anice's temper tantrums were the gossip of the servants. The entire keep, the entire village would hear of this by the evening meal. Alex keeping his leman here was one thing, but if everyone thought she was pregnant with his child?

''Maggie?'' A whispered voice floated in from the hallway.

''Rachelle?'' As the woman stepped into view, Maggie motioned to her to enter. ''Close the door.''

''Are ye ill?'' Rachelle's concern showed in her expression. ''I havna seen ye since . . .''

''Since Alex dragged me up here and beat me?'' She watched as the young woman drew her bottom lip between her teeth and worried it.

''Was there bleeding? Do ye need me to help with yer . . . ?'' She reached out her hand as her words drifted off. Maggie recognized that Rachelle didn't know what to do but wanted to do something to help. Rachelle probably thought she was overstepping herself since it was clearly Alex's right to discipline where and when and who he saw fit.

''No, Rachelle, Alex's belt did not damage my skin. I am suffering from head pains, and they make my stomach roll and clench.''

''So, ye are no' breeding?'' The question came out on a whisper.

''No, Rachelle, I am not carrying a babe. Not Alex's nor anyone else's.'' Maggie struggled to sit up, and moments later, she was retching into the pot again. She felt a cool hand on her brow and then a wet piece of linen was thrust into her hand. When her stomach calmed, she sat back on her heels. Looking into Rachelle's disbelieving face, she repeated her denial.

''No baby.''

Rachelle helped her to her feet and back to the bed. ''Alex told Odara ye were not weel and wouldna work this day. Everyone thought it was because he beat ye and ye were too embarrassed to come down."

Maggie shook her head in reply. What a time for a full-blown migraine attack. She could not remember one this severe. The arch and its mysterious vibrations were behind this. Her head had started pounding as she neared it. The longer she stayed near it, the stronger the pain. It had triggered this attack.

"I was ashamed to come to the kitchen today, but it was my headache that kept me in bed."

"Mayhap Moira would have a potion to help yer pain?"

"Moira?"

"The healer. She lives in the village. Shall I go and ask her for something to ease yer pain?"

A healer? An herbalist, more than likely, at this time in history. Would a healer's concoction help or harm her? She wondered. Well, at least it would give Rachelle something to do.

"Yes, please. Ask for something to help the pain in my head and my stomach's upset."

Rachelle drew the bedcovers up over her and tucked them around her. "I will return as soon as I can."

"Rachelle, please don't get into trouble for me."

"I hiv time since the men return now for the noon meal. I will find Moira and ask for her help. She will not deny ye."

The door closed slowly and softly, no loud noise to jar her senses.

Rachelle's words penetrated her fog—the noon meal. She had spent the morning in bed, unheard of for a servant, even one who had been punished just yesterday. Well, she would wait and see what this healer's potion looked and smelled like. Then she would decide whether or not to drink it. But, with the throbbing in her head making her dizzy again, she thought that even the death that might follow the unknown brew would be preferable to this pain.

''What did ye do to her, Alex?''

''Who are ye talking aboot, Brodie?''

''Ye ken, Alex. I am asking ye aboot Maggie.''

The bright sun shone directly down from overhead. Alex shielded his eyes and looked into Brodie's face. His friend's glare and angry eyes were obvious. Alex returned the glare and raised his eyebrows, challenging Brodie to continue at his own risk.

''Ye beat her so much that she is still abed and ill. Rachelle is on her way to Moira now for a potion to help her pain.''

''Who told ye that?''

''Rachelle went to check on her and found her retching in yer chamber.''

Alex couldn't share the truth of the matter with Brodie. He knew that Maggie's response to the arch was the cause of her pain.

Brodie drew up to his full height before Alex. ''Did ye use yer fists on the lass?''

''Brodie, ye dinna need to take her side in this. And, nay, I dinna use my fists.'' Brodie's eyes bespoke his disbelief. ''She is mine and ye hiv no right to interfere wi' my handling of her.'' Alex stood taller and continued, ''Do ye ken?''

''She is an outsider, she doesna ken our ways, Alex. Go a bit softly wi' her.''

''This from the mon who strangled her a little while after meeting her? Ye are overstepping yer bounds, Brodie.''

''Was her offense so grievous that ye haid to beat her senseless?''

''Brodie,'' he growled in warning. He stood, legs spread and hands on his hips. ''She was rude to Anice.'' Brodie's snort made him pause. ''She dinna ken her place and called for me in front of Anice and the villagers. I haid to correct her.''

''Weel, who else would she call for? Ye are the only one who she kens.''

''From the look on yer face, she could call ye.''

''Aye, I would aid her, not beat her. And Rachelle would, also.''

Alex slapped Brodie on his shoulder and smiled, breaking the growing tension.

''Good. Maggie needs friends here. Come, walk to the hall wi' me and I will look in on her now. And ye can ask her yerself if I used my fists as ye believe.''

''Alex. Join me at the table.'' Laird Struan's voice carried clearly in the hall, which Alex was trying to sneak through without being seen. The hall quieted, and all eyes looked to him. Changing his direction, he strode to the dais and climbed the steps to the high table. With his attention on Brodie's figure going in the opposite direction, he never saw Anice enter from behind and take her seat.

''Good day, Faither.'' He nodded his head and then spotted Anice. ''And good day to ye, Anice.'' He paused and noticed a blush spreading over her cheeks as she returned his greeting. She was so young. She would be in her first year of high school in his time. The thought that it was acceptable to marry a girl of that age in this time bothered him. And the fact that everyone here thought he was the man who would do it bothered him even more.

Struan leaned over toward him and beckoned him closer with a crook of a finger. Alex leaned over and turned his head to hear the coming whisper.

'' 'Tis said that yer mistress—'' Struan began.

''Faither, Maggie is my concern,'' Alex interrupted.

''She is the clan's concern if she is carrying yer child.''

Alex sucked in air so fast and hard that he choked. Coughs, loud violent ones, followed the gasp that started it all. Struan whacked Alex on the back a few times to help, but it didn't. Finally, Alex grabbed a mug of ale and took a gulp. After a few more coughs, he could breathe.

"Faither, I think we need to speak privately aboot this matter. Anice, would ye pardon us for a bit?"

"Of course, Alex, Laird Struan." Her soft voice was accompanied by a dutiful nod, first at him, then the laird. "Firtha can keep me company until yer return."

Anice's maid, the tall one who could scare a Scots warrior out of his kilt, took a seat next to her lady. Alex noticed an unreadable look pass between the laird and the lady's maid. What could that be about?

Struan set the course, off the dais, through the hall, to the solar. Alex matched the laird's long strides step for step. Struan preceded him into the room, so Alex closed the door behind them. Struan turned and faced him, the laird's face hard and ungiving.

"So, is it true?"

"What is it that ye've heard now aboot Maggie?"

"That she carries yer babe, a bastard for the clan's heir."

How could this be happening? He was an accountant from New Jersey, for God sake. He should be doing lunch with one of the firm's major clients right now. Instead, through some unknown, unbelievable twist of fate and time, he was standing here, playing out a charade with a man supposed to be his father. He raised his hand and rubbed his forehead, then slid his hand through his hair. He wasn't prepared to deal with this problem or any of the problems they had encountered so far. Like Maggie, he kept hoping that he would wake up and find that it was all a dream, a bad dream.

Now this, a rumor about Maggie. The laird would reach the end of his tolerance soon. They had been warned already. So, would this be the straw that broke the camel's back? What would happen to Maggie if Struan's limits had been reached?

"Nay, Faither," Alex said calmly, "Maggie isna breeding."

"Weel, I ken that she was found pale and retching over a chamber pot this morn."

"Who told ye this?" Alex could not imagine that Rachelle had spread such news to the laird.

"Anice's maid brought the news to me."

"The tall one who spread tales before?"

"Aye, that one. She came to me, kenning that Anice would be distraught if this reached her ears."

"Faither, Anice's maid is trying to cause trouble for Maggie again. I am swearing to ye that Maggie is not carrying my bairn."

"Why is she ill?" Struan cast him a questioning look, and for a moment, Alex thought he heard a note of true concern in his voice. Concern for Maggie?

"She suffers from pains in her head that make her ill. She complained of them last eve in our chamber."

"Was that before or after ye beat her?"

Although spoken in an even tone, Alex could hear the censure in Struan's question. Did everyone here believe him capable of beating a woman? That answer was obvious: yes. And he should have been within his rights to correct his leman any way he chose. Even Maggie had told him that much. But now his friend and his father were questioning him about his actions. Was this more about the real Alex than about himself? Did the real Alex have a streak of cruelty that worried his family and friends? Or had Maggie's warmth and personality won these people over as she was winning him as well? He needed to think about this. He took a deep breath and let it out slowly, trying to rid himself of anger.

"I took my belt to her back, Faither, three strokes on her back. She was alive but sleeping when I left our chamber this morn."

"Did ye also take yer ease on her after ye . . . used yer belt?"

"Nay. I amna such an animal that I would take from her when she is unable to give to me of her own will. I hiv never forced myself on her."

Struan's tense stance relaxed before Alex's eyes. Apparently, his words had appeased the laird in some way.

"We maun rejoin Anice and the meal, Alex." Struan headed for the door.

"I would like to look in on Maggie first."

"Nay, Alex. After the meal, ye can see to her. Yer worry for her is admirable, but I canna permit ye to put her first before consideration of Anice. Ye maun learn to balance yer concern for yer leman with yer betrothed's right to yer attentions. Otherwise, trouble will follow for all involved."

Although he strongly disagreed with Struan, Alex could not refuse his order. As they walked back into the hall, Alex saw Rachelle edging her way along the back of the hall. She paused briefly, her eyes widening, as she caught his look. He turned his glance to the front of the hall and the high table after he watched her path to the stairs. She would watch over Maggie until he could get there.

Chapter 21

THE WHITE TOWER, LONDON, ENGLAND

THE SOUND OF soft leather slapping on the stone floor accompanied the young man's strutting steps into the audience room. The quality of his clothing, from his velvet tunic with richly decorated sleeves and shoulder cape, to his parti-colored hose and short leather boots, spoke of his wealth and position. Only the lack of an appropriate head covering denoted the informality of this visit

"You have summoned me, Your Highness?" The young Scot made an impressive bow before his sovereign, King David of Scotland and current guest of the English King Edward, the third bearing that name.

"Aye, Sandy, I received some puzzling news from your betrothed's clan, the MacNabs."

"Are they trying to change the betrothal agreement?"

"Nay. They hiv sent to me a letter of thanks for the original betrothal and their regrets that I cannot attend the wedding. It appears that felicitations are due you on your impending wedding."

"Wedding? I know nothing of a wedding!" Alesander Robert MacKendimen strode up and tore the letter from his king's grasp. Their familiarity and camaraderie was obvious in the exchange and in the lack of distance between king and subject. Sandy, as he preferred to be called, read the parchment and cursed vehemently from between clenched teeth.

"So, you know nothing about this? How it came to be arranged?"

"None, David. I've been here with you for five years with nary a word to or from my clan. What do you think this means?" Sandy held out the letter.

The king took the parchment back and rolled it up tightly. Handing it to a servant, David cleared the room with a sweep of his hand.

"The MacNab is marrying his beloved only daughter to the heir of the clan MacKendimen in a fortnight. The MacNab is apparently unaware that the heir of the MacKendimens stands before me here in London and is not in . . . What's the name of your clan's town?"

"Dunnedin."

"Dunnedin. I was going to send my own messenger, but perhaps you would prefer to see to this on your own?"

"Aye, I would. With your permission, of course." Alesander made a courtier's bow to the king.

"You have my permission and an escort from Edward to the Scottish borders. Take several of your soldier friends with you as well, and discover what is going on at your home. I will have letters prepared to ease your way. Get to the bottom of this."

"Aye, David, I will." Sandy backed up several steps in respect, turned, and strode for the door.

"And, Sandy, my friend?" He paused at the raised voice and faced his sovereign. "Come back to serve me here when you have discovered the truth."

''Shall I return with the MacNab wench at my side, sire?''

''Nay, Sandy. There are still too many good English wenches we have not tried yet. Your wife at court may be a constraint on our good times.''

''As you command. I will return posthaste and unbridled by a wife.'' He winked at David and continued, ''for if I do not, you'll wear out all the good wenches alone!''

The king's loud laughter and Sandy's steps echoed through the chamber and halls as the heir of the MacKendimen left for home.

Chapter 22

"STAY AWAY FROM her, Alex."

The soft words of warning brought him to a halt. Rachelle stood next to the bed like a lioness protecting an injured cub. He looked past her and saw that Maggie was sleeping, her breaths coming deep and even, no frown of pain on her brow or face. Then he locked gazes with Rachelle.

"She said ye haid changed." Rachelle tilted her head in Maggie's direction. "But, from the looks of things, ye are still the bully who left here nigh onto five years ago, Alex MacKendimen." Her raised chin, crossed arms, and defiant expression were meant to insult him more than her words.

He stepped closer to her and her answering backstep brought her legs up against the bed. This was no wilting flower; this Rachelle was every bit enough woman to protect her friend. A smile turned up the corners of his mouth.

"Nay, Rachelle, I am different in ways ye canna even imagine from the Alex MacKendimen who left here with the king."

She snorted in reply, so much like Brodie's sound that Alex laughed.

"I will let ye in on our secret," Alex tipped his head in the sleeping woman's direction, "I didna lay a hand on her yesterday, nor did she feel the bite of my leather belt."

"I dinna believe ye, Alex. Maggie was overcome with pain when I found her this morn."

"From her head, Rachelle, not her back. Her back is unblemished by my hand."

Rachelle looked back and forth between the two, and it was clear she didn't know what to believe. But she hadn't relaxed her stance or let him closer to Maggie.

"My only sin was in not recognizing how ill she was this morn before I left her. I came now to see to her." After a delay of several seconds, Rachelle relented and stepped aside enough for him to take a closer look, and he noticed how pale Maggie was, even in sleep. He sat on the side of the bed and leaned to her, pressing a kiss on her forehead. "No fever, that's good."

"Maggie asked me to go to Moira for a potion. When she said the pains in her head haid made her ill, I . . ." Rachelle paused and swallowed, "I thought ye haid struck her there as well as on her back."

Alex shook his head in denial. Damn, but the real Alex was no man he wanted to be compared with. An uncaring bully, a cruel and undisciplined lecher. A great heir for the MacKendimens. No wonder Struan had sent him away.

"I didna strike her. I willna raise my hand to her or any other woman in anger, Rachelle."

Rachelle stepped soundlessly to the door. "I will leave ye then. Moira said she should sleep the day and night through. Call on me if ye need anything for her, Alex."

"Rachelle." She paused at her name. "Can ye look in on her later? Before the evening meal? I may not get back here until then."

"Aye, Alex, I will see to her for ye."

"Rachelle, ye hiv my thanks. For this and for being her friend."

Rachelle's fair cheeks blossomed with color as she smiled and pulled the door closed. Alex smoothed back the loose tendrils of Maggie's hair and tucked the covers a bit tighter around her. He pressed his lips again to her forehead and whispered to her.

"Sleep, Maggie. Get yer strength back. I fear ye will need it for what we are to face here."

Straightening up, he walked to the door, and after one final check, he left the chamber.

The first thing she noticed as she fought to open her eyes was that she was so warm and comfortable that maybe she didn't want to wake from her sleep. The second thing was the rhythmic snoring, low and metered, that came from behind her and entered her ear. Her breathing began to pace itself with the inhalations and exhalations. The next thing she realized was that an arm and a leg were wrapped around her in the tangle of sheets and held her firmly in place. Alex's arm encircled her tightly at the waist, and his hand rested across her breasts. His leg lay across hers, anchoring her firmly at his side.

It was when she noticed that those limbs and everything else pressed against her were naked that she really woke up.

"Alex. *Alex!*"

"Hmmm." He mumbled an answer to her call.

"What are you doing?"

"Weel, Maggie, I'm trying to get some sleep. What are ye doing?"

He had not moved a muscle so, to get his attention, she did. Unfortunately, when she wiggled her bottom against his groin, he moaned and came awake, his body reacting quickly to her movements.

"Maggie, unless it's an invitation ye are makin, I wouldna move too much more like that."

Without regard for the condition of her head, Maggie scurried out from under the covers and knelt at the bottom of the bed. Pulling the twisted linen shirt from around her waist, she smoothed it down the length of her thighs, covering her limbs. Her hair had come loose from her braid and fell in waves over her shoulders. Alex sat up, finally awake, but thankfully, still under the bedcovers.

"Alex, what were you thinking?"

"Weel, lass, I dinna think I was thinking at all." He dragged his hands through his sleep-bedraggled hair and rubbed his half-opened eyes. "I think I was asleep and comfortable. Were ye hiving a bad dream?"

"No. I woke up and found you wrapped around me. I didn't expect it, that's all." She crawled back toward the pillows.

"I am sorry, Maggie, if I scared ye. My body just haes a mind of its own when I am asleep. I'll try to stay on my side of the bed from now on."

"You're not wearing anything."

"I guess I got too warm and took it off." He reached over the side of the bed to the floor and grabbed at the fallen shirt. As she got settled back under the covers, he yanked the covering over his head and chest. Without glancing at her, he slid back under the covers and turned on his side, away from her.

Silence filled the chamber as Maggie sought a new comfortable position. She was a little embarrassed by her reaction to waking in his arms. Feeling his skin, naked and hot against hers had caused an ache to form in her center. His erection, pulsing against her buttocks, stirred a heat within her. This physical attraction between them was growing. The kisses, the embraces, the caresses. They were all enhancing an increasing temptation between them. One that was becoming difficult to ignore. One that Maggie wasn't sure she wanted to ignore.

Sighing deeply, Maggie turned and punched and fluffed the pillow. She had told Alex that they should avoid anything emotional between them, and she believed it herself when she said it. But now, facing an even more uncertain future, she felt drawn to his strength. If they were to survive here in the past, it would have to be together. The arch was the doorway back home; she knew it for certain. If it didn't work for them, if they couldn't pass back through . . . She couldn't even crystallize the complete thought. A shudder passed through her, a sensation of deep dread. Her movement must have disturbed Alex. He rolled over to face her.

"How is yer head? Is the pain gone?"

Maggie carefully touched her forehead and then her temples. No area hurt, no painful tightening remained.

"The pain is gone."

"Ye sound surprised."

"I am. When I drank the healer's brew, I wasn't sure I would wake up. I can only imagine what was in it."

"Bat's wing and eye of newt?"

"From the smell and taste, something probably far worse."

"Weel, she said it would make ye sleep, and it did. How does yer stomach fare?"

"Good. I actually feel better than I usually do when a migraine lifts."

"Ye scared me, Maggie. I dinna ken what I would do wi'oot ye." She heard the fear in his voice.

"I didn't mean to frighten you. I've never had a headache like that before. I think that being too near to the arch intensified my headache."

"I guess that ye should stay far away from the arch for now. If ye keep reacting to it like this, the entire clan will believe that I beat ye senseless."

She sat up and peered through the darkened room. "Is that what they think now?"

"I fear so, lass. Rachelle, Brodie, and Struan all confronted me aboot abusing ye."

"Oh, Alex. I'm sorry. I didn't mean for this to happen."

He held out his arms to her and she moved into his embrace. She lay against his chest, his slow and even breathing and his hand smoothing her hair comforted her.

"The important thing is that ye are well. I ken ye are disappointed that the arch dinna work for us the way we wanted, but we will find out more. I just ken that we will."

"Alex, if we can't get back home . . ."

"Nay, Maggie, I amna ready to even let that thought enter my mind. We will keep watching and listening for clues. Maybe this haes happened before, maybe someone else haes knowledge of this arch. We will find our way home." He tightened his arms around her.

Pulling out of his arms, Maggie settled back on her side of the bed. She didn't have any words to answer his because she didn't share his conviction of them returning home. It looked more and more as if they were trapped here.

Closing her eyes, Maggie took a few deep, relaxing breaths and tried to fall asleep. Another morning would be here too soon and she needed her full strength to face it. She had to watch every step she took. She and Alex could afford no mistakes. Finally, sleep began to overtake her, and she thought she felt Alex's strong arms holding her close once more.

Chapter 23

"REMEMBER, MAGGIE, ACT as if yer back is injured."

"I know, Alex. Everyone believes that you beat me. I will be careful."

"Are ye sure ye are feeling better?" He looked closely at her face.

"Yes, Alex. I am fine." The monotone of her voice did nothing to reassure him. She seemed low in spirits this morning.

"By the way, Alex. I have my medications in my bag if anything like that happens again. They must be safer than whatever the healer gave me."

He nodded at the information, but that still didn't explain her quietness. She was silent as she began to separate her hair into sections to braid it. He closed his eyes for a moment and could feel the tension emanating from her in spite of her calm appearance.

"Rachelle kens the truth of the matter."

"What do you mean?" Maggie walked to his side as she braided her hair.

"I told her the truth—that I hadna beaten ye at all. That it was the pain in yer head that was making ye sick."

"Did she believe you?" She wrapped her kerchief around her head and tied it under her long braid. He watched every move, saw every motion of her body.

"Nay. Not at first. She claimed I hadna changed from when I left with the king." He chuckled, thinking of how different he was from that Alex. Maggie did not crack a smile. "Ye are certain ye feel better?" He lifted her chin to look at her eyes.

"I said I'm fine. Now, I've got to get to the kitchen. Are you coming down to eat?"

"Aye, I am following ye now."

Alex pulled the door open and entered the stone passageway, walking next to her. She resisted his attempt to take her hand, so he walked by her side until they reached the entry to the great hall. A momentary burst of irritation occurred when he noticed that she waited for him to enter the room first. Frowning, he watched as she stepped close to the back wall and made her way silently to the kitchen, never sparing him another glance.

Hmmm. Something was still wrong with her. Or maybe she was just acting the part of the disciplined leman. Maggie? No. Something was still amiss and he wouldn't be able to talk with her until much later in the day.

Glancing around the room as he strode toward the dais, he nodded to those who greeted him. Their good days sounded a bit muted, but they were all respectful, as befitted his position in the clan. The last two days had altered his standing somehow. He was still thinking about the kind of man the real Alex was when he reached his destination.

"Good day to ye, Alex." Anice's soft voice reached him from the raised platform. Clearing his thoughts, he moved briskly up the steps to his designated seat at the high table. No one else was present.

"Good morn, Anice." He motioned to one of the servants to begin serving them. Bowls of steaming oatmeal were placed before them. Loaves of warm bread, wedges of dark yellow cheese, and crocks of honey and butter were added to the table to complete the meal.

Anice began to chatter amicably, and Alex's glance and thoughts drifted back to the woman making her way into the kitchen. God, he hoped she'd make it through the day. Her lack of spirit worried him. They had to stick together and figure out this puzzle. He needed her sharp mind to find answers to the obvious questions about their situation. How? Who? More importantly, why?

He reached out to the platter closest to him and took a small loaf of bread. Tearing it in two, he handed one piece to Anice. He was learning his place, his role in this place and time, as impossible as that sounded. But what if they could not leave here? What if he had to stay in this barbaric place and never return to his real life? What would happen to them? To Maggie? To Anice? To the real Alex? He shook his head in denial. He could not stay here. He had a life to get back to: his job, his career, his goals.

Anice's frown and worried voice pierced through his reverie.

"Did I say something to displease ye, Alex?"

"Nay, lass, ye didna. I was just lost in my thoughts."

Her lips began to curve into a timid smile. He remembered how young she was and smiled back. "Tell me, Anice, aboot yer plans for the wedding."

How could they survive here . . . now? If they couldn't find a way back through the arch and were stuck here . . . Maggie shook her head at the mere thought of spending her life here.

"Mistress Hobbs, do ye hiv trouble with what yer supposed to do?"

Maggie snapped out of her daydreaming and realized that Odara was speaking to her.

"I beg your pardon, mistress. I didn't hear what you said."

"Ye havna completed even yer first task, and ye were shaking yer head at me. Do ye ken yer duties for the day?" The older woman spoke quietly and everyone working in the kitchen shamelessly listened to the conversation.

"Yes, mistress, I understand what I have to do."

"Then, do it, lass." With a curt nod of her head, Odara turned back to her own duties. Maggie looked around her at the audience of kitchen workers and picked up another ball of dough. Once she started the familiar push-pull of kneading the mixture, her thoughts cleared. She worked hard at not letting the desperation that lurked on the fringes of her consciousness get too close or too strong.

It was then that she spotted Rachelle entering the room. The pretty blond negotiated her way around tables and hearths and workers and soon stood next to Maggie. Rachelle's furrowed brow revealed her concern. Maggie's heart lightened a bit when Rachelle placed her hand over Maggie's in a gesture of friendship. Not just a gesture, but one that she made in front of the entire group of kitchen workers—and none missed it.

"Are ye well?" Rachelle's voice was a whisper as she picked up a knife and selected vegetables from the basket before her.

"I am well, Rachelle. My head no longer aches, nor my back."

"Did Alex tell me true?" Rachelle did not turn to look at her, but Maggie could see the tenseness in the woman's body as she waited for confirmation or denial.

"Yes, he did. But you must not tell anyone else. It's important."

Rachelle did look at her then, with eyebrows upraised in question.

"It was not my place to question or offend the lady Anice. I know that now."

"If ye were of the clan, ye could have done what ye did wi'oot fear of punishment. But ye are not MacKendimen."

"No, I am not. I am a servant of the MacKendimens.

An outsider, and Alex's leman at that. I should have known not to approach Alex while Anice was present.''

''But why will ye let the clan believe that Alex beat ye?''

Maggie looked around at the nearby women who were also assigned to the kitchen. Most were of the clan and did their work in exchange for their keep and their place in the extended family. Although a few were servants like her and clearly not treated as family, she had seen none that were openly abused or beaten. She let out a deep sigh as she pieced together an explanation for Rachelle.

''Struan has made it clear to Alex and me that if there's trouble, I will be thrown out. He knows that Anice is not happy with me being here, but he believes Alex has a right to my . . . presence here.''

''So, if Anice and Struan believe ye hiv been chastised for yer insolence . . .''

''I am still safe and can stay with Alex.''

At Rachelle's silence, she continued. ''And I have been chastised, Rachelle. Alex made it very clear that I was not to approach him if Anice is near, and I am not to offend her or even speak to her in any way. I will know my place from now on.''

They worked on in companionable silence and soon the baskets were empty and the stew pots and ovens were full from their efforts. The sweat that dampened her brow and back and her chemise reminded her of a question for Rachelle.

''Do you ever take a hot bath here?''

Rachelle laughed at her questioning frown. ''Do ye do things differently in England?''

''I am accustomed to bathing daily. I have missed those baths the most since I arrived here.''

Maggie's supply of toiletries had run out quickly. She had managed over the last weeks with sponge bathing with a tub of heated water in the room she shared with Alex, but she longed for a long soak in a steaming bathtub with lots of her shampoo and soap. Unfortunately, that privilege belonged to very few of the inhabitants of the castle. Most used the nearby loch to bathe, but its bone-chilling temperature did not make it an option for her.

''We use the loch until it gets cold in the fall.'' Rachelle's eyes twinkled with mischief.

''Until it gets cold? Does it ever get warm is my question.''

''There is a spot where the sun warms the water a bit more than the rest of the loch. Even a Sassenach like yerself might find it comfortable.'' They both laughed at the friendly insult.

''Do you remember where we watched Brodie and Alex swim?''

''Is that what you call it? Swimming?'' Maggie watched a blush spread upward over Rachelle's neck and face. The blush was contagious, for she felt the heat of it creep up to her cheeks as she remembered how Alex looked as he walked from the lake, naked, standing tall in the sunlight.

''Ye go past it, traveling away from the castle. The loch runs off to the left and forms a small pond. The water warms there because 'tis shallow.''

''Is it safe for me to go there alone?''

'' 'Tis on MacKendimen land, so ye will be safe.''

''Even me, an outsider?''

''Everyone kens yer importance to Alex, even if they believe he beat ye. No one will bother ye there.''

Finally, she thought, a bath. She could gather some soap and a linen for drying. If she only had a change of clothes to use after her bath. The seams in her chemise were beginning to fray from wearing and washing it constantly since her arrival here. She sewed it as best she could and the separate bodice held everything together, but she needed a new one.

The thought of a real bath lightened her spirits and she started on her next assignment of the day, kneading more loaves of bread.

Chapter 24

SURELY, THIS MUST be heaven.

The sky was the color of robins' eggs without a cloud in sight. The sun's rays still warmed the glade and the branches of the trees waved gently in the breezes that moved along the shoreline. The water was lukewarm, but it covered her skin, and she felt the dirt and grime just melting off. She dipped her head under the water, staying under longer than necessary because it felt *so good.* When she closed her eyes, she could almost believe she was home in the huge bathtub in her house.

Almost.

Maggie sat in the shallows with her back to the path she had followed to get to this pond. The soap she found to use certainly didn't feel or smell like her scented bath soap at home, but it would do the job. She reached back and dipped her hand into the small container of soft cleanser. Spreading it through her wet hair, she began to hum a song from *South Pacific*.

After lathering up and scrubbing her hair and scalp, Maggie dipped under the water to rinse it clean. A wave moving through the pool washed over her and she slipped along the bottom losing her hold on the soap and causing her to fall deeper under the water. After a few frantic seconds of freeing her hands and finding a foothold, Maggie emerged from the water, coughing and sputtering mouthfuls of suds and water.

"Here, lass, take this afore ye drown."

She grabbed at the cloth pushed into her hand and then gasped, remembering her nakedness. Sinking into the water, she rubbed at her eyes, clearing out the bubbles.

"Alex! What are you doing here?" She knelt lower in the water and held the small linen in front of her.

"Rachelle told me ye were coming here and for what, so I followed to make sure ye were well."

She pushed the dripping mass of hair over her head and shoulders with one hand. "I'm fine, Alex. You can go now."

"And what if ye try to drown yerself after I leave?"

"I wasn't trying to drown myself. I slipped on the bottom."

"And what if someone else comes upon ye while ye are still bathing? Who will warn ye?" She saw his eyes focus on the small towel in front of her. The very small towel.

"Everyone else bathes over in the lake, Alex. Rachelle told me I'm very safe here."

"Weel, if it's all the same to ye, I'm staying until ye finish. We can talk while ye wash."

She couldn't help it. Her eyebrows just about crashed off her forehead as she thought about Alex sitting nearby while she splashed around naked in this pond.

"I didna say I would watch ye, Maggie. I'll give ye yer privacy." He turned his back on her and sat on a log. She looked for the larger piece of linen to dry off her body and realized she'd drifted away from the place where it was draped over a low branch. She would have to stand and walk over to get it.

"What do you want to talk about, Alex?" She waited until he started to respond before rising from the water.

"You. I want to talk about you."

"Alex, did you hear yourself?"

"Aye, I did."

"You said 'you' not 'ye.' " She took the final few steps to the linen and wrapped it around herself. She waded through the last few feet to the shore and approached him from the side.

"Sometimes, when I focus my efforts, I can speak without the brogue." He turned to face her as she came closer. "But I fall back to the brogue verra fast."

"Why do you think it happened?" She stepped carefully to the log where he sat.

"The brogue?"

"No, this, us, here?" She leaned over and twisted her hair to squeeze more water from it.

"I dinna hiv a clue. Do ye?"

"I don't even know if this is really happening, Alex. I still have the feeling that I'm going to wake and find it was a dream."

"Get dressed, lass, afore ye catch a chill. The sun is going down, and it willna stay warm much longer in the shade." He helped her to stand, and she picked her way over to the pile of clothes. She wondered as she stepped behind a tree if he would notice that she was wearing his shirt. Since Anice kept up a steady stream of new clothes into *his* trunk, she doubted he would mind. After all, she was already using one of his new shirts as a nightgown.

She wrung out her hair, dried it more with her worn chemise, and braided it. Then Maggie pulled on the new shirt, followed it with her skirt, and tied the bodice in place. The other clothes held the large shirt in place. The sleeves were too long, but she'd been rolling hers up to keep them out of her way. Dried and covered, she made her way back to Alex with the old shift in her pocket.

''Ye look comfortable now.'' He stood when she approached.

''And I feel *clean.* I didn't think I'd ever get rid of the dirt.''

''I haid forgotten that ye hiv been unable to get a real bath. I beg yer pardon for ignoring yer needs.''

''Why should you be responsible for that?'' She sat back down on the log and patted the space beside her.

''Because ye are supposed to be my mistress. I should be looking out for ye.'' His eyes darkened as he spoke. Anger flared in their blue depths.

''That's probably the thing I like least about where we are.''

''What's that?'' he growled.

''That a man has to look out for me! I am quite capable of doing that for myself, you know.''

''Not here. The roles are verra different than the ones we left behind. Ye are beholden to me for everything. If not to me, then to another man.''

''Well, isn't that just wonderful? I've fallen through a hole in time to a place where the thing I detest the most is the norm.'' Her eyes and throat burned with unreleased tears. She was mad, damn it, and she wouldn't cry. Not again, not in front of him.

''What is it that ye detest, Maggie?'' His voice was softer now, enticing her to reveal her secrets. It had been so long since she'd been able to talk unguardedly. His arm slipped around her shoulders, inviting her into his embrace. She accepted the invitation.

''I have finally reclaimed my life. No one can put any demands on me. Not school, not family, not . . . anyone. And now, I'm living my worst nightmare.''

''Did yer mon . . . ?''

''My man? Oh, you mean Don? Did he what?''

''Aye. Don. Did he put demands on ye?'' His grip on her tightened briefly, then relaxed.

''Yes, he tried. He thought I was too smart to continue

in teaching. He thought I should be something else.'' Bitterness spilled into her voice. Even she could hear it. ''He tried to force me to choose between what I loved to do and who I thought I loved, and all for his own reasons.''

''And?''

''We broke up almost a year ago and I have my life back.''

''Ye sound like me, Maggie.'' He shifted on the log and faced her now. ''I feel as if I just reclaimed my life, too.''

''From who or what?'' She thought about the little she knew of his life. Finally, some answers.

''I was engaged to someone. She wasna pleased about this trip wi' my aunt. She broke off the engagement when she found out about it.''

''She broke off an engagement over a trip? That sounds a bit simplistic, doesn't it?''

He wouldn't meet her glance and got up from their seat. *Pace, go ahead, pace,* she thought. And the funniest thing was that he didn't even realize he did it.

''Yer right. There's more to it than the trip. Nancy offered me a certain comfort; we both knew what we expected of the other. She expected a fiancé who would spend money on her and look good in public and be good in bed.''

''And?'' The good in bed part intrigued her.

''I met her requirements.'' His blue eyes sparkled. A smile threatened to break onto his mouth. He knew what she was thinking and knew she was dying to comment. She controlled herself for the moment.

''What did you expect from her?'' That was good, she thought, not even a quiver in her voice.

''I expected pretty much the same thing from her except for the spending part. I fully anticipated being able to provide for her after I become a full partner in the firm.''

''You haven't mentioned love or caring.''

"What about ye?" He stopped pacing long enough to raise an eyebrow at her and she felt his challenge.

"I thought I loved him. I know now that I didn't." She jutted her chin, returning his challenge.

"Love never entered into it for us. It was more a matter of mutual attraction and mutual convenience. At least until lately." He paused now and leaned against a tree. She felt his hesitation. He dragged it out by drawing his dagger and inspecting it closely. Then he raised his eyes to her.

"Afore ye ask . . . in the last few months we were together, I hiv felt as though something was missing. I wanted more. But, I do no' ken what."

"So, here we are—both failures at relationships. Do you think that has anything to do with why we're here?" She walked closer to him and looked up at him.

"I hiv no idea." He shook his head at her question.

"The old woman at the festival told me I had to teach a MacKendimen."

"Teach a MacKendimen? Teach a MacKendimen what?" His eyes glazed over, and he looked momentarily lost in his thoughts.

"I don't know, but it may be a clue to the why, if not the how. What do you need to learn?"

"Besides what this is all aboot or how to get home? Not a thing I can think of. Come." He took her hand and started leading her back to the castle. "It's almost time for the evening meal."

He'd lied to her. There were so many things she could teach him. She could teach him how to make her gasp in pleasure. She could teach him how she liked to be touched, how she tasted, which areas of her body were most sensitive to fingers, lips, tongue. She could teach him how to step back and enjoy life. He wanted to learn of her spontaneity, her caring, her sense of humor. He wanted . . . her.

They walked back in silence, and he held onto her hand until they approached the entryway into the castle grounds. Without words or directions, she paused in the brush near the path and waited for him to enter alone.

That's what he hated about this time and place. Even if the role he played here was more physical, less dependent on technology and modern conveniences, it was still as restrictive. He was as much a peg jammed in a hole here as he had been at home. How to change that? He did not have a clue.

Chapter 25

THEY FELL INTO a pattern of normalcy—well, a kind of strained pattern of normalcy—over the next few weeks. Alex became more of a warrior while Maggie won over more of the castle folk each day with her unassuming ways and pleasant personality. No one in the castle muttered curses as she passed or called her vile names anymore. She did what was expected and never complained about her work or the treatment she received. She talked to one and all, except for Anice. They agreed that she avoid her at all costs, there was no sense in looking for trouble.

He waited and watched—watched for any clues to how this had happened and, more importantly, how they could return to their own time. He even found himself staring at the arch whenever he was near it. He touched it once and waited for a reaction. None came. Maggie avoided it as much as she did Anice. Others walked through and around it without anything untoward happening. He didn't; there was no sense in looking for trouble.

And Alex lusted in those weeks. He'd convinced himself that it was *just* lust, nothing more involved than the increasingly strong yearnings of his body for Maggie. He swam more than ever in the damned icy water of the loch and many nights, as many as he could without raising suspicions, he slept outside or in the barracks. And, when he could not, he slept on the floor . . . on the rushes . . . in spite of the creatures he knew lived there. The noises in the rushes were not enough to force him back into the bed where Maggie would seek his heat and comfort during the night. At least, he got some measure of sleep on the floor, in the barracks, or outside by the loch. Maggie was a temptation that chased the sleep from his mind and body.

His equilibrium was faltering, and he knew it. He had to seemingly accept Anice's attentions, and he fought his own reaction to Maggie: to her smile, to her ripe body in the bed at night, to her warmth during the day. It was getting to him.

Alex knew, though, that even more trouble was coming. He felt the shiver of its warning deep in his bones and in his heart. He didn't know where it would come from or what would happen, but he was sure it was coming for them. Maggie might be the one to feel the power of the arch, but he could feel the power and tension of trouble in the air.

He recognized the signs were growing when Maggie was given duties that took her into the village one night. Trouble, he knew, would be at his door soon.

The soft knock at the door brought Alex to full awareness. He felt next to him on the bed and realized that it was empty. Where could Maggie be at this time of night? She should have returned from the village by now. Worrying that something might have happened to her, he covered the distance between the bed and the door in a few paces. He tugged hard on the heavy door, and it swung toward him. The short, hooded figure in the hallway ducked under his arm, blowing out the candle, as Alex closed the door. When Alex turned around, he faced the firelit figure of a girl, hair flowing loosely, in a mostly transparent nightgown.

"Anice? What the hell are ye doing here? It's the middle of the night!"

She dropped the robe and slowly approached him. He could see her nipples through the clinging material of the gown, nipples drawn into tight little buds by the chill in the air and probably the excitement of her midnight rendezvous. A triangle deeper in color than her hair was also clearly visible to his sight as he looked her over from head to toe. Her toes were bare, too, he noticed, as they peeked out from under the gossamer thin excuse for a cover.

Anice stopped an arm's length away and shook her head, causing her rich, flame-red hair to cascade in enticing ripples over her shoulders and down her back. He swallowed a large gulp of air as his awakening body reacted to the sight of those curls sliding over her curved bottom and down the backs of her thighs. Alex licked his dry lips and took a step back away from the temptation that she was creating. *By God,* he thought, *she only has fifteen years!* That thought should have scared him free of the spell she was weaving, but it didn't.

Anice launched herself into his arms and molded herself to his body. She squirmed over him and wrapped her legs around his thighs as though trying to mount him. The comparison was not lost on him as his body reacted and increased in hardness with every move that her soft, young body made. Anice pulled his head in close and attacked his mouth with her inexperienced one. She sucked at his lips with hers but kept hers closed tightly, obviously too unpracticed to know that there was much more to kissing.

The strength of her movements forced them the few feet across the room to the bed. Caught off balance, he fell backward, taking Anice with him. The breath was knocked from his body as she landed on top of him and continued her vigorous assault. Comprehending that he had to get control of the situation, Alex rolled until he was on top and pulled his face from hers. He gasped for air as he pinned her shoulders to the bed. She was just as breathless.

It wasn't until she started wiggling again that he realized his erection lay directly at the junction of her thighs. The thin linen of his tunic did nothing to hide her heat or wetness. His rock-hard maleness, deprived of feminine warmth for too long, had a mind of its own, it seemed, and Alex fought against it and her determination to keep him in intimate contact.

Finally, a moment of cold clarity controlled his brain and Alex realized that he was lying on top of his scantily clad, fifteen-year-old fiancée! He jumped off her and ran to the other side of the room. Anice pushed up on her elbows, her unfairly enticing breasts jutting out against the nightgown and heaving with every deep breath she took. She started to get up from the bed and he whispered harshly, "If ye wish to protect yer life, Anice, dinna move from that bed." She gasped and remained as still as a statue as he began to pace the room.

"Would ye tell me what ye are doing here?"

"We are betrothed, Alex." Her voice was husky, her arousal making her sound older than her years.

"I ken we are betrothed, Anice, but that doesna explain what in the hell ye are doing in my room in the middle of the night."

"I think that should be verra clear to ye, Alex. I've come to share yer bed."

Now it was his turn to stand motionless in response. He waited for more of an explanation, but none came.

"Anice, we're to be wed in a short time. Dinna ye think it might be better to wait until our wedding night?"

"But, Alex, I hiv waited for nigh unto five years for yer return. Do we hiv to wait any longer?" She stood next to the bed but continued to rub her hand lightly on the covering. ''Or, is it that ye dinna want me in yer bed?''

Her eyes were wide and expectant as she waited for his acceptance or refusal. She was clearly too naive if she hadn't been able to tell how much his body had responded to her attempt at seduction. Maybe she had given him an opening he could use to get her out of his room before someone found them.

''Anice, our marriage has been long planned by our families. 'Tis no' the time to take ye to my bed, even if we are betrothed.'' He paused for effect. ''My heirs maun be legitimate and I willna take any chances of them being born too soon after our joining. I will marry ye and honor ye and bed ye as my lawful wife, but Maggie is here for my pleasure.''

Her face froze and then her expression sagged. Tears formed and poured out of her eyes, rolling down her face. He cringed inwardly at her pain. He couldn't stand to see a woman cry. Her voice cracked as she spoke to him.

''So, ye would bed yer leman but not yer betrothed?''

''Aye, I would.''

Before she could respond, the door opened, and Maggie walked in. She looked around the room; her glance took in the silently sobbing Anice first, then him.

''Pardon me, have I disturbed you?''

''No, Maggie, Anice was just leaving.'' Alex looked at Anice and motioned, with his head, to the door. She bent over and grabbed her robe from the floor. Clutching it to her chest, she ran from the room. Her sobs could be heard as she made her way down the hall to her room.

''My God, Alex, what did you do to her?''

What had he done? The sinking feeling in his stomach told him he may have overplayed his hand with Anice. Alex ran his hands through his hair and grunted in self-disgust. He grabbed a length of plaid off one of the trunks and decided that now was as good a time as any to go for a swim in the very cold waters of the loch.

Without meeting Maggie's stare, Alex replied through gritted teeth, "I didna do what ye may think or what she may have wanted. I was the one in control! And," he said as he took hold of the door handle, "she is no' the one I want." He met her eyes and the widening he saw told him that she got the message. Then he stormed into the hallway and pulled the door behind him. Anice's sobs followed him long after the echo of the slamming door had ceased.

Chapter 26

THE SUNLIGHT PIERCING through the window wakened Maggie the next morning. Sliding her hand across the bed, she discovered that Alex was gone. She sat up and looked around the room to see if he had slept on the floor by the fire. The room was empty but for her. She slid off the bed and gathered her skirt and bodice from the trunks. Reaching into the skirt pocket, she took out her linen chemise and realized she had better find a new one soon. Her only undergarment had become worn and thin from the constant wearing and washing. She left on Alex's shirt and dressed quickly in the chilly room. After braiding her hair and wrapping it in a cloth, she was ready to break her fast and to begin her day in the kitchens.

Break her fast! She was beginning to sound like these Scots in her thoughts now. Most of the servants in the kitchen had stopped snickering behind her back in Gaelic and started speaking in a Scots-English once the newness of the situation wore off. There were still a few men who pinched her behind or pulled at her breasts, but they didn't try it very often. Alex made his possession of her very clear in public and to touch her in his or his friends' sight would be a direct challenge. The cowards who still tormented her would never want to face the laird's son in a fight.

The only time, she thought, that Alex did not proclaim his ownership of her was in the presence of Anice. They had agreed not to humiliate her in front of the clan since they would hopefully not be here forever, and she would. She would have to live out the embarrassment they caused while they were here in her time.

Maggie walked through the hall on her way to the kitchens. The tables were in place and soldiers, servants, and some family members were starting to drift in to eat. She still couldn't face the porridge the cooks made for breakfast. She entered the kitchen, poured a mug of water, and took some bannocks from a large platter that was ready to be served. The bannock cakes reminded her of rice cakes, moister and heavier, but very definitely palatable. She finished her quick meal and started her duties.

A few minutes later, one of Anice's serving women came into the room and asked the cook to have food delivered to Anice's room. At the cook's nod, Maggie began organizing a tray. The woman's voice rang out through the relative quiet in response.

"Nay! I'll not hiv my lady's food touched by that whore. Odara, find another to prepare and deliver it now. The lady is waiting." Without waiting for an answer, the woman turned and left.

Maggie came to a complete stop, her hand still extended to pick up a small loaf of bread. Even though she knew that she was not actually Alex's lover, the words sliced through her. The flush and heat of humiliation crept up to color her cheeks. She dropped her hands to her sides and lowered her head so that those in the kitchen couldn't see her tears.

"Maggie," Odara called out to her, "let that be, and

knead the loaves for me. The bread has done its rising."
Maggie nodded and moved off, grateful for something to do.

After she picked up one of the mounds of dough and started to work it on the table's surface, Odara pointed at one of the other girls who took up the task of serving Anice's breakfast. Soon, the normal hubbub of the kitchen began to cover the awkward silence. Maggie only looked up when she heard Rachelle's voice.

Rachelle stood close by and pulled a lump of dough toward her. Rachelle had been the one to give Maggie the errand last night. In the light of day, Maggie could see that it was part of Anice's ploy to get her out of Alex's room last night. What had happened between Alex and Anice? Could he have made love to her? Did they argue? She had to find him and ask him.

"So, did ye and Alex hiv a wee bit of a fight?" Rachelle whispered.

"A fight? Us? No. What makes you think that?"

"Weel, the whole keep could hear the slamming of the door in the middle of the night. Then, Alex made enough noise wi' his cursing and his leavin' the hall to wake up those few who hivna heard the door."

Maggie's mouth dropped open wider and wider with each sentence Rachelle uttered.

"Then, he came back soaked from the loch and slept wi' the men in the barracks. Now, are ye really trying to tell me ye dinna hiv a fight?"

Maggie closed her mouth and swallowed. To all outward appearances, it must seem as though they had a whopper of a fight. But, Maggie couldn't reveal what or who she had found with Alex. An argument was an easier excuse . . . and Alex had been angry when he left the room last night.

"Weel, mayhap a wee one." She imitated Rachelle's brogue and Rachelle laughed. "Things canna go smoothly all the time, ye ken." When they were kneading the loaves again, Maggie nudged Rachelle's elbow. "How did you find out about it? You don't sleep in the hall."

Rachelle's blush would have been an answer by itself. But her words confirmed it. "Brodie told me this morn."

"Oh, no. Are all the men talking about it?"

"Maggie, I am sure not all the men ken. But the warriors all sleep in the barracks so they heard of it."

"That means that the entire village will hear of it by noon."

"Oh, Maggie, dinna worry. They will probably not ken of it . . . until the evening meal." Rachelle laughed right in her shocked face.

"Rachelle. Maggie. The bread would get done faster if ye would knead as much as ye blabber." Odara's voice was what she needed to get back to her task.

Well, she thought, now she and Alex had to talk themselves out of another corner.

It was mid-morning when the summons came. Maggie was to answer the lady Anice's call to the solar. Maggie had hoped that this morning's insult would have been the end of it, but she was wrong. Odara's eyes were filled with sympathy, but she could do nothing to interfere. The lady's word was law, second only to the laird and his son's.

Maggie washed her hands and face with water from the stone basin in the corner of the kitchen and retied the scarf around her head. She had not yet been in the solar, but she knew where it was. The hall was empty but for a few servants when she made her way through it. She paused at the door of the women's room and knocked lightly. The door swung inwardly, and she was called into the chamber.

"Is it her?" Anice's icy voice came from the far side of the room. The door's direction blocked her from Maggie's view.

"Yes, milady." The servant turned to look at her mistress.

"Let her in, Iseabel, and close the door."

The young girl waved her in and pointed to Anice who was seated with a group of women near the windows. As Maggie walked toward the women, she realized that the windows were real glass, the first she had seen in the keep. As a result of the glass, the solar was a sun-filled room and one where the ladies of the clan gathered to sew and weave and embroider. Maggie stopped a few paces away from the industrious group. In addition to Anice, she recognized a woman of about forty who she knew to be Alex's aunt Gunna and another who was Anice's elder cousin Wynda. Standing off to Anice's left side was Firtha, Anice's personal maid, the woman who had insulted her in the kitchen and in her room.

Gunna opened the conversation abruptly.

"Are ye noble born?" Gunna squinted at Maggie as she barked out her question in a high, whiny voice.

"No," Maggie stuttered.

"Then ye had better learn yer manners here and now." Gunna nodded at Firtha who walked over and took Maggie's shoulders in a hard grip and forced her to her knees before the others. "That's the place for someone of yer position—on yer knees afore yer betters. And ye had best address those higher than ye as 'milady' if ye want to keep yer teeth."

Gunna smiled smugly and leaned over her embroidery frame and continued adding stitches as if nothing had happened. Firtha went back to stand beside Anice. Her smile foretold that this was the beginning of a long visit to the solar for Maggie.

Maggie stubbornly refused to cower before these medieval witches and started to struggle up to her feet, twisting the scarf that had come loose in her hands.

"Stay there, as ye are," hissed Firtha. The maid stepped toward her, hand raised, and Maggie dropped back to her knees. "My lady has not given ye permission to rise, ye filthy whore."

"Now, Firtha," Anice said in a syrupy-sweet voice that dripped with malice, "this Sassenach doesna ken our ways. I am certain that she'll learn quickly to ken her place, or she'll be leaving Dunnedin verra soon."

"Sooner than she thinks," chimed in Wynda. The other women joined Anice in an apparent private joke that left Maggie with a queasy feeling in her gut. She clenched her teeth, trying not to lash out in anger—an anger that would have been unacceptable in this day and age. Where the hell was Alex when she needed him?

"If ye continue to displease our laird's son as ye did last even, ye will be gone afore our wedding takes place." Anice leaned forward and looked Maggie directly in the eyes, daring her to reveal the truth they both knew. "It would be a shame since I was beginning to look forward to correctin' yer insulting ways myself. After I marry Alex, yer place will be in the village wi' the other sluts, who service the men in our clan and our visitors. That is the best place for a Sassenach whore, is it not?"

Maggie flinched at the venom in her words. The whole group laughed at her reaction. It was as if Anice was telling amusing stories instead of threatening someone's life! She thought that young unmarried women of this era never discussed things like whores or sex or whatever. Where were the virginal maidens she had read about?

Anice rose from her chair and handed her sewing to her maid. She inched her way over to where Maggie knelt and motioned her to her feet. When Maggie stood and Anice was close enough so that no one else could be privy to her words, she whispered under her breath, "If ye ever breathe a word of what happened last night, I'll find a way to kill ye." Maggie started to back away, but Anice grabbed at her arm, ripping her sleeve, to keep her close. "And nothing the laird or Alex says or does will stop me."

Maggie yanked her arm away and stumbled to the door. The maid standing nearby didn't move as Maggie grabbed the knob and pulled it open. As she ran across the room, Maggie heard Gunna's irritating voice: ''Ye canna teach a whore the manners of a lady, Anice.''

But it was Anice's shrieking laughter that scared her the most.

Chapter 27

WHOOSH! CRACK! WHOOSH! *Crack!* The long wooden staffs met and reverberated with each blow given and received by the two iron-muscled warriors opposing each other.

"Harder. *Harder!*" yelled Alex, forcing his voice over the cheers of the onlookers to this fight. "Faster. Move yer feet, Braden. He's going to knock ye over again if ye don't start moving."

Alex paced around the fighters, calling out instructions as he coached both men.

"Iain, I canna help ye if ye dinna listen to me. Lean in, shift yer weight. Watch out for yer legs."

Alex threw his hand over his eyes in frustration as he watched Braden finally follow his commands and upend Iain in the dirt. The other soldiers and servants, who had gravitated out to watch the fight, cheered loudly for the winner or commiserated with the loser.

Alex sat down on the ground with the two warriors. All three were drenched in sweat and breathing heavily. As the throng drifted away, Alex reviewed the fighters' strategies and made suggestions for the next time. He stood and was dusting himself off when he caught sight of Maggie running out the gate and into the woods. She was too far to hear him, so he didn't yell. He mumbled excuses to the two men, grabbed his tunic off the nearby fence, and trotted after her. When he approached the gate, the guard smiled knowingly and pointed in the direction of Maggie's path.

He had a feeling she was headed for the loch, so he slowed to a walk to catch his breath. Thank God he'd been in decent physical shape when he arrived here, or he would be dead by now from the training. After just a few weeks, he knew his upper body was much stronger from all the practice and drilling with the large two-handed claymore. The running and swimming had added to the strength in his legs, too. His body was changing, just as his voice and accent had already.

He also decided to let his hair and beard grow and both of the women in his life had responded favorably. Maggie said he looked like the barbarian he was becoming. But it was the inflection and throatiness in her voice that made it clear she found it and him attractive. Anice just blushed and stammered when he asked if she liked his beard.

It was getting hard to believe that a few short weeks ago, he had worked behind a desk, crunching numbers for clients in his stable, well-ordered life. Now he was a different person, freed from constraints, stronger, and more self-reliant. Unfortunately, he was living over six hundred years in the past. He laughed at the absurdity of this twist of fate and time.

The choking sobs traveled through the quiet glen to him and alerted him that Maggie was close by. He stopped and listened and then jogged in the direction of her crying. He broke into the clearing and spied her sitting on a boulder by the end of the lake. Her hair, freed from her braid, tumbled around her face and over her shoulders. Her face was hidden by her hands, and she rocked ever so slightly as she wept. He approached her quietly and spoke softly, trying not to frighten her.

"Maggie? What has happened to ye?"

She started at the sound of his voice, barely moving her hands to see who had followed her. He opened his arms to her, offering the comfort she needed desperately. She didn't hesitate to scramble off the rock and dash into his arms. He wrapped his arms around her, and unconsciously imitated her earlier rocking to and fro. Her crying intensified, and he swallowed deeply to get rid of the lump in his throat.

Maggie was strong and resourceful. She was an equal to him in their efforts to survive and find a way home. It took a tremendous amount of stress for her to reach the point of weeping. He'd only seen it twice before: on the day they arrived and when they tried to get through the arch. He needed to discover what had driven her to this state, and he had a strong suspicion that the cause's name was Anice.

"Maggie, love," he murmured, stroking her hair and pushing it away from her face. "Dinna greet, Maggie. Tell me what happened." He continued their rocking, holding her close and wrapping his arms more tightly around her.

"You don't understand, Alex. It's not supposed to be this way." She hiccuped as she drew a deep breath into her lungs. She leaned her head back to look into his eyes, revealing that her eyes were tear-swollen and her nose was running.

"Wait, Maggie. Let's get ye cleaned up a bit, then we can talk." At her stiff nod, he led her carefully down to the water's edge and sat down next to her on the ground. He wet his hands and stroked them down her face, wiping off the tears. He gentled his touch when she winced. With the lightest dab possible, he cleaned her face and then dried it with the scarf she had twisted around her hand. She stopped sobbing and now sat motionless as he tended to her. He smoothed back her unruly hair. Then, he moved behind her and began to braid it.

"Alex, what are you doing?" She tried to turn around.

"I canna finish this if ye keep twisting aboot." He grasped her shoulders and straightened her body. They sat facing the loch as he braided her hair. "I watch ye do this every night afore ye sleep. I dinna think it can be too difficult even for a mon to do."

"You . . . watch . . . me?"

"There isna television here, if ye dinna notice. Wi'oot lights in the room, there isna much to watch by the light of the fire." The tremulous smile she gave him over her shoulder made his stomach tighten. He weaved the portions of her hair over and under until a long, uneven braid appeared. He pulled it side to side, trying to center it on her back, and then gave up. He tied the strip of leather around the end again and let it drop, satisfied at his result.

" 'Tis no' perfect, but it will hold the hair out of yer face." Before he knew it, Maggie had leaned against him, her back against his chest. "Now, tell me what's no' as it should be."

Maggie took a deep breath, filling her lungs and releasing it slowly. Alex wrapped his arms around her from behind, lifting her arms and resting on her waist.

"Oh, Alex, I always thought that the Middle Ages were so romantic. I've read a lot of books set in medieval times, and I always dreamed of being the lady of a castle and wearing beautiful clothes. The brave, handsome knights would vie for my hand, and I would choose the lucky winner."

"And would ye live happily ever after in this dream of yers?" The corners of his mouth turned up as he asked.

"Well, of course, this is a romantic fantasy I'm telling you about. It *has* to end happily."

"And?"

"And what?"

"And, what part of yer fantasy hasna come true for ye?"

Maggie's spine stiffened, pulling her out of his embrace. He knew he should not tease her, but he just couldn't resist the urge.

"Would ye believe none of it?" she asked, imitating his accent. He still couldn't hear it when he spoke.

"Aye, Maggie, I believe ye." He experienced some disappointment when, instead of leaning back against him, she removed her shoes and stood and walked to the lake's edge. Once there, she stepped into the shallow water and splashed around in the few inches at the edge. He pulled his sweaty boots free and flexed his toes. The icy water would feel good on his overheated feet. He followed Maggie to the edge and took her by the hand. He intertwined their fingers and pulled her into a walking gait.

"But, are no' fantasies just that? Yer an educated woman. Ye canna believe that only good existed at that time, or should I say, *this* time?"

With her free hand, Maggie pointed at her head. "I knew it here." She moved her hand to her chest. "But not here. In my heart, I kept the romantic dreams alive."

"Aahh, Maggie," he squeezed the hand he was holding, "keep yer dreams, never let go of them. But we canna ignore the reality and the dangers of this time." He gently outlined her lips, hoping that she would finally confide in him about the cause of her unhappiness. "Let's sit in the shade and talk."

They walked away from the edge of the water and sat down on the grass. The thick shading of the tree above them and the cool breeze off the loch made it very comfortable for an August afternoon. Alex drew Maggie down to sit between his legs, and he leaned against the tree. Lucky for him, this tree had smooth bark. He didn't want to break the quiet of the moment by leaving to retrieve his tunic, and the thought of Maggie's body against his bare skin was something he looked forward to.

They sat for a few minutes, without speaking, enjoying the pleasant quiet. When Maggie rested her head back on his shoulder, he took advantage of the nearness of her ear.

"Now's as good a time as any to tell me what happened." After just a slight hesitation, Maggie started.

"I think we have underestimated Anice."

"How so?"

"She is not a fifteen-year-old girl. She's really a five-star general in disguise."

Alex let out a bark of laughter at her comment. Maggie turned sideways in his arms to face him. Her face was devoid of humor as she continued.

"It's easy for you to find humor in this. Every time you see her, she's Miss Sweetness to you. And you've been spending a lot of time with her, Alex."

"That is what this is aboot—the time I spend wi' Anice?"

"Well, her campaign to win your affections and keep you in her company was to be expected; she is your fiancée, after all, but her latest moves show a determination and strategic planning that the army would love."

He could not help himself; he laughed loudly again. It irritated her, and Maggie tried to escape his embrace. He grabbed her hand and wrapped their fingers together to prevent her leaving. Jealous? Could Maggie be jealous of Anice?

"Nay, Maggie, dinna move away. I dinna mean to laugh at yer ideas. It was just the verra serious look on yer face and yer speaking of Anice this way that seemed funny to me. Just tell me what happened."

Maggie leaned against the leg he had drawn up behind her. "Well, Alex, you know I've been trying to avoid her since the scene in the village?" Alex nodded in answer. "And, for the last two weeks, I've done a pretty good job of staying out of her sight." Alex nodded again.

"Well, I think the uneasy truce is over."

"What makes ye say that?"

"Last night and this morning."

"Last night?"

"Whatever happened between you and Anice has stirred up a lot of anger. And this morning, she summoned me to her solar and threatened me with all kinds of terrible things once you two are wed. And, in spite of anything you or Struan could do to protect me."

Alex pulled his leg from behind her and scrambled to his feet. He paced around the small clearing while he thought of Anice's latest machinations. Maggie's laughter got his attention.

"What do ye think is so funny?"

"Alex, you always pace when you are thinking or worried. I was just thinking about what a habit it is for you." He frowned at her and she smiled in retaliation. "So, what did you and Anice do before I got to the room?"

"Ye ken that I am no' interested in her for other than the roles we play? And that she's really just a bairn to me?"

"Really?" Maggie's eyebrows raised at the word.

"Of course! What kind of self-respecting man do you think I am? She's only fifteen for God's sake. *Fifteen!* 'Tis bad enough that I hae to pay court to her every day and spend more and more time wi' her. And I only spend the time wi' her that I need to so that Struan and the others will no' become suspicious."

Alex bellowed out the last word. His anger at the way his body had not bothered to consider her age last night grew. He was ashamed that his growing desire for Maggie had wrecked his control, and, for a split second in that bed, all his body wanted to do was to drive into Anice.

"Fifteen would be jailbait in our time, Alex, but not here. She should have been married almost three years ago and had a baby or two by now. She's ready, *in all important ways*, to be married." Maggie paused. "But you didn't make love to her last night, did you?"

Alex was stopped dead by her question. For a brief few seconds last night, he admitted that his body had almost gotten the better of him. But the woman in front of him now was the one he really wanted. He shook his head, answering her in the gesture.

He'd wanted to make love to *Maggie* so badly that he took to sleeping on the floor to avoid wrapping himself around her while she slept. He wanted to peel off her clothes and make love to her right now, right here. He felt his body respond to his thoughts quickly, hardening and enlarging, ready to make her his own, for real. He couldn't help the pure wanting that was showing on his face. Maggie reacted when she caught sight of his erection, apparent in the tight breeches he was wearing.

"Alex, this isn't about Anice, is it?"

He reached down, took her hands, and pulled her up to stand in front of him.

"Nay, Maggie, no' aboot her at all. This is aboot ye and me, and I'm thinking aboot what I'd like to do to ye." He took her face in his hands and slowly lowered his head. Her eyes fluttered shut as his lips brushed her cheek, tracing an erotic pattern all over her face. He smiled at the shiver she gifted him with in return.

"I havna wanted her the way I want ye, Maggie." He kissed her chin and trailed the tip of his warm, wet tongue over to her ear. "I havna touched her other than an expected kiss or an embrace.

"I've wanted ye for a long time now." He bit her ear with enough force to gain another full-body shudder. "And," he whispered into her ear while he moved one hand down her back to rest on the incredibly arousing curves of her bottom and press her into his engorged arousal, "I want ye *now.*"

Chapter 28

HE COULD NO longer fight against the attraction that burned between them. He outlined her trembling mouth with his tongue. Reaching around, he loosened the tie on her braid that he had so recently placed there. As he worked his fingers into her hair, savoring the feel of the silky curls, he felt her arms come up on his bare back and pull him even closer.

"I have wanted to do that ever since I watched you braid it the first night we were here."

"You like my hair?" Her voice was a throaty whisper.

"I've thought of rubbing it over my body and yer's when I make love to ye."

Maggie arched against him, pressing her curves against his hard body and her eager response destroyed the last of his control. He slid down to his knees and pulled her with him. Her breasts were tight points against his bare skin, the thin layers of material hardly even noticeable. A moment later, he was guiding her down to lie on the grass with him.

Using his arm to pillow her head, Alex pulled Maggie

close and wrapped one of his legs over hers. He felt the pounding in his groin grow until he knew he had to be inside of her. He rubbed his hardened flesh against her, relishing her passionate response. Her tongue darted inside his mouth to explore it hungrily, and the feel of it drove him wild with a desire that was beyond anything he'd ever experienced before.

Alex pulled his mouth away and looked into her passion-glazed eyes. Keeping their lower bodies melded together, he eased back from her chest. He slid his hand around and teased the hardened nipples that had teased him for too long. Maggie whimpered as he rubbed his palm over one and then the other. She arched into his grasp and moaned from deep in her throat as he pressed harder against her heated flesh.

His mouth was watering in anticipation of tasting them, so he tugged at the laces on her bodice, loosening them. Now, the only thing that stood between his tongue and the enticing points was the thin layer of chemise that Maggie wore. Rather than delay, Alex opened his mouth over one tip and drew it in. He chuckled as Maggie gasped in surprise. He looked up and saw that her eyes were tightly closed and she was breathing in short, hitching gasps as he continued his vigorous attention to her breasts. His pride and his arousal both swelled at the compliment given by her responsive body.

Maggie was rocking her pelvis against his groin as he suckled one breast, then the other, still not bothering to move the material aside. He was thrilled when she reached up to her neckline and untied the smock's ribbon. She loosened it and pulled it down to expose her breasts to him, but before he could respond, she lifted one breast to him in invitation. He didn't hesitate a moment to take what she offered.

The taste of it was incredibly sweet, and he laved and swirled his tongue around the first nipple before biting it gently. He applied the same attention to the second before rolling Maggie onto her back and covering her with his heated body. Now nothing separated their bare chests, and they both moaned at the pleasure of it.

Maggie luxuriated in the feeling of Alex's weight on top of her. She arched her hips and felt the evidence of his passion thrusting against her mons. She wrapped her legs around his to keep the contact as tight as possible. When Alex loosed his legs and knelt over her, she cried out for his heat. She grabbed his hips to pull him down, but he resisted and instead tugged the chemise free from her skirt and pulled it over her head. She was left naked from the waist up. She didn't resist when he slid his hands up under her skirt to pull off the silk panties she still wore underneath the coarsely woven material. And, when he skimmed his fingers up the skin of her inner thigh to touch the center of her building heat, her body tightened, coiling and writhing at his touch. His fingers, callused from working with sword and staff, created a wonderful friction on the moist flesh between her nether lips. Maggie couldn't keep her thighs together as Alex insinuated first one finger then two into the place that led to her woman's core. He plunged them in and out at a furious pace, drawing the moisture he found out and spreading it on the outer lips.

"Alex," she cried out, not sure what she was asking for. Her brain had stopped working and she could only feel—feel every response her body offered to his touches, his caresses.

"Alex," she moaned again as he found the little pearl between the outer layers of flesh. She grabbed him by the hair and pulled him down closer to her body. He slid down next to her, continuing to wreak havoc on her senses. Her skin was on fire; every crevice of her body ached to be filled. She could feel the pulling inside her core tightening, building to an impossible height.

Every part of her, from head to toe and especially the places that Alex was touching, screamed for release. He leaned over and kissed her deeply, the plunging of his tongue imitating his fingers until she couldn't breathe. And, with one final stroke of his thumb against the center of her arousal, she climaxed, not able or wanting to control the loud groan that escaped from her lips. Wave after wave of intense pleasure swept through her body leaving her satisfied . . . for the moment.

When she could finally breathe again, she looked up to find him staring at her. He was smiling, his eyes sparkling and his breathing a bit labored, too. She felt very pleased by that for some reason. Then, she frowned at him.

"It's not fair!"

"Maggie, what do ye not find fair now?" He pushed his hair back from his face and scratched his beard.

"I've been watching you, too. I've watched you training with the men in just those tight breeches or in the plaid. I've wanted to feel the strength of your thighs." She slipped her hand down onto his muscled thigh. "And I wanted to feel your chest." She rubbed her hand over the now-sweaty skin of his chest. "Hhhmmm . . ." she teased, "I think your chest and thighs are bigger now than when we arrived here. Has anything else grown bigger?"

His response to her teasing was a groan of his own. Maggie allowed him to take her hand and put it on his erection. She squeezed it firmly, massaging the ridge of hardened flesh until his breathing became irregular.

"Now, this is a bit more fair. But, we've still a ways to go." Maggie knelt up and leaned over Alex's body, kissing and licking her way down his chest and stomach to the waistband of the pants he wore. She returned to his flat, male nipples and played with them as he had hers, licking, sucking, and nipping with her lips, tongue, and teeth. The salty taste of his skin and musky odor aroused her senses and encouraged her teasing. By the time her tongue slid back down to his waist, Alex was gasping. Leaning down and arching her back, she rested her naked breasts with their very sensitive pebbled tips on his chest and used her hair to tickle his skin.

"I want to see you naked, Alex."

Maggie moved between his legs and yanked on his pants. He untied the belting at his waist and helped her to ease them down by lifting his hips. The second tug exposed his hipbones; she paused to bend over and kiss them, rubbing her cheek in the springy hair below his waist. The third tug freed his penis; she encircled it with her hands and stroked the velvety length of it and watched Alex's face tighten in pleasure. The fourth tug revealed the sac under his erection; as she gently rolled and squeezed it, Maggie saw and heard his breaths become labored. Maggie crawled backward and pulled the trews the rest of the way down and off his legs.

"Take off your skirt," Alex ordered gruffly.

She nodded, thrilled that his reaction was so strong. She stood and allowed the skirt to drop down her hips and legs. Stepping out of it, she moved closer and stood over him, her legs spread to stand outside his thighs. His gaze moved over her and made the heat rise within her again. The aching and wanting began anew and the deep growl was the only warning she got that his patience was at an end.

She looked like a Greek goddess to him. He'd seen a statue in a museum that looked as she did now: her breasts thrust out, firm and high, and her hair flowing and curling down her back. Her other curls made his hands itch to touch them again as they guarded the entrance to her womanhood. Her buttocks were firm and he was dying—absolutely dying—to touch them. His loins felt ready to burst, so he grabbed her legs and pulled her down to straddle his hips. Her inner lips were hot and wet as he placed her over his raging flesh. He rubbed his hardness along her cleft and looked to her for a signal to stop. When all she did was arch her back and let out a long, breathy moan, he eased into her and watched her slide down his erection. He was plunged to the hilt when she opened her eyes and gave him a dreamy smile.

"This is fair, Alex, very fair now," she said on another moan.

He held her by her hips and began a rhythm for her to match. She leaned forward, dipping her breasts close to his mouth. He obliged her request and took one turgid tip and then the other into his hungry mouth and suckled them. Caught up in the excitement, Maggie began to match the rotating and surging motions of his hips with her own.

Alex knew he was close to exploding within her. He could feel the pressure building, his sac tightened in anticipation, and his erection swelled even more. He reached between their bodies and searched for the sensitive bud that would stir her to the same level. He found it, and Maggie raced toward another orgasm with him. When he felt the first quivers of her release, he rolled her onto her back and thrust as deeply as he could into her molten passage. He felt his seed begin to escape as he plunged a few more times to gain his release.

He knew he yelled out her name as he surged inside her. Then he collapsed on top of her and prayed that he would still be alive after he calmed down. He eased off to one side, allowing her to catch her breath, too.

Alex knew that time had passed, but he couldn't tell how much. What had occurred between him and Maggie was more than just having sex. He knew that deep within himself. But he hesitated to speak, not knowing the right thing to say to her. He didn't know what this meant to her: A commitment? A physical release only? He knew it felt so right, being inside of her, joined to her body. Nothing he and Nancy had ever done came close to what he experienced with Maggie just now.

It felt so right, so good.

He must have dozed off because Maggie lay curled up at his side, her head resting on his chest. He smoothed the hair back from her face and shook her gently.

"Maggie. Maggie, love. It's time to wake."

It didn't work. He groaned. She was a bear to wake up. He shook her again, this time more firmly. When he got no response, he looked around and remembered where they were. He slid out from under her and ran down to the loch. He grabbed their shoes and his tunic and he dipped his tunic in the cold water. With it still dripping freely, he dashed back to the grove where Maggie lay, snoring and oblivious to the world.

"Maggie," he called once more. Alex knew what he was going to do was cruel, but he couldn't resist. He twisted the tunic and let the cold water drip onto her. The icy droplets hit her face and stomach and legs, and Maggie woke up screaming. When she realized who had done what to her, she jumped to her feet and started chasing him. Alex was not about to point out that she was as naked as he was!

They'd reached the water's edge when he stopped and let her catch him. He pulled her into his arms and they fell into the lake together. She was momentarily silenced as they went under the surface, but her screams pierced the air as they came back up.

"What the bloody hell do you think you're doing, Alex MacKendimen?" She stood up in the shallows and pushed the mass of sopping hair out of her eyes and over her shoulders. "It's freezing in this damned lake."

He clucked his tongue at her. "Maggie, lass, that's not the kind of language I would expect from a lady, ye ken?"

He didn't know exactly what he had said to cause the change in her, but from her stricken look, he knew it involved Anice. She started to walk out of the lake when a loud cough startled them both.

"Alex, the laird thought it best if ye came back and practiced yer swordplay wi' the men instead of yer wench."

Brodie's voice was loud and mocking. He was sitting on the large, flat rock where Alex had first found Maggie.

It only took an instant for her to sink into the covering water with a squeak.

"I thank ye, Brodie, for delivering my faither's message. Ye can go now."

"But, Alex, I'm supposed to wait for ye and bring ye back."

"Thank ye agin, Brodie, I can find my way back to the practice yard," Alex growled out from behind clenched teeth.

Brodie got to his feet. "Weel, if ye think ye can find yer way . . . I'll tell yer faither that ye be on yer way back." He ambled off into the woods, whistling a tune.

Maggie had already stumbled out of the water and was running for her clothes when Alex walked from the lake. He got to the clearing in the trees as she was squeezing the water from her hair.

"Ye are difficult to wake, and using the water was a cruel trick to use on ye. And I am sorry for Brodie finding us like that, Maggie. Can ye forgive me?"

"It wasn't your fault that Brodie came upon us like that, Alex. Our disappearance from the keep together was obviously noted. I'm just glad it was Brodie and not one of Anice's maids who found us like this." She gestured to their lack of covering.

He pulled on his breeches and tied them. He fought his boots on and then tugged his tunic over his head. "I think it might be a good idea if we dinna return together. Why dinna ye take yer time getting dressed, and I'll see ye back at the keep later?"

At her nod, he started to leave. He turned and watched her stand and put her chemise back on. He covered the small distance between them in a few steps and wrapped her in his embrace. He placed his lips very gently on hers, and he kissed her slowly and deeply. She sighed as he stepped away from her.

"And, Maggie, I dinna."

"You dinna, I mean, didn't what, Alex?"

"I dinna make love to Anice last night. I havna made love to any other woman or wanted to since I got to Scotland and met ye."

She blushed at his words. "Thank you for answering my question." He turned to go when he heard her say his words back to him. "And, Alex, I havna made love to any other mon or wanted to since I got to Scotland."

He liked the accent he heard in her voice. He smiled and waved and ran into the woods to catch up with Brodie.

Well, they would talk more tonight. And, he hoped, make love more tonight, too.

Chapter 29

"IT LOOKS TO me that the first time was a good one for ye and yer Alex."

Maggie wheeled around to identify the intrusion into her privacy. She had been lost in her thoughts about what had just happened between her and Alex and never heard the woman approach.

"What did you say?" she asked.

"I said that it looks to me that ye and yer Alex finally took the step."

Maggie could feel the blood drain from her face and was helpless to stop her reaction.

"I don't know what you mean. Who are you?" She clenched her hands together, trying to stop their trembling, but nothing could stop the god-awful fear that she and Alex had been exposed.

"I am called Moira. I'm the healer of the clan MacKendimen." The woman paused for a moment. "And some in the clan say I hiv the *an-da-shealladh*."

Maggie regretted not taking time yet to learn more of those tongue-twisting Gaelic words.

"The healer? The one who made the potion for me?" At her nod, Maggie continued, "You have my thanks for your help." Moira simply smiled in response.

"And-a-shee-lad?" Maggie stumbled over the words. "What does that mean?"

Moira chuckled at her pronunciation. "Nay, lass, no' even close! But I thank ye for trying to wrap that outlander's tongue of yers around our good *Gaidhlig* words." Moira bent over and picked up one of the baskets at her feet. Maggie was so startled by this woman's sudden appearance that she had failed to notice them. Moira surprised her again by holding out one of the baskets for her to carry. "Come, lass, help an old woman in her task."

"You don't look old to me," Maggie said, not seeing a gray hair among the thick brown hair on the woman's head. She stuffed her scarf into the pocket of her skirt and held out her hand.

"And, ye dinna sound English to me, lass."

Moira dropped the handle of the basket into Maggie's outstretched palm. Not able or willing to respond to her taunt, Maggie lifted the basket closer to her face and inhaled deeply, enjoying the freshness and fullness of the scents. She examined the contents and recognized several plants and flowers from nearby fields. Others didn't look familiar at all. She looked up to catch sight of Moira disappearing through the trees. After looking around the area to see if she'd left anything behind, Maggie then raced to catch up.

"You didn't tell me what *anda*-whatever means."

Moira continued at her brisk pace, never slowing down. She looked back over her shoulder at Maggie, smiled enigmatically, and said, "Two sights."

"Two sights?" Maggie asked again.

"Weel, that's what the words mean, but ye probably ken it as the second sight."

Maggie stopped dead in her tracks. Whatever confusion she had suffered before now turned to unadulterated terror. Those words were exactly what Mairi used to describe her gift: *second sight.* Was there a connection? What could or did Moira know?

"Come, lass. Visit awhile. I have ointments to make, and we can talk about ye and yer Alex." Moira's melodic voice drifted back to Maggie and shook her from her fear. As she looked around, Maggie didn't see anything that seemed familiar in this part of the woods. "And bring my basket wi' ye." Maggie followed the bits of conversation as though she were following a road map, weaving through trees and bushes with Moira always just ahead, just out of sight.

Then, as if she opened a door into another world, Maggie broke into a clearing and the village was spread out before her. Clusters of four or five cottages each spread out between her and the castle wall. Smoke curled from openings in the roofs and added to the other smells she was just beginning to notice. The animal sounds and odors she had detected on her ride through the village were now amplified, louder and stronger because they were closer. Pigs snorted and rooted the ground in their pens. The shaggy cattle being driven to another roughly fenced yard made a sound unlike any moo she had ever heard. Maggie jumped back from their path and watched them tamely meander where they were guided by the man in charge.

After the herd passed by, Maggie turned and looked for signs of Moira. She followed a well-worn path that led around some of the cottages and toward a group of people who she could not understand. Approaching from behind, she came upon a small group of young women who were giggling and blushing and primping. She didn't comprehend the words, but the actions were a constant through time and place. There must be a man around, a good-looking man, who they were trying to impress. She sidestepped the ensemble and was granted an unimpeded view of the village blacksmith at work.

He stood near a fire, working a piece of metal over the

white-hot flame. *Bang, bang, bang.* The noise echoed out past her into the village. Even from this distance, she could feel the sweltering heat pouring from the forge and smell the odor of the heated metal as he worked it into a new shape with heat and water and brute force.

He wore no shirt, and the black trews he did wear were plastered to his lower body by the sweat that constantly flowed down his chest, stomach, and back. His long, black hair was braided back to keep it out of his face while working near the dangerous fire. Hair the same shade created a furry covering over his well-developed chest and spread down into those pants. Maggie swallowed deeply and tried to look unaffected by this display of blatant, sensual manliness. She completely understood why the fair maidens of the village spent their time ogling this guy.

"What's his name?" she whispered to the girl nearest to her. After a moment's hesitation and no response, she gently nudged the girl nearest to her with her elbow and repeated her question.

"Pol," the young woman stammered out, "the blacksmith." The words ended on a feminine sigh that she had heard many times in the junior high hallway.

Pol paused in his work to wipe his eyes. Never putting his tool down, he dragged his forearm across his forehead and bridge of his nose. Before wielding his heavy hammer again, he stretched his arms over his head and then rotated them down, exposing his extremely well-shaped, muscular chest and back to his gathered fans. As Maggie watched him work his crowd, she couldn't help but appreciate his well-formed legs and behind and . . . Damn, this was fun, but it wasn't helping her find Moira. With Moira's basket still in her hand, Maggie stepped away from the adoring crowd and approached the blacksmith.

"Good day, Pol." Maggie heard the surprised gasps behind her.

"Good day to ye." His voice was deeper than the echo

in the village well and his eyes were bluer than the loch on a sunny day.

"Can you tell me how to find Moira's cottage?" She held out the basket. "I have her herbs."

"Weel, lass, ye follow this path until it leaves the village, and ye will see Moira's place just afore ye enter the forest." He used one his of massive arms to point the direction.

"My thanks for the aid." Maggie gave a modest bow of her head to express her appreciation. Just before she took her first step on the indicated trail, Pol grabbed her hand. The onlookers hissed their disapproval.

"Ye should have a care wandering through the village alone. Some men willna respect yer place in Alex's life."

She shook her hand free from his strong but not hurtful grip. "And you, are you one of those men?"

"Nay. I hiv all I could want," he answered with a genuine smile that revealed extremely attractive dimples and a cleft in his sculpted chin. "I dinna need to go looking fer trouble wi' Alex's woman." Maggie relaxed her guard a bit and returned his smile. "But ye best be on yer way afore my watchers tell tales that are no' true." He nodded toward the bevy of beauties watching his every move.

"Again, I thank you. Have a good day, Pol."

"And a good day to ye, mistress."

As Maggie turned toward the edge of the work area, she heard an older woman yelling at the girls. Waving her arms and using a voice that Attila the Hun would have been proud of, she dispersed the crowd around the smithy. Pol, she noticed, went back to his work, but not without a farewell wink and nod to her.

A few minutes more of walking, and Maggie reached the edge of the village. There, tucked into the encroaching trees, was Moira's cottage. Maggie expected seven little men to come parading out at any moment, whistling their way off to work. She'd noticed that most doorways were smaller here, or should she say *now.* Another big difference was that each croft had an enclosed area for the animals to use when the weather was too cold. Luckily, it was the middle of summer, so they could keep the creatures outside. She didn't think she could ever get used to sleeping with those cattle!

At her approach, the door swung open, and Moira greeted her.

"Here, lass, let me take those." Moira took the basket and waved Maggie inside. "The water is still cool in that pitcher, if ye want to refresh yerself."

"Thank you, I am thirsty." Maggie took an earthenware mug and filled it. "Can I get you some?"

"Nay, lass, I already quenched my thirst afore ye got here. What took ye so long?" Moira began to sort the various plants into separate piles on the high worktable on one side of the room.

"I lost sight of you when we entered the village. I had to ask directions."

"Who did ye ask?"

"Pol, the blacksmith."

"Ah," Moira sighed, "he's a good mon."

Maggie could not believe her ears. She could swear that Moira meant more than just a simple comment.

"You know him well?" she asked innocently.

"Verra well, lass. And he's good, verra, verra good." Her voice lowered to a very throaty tone.

Maggie choked on the mouthful of water that almost made it down her throat. Moira smiled. "Are ye shocked? Ye, of all people, shouldna be."

"What do you mean, 'me, of all people'?"

"Weel, yer place is sleeping wi' the son of the laird. Why should someone else sharing their bed wi' another be such a shock to ye?" Moira's eyes and hands never left the task of sorting the contents of the baskets, but

Maggie could feel that Moira was paying complete attention to her answers.

''It really isn't any of my business who you sleep with, Moira. It just surprised me that you would be so open about it to me.''

''To ye?''

''I'm sure the rest of the village knows about your er . . . relationship with Pol. But I'm a stranger to you. Why share that with me?''

''Yer not a stranger to me, Maggie Hobbs. I hiv been waiting for ye and yer Alex for a long time.'' The words sounded very familiar to her, and Maggie noticed that Moira was staring directly at her as she spoke now. The woman's eyes had taken on an unnerving glow.

''Why do you call him 'my Alex'?''

''He isna ours, is he?''

Maggie couldn't focus her eyes, once the room started to spin around her. She couldn't stand up, either. She was falling to the floor when the darkness crept up and claimed her.

''Here, lass, take a wee sip of this. It will clear yer head.''

Maggie felt a gentle but strong hand lift her head and a cup at her lips. She managed a small taste before choking. The liquid burned its way down her throat, into her unsuspecting stomach, forcing tears to her eyes. Even the air pouring into her lungs burned like the fiery liquid. After a few coughing spasms, the burning subsided, and she tried to speak.

''What did you give me?'' she asked hoarsely.

''Just a wee dram of the *usig-beathe*.''

''Whiskey?''

''Is that what *ye* call it? How do ye feel, lass?''

Maggie sat up and touched her forehead. With Moira's help, she stood, swaying slightly. She grasped the edge of the nearby table to get her balance. She closed her eyes and waited for the room to stop moving. "I think I'm all right now. I don't know what happened."

Moira took Maggie's hand and Maggie felt a wave of warmth and comfort spread through her whole body. Moira reached up and placed her palm to Maggie's cheek, pushing the hair away from her face in a motherly gesture.

"Ye hiv nothing to fear from me, lass. I amna a threat to ye or yer Alex. I may be the one able to help ye both." Moira moved away from her and went back to sorting the plants, and Maggie stood forgotten for the moment.

Before they could continue, a small boy stuck his head into the cottage through the top half of the door that Moira had left opened and called out to Moira.

"Is the Sassenach woman still here, Moira?"

"Aye, Robbie, and ye best be watching yer mouth. Ye dinna hiv to insult the puir lass. I ken that yer maither taught ye better than that."

The boy's eyes widened and his bottom lip trembled a bit, but he nodded his head, accepting Moira's correction.

"The cook said she's needed for the noon meal."

"Thank you for coming for me, Robbie. I'm on my way." The boy smiled and was off running in the direction of the keep before she could complete her answer. Maggie looked over at Moira, who was still sorting the bounty of herbs she had collected. Maggie took in a deep breath, enjoying the many scents that filled the air of the small croft.

"There is a *ceilidh* planned three nights from this night. Bring yer Alex, and we can speak then."

"A *kaylee*?"

"A gathering of song and dance. The whole village comes out fer it."

"But that means Anice will be there."

"Nay, Anice niver comes to the *ceilidh*. She likes to play the noble lady too much to lower herself." A trace of bitterness entered Moira's voice. Maggie looked her in the eyes. "Anice may weel like the courtier Alex who's been living in England far better than the one who has shown up here. Yer Alex is a true Scotsman in his heart."

"What do you mean by that?"

Without answering her question, Moira walked over, opened the bottom of the door, and left the cottage. Maggie followed her out into the clearing.

"If ye take this path until ye see the tanner's cottage and then go to the right, it will take ye but a few minutes to reach the keep."

"You're not going to answer me, are you?"

"Nay, lass. There will be plenty of time to answer yer questions at the *ceilidh*. Good day to ye now." Without a pause, Moira walked back into her home and closed the door, both parts, behind her.

Just great, Maggie thought. *More to this mystery and more that I don't understand.* And one more thing that she and Alex had to add to their discussions tonight.

Tonight . . .

Her mouth went dry at the memory of what they had just shared at the loch. Shaking off her reverie, she headed off in the direction Moira had suggested. She really shouldn't keep Odara waiting.

Chapter 30

THE FIRE CRACKLED in the corner hearth, wisps of smoke curling up into the narrow chimney and escaping out a small vent in the wall. Maggie wrapped the plaid tighter around her shoulders against the coolness of the room and continued to mend her skirt.

August? It couldn't be August and this cold.

The bodice lay waiting for her experience with needle and thread. She grimaced as she examined the extent of the damage to her clothes, first by Anice and then by her adventures in the woods with Alex. At this rate, she'd be bare save for Alex's shirts.

She was so intent on her repairs that she never heard the door swing open. It was the draft of cool air entering through the opening that grabbed her attention.

"Close the door, Alex. I finally got this room warm enough to be comfortable." She pulled the plaid tighter around her shoulders again and dipped closer to the candle to see the small stitches better.

Alex took the fabric and needle from her hands and threw it on the table and pulled her to her feet. Then he took her face in his hands and brought it close to his.

"Ye dinna need a fire to warm ye, Maggie. I plan to do that for ye." He dipped his head and touched his lips to hers. The plaid dropped to the floor, completely ignored.

She truly must have lost her mind, because the next thing she knew she was under Alex's long and muscular body, their legs entwined, on the bed. He continued kissing her, and the heat and passion of those kisses drew her breath and her wits right out of her. She opened her mouth as his tongue gently encircled her lips.

He continued the kiss until she finally thought to push him away. He pulled back and looked at her.

"I'm sorry, lass. Was I a bit too rough?"

She noticed right away that he was still on top of her.

"Are you going to move, Alex?"

"Like this, Maggie?" He arched his back, sliding his hardness into a deeper caress between her thighs. And, damn her, she let out a moan at the pleasure of that move.

"Alex, I think we should talk about this."

"I dinna hiv the strength to stop and talk now, Maggie. Mayhap later?" He aimed his kisses with devilish intent all the way down her neck and into the valley between her breasts. How could she resist this? Warmth spread in and down through her body, following the pulses of pleasure that he created. Soon, even her toes were warmed.

"But, Alex . . ."

"Aye, lass, I'll touch ye there." The scoundrel! He was purposefully misinterpreting her words.

His hands moved down past her hips and slipped beneath her buttocks. First, gliding over the sensitive area, then he used his fingertips to start the tingling. Next his hot hands slid over her skin and cupped her bottom, pressing her against his erection even more firmly.

"Alex, your shirt . . ." After ripping her own clothes she was concerned that his shirt that she wore would get damaged.

"Aye, lass, let me help ye."

Thinking that he meant to stop, she untangled her legs from his and waited. In one brief moment, he yanked the shirt over her head, leaving her naked on the bed. He was fast, she would give him that! She swallowed convulsively as, with one more yank, this one on his belt and plaid, he was as naked and as aroused as she was. She reached her hand up to stop his body's descent to hers. She didn't stand a chance.

His chest, furred and heated, brushed against her breasts and she felt the tips of them harden. He knelt between her thighs, bringing the rest of him into intimate contact with her tingling flesh. A throbbing intensified in her core, and she was panting as her breathing became ragged with desire. She had to try one more time.

"Alex, please stop. Now." The words were spoken in broken syllables, her hands both clutched and pushed on his shoulders. He paused in his attentions to her trembling body and raised his head.

"If ye mean it, Maggie, I will stop." He took a deep breath and let it out. She could feel that his desire had not waned one iota.

"I do, Alex." Her body cried out in protest when he slid off her and put his body next to hers on the bed.

"Tell me what concerns ye?" His voice was just above a whisper, and it sent shivers through her body.

"What concerns me? What do you think concerns me?"

"I canna read yer mind, Maggie. I was looking forward to being with ye again this night. I was looking forward to sharing the bed with ye and keeping ye warm."

Damn his blue eyes! He had the nerve to wink at her again.

"Alex, I think it was a mistake. This afternoon . . ." she began.

"It wasna a mistake. It felt right between us, Maggie. Nothing has felt more right in my life in a long time."

He pulled her closer, wrapping his arms around her and anchoring her legs with one of his own. "Do ye deny that ye felt it, too?"

She couldn't. The attraction had been growing, but she felt more than just the physical part. She cared for this man, cared deeply.

"I can't deny it, Alex. But it's more than just good physically. I feel more than that."

"I do, too, lass. I don't understaun it yet tho'."

"So, what do we do in the meantime?"

"I ken what I want to do and what I dinna want to do." His eyes flashed and moved over her in a clear message of what he'd like to do.

"What dinna ye want to do?" she teased him.

"I dinna want to sleep on the floor anymore." He laughed when she frowned at him.

Was her conscience soothed? Did she really not want Alex in her bed making love to her? He would stop, he had shown he would control his passion if she wanted him to. Thinking about it, she knew deep down that a door opened for them. The one time this afternoon would not be enough. She wanted him . . . and all that he had to offer.

"You don't have to sleep on the floor, Alex. You are welcome in this bed." She raised her hand and caressed his cheek, feeling the growing beard that was both soft and springy to the touch.

"Are ye certain, Maggie? I dinna want to think that I forced ye to this."

"You have not forced me to do anything but realize how important you are to me . . . and how much I'd like to continue your warming of me."

She gave herself up to him, and he took her with gentleness—the first time. The second time was a bit more heated. And the third time . . . well, she fell asleep with a smile on her face after the third time.

* * *

Alex peeled his body from Maggie's and climbed from the bed. She protested, grumbling about the time of day and how cold it was in the room. He laughed at her difficulty awakening. Padding around the room, he picked up the clothes he had tossed last night in his rush to make love to her. He looked down at that easy-to-arouse part of him that was warming to his thoughts of last night's loving. Better to think about something else. The sight of her mangled clothes wiped away any amorous thoughts.

Examining the skirt and bodice, he realized that she had been wearing the same clothes since they arrived, three weeks before. The only things new to her wardrobe were the few shirts of his she wore as bedclothes and under her skirt as a blouse. Damn him! Just as he'd failed to secure her something as simple as a bath, he had also totally overlooked her day-to-day needs. His clothing had been replenished almost daily by Anice and her women, but Maggie had been completely ignored.

It was about time he took care of her.

He strode to the door and yanked it open. Summoning one of the passing women, he asked her to bring Dougal immediately. He finished dressing while he waited and covered Maggie with the thick blanket. At the knock, he opened the door to an irritated steward.

"Thank ye for coming, Dougal." He motioned the man inside, but his steward refused with a curt shake of his head. "Verra well." Alex stood in the doorway. "Do ye hiv a supply of clothing for use by the servants?"

"Of course, Alex. Each servant is provided with two sets of clothing, a cloak, and a pair of shoes on Michaelmas Day. The laird is generous with those who serve him."

"I would like ye to provide the two sets of clothing to Maggie now. Hers were stolen in the attack on our way here, and she has none but the ones she wore." At his hesitation, Alex yelled, "She canna go aboot naked, Dougal. Find some clothes that will fit her and find them now.''

He slammed the door so quickly that he never noticed the look of repugnance that covered the other man's face.

''Well, that's certainly the way to win friends and influence people, Alex.''

She was awake and sitting up in the bed, her hair falling over her shoulders in waves. No one, *no one,* should ever look this good in the morning. The thought of Maggie going about naked had more appeal to him suddenly.

''He was being unpleasant.''

''No, he was being Dougal. He doesn't like to be reminded that I exist.''

''Weel, I dinna care what he thinks. Why didna ye tell me aboot the sad state of yer clothes?'' He held out the torn skirt.

''I've been sewing it as it needs to be fixed. I really didn't want to cause an uproar by asking for clothes. And I didn't know who to ask.'' She shrugged as though it was not important.

''Maggie, yer a teacher?'' At her nod, he continued, ''Ye know how to go through proper channels in asking for something to use in yer classroom?'' She nodded again, but her eyes took on a suspicious glint. ''Here, now . . . I am the proper channels. Ye must tell me when ye need something. I will make sure ye hiv what ye need.''

''But, Alex,'' she began. He could see her spine stiffening at what she perceived as an insult. He had to make her understand that it was nothing personal. It was just the way things were done.

''Aye, Maggie, I'll touch ye there again.'' He repeated his words from the night before. For a moment he didn't know if she would laugh or scream at him. The laughter won. ''This is not personal, Maggie. It's just the way we hiv to do it while we're here. When we get home, ye can tell me what to do.''

"All right, Alex. I'll try to remember that it's just the way things are done." She threw back the covers and climbed out of bed, looking for the shirt she used as a shift. He let his glance linger on those legs, long and sleek. His mouth watered at the way his thoughts were moving. Only the knock at the door saved her from being thrown back on the bed with him on top of her, between those legs. She stood back in the corner and waited for him to answer the door.

He opened the door to find Jean, the woman who showed them to this room, with a pile of clothes in her arms.

"Dougal said to give these to ye, Alex. He was muttering something aboot naked women when he told me to pick out some clothes for Maggie."

"Thank ye, Jean." He nodded at her and began to close the door.

"I'm sorry that I didna think to get clothes for her, Alex. We treat the servants better than we've treated her." Jean whispered, shaking her head in dismay. "If any of these dinna fit, tell her to come to me and we can get something that does."

"I will tell her, Jean." Alex backed into the room and shut the door.

Maggie walked to him and took the pile and put it on the bed. He was treated to another look at those legs and memories of them wrapped around his waist while they . . . He shook his head, trying to break the spell her presence wove around him.

"I need to get to the hall now, Maggie. I will see ye tonight?"

"Yes, Alex, I'll be here." Then the temptress had the nerve to rub her hand over the surface of the bed next to her. "Right here."

He gulped and coughed . . . and ran.

Chapter 31

THE DAY OF the *ceilidh* dawned clear and stayed that way as it progressed past noon. The castle folk went about their duties with a lift in their step and a tune under their breath. Rachelle told her that most of the clan living in the castle did attend the *ceilidh* in the village. The biggest exception was Anice and her women. Even Struan was expected to make an appearance at the gathering. Alex told her he would join her as soon as the laird left the village.

After the workers cleared the evening meal from the tables and cleaned and dismantled the tables, Maggie watched as they gathered with family and friends and hurried to the village. At their invitation, she joined Brodie and Rachelle on the short trek to the center of the clan's town. Drawn by the music and the soaring flames of a bonfire, the clan gathered.

The melancholy lilting of a pipe captured her attention. Maggie left her friends and followed its call. A lone piper sat, not with bagpipes, but with a small instrument that resembled a flute. She sat on the ground nearby and let the soul-touching melody pour over her. The music soothed her soul, and she took in the comfort it had to offer. After a few minutes, the song ceased, and the piper was rewarded with plentiful applause. A man with a drum placed himself next to the piper and joined him in the next song.

As the crowd gathered and the music quickened its pace, the villagers began to dance around the huge fire. Maggie clapped to the beat and laughed as the young and old, married and single, male and female, circled around and around. Brodie and Rachelle swept by and waved to her. She gasped in surprise as Pol pulled her to her feet and swung her into the steps of the dance. He laughed and kept hold of her hand until she imitated his movements and kept pace. In spite of his size and strength, the blacksmith could dance! He moved in synch with the rest of the dancers, and his steps were sure and fast. Maggie was puffing deeply when the music stopped.

"Thank ye for the dance, mistress." He gave a slight nod, but Maggie was mesmerized by his blue eyes and warm smile.

Maggie curtsied before him and returned the smile. "And, I thank you for taking pity on an outsider . . . again, Pol."

" 'Twas not pity. Definitely not pity." Pol winked at the admission.

"Well, I thank you for doing it . . . whatever the cause." She winked back at him.

"Moira said she will speak to ye when Alex arrives. Join her near the food tables." His voice lowered a bit as he gave her the message.

She nodded in response, and he walked away. Before she could sit, a man, a stranger to her, reached out his hand in invitation to her. Looking around, she saw no one discriminating in their dance partners. She accepted his offer and enjoyed the music and the movements of another dance. The dances moved quickly, and the whole of the village joined in. Maggie even saw Struan kicking up his feet and clapping his hands during the last song. Then the piper and drummer were presented with huge mugs of ale, and the musicians took a break.

It was then that Maggie caught a glimpse of Alex making his way through the crowd. Watching his movements and the greeting given him by the villagers, Maggie knew that he had been successful in playing his role. Young and old, villager or castle folk, they shook his hand, patted his shoulder, slapped his back. From the gossip already heard, she knew that this was not the way the real Alex was treated before he left Dunnedin. Everyone marveled at how the lad had grown up and matured. Little did they know!

He reached the place where she stood and held out his hand to her. Scanning the gathering, she saw Struan striding up the path to the castle. Giving him a smile first, she then accepted his hand. Alex pulled her close and tucked her arm under his.

"So, this is a *ceilidh?*" His voice was low and whispery as he asked his question. Her body shivered as his breath tickled her ear.

"Apparently so."

"Ye hiv been dancing?"

She pushed a few sweaty tendrils of hair from her forehead and shook her head. "It's been fun."

"Weel, the piper is starting agin. Come, fit the flair wi' me."

"Did you just ask me to dance?" She turned to face him as couples formed around them, tapping their feet to the beginning strains of the music. The drummer joined in and the reel started.

"Aye, lass, I'm asking." With that short notice, he wrapped his arm around her waist and swung her in a circle.

The rest of the dance took all her concentration, so small talk was out of the question. They changed partners several times during the lively jig but ended together, both out of breath.

"And I thought I was in good shape." Alex panted as he forced out the words. "Ye are no' breathing hard at all."

"I must be in better shape than you are, Alex. Come to think of it, you have difficulty keeping up with me in other things." She smirked at him as comprehension of her challenge showed on his face.

"Ye best take care in challenging me, lass." He leaned closer and whispered again, only for her to hear. "I was being considerate of yer general weak state last night."

Maggie felt the creeping wave of heat move up her face. Another wave of heat headed down her body to another spot where it joined with a throbbing deep in her core. Last night . . . Just the thought of what they had done together and how they had done it renewed the aching in her body. Even her skin tingled with a desire to be touched . . . tasted . . . caressed. It was no surprise that her voice sounded strained when she finally made her rebuttal.

"General weak state? I think not."

"Come then. Let's go a bit deeper in the forest. We can find a private spot, and I will test yer strength and endurance now." He matched his words with a step toward the perimeter of the village.

The wicked man, she thought. He knew what even his words alone did to her body. His breathing had slowed, but now she was panting and out of breath.

"No, Alex, wait." She pulled him to a stop, regretfully.

"Ah, ye see the foolishness to yer words?" He raised an eyebrow, mocking her weakness.

"I will accept your challenge later, Alex. Did you forget why we came tonight?"

"To dance, to sing, to share good times with family and friends?"

Still holding his hand, she pulled him in the direction where the tables of food and drink were. "Alex, we must meet with Moira. She knows about us. More importantly, she may know the way home for us."

"Aye, lass, lead on. Take me to the woman."

It took a few minutes of weaving through the crowd to reach the food tables. Maggie stood on her toes and searched around the area.

"Alex, do you know the blacksmith?"

"Aye, Maggie. Why?"

"Can you see him?"

"Aye, he's sitting across the way." He pointed off to one side. "Is that who yer looking for?"

"Is he with anyone?" She gave up trying to see over the crowd.

"He is with a woman." He cleared his throat. "Verra much with a woman. Are ye sure ye want to interrupt them?"

"It must be Moira. Let's go." A few moments later, Maggie found that it was indeed Moira with Pol. Actually, *on Pol* would have been a better description of the scene. She cleared her throat this time to gain their attention.

"Moira, Pol." She nodded to each of them.

"Maggie and Alex. Are ye having a good time at the gathering?"

"No' as good as ye are, from the looks of it," Alex chimed in, and the two men broke out in loud laughter. Pol lifted Moira to her feet and stood next to her. Moira barely came to the man's chest and must be years older than him. She shook her head as the tall man bent and kissed Moira on the lips. He whispered in her ear and they chuckled at his words . . . a private joke of some kind.

"I will leave ye to yer talk. Alex. Maggie." He nodded his head and walked off into the crowd.

"Come, walk with me to my house."

She wondered if Alex was as apprehensive as she was at this moment. This was the only person in this time who seemed to know what happened to them. This might be their only lead to a way home. This might be their only chance. She felt him squeeze her hand tighter as they followed the woman through the village.

A coil of tension wound in his stomach as they left the *ceilidh* behind them. Moira gestured to some boulders outside her small cottage.

"The weather 'tis fair. Let's sit awhile here." He waited for the two women to sit first. There was still a little of the civilized gentleman left inside this barbarian. He waited for Moira to begin; this was very much her show. She did not keep him waiting long.

"Ye really do look as he does." She squinted at him, examining his features slowly, carefully.

"So I hiv been told."

"And, ye e'en sound like him. 'Tis a marvel."

"What else can ye tell us that we dinna already ken?"

Maggie gasped. "Alex, there's no reason to be rude."

Moira patted Maggie's hand before he could answer. "He no' rude, Maggie lass. He's impatient."

He had little liking for being taken apart and appraised by them. "Aye, I am impatient. So, what can ye tell us aboot the arch?"

" 'Tis made of stone and ye can walk underneath it." Moira raised an eyebrow at him as she spoke. The sarcasm in her tone was her answer to the rudeness in his. Time for a strategic retreat.

"I beg yer pardon, Moira. Please tell us what ye ken aboot the arch?" He removed all traces of sarcasm and displeasure from his voice. Truth be told, if she could help them get home, he would do anything she asked.

"The real Alex would hiv struck me and demanded an answer. Ye are truly a better heir for this clan than he."

It was still hard to believe that there was another one of him running around here in old Scotland. Well, not truly another but a look-alike ancestor.

''So, I hiv heard. But ye ken we are no' of this place, and I amna the clan's heir.''

She sighed deeply, sounding much older than her real years. ''Ah, weel, I can hope that the fates play the same kind of trick on him, and it helps him to change to who he should be.''

''The fates?'' Maggie interrupted. ''What do you mean?''

''Ye may call them many things: fate, God, the almighty. But whatever ye call them,'' she paused and pointed at him. ''Ye hiv offended them mightily, Alex MacKendimen. 'Tis yer fault that ye are in this trouble and here at all.''

Chapter 32

HIS HEAD WAS spinning, his thoughts scattered in his brain, and he could not grab hold of even one clear one. His fault? How could it be his fault? He closed his eyes and counted to ten. It always helped him to cool his temper. It didn't help this time.

"What right do ye hiv to blame me for . . . this?" He motioned with his hand at himself and Maggie. She looked as stunned as he felt at the moment. "What did I do to cause this?"

Moira rose from her place and approached him. She took his hand in hers, and stroked it, slowly, soothingly. He felt a calmness pierce through his anger and frustration. Her voice was all he could hear.

"*I* do no' blame ye, Alex. Ye asked, and I but answered ye. Do no' fear. This is but a lesson given to ye. Open to what ye are being shown, and ye will succeed in this."

Try as he might, he couldn't turn away from this woman or her words. He expected his anger to rise, but it didn't. Instead, the deep truth of her message sank into him. Instead of his heart racing as it had been, his breathing and his heartbeat slowed their paces. Instead of being alone in this, he saw Maggie . . . waiting.

Maggie! Whatever his transgression, it had pulled her back with him. Was she part of this? Was she the solution?

"Aye, Alex. She plays a part, too. She is here wi' ye for a reason."

"I dinna understaun. What hiv I done?"

"Mayhap ye are no' following the path laid out for ye? By pursuing a different life, ye hiv offended that which sets the course. Mayhap ye turned yer back on something when ye shouldna?" Her eyes seemed to glow as she spoke. It couldn't be.

He was lost. None of this made sense to him. He needed time to think about this. Moira still had his hand in hers, stroking it. All the tension that twisted in his gut was loosening. It flowed out of him as she continued her movements on his hand.

"I need to think on yer words, Moira. But, do ye ken other things aboot what's happening with us?"

"Aye, I can. Come closer, Maggie."

Maggie stood and walked the few steps to his side. He took her hand in his free one and pulled her close. She looked shocked, her eyes were glazed and unfocused. He wrapped his arm around her waist and held her tightly, resting his head against her chest. Shaking her head, she broke free of the reverie surrounding her and looked at him and then Moira.

"The arch was built but a few months ago and, from that time, strange things hiv occurred near to it. Voices and noises come from it when no one is nearby. Lights shine from it in the day and night. I amna the only one who feels the power of the arch."

"I can feel it, too," Maggie said. "But I don't hear or see things in it. Do you?"

"Ye ken, I hiv the second sight. My visions usually come in the flames of my hearth, but I now see them in the arch. It calls to me and willna brook my resistance." She paused and Alex felt her hesitation.

"What else do ye ken?"

"That Alex MacKendimen will ride from London and return soon to Dunnedin."

"What?" His voice joined with Maggie's. Even Moira's calming force could not quiet his fear now. "When? When does he return?"

"I ken no' the time of his coming, only that he comes this way."

"But, what will happen to us when he comes back? Alex, we must make plans to leave. Now." The frantic worry was back in Maggie's voice as she spoke. He knew that her fear was as strong as his. But, Moira was not done.

"Nay, lass. Ye canna run from the fates. Stay and live yer lives as ye hiv. I feel it deep in my being that ye maun keep to the roles ye play. Ye maun."

"Is there more to tell us, Moira?" Maggie's voice shook.

"No' at this time, lass. But I ken that my part in this is to aid ye both in this journey ye make. I will tell if there are more visions, more wisdom. Keep to yer roles and . . ."

"And?" he asked.

"Take care when yer around the lady Anice."

"That goes wi'oot saying." He looked to Maggie for her agreement.

Moira pointed at Maggie and warned, "Ye maun watch yer step carefully. Trouble is coming to ye from Anice."

He saw Maggie tremble at Moira's words. He stood and put his arm on her shoulder. "We are aware of the problems that Anice could cause. She haes started trouble already. We will be careful."

Before any of them could move, a small boy came running full-tilt into the clearing next to Moira's cottage. He stopped in front of Alex.

"Alex, I come from the castle wi' a message from the laird."

"Aye, Kenneth, I ken ye live at the castle." He could not help teasing the boy who served as Struan's page. He ran his fingers through the mop of unruly red curls on the boy's head and mussed them even more.

"*Alex.* I am trying to carry out my duties," Kenneth whined and stepped away before continuing. "The laird said ye maun come at once," the boy's voice was even and serious and grossly out of place for a body so small. "There be a messenger just arrived from the MacNab."

Alex waited for more, but none came. At the end of his words, the boy bowed and ran back as fast as he had come. *Trouble thy name is Anice,* Alex thought, amending Shakespeare's line. It seemed absurd that he was remembering it before Shakespeare wrote it. He had accepted weeks ago that this whole situation was beyond absurd.

"Weel, I better go and find out what else awaits at the castle. Maggie?"

"I will find Rachelle and Brodie and come back with them, Alex. It's best if I'm not seen there with you."

"That may be a good idea, but I doubt ye will find them now." She frowned at him and he laughed. "Most of the couples hiv drifted away to the same bit of privacy I mentioned earlier to ye."

Her laughter, when it came, was a welcome thing to him. He turned to Moira before leaving. He wanted to say something to her but didn't know the words.

"I ken, Alex. If anything happens to ye, I will help Maggie as best I can."

"Ye hiv my thanks for that assurance, Moira, and for being with us in this. It feels good to hiv a friend and ally."

"Alex, I will follow in a few minutes and meet you in our room when you've finished with the laird."

He nodded and reached down for a quick kiss. He needed the touch of her lips at that moment. The feel of something real in this world of what should be make-believe. It reassured him that she would be waiting for him.

Taking a deep breath, he started for the path leading to the castle. He'd been able to completely block from his mind the impending wedding to Anice. He thought about it as he hiked along. One week, that's all that was left before the wedding. He could think of no way to postpone the ceremony, and yet he could not even consider taking Anice to wife. What would happen then? Would the other Alex arrive before or after the wedding? Would they make their way back home? More importantly, would they be alive to go back home? One more week . . .

Four more weeks?! Alex wanted to shout out his relief but, in the face of the information about the unfortunate MacNab, it didn't seem right. He kept his expression blank as the messenger completed his duty and bowed to the MacKendimen, to him and then to Anice. Struan, seated in his high chair looked at Anice and Alex. Plainly uncomfortable with facing Anice after the news of the accident, Struan cleared his throat and coughed a few times.

Anice sat on a stool at Struan's side, immobile, tears running down her face. At that moment, she looked her young age. He had to do something to ease this awkwardness.

"Anice?" He waited to catch her glance. She rubbed her eyes with a handkerchief and looked at him. "I am glad that yer faither wasna hurt badly. His leg should heal quickly."

"Yes, Alex," she whispered.

"It will be but a short delay, a few weeks. Ye hiv been mightily patient waiting for me. Can ye wait just a bit more?" He smiled at her, trying a little charm to ease the way. He could see her lips trembling before she answered. She nodded her head and rose from her seat.

"Aye, Alex, I will wait a few more weeks." She turned to Struan and curtsied. "By yer leave, laird Struan?"

"Of course, lass." Struan stood and waved Alex over to her side. "Alex, 'tis late. Escort Anice to her chamber."

He owed her some attention and some soft words; she was devastated by this news. He did not know whether she was more upset by the news of her father's broken leg or by the delay in the ceremony. He had his own idea, but he held his tongue and offered her his arm.

"Come, Anice, I will walk ye to yer room."

She wrapped her arm around his and allowed him to lead her down from the dais and through the darkened great hall. As they made their way up the steps and down the passageway to her room, Alex spotted Maggie just closing their door. It was quiet as they passed by and walked to Anice's doorway. He paused when they arrived and thought about what to say. She beat him to it.

"Alex, aboot the other night . . . in yer room. I was . . ."

"Anice, there is no need to talk aboot what happened then." He leaned over and kissed her forehead. "A few short weeks, and I'll make ye my wife. Things will work out for the best." He stepped away and turned the knob to open the door. It pulled from his hand as Anice's maid, the tall one, opened the door and waited for her mistress to enter.

"I will see ye in the morn, Anice. Mayhap we can ride out to the other side of the loch one afternoon soon?"

And, as Firtha closed the door in his face, he made his getaway. Running down the hall, he threw open their door and grabbed a very startled Maggie. She screeched as he swung her around in a circle.

"Alex, what has gotten into you?"

"Four more weeks, Maggie. We got a reprieve! No wedding for four more weeks!"

Maggie reached out and wrapped her arms around

Alex's neck and hugged him to her. He kissed her and used his other foot to close the door to their room. In their excitement and relief, neither one saw that Anice's maid had followed him down the darkened hallway, and neither one knew that she overheard their words of joy at the postponement of the wedding to her mistress.

But by morning, her mistress knew.

Chapter 33

AS SILENT AS a tomb, she thought as she made her way from the stairway to the great hall's entrance. She'd like to believe that the quiet, subdued atmosphere was the result of too much ale and too much dancing, but she knew better. Gossip swirled through the entire clan within minutes of the messenger's arrival from the MacNab. All knew of the delay in the coming marriage of Alex to Anice. And all knew of the lady's fiery reaction that came this morning in the hall.

Maggie had waited for Anice to leave the hall so she could get to the kitchen without being seen by the angry fiancée, but she could wait no longer. Shaking her head about this situation, she decided to go out to the bailey and walk to the back entrance. Passing through the dusty courtyard, she met Brodie and Rachelle coming in from the village.

"So, Alex was right?" She tried to keep a straight face as guilty grins crossed both faces in front of her. "You didn't come back from the *ceilidh* last night, did you?"

"Weel, Maggie, we . . ." Rachelle stammered and blushed as she tried to answer.

"Aye, Alex was right," Brodie broke in. "I am surprised to find ye here as weel."

"Alex got called back last night by Struan. A messenger came from the MacNab."

"We heard the news in the village. Ye may be the only one happy aboot it." Brodie's stern expression now matched the others inside the castle.

"Happy about it? Why would you think I'd be happy that the MacNab had an accident?"

"No' aboot that, Maggie, aboot the rest of it." Rachelle was still smiling.

"That the wedding has been delayed?"

"Aye, lass, how do you feel aboot *that?*" Brodie demanded to know.

"Well, I'm not completely unhappy about it." She chuckled after her words.

"Nay, I guess ye are no' unhappy to hiv Alex to yerself for a few more weeks. But ye better keep it to yerself. There are those in the clan who will watch for yer reaction."

"My reaction? But, Brodie, I am just an outsider. Why should my thoughts on this matter be of importance?" She stopped and turned to face them.

"Maggie, Anice will be waiting for yer words and actions. She is deeply hurt by yer presence here and now by this."

"I keep out of her way." There was more bitterness in her response than she expected. "There is no insult intended by my being here with Alex. It's just . . . the way it is for now."

"Aye, for now. But, that will change with Alex's marriage."

"Brodie, are ye against her now? Have ye changed yer mind?" Rachelle stepped closer to the big man, her hands on her hips, legs spread. "I thought ye had no objections to her."

"Objections? I hiv no objections to Maggie or her being wi' Alex. But, Rachelle, ye hiv seen Anice's behavior since they came back. The clan will suffer for her displeasure."

"Weel, if ye are now turned coward and will not stand by Maggie and Alex as yer friends, then we hiv nothing to talk aboot. Come, Maggie, we hiv our chores to attend to."

Maggie stared open-mouthed as the petite blond grabbed her hand and pulled her toward the kitchen. She turned back and saw a dumfounded Brodie scratching his head while he watched them walk away. He shrugged at her glance and strode off in the direction of the practice yards. She turned back to Rachelle.

"Rachelle, I don't want you fighting with Brodie over this."

"We are no' fighting, Maggie. Dinna worry aboot us. And, I didna want him to hear this, but Brodie is right aboot Anice," Rachelle whispered after tilting her head to Maggie's.

"How so?" Maggie wanted to hear this explanation.

"Anice has been here for nigh unto five years, working for the good of the clan. Many of us do no' like her ways or the airs she puts on, but she has done much for the clan." Rachelle paused and looked at Maggie. Maggie nodded that she was listening.

"She is but fifteen years and inexpairienced in dealing with men, especially the likes of Alex and ye. I ken ye try to stay out of her way, to not hurt her feelings. I fear 'tis too late for that now."

"Rachelle, I told you that Alex and I were taking care not to be seen together by her. I know her place and I know mine." Maggie took a deep breath and let it out. "She will have Alex and his name in a few short weeks . . . and I will not. Nothing else matters."

"I will give ye warning, Maggie, as a friend. Ye will no longer be welcome in the castle once the marriage takes place."

"But, I thought . . ."

"I ken what ye thought. I heard Struan tell Dougal that ye would be moved into the village the day the MacNab arrives for the wedding. That, if Alex wants yer . . . company, he will hiv to seek ye out there. He also told Dougal that he and Anice plan to give Alex verra little chance to seek ye out at all."

Maggie's stomach tightened in reaction to this news. What would happen to her in the village without Alex's 'protection'? She would be prey to all those who held their words and actions now. She needed to talk this over with Alex and Moira, who knew their secrets. They had four weeks left. They needed to use every day left to them to find a way home.

Instead of answering Rachelle, she dug into her pocket, pulled out her scarf, and wrapped it around her head and under her braid. Without a word, she crossed to the entrance of the kitchen and entered the busy rooms. All movement stopped as the kitchen workers saw who it was that had entered. She heard not a sound or breath as she walked to the table where she worked. And, at that moment, she didn't have the courage to look anyone in the eye.

Part of her wanted to laugh and enjoy the news of the delay. Part of her knew the danger in showing mirth in light of Anice's outburst in the hall earlier.

If they only knew . . . if they only knew.

She wasn't happy for selfish reasons over this delay of the ceremonies, at least not for the reasons that the entire clan thought. She was happy to have more time to look for a way home. Happy to have more time before Alex was forced to take a fifteen-year-old as his wife. Happy to have more time before facing the thought of being entirely alone in a godforsaken medieval village where all the men thought she was fair game. Her body shivered at that thought.

Alone.

All alone.

"Odara? The dough again?" Maggie raised her voice without raising her eyes. From somewhere across the room came the response she expected.

"Aye, mistress, the dough. We need more loaves for the noon meal. The rest of ye get back to yer work." Odara's voice filled the hushed room.

Maggie acknowledged her assignment with a nod and pulled the ever-present basket of dough to her. Rachelle touched her arm lightly.

"I am sorry if I upset ye, Maggie. I thought ye would want to be warned."

"I am upset, Rachelle, but I needed to know Struan's plans. Thank you for telling me."

"What will ye do?"

"I will go home after Alex marries. I told you before that if Alex doesn't want me, I will return to my family." If she only could do it. If it was only as easy as she made it sound.

"Ye wouldna stay and settle here?"

"Here? No, Rachelle, I couldn't live here with Alex married to Anice. I will find a way home." She had to. *They* had to before this wedding came to pass.

"Find a way home, Maggie? I am sure that Struan will make arrangements for yer travel back home." Rachelle patted her arm again. "He may do this for the clan but ye still saved his son's life. He owes ye at least a way home."

If it were only that easy.

"I tell ye, Alex, ye should place her in the village now. Do no' wait until the wedding." Brodie swung his sword over his head and around and came at Alex from the side. It was just practice, but only a quick twist to the side left Alex unbloodied.

"Why?" Panting, he lifted the claymore and swung it as he threw himself at his larger opponent. Brodie barely moved back and took the hit on his sword. The weapons clashed and slid down to the hilts against each other. Placing his free hand on the handle, he pushed with all his strength, trying to unbalance Brodie more. The movement worked, and the two warriors rolled head over feet and hit the ground. Alex didn't bother moving. He was struggling just to breathe.

Brodie pushed up into a sitting position and dusted off his face. "I will agree that things were fine afore. But this news from the MacNab put a new look on the trouble. Ye can see the steam coming from Anice's ears, and she willna let this go quietly."

"So, Maggie is to pay because Anice's faither haid an accident and canna come now? Come now, Brodie. Does that seem fair to ye?"

" 'Tis not fair. 'Tis the way of things here." Brodie thumped Alex on the shoulder and offered him a hand up. "Ye ken that, Alex. 'Tis no different than when ye left. The clan comes first."

"Aye, I ken. But what aboot Maggie? She'll be made to suffer if I abandon her in the village now." Alex swiped at the dirt and mud on his tunic and pushed his tangled hair out of his eyes. He couldn't believe he was even talking about this with Brodie.

"Ye dinna hiv to abandon her. Find her a place to live and ye can . . . visit her there."

"Would it surprise ye if I tell ye that I need Maggie for more than just the bedplay she gives?" The words were out before he could stop them.

"Nay, Alex, I amna surprised. She is a good-looking lass, pleasant to be with, and she enjoys yer company. But Anice will grow up and, with yer firm hand to guide her, soon be the wife ye want her to be."

Alex exploded. Fear of what could happen to Maggie in the village unprotected surged through him and gave him a strength born from anger. He swung barehanded and connected with Brodie's jaw. Pain screamed up his arm into his hand from the force of his blow.

"I dinna want Anice as wife. And I dinna want Maggie in the village. Now, leave me be."

He had lowered his voice but the sight of Brodie laid low by Alex brought the other men running. Alex pushed through the crowd and trotted out of the gate. The loch seemed the right place for the time being. It would cool his temper and his fist. Then he'd better find Maggie. This was getting dangerous.

"I guess our relief was short-lived."

Nodding, Maggie put down her mending and walked into his outstretched arms. He rubbed her back and shoulders and then brought his hands into her hair. Untying the lace at the bottom of her braid, he moved his fingers through it, loosening the curls with each stroke.

She leaned back and accepted his kiss, the one that she knew would follow his playing with her hair. In their short time together they already had developed their own rituals. Maggie moved closer to Alex's body, and he wrapped his arms around her, pulling her close. His erection was noticeable through the thin shift she wore as their hips ground against each other. His hands moved down to her bottom and caressed her thighs, pressing her against him.

Their mouths touched, and when he opened to her, she moved her tongue into his, exploring the welcoming warmth he offered. She heard a moan and realized it came from her. He was good at this, and she so enjoyed slow, deep, wet, hot kissing. Seconds, minutes passed, and then the moment was gone. Alex stepped back away from her. A chill invaded in the absence of his embrace.

She touched her mouth and took control of her breathing, gradually slowing down to almost normal. She turned and saw Alex pacing in front of the fireplace. He was worried—probably about all the gossip that moved through the clan today. Instead of going to him, she picked up the plaid that she dropped and wrapped it back around her shoulders.

"Ye were no' at the meal?" He stopped in front of the small fire burning in the hearth.

"No, I brought my meal here."

"Why?"

Still he didn't face her. He stood searching the flames as though the answer he sought was there.

"I think for the same reason you were pacing."

He looked at her with a frown. "I wasna pacing."

"Aye, Alex, ye were." She laughed at his puzzlement. "Anyway, the atmosphere is very tense today, so I thought it would be best to keep myself out of the way."

"Good idea, Maggie. But I fear 'tis too little, too late." He turned back to the fire, moving his hands in front of its heat.

"Did you hear about Anice's tirade in the hall this morning?"

"Aye. Dougal told me aboot it. He also shared with me the real reason for her outburst. He was overjoyed to tell me what Anice had heard."

"Heard? From who?" Maggie sat on the bed and pulled the brush through her tangled hair.

"Firtha."

"Her, again? This doesn't sound good." She waited as he struggled with the words. Was this the trouble Moira meant in her words of warning?

"When I left Anice at her door last night, I dropped something on the floor. After closing the door, Firtha picked it up and told Anice she would bring it here. She followed me down to the doorway of this room."

Maggie thought about Alex's words after she opened their door last night. She gasped as his words came to mind: "Four more weeks, Maggie. We got a reprieve . . ."

"Oh, Alex. She heard us?"

"Worse. She saw us kissing and dancing around the

room in joy of the news.'' He walked to the bed. ''Firtha was so outraged she told Anice and, weel, ye ken the rest of it.''

''So, what do we do now?'' Even as she asked the question, Maggie knew they needed to talk to Moira.

''I think it's best if we speak to Moira aboot this. She may be able to help us come up wi' a plan.''

''Maybe I should move to the village? Rachelle said that it's what Struan plans soon, anyway.''

Her voice surprised her with its calmness. She wanted to scream. For weeks, in spite of the insults and bad behavior aimed at her, she had kept quiet. Knowing the dangers they faced, she had borne the indignity because it was their only way. Hours and hours of intense physical work in the kitchen, days and days of worry and fear. And, always, she was controlled by others. She had done nothing to instigate their newest problem, but she was left to bear the results. She was mightily tired of it.

''Brodie suggested the same thing to me today.'' Alex rolled his arm and shoulder, rubbing the muscles. By the looks of the bruises on his face and the stiffness as he moved, Brodie did more than just suggest.

''Let's talk to Moira tomorrow, Alex. I can go to the village after the noon meal to see her. Join me if you can.''

''Aye, I will try to be there. Now, I am exhausted. Are ye ready for bed?''

Alex peeled off his clothes, dropping them as he rounded the bed. He stood naked before her and she scrutinized him from head to toe and every place in between. He said he was tired, but his body responded to the invitation in her expression. She stood up and ran her fingers over his arms and chest, swirling the dark red curls of hair between her fingers. Standing on her toes, she leaned up and offered her mouth to him. He took it without hesitation.

For a long moment, they ignored all of their worries

and lost themselves in the pure pleasure of kissing each other.

''Alex, if you're so tired, maybe we'd best get into bed,'' Maggie murmured against his lips.

''Aye, lass, that's a good idea.'' He stepped back away from her and grasped the edges of her nightshirt. A quick raise of her arms, and their completely naked bodies touched skin to skin. He wrapped his arms around her and walked her back to the bed. She molded her body to his: thighs to thighs, belly to belly, chest to chest. She loved the feel of the hardness of his body, all of it. She loved the way he touched and caressed her when they made love. She loved him.

She pulled her mouth from his at the frightening thought. She loved him? How could she? They'd been together for only a matter of weeks and not by their own choice. He was stuffy and regimented and liked order in his real life. He was a warrior and strong and fair and struggling to break out of his self-enforced role while in this life. She looked into his questioning gaze and saw the blue eyes that looked at her with concern.

They reclined on the bed, and he moved to cover her body with his. She gazed into his eyes as he leaned down to kiss her again, his hips settling between her legs and bringing them into closer contact. *Aye, Alex MacKendimen of the Clan MacKendimen, I do love you,* she thought with dawning wonder and joy. She surrendered to his passion and to her love.

Chapter 34

THE FIRST THING that penetrated Maggie's consciousness was the whispering around her. She opened her eyes to see four very stout laundry maids standing around the bed, staring at her. A couple more wore expressions of sympathy, the others envy and disapproval. She scrambled to sit up, pulling the covers to her chin when Anice stalked into the room and shut and secured the door firmly behind her. The rage burning in those Celtic green eyes sent a chill up Maggie's spine, and a knot of dread tightened her gut.

"I've tried to give ye the benefit of the doubt, ye being a Sassenach and all. But I canna have ye putting on airs that ye shouldna be having, and I canna allow ye to mock me in front of the clan. Ye may be the leman of the laird's firstborn and heir, but I am his betrothed and soon to be his wife. As his betrothed, I have been given the run of the castle and control of all of the women in it, even ye."

Maggie began to shake as the serving women edged closer to her. Anice nodded at them. Maggie froze in shock as they grabbed her hands and feet, turned her over on her stomach, and quickly tied her to the bedposts. She craned her neck, trying to see what was happening, but one of the women climbed on the bed and held her head down between two pillows. The maid tied a strip of fabric across her mouth to muffle any sounds she might make and then moved away. Maggie struggled against the leather bands encircling her wrists and ankles. It did no good.

"I have decided to teach ye a lesson now so that we can all live peaceably later and so that ye ken yer place, Sassenach. Ye hiv disrupted the clan and will learn from this."

Anice approached the bed and held out her hand to one of the maids, who placed the hilt of a dagger in her palm. She leaned over Maggie and grabbed her braid, yanking it and Maggie's head back. Without pausing, she cut through the braid and threw it on the bed. Maggie stopped struggling as the sharp blade passed nearer and nearer to her face. Then, Anice hacked at the remaining hair.

Unable to move, Maggie's fear turned to terror. She was tied to a bed by a medieval madwoman and helpless to stop anything that the outraged Anice ordered done to her. Where was Alex when she needed him?

"Now, ye willna be quite so pleasing to look upon, will ye? Mayhap, ye willna keep his attention without yer lovely locks?" Maggie turned as far as she could and watched Anice back away from the bed, straighten her hair back from her face, and press her hands against her skirt, wiping off her palms.

"I am mistress of this castle since Edana's passing, and I am in charge of punishing any servant who doesna follow orders or shows disrespect to their betters. Ye hiv been disrespectful to me since ye came here, and it will end now. Ye will do as I bid ye to do. To help ye remember, I will give you five strokes. Ye should ken I am showing ye mercy by only giving ye five."

Now that Maggie knew what Anice planned to do, she

started to scream against the gag. Terror spread through her, her lungs refused to take in air, and her body tightened in anticipation of being beaten. The gag between her teeth muffled most of the sounds she forced out, and only those in the bedchamber could hear her. One of the women leaned over and pulled the entangled covers from her legs, exposing her to the cool air in the chamber.

Maggie turned at the movement and watched in horror as Anice picked up the thick cane and stood next to the bed. She closed her eyes when Anice raised her arm high and brought it down. Maggie screamed and bucked against her bindings. Anice continued with the cane, each stroke burning her skin more than the last. She stopped counting when Anice passed ten strokes. The world around her spun and her stomach gripped and heaved from the pain in her back and hips and shoulders.

She slipped into the darkness swirling around her.

Anice was out of breath. Her jealousy and anger at this outsider who dared to draw Alex's attention away from her was greatly relieved. As she glanced at the other women in the room, Anice noticed that they averted their eyes from the still form lying on the bed. Disregarding their shamed expressions, she looked down to admire her handiwork. The slut should trouble her no more. Anice gasped and felt the blood drain from her own face as she saw the damage to Maggie's back. Oh, God, what had she done, what had she done?

She had only meant to teach the whore a lesson. But her fury at being humiliated by Alex in front of the entire clan had inflamed her anger and increased her strength. Maggie's back was already bruising and she bled from several wounds. Anice had gone farther than she had intended. What would Alex say to this?

Before she could do anything else, the door to the chamber was kicked in, and two men stormed into the chamber. Alex was first into the room, and he took one look at Maggie on the bed and roared in fury. One of the women braved his anger and started to untie Maggie's hands and feet from the bedposts.

Maggie moaned as she was released, causing the servant to drop her hands and run from the room. Anice could not move from her spot. Her body shook in fear of Alex's retaliation against her. Only Struan's motion to the door broke her free from her place. She walked as quickly as she could without running. She must hold her head up in front of the clan—she had the right. She had the right. The words became a chant in her mind as she entered her solar and closed the door behind her.

She had the right.

The laird had followed Alex into the room and remained at the door, watching how his son reacted to this scene. He had tried to warn Alex that he must be wary of shaming Anice with his leman, but Alex had been away from his clan for too long and had picked up too many foreign customs. Anice had behaved as any well-bred Highland lass would. As mistress of the castle, she would see to the women however she saw fit. Although his beloved Edana had ignored his liaisons and the many lemans he had over the years, even she would have been within her rights to strike out as Anice had today.

He motioned to the maid who stood outside the door. He whispered directions to her and she gathered her skirts and ran down the hallway on her errand. The MacKendimen approached the bed. The results of Anice's jealous tirade looked much worse than the injuries really were. Cleaned up, the wench would be sore for a few days, but there did not look to be any permanent damage. By God, Anice and Alex would breed some fiery sons!

"Alex?"

Alex was leaning over the bed, whispering to Maggie. As Struan waited for a response, he observed Alex put his hand on her head and gently rub her shorn head. *'Twas a shame,* he thought as he watched Alex's gesture, *such a lovely lass.*

"Alex!" The laird raised his voice to get Alex's attention. Alex finally stood up and faced the laird.

"I tried to warn ye about Anice's temper and about yer decision to flaunt this woman in her face. Ye ken 'tis yer right to have any leman ye want, but ye should probably have waited until after the wedding to bring her to the castle."

Alex's face turned red with barely suppressed rage. He clenched his fists and gritted his teeth.

"Ye canna take any action agin Anice. Ye must treat her with the respect due to yer betrothed wife. I told Jean to bring some of the men here to take Maggie to the healer's cottage. Moira will tend to your woman's injuries. When they get here, ye are to go back to working wi' the men. Ye need to regain yer strength wi' the sword."

The laird turned and left the room, fully expecting that Alex would obey his orders without question. Struan rubbed his hands together in glee, just contemplating all the brawny bairns he would soon have from Alex on Anice. If only Edana were here to enjoy them.

Alex sat gently on the end of the bed, trying not to disturb or move Maggie at all. But even the shift of his weight made her moan in pain. It was good that she had not regained consciousness yet. There would be more pain in moving her to the village and in cleaning and tending to the bleeding wounds crisscrossing her back. He rubbed her head again. Let her sleep through this.

Easing her onto her side, he pulled a sheet up and covered her with it. He shook his head in anguish at the scene before him. He could barely believe that just a few short weeks ago, he had lived in another time and place as a mild-mannered accountant. The longer he lived here, the more unrestrained he felt, the more Gaelic warrior he became. And the fury this beating aroused in him made him almost unrecognizable to himself. Yet he knew something more complex than rage was transforming him.

His feelings for Maggie were more than just concern over the beating. More than just friend for friend. At some point, as he watched her struggle to maintain control over her feelings and struggle to fit in, as he watched her dance, watched her sleep, his emotions had deepened in ways totally unfamiliar to him. He . . . loved her? Shaking his head, he tried to deny it. It couldn't be love, could it? He wasn't looking for love, didn't want it. He had too many other things to accomplish in his life before he let something like love slow him down. He wanted . . .

His mind drew a blank. He fought to find the words. The partnership? No, that lost its importance long ago when compared to survival here. The money, the house, the car? No, he was happy here with the clothes on his back.

Maggie.

She was the only thing important to him now. Caring for her and keeping her safe from further harm. Getting her well and finding a way home. Keeping her close and loving her. *Loving her.*

The sounds of tromping feet coming toward the room cut into his thoughts. Looking to the broken door, Alex saw several men with a litter waiting for his signal. To his relief, he saw Jean led them.

"Jean, will ye help me cover her afore they take her?"

Jean stepped into the room. "Of course, Alex." The woman stepped closer to the bed and gasped at the sight before her. She swallowed a few times and then spoke, her words in a whisper.

"What in God's name did she do, Alex? What could Maggie hiv done to Anice to deserve this treatment?"

"She was with me, Jean. That was Maggie's misfortune. Now, do ye hiv any ideas aboot how to make this any easier?"

''Nay, Alex. Mayhap if we dress her in one of your shirts and cover her wi' a blanket? What do ye think?'' She looked to him for direction.

''That may work, Jean. Get one of my shirts from the trunk, and we can slide it over her head together.''

After much shifting and adjusting, they had Maggie decently covered. It took a few minutes more to get her onto the litter and covered for the journey to Moira's. He started to follow the men when Jean grabbed his arm.

''Nay, Alex, ye canna come to the village. Everyone heard Struan's orders to ye. Struan said to go to the practice yard and ye maun.''

Alex gritted his teeth again and tried to tamp down his rising anger. He wanted to make sure she was going to be all right. His place was with her, not playing warrior in a practice yard. Didn't Struan understand that simple fact?

''I will walk wi' her and get her settled at Moira's,'' Jean whispered. ''One of the lads ran ahead to prepare Moira aboot Maggie's coming. I will tell ye how she fares when I return.''

Alex stood there, torn between his need to see to her comfort and their need to stay in character and follow the rules. She had been endangered by his behavior already; he could not do it to her again. He looked into the great hall and saw everyone there watching him, waiting for his reaction.

He knew what he had to do, and he did it.

He turned in the other direction and slowly walked to the practice yard. The onlookers parted to let him through, although no one would meet his eyes as he passed by. He didn't know who felt guiltier, he or the clan who stood by and observed.

Chapter 35

THERE WAS NO way that he could eat this meal. His stomach churned with anger, frustration, and worry. He was supposed to sit here and converse with the witch who had beaten Maggie? While Maggie still lay unconscious in Moira's cottage? He thought not. He scowled at the serving woman who offered him ale. He growled at the one who offered him a platter of meat. He frowned as he watched Struan approach the table. But he stood and nodded at the man in spite of his feelings.

"I can see that yer work in the yards didna improve yer attitude at all, Alex. Yer face and yer grumbling is heard and seen by all here." Struan motioned out at those eating below them.

"I canna pretend I am happy aboot what has happened. I amna." Alex drank deeply from the mug of ale and held it out for more. "And I amna pleased that ye won't permit me to go to her." He knew he was pushing it with Struan, but he did it, anyway.

"I told ye afore: Yer responsibility to the clan comes first, just as mine did all those years ago. When I give the word, ye may go to her. And,'' Struan eyed him over the edge of his mug, ''that willna happen verra soon.''

Alex slammed his mug down, splashing the newly poured ale onto the table and his clothes. He started to rise when Struan grabbed him by the wrist.

''Dinna e'en think to defy me. If ye try to, I will send her back to England wi'oot a moment of hesitation.'' Struan's grasp was strong. Alex was forced to stay seated. As soon as he stopped resisting, Struan released him. ''Now, here comes Anice. Ye will treat her right or yer leman will pay the price.''

''Dinna ye think Maggie haes paid enough? Damn ye, Struan, I willna be kept from her.'' He watched Struan's eyes light with fury. The man might be old but, as he straightened his back and glared at him, Alex knew he'd best pick his fights carefully. Silence filled the hall; the tension was palpable. He felt all eyes on him and the scene about to unfold.

''Ye better keep yer head on yer shoulders and mind yer treatment of Anice. 'Tis the last time I will warn ye.'' Struan had lowered his voice, but the threat was there. Maggie's presence and well-being was contingent on his good behavior. He could not let her down. Her life, their lives depended on his actions. Alex breathed deeply and watched Anice make her way through the hall. As she approached the steps, he left his seat and walked to the edge of the platform. He held out his hand to escort her the rest of the way. She didn't meet his gaze as she made her way to her seat.

It wasn't until she reached out for a goblet of ale that he saw her hands shake. He looked at her face, which she kept bowed, and saw that her skin was pale, very pale. And her lip trembled as she took a drink of her ale. He reached over to move a lock of hair that was loose from her braid and, for an instant, she cringed away from him. He thought he was mistaken until he saw the effort it took for her not to move from his touch.

She was scared! Of him! She must know how furious he was about her punishment of Maggie. Good. Let her stew a bit.

The rest of the meal was pure torture, not only for him but for all in the room. No one dared say much or speak too loudly for fear of touching off an explosion. Struan threw him angry glares but held his tongue. At last, bowls of fruit and wedges of cheese were put on the tables, signaling the end of dinner. To Alex's surprise, or perhaps not, not many of the clan left the room. He smiled grimly to himself. They didn't wish to miss a show. Clearing his throat, he pushed back his stool and stood. With his arm outstretched, he leaned to Anice.

"If I might hiv a word wi' ye, Anice? In yer solar?"

She was startled by his invitation. Her eyes darted to Struan for guidance. Struan nodded at her.

"Alex?" Struan growled.

"Aye, Faither?"

"Ye heard my words. Dinna cross me on this."

"Aye, Faither, I heard ye. I ken what I maun do."

Anice's head turned back and forth, following their words. He stepped away from the table, taking her with him. His long strides forced her to trot to keep with his pace. When they arrived at the solar's door, she was out of breath. Alex pushed open the heavy door and led her into the sun-filled room. Gazing around the room, he found Firtha standing in the shadows, awaiting Anice's orders. Anice lifted her arm from his, but he grasped it firmly and held her at his side. The servant stepped toward them, bringing her height and bulk as an unspoken threat.

"Ye may go," he said, as he covered Anice's hand with his.

"My lady may hiv need of me. I will stay." She challenged him with her tone, her stance, and her glare.

"If ye do no' obey me, yer lady will be looking for a new companion. Ye *will* be sent back to live wi' the MacNab."

''Alex,'' Anice's voice trembled as she defended Firtha, ''she didna mean to question ye. She was trying to help me.''

''Anice, she is disputing my authority over ye and her, and I willna stand for it.'' He would not let a servant intimidate him. ''I said to go. Now.'' He tilted his head in the direction of the entry.

Anice clutched his arm tightly, shaking at the cold fury in his words. The maid finally gave in and ran past the couple and out the door. Alex remained still until he heard the slam of the door. He threw off Anice's arm and strode across the room. When he turned back, she stood, head down, wringing her hands. He waited for her to look at him instead of the floor. After a few minutes of tense silence, she raised her eyes to meet his gaze.

He'd thought long and hard about how to handle this. Although a part of him would feel deep satisfaction from giving her a beating like she had given to Maggie, he knew he could not use force against her. 'Twas his right, but Struan made it clear he should not exercise that particular right until after the wedding. No, violence was not the answer here. Her fear of him and her now biddable appearance told him that the threat of retaliation, especially in full view of the waiting clan, would be enough. Her pride and fear of his violence and her humiliation would keep her in line.

''I amna pleased wi' ye, Anice.''

She didn't answer, she just nodded, and her body shook with deeper tremors. He took a step closer to her and heard her loud gasp. Her breath was hitching and the shine of tears filled her wide, green eyes. Another part of him was horrified that he would terrorize this babe of but fifteen years. But she had amply demonstrated that she could be an admirable enemy when she chose to be.

He lowered his voice and growled his words. ''I amna pleased wi' ye *at all,* Anice. After I told ye that I would handle any problems wi' Maggie's behavior, ye chose to ignore my wishes?"

He took a few more steps, and she recoiled from him, still wringing her hands in front of her.

"I willna hiv a wife who disobeys my word, Anice."

"Alex. I, er . . . I . . ." She backed away from his every step until she could move no more. He trapped her against the table in the middle of the room. He raised his hand in front of her as a threat and she lost all color. She sank to her knees on the floor before him.

" 'Tis my right, Anice."

"Alex, please dinna hit my face," she cried, "please no' my face. Use the rod if ye maun, but I beg ye, dinna strike my face." She crumpled at his feet, sobbing, clutching at his foot in supplication.

It was a pitiable sight. He had used her fear and pride against her. Even though he knew what Anice had done to Maggie, he couldn't really hurt her in the same way. He reached down and grabbed her shoulders, dragging her to her feet. She was still crying and fought to hold her face out of his striking range. Alex shook her forcefully a few times until she finally raised her face to him.

He gritted his teeth and forced an angry whisper through them. "I willna hit ye, Anice, at least not now." He shoved her away, against the nearby table. "Now, stop this crying and take hold of yerself."

Regaining her balance, she pulled a rag from her pocket and wiped her swollen eyes and drippy nose. She pushed the loose tendrils of hair from her braid over her shoulders and straightened her dress.

"Why not, Alex?"

"Why no' what?"

"Why will ye no' punish me if yer angry aboot what I did? 'Tis yer right."

"Striking ye willna make things right. Just as ye beating Maggie was wrong, so would my beating ye be."

''I dinna understaun, Alex. Afore ye left wi' the king, ye didna hesitate to strike out in anger.''

''Things hiv changed in me since then, Anice. But, if ye continue to defy me, I *will* give ye the beating I am itching to give right now.'' He clenched his fists and released them several times in front of her face and watched as she grew paler and paler with each movement. ''So hiv a care and do what I tell ye to do.''

''Will ye return her to the castle, Alex? To yer room?'' Her voice trembled. She was pushing him, and she knew it.

''Nay, Anice, she willna return here.'' She stopped sniffling and looked at him expectantly. ''But, I will see her in the village when I wish to. Dinna think to stop me.''

''Aye, Alex, 'tis yer right to that, too.'' She paused and stared past him for a moment. '' 'Twas so embarrassing to hiv her here, under my gaze. Ye hiving her at yer beck and call for all the clan to see. I couldna bear the humiliation any longer.''

''I will decide who I seek pleasure wi' and where and when I do it. Do no' voice yer objections again.'' He clenched his fists again, making sure she noticed.

''Aye, Alex, I will do as ye say.'' She nodded her acceptance, her glance never leaving his hands.

''Now, wipe yer eyes and come back wi' me to the hall. We maun show Struan and the clan that ye are still alive.''

He smiled grimly as she gasped at his words. She did walk to his side as he ordered. That was a good sign. He placed her arm around his forearm and led her to the door.

''Anice, do no' fear me raising my hand to ye if ye ken and stay in yer rightful place. As my wife, I will treat ye wi' the respect ye are due.''

He watched her lift her chin and regain her pride as they approached the door to the great hall. Pulling it open, all those who perched near it, trying in vain to hear the conversation on the other side, went running in different directions. They walked into the huge room and came face-to-face with Struan.

"Did ye beat her?" Struan's arms were crossed over his chest, his gaze hard on both of them. Alex turned in time to see Anice blush at his question. She looked back at him for a response.

"No' yet." He paused and glared back at Struan. His bravado was a bluff but his only weapon for now. He felt strong enough in his fighting skills, should Struan challenge him over this.

"No? Ye are a changed mon since yer stay wi' David. Ye surprise us all." Struan stepped aside and slapped him on the back. "Go to the yard now. Four of the clan's best warriors await yer instruction in the long staff. Anice," he pointed across the room, "yer maid awaits yer orders there."

Alex dropped Anice's arm, and she curtsied to him and Struan before walking to Firtha. Then Alex walked away, toward the yard.

He thought he understood Struan now—clan and one's duty to it came first, all else after. Struan upheld the hierarchy of the clan's life, too. Everyone had a place, knew it, and stayed within it. Thank God he didn't have to live his life that way.

Or . . . did he?

Instead of blind allegiance to a clan, he devoted himself to his job and his pursuit of a partnership. Just as Struan did not let anything change his world, Alex did not let anything deflect him from his path. Anything, anyone that did not further his goal was disregarded. Family, relationships, *love:* all ignored because he couldn't waste his time, his energy, his concentration on anything that would not move him closer to that partnership.

He stopped at the fence surrounding the yard, not seeing the men there as he searched within his soul. He ran his fingers through his hair, now much longer than when he arrived in Scotland.

It was not as bad as all that, he thought. Wouldn't he gain everything else he desired by attaining his goal? He would soon have a wife—he was sure he could work things out with Nancy. They would marry and have children. Shaking his head, he tried to visualize a future with her.

No, their time was done.

Thinking about his future, he could only picture Maggie with him. Maggie greeting him at the door with a baby in her arms. Maggie laughing at his seriousness. Maggie, in his bed, moaning at his touch, arching toward him as he entered her body. He shook his head to clear away the images.

No, they had not spoken of a future together once they got back home. They would go their separate ways, and he would go back to . . . What? Who? How? He couldn't think about this now. The men were waiting for him. He would speak to Maggie tonight. She could help him sort out his confusion. Tonight, he would go to her, regardless of Struan's threats.

"Here, lass, let me help ye raise yer head a bit."

She felt a hand slip under her head and lift it gently. At that slight move, she groaned in agony as waves of pain pierced through the darkness to her.

"Easy now, lass, drink a bit of this. It will ease yer suffering."

Maggie struggled to sip the liquid held before her lips. Its bitter taste and smell repelled her, but she had neither the will nor the strength to say no. A small sample was all she could swallow before the darkness threatened to claim her again. The darkness was her refuge for now; she could not see or hear or *feel.* She welcomed it and sank back into its murky grasp.

* * *

"Will she live?"

"Aye, Alex, 'tis as Struan first said, her back looks and feels much worse than it truly is."

Moira opened her door quietly and allowed Alex access to her cottage. This was a good sign—defying Struan to see Maggie.

"Where is she?" She could hear the worry in his voice, true concern for this woman of his time.

"Ye can look in on her, but she willna awaken for several hours, probably no' afore the dawn." Moira pointed to the smaller room.

"Ye hae given her something for the pain?" Alex's face was twisted in anguish once he saw the extent of Maggie's injuries. He knelt next to her and lifted her hand in his, waiting for Moira to answer.

"I hae done what needed to be done here, what hae ye done to Anice?" She knew what the real Alex would have done. Anice would be in worse shape than Maggie if she had challenged the real Alex.

"I threatened her wi' my fists if she should come near Maggie again. From the look on her face, it should work."

"Ye can stay a few minutes and no more, Alex. I dinna want her disturbed."

She watched from the doorway as he stroked Maggie's hand over and over again, whispering her name in a pleading tone. Shaking her head, Moira knew that good would come from this bad. But would it come in time?

She was on her stomach, lying on a low mattress of some kind. She tested her strength by turning her head to the other side. The place was dark; a small peat fire burned close by, giving off heat and the unmistakable odor but not enough light for her use. The earthy smell of the room told her she was not in the castle any longer, but where was she?

Maggie tried to raise herself up on her elbows, but her

body resisted her mind's best efforts. It took a few moments of struggling before she was successful in leaning up. Even from her new position, it was too damn dark to see much at all.

She heard scuffling footsteps coming toward her and braced for another attack. None came.

"Are ye awake, lass?"

"Moira, is that you?" She thought the voice was familiar. Was she in Moira's cottage?

"Aye, Maggie, 'tis me." A torch flared, its brightness forced her eyes closed. Laying her head back down, she waited to become accustomed to the light.

"Where am I, Moira? Is this your home?"

"Aye, ye are safe here. And welcome." She felt Moira's soft touch on her forehead. "Ye still hae a fever. Ye should drink."

"Not more of that bitter drink. I will get sick."

"Ye are no' a gracious patient, are ye, Maggie?"

Maggie heard the humor in Moira's voice. How long had she been here in Moira's care? How much of a pain in the neck had she been to the woman?

"I beg your pardon, Moira, if I have not been." She lifted her head to drink from the mug held in front of her mouth. "Thank you for your kindness to me." The cool water poured into her mouth, and she swallowed deeply, her thirst stronger than she realized. The cup tipped away and was gone after a few gulps.

"Take just a bit at a time, no' too fast. Ye will suffer belly-thraw if ye drink too much."

"I don't even like the sound of that. Can you help me to turn over, Moira?"

"Ye may like that e'en less, lass. Why do ye no' wait till morn to try to move? Ye will hae more strength by then."

"Is it night, Moira? How long have I been here?" She settled back down on her stomach on the pallet.

" 'Tis the middle of the night. Ye were brought here early this morn, still unconscious."

"How did I get here?"

"Struan haid some of the men carry ye here on a litter from the castle."

"And Alex? Has he been here?"

Moira did not respond right away. Was her hesitation the answer? Had Struan kept him away? Or Anice? They were her best guesses. She fought the burning tears that stung her eyes and nose. Rubbing her hand across her eyes, she took a deep breath and let it out, trying to regain some control. Moira laid her hand on Maggie's head and rubbed it gently.

"He didna stay away. He was here for a short visit while ye slept, Maggie. Do ye ken 'tis said his roar at the sight of ye on that bed scared the pigeons from their roosting places in the castle walls. He couldna stay this time, but that doesna sound like a man who cares too little."

"I know he cares, Moira."

"Good. Now, rest till morn and then we'll get ye up from yer pallet and moving."

Maggie still had so many questions to ask about her injuries, about Anice and Alex. But her strength was depleted that quickly—after just leaning up and taking a drink of water. In the morning, she would ask. She would ask about . . .

Chapter 36

FAINT DAYLIGHT PIERCED the darkness. Maggie tried to turn onto her side, but waves of pain stopped her. A groan escaped her best efforts to remain quiet. The need to empty her bladder grew, forcing her into action. She pushed up on her elbows, grunting with every move. Fighting the anguish that threatened her success, she tried to recall those Lamaze instructions she learned as labor coach to her sister. Blowing in short breaths, she managed to roll on one side and get onto her hands and knees. Her shoulders and back burned unlike anything she had ever felt; the pain was worse than even her recent migraine. It surged through her, and an urge to vomit grew. She looked for a chamber pot, something to use as she felt the retching reflex begin.

Without warning, she was surrounded by a massive arm, crossing under her and bracing her stomach. He held her secure, protected her from falling face first into the basin he placed before her.

"Go ahead, lass, I hiv ye."

She wanted to laugh at the sheer embarrassment of this

scene. She didn't know what bothered her more: vomiting in front of a stranger or that the stranger was the gorgeous blacksmith. Her body forced her stomach to empty before she could think about anything else. After the convulsions ceased, he eased her back into a sitting position on the pallet and took the basin from the room. Without thinking, she tried to twist her hair—hair that was no longer there. Short, uneven curls covered her head.

Could this get any worse? She shook her head, fighting the urge to cry now. Pol stooped down in the doorway and entered the room. Now he carried a cup, the basin, and a piece of linen.

"Pol, I . . . Well, I mean, thank you for your help. You don't have to do this."

" 'Tis fine, mistress. I often lend a hand when Moira tends the ill."

"You do?" She was astounded by this information. Most men she knew would run in the other direction from anyone sick. "I think you can call me Maggie. I feel silly now that you've seen me like this to have you speak so formally to me."

He handed her the cup and leaned to hold the basin closer. "I wouldna suggest that ye drink the water now, Maggie. Ye may wish to rinse yer mouth only." She nodded, swished a mouthful of water, and spat it into the bowl. Pol held out the damp linen to her, which she used to wipe her face and hands.

"Thank you, again, for your help. Could you help me to my feet?" She had to find a place outside to . . . oh, no, she couldn't ask his help for *that.* Where was Moira?

"I will, if ye take it slowly. Yer back and shoulders are badly bruised and willna want to move at all." He moved in front of her and grasped her arms. Standing up in one fluid motion, he brought her to her feet. She closed her eyes and gritted her teeth against the pain. Her knees shook as she swayed within his hold.

"It may help if ye open yer eyes and concentrate on

the room around ye, lass.'' Moira's voice! *Oh, thank you, God,* she offered up under her breath.

She followed Moira's instructions and soon the room stopped spinning and her legs grew more steady. Maggie had a death grip on Pol's arm and, with his support, she wobbled the final few steps into the other room of the cottage. Moira positioned a chair by the hearth, and Maggie sat the only way she could: she straddled the seat and held on to the spindle back.

It was then she noticed her near naked condition. She wore one of Alex's shirts, but it was on backward, unlacing down her back. At least she had underwear on. She felt her face heating as she pulled on the hem of the garment, trying to cover more of her legs. Pol chuckled at her actions.

''Moira, I will be on my way, if ye dinna need anything else.'' He smiled at Maggie and waited on Moira's response. Moira walked with him to the door of the cottage, whispering to him and smiling at his words. He leaned closer and kissed her deeply before leaving. Maggie looked at the floor, the ceiling, the fire, anything to withdraw from this private moment. A few more hushed words and he left, winking at her as he pulled the lower part of the door closed. Moira watched him leave, waving several times through the open portal.

''I have never been so embarrassed in my life.''

''By Pol's help?'' Moira looked at her. ''Why?''

Maggie's mouth dropped open in shock. ''Do you know what he did? Do you see how I'm dressed? How I look?''

''Do ye really fret over such things in the place yer from? Ye needed help, he helped ye. 'Tis simple.''

''I don't think so. I cannot see Struan holding a basin while I got sick.''

''Nay, lass, neither can I. Yer right, Pol is special.'' Moira walked to her worktable and gathered some herbs and a bowl. Mixing and crushing the leaves, she added liquid from a small crock. She produced a gooey concoction that smelled better, much better, than it looked. She carried the ointment to Maggie.

"Moira, I really need to . . . um . . ."

"Pish?"

Maggie laughed even though the movement of expanding her lungs brought with it pain. "Oh, is that how you say it? Pish? That sounds so funny."

Moira loosened the ties on the shirt and eased it off of Maggie's shoulders. "Let me put this on yer back. It will ease yer suffering and let ye tend to yer other needs wi'oot so much pain."

Maggie braced for Moira's touch, ready for the pain. After the first stroke, she was amazed to find her discomfort lessening. The ointment felt icy then warm and soothed the burning and tightness.

"How bad is it?"

"Weel, a few places hiv broken open and bled. They looked much worse than they really are. Ye still hiv a fever, so I want ye to drink some of my tea when yer stomach settles. When yer ready to lie down and rest, I hiv a different salve to keep the open wounds from festering."

Maggie wrapped her arms around the back of the chair and rested her head on her arm. The cool, fresh air rippled across her neck and over her scalp, rustling the curls. Running her hand over them, she grimaced.

"Ye are fortunate that she only cut yer hair. Others, afore ye and her, hiv been tarred as weel."

"Tarred? You're joking." Maggie sat up.

"Nay, lass, I speak the truth. Lemans may hiv to be allowed but they are never treated weel by the lady whose place they take. Here, now, I am nearly done." Moira spread a little more ointment over some of the welts, pulled the garment up onto Maggie's shoulders, and tied the laces. Maggie flexed her shoulders back and lowered her arms—no more burning or stinging. She was almost comfortable. Almost.

With some help, she stood and backed off the chair, pulling the shirt down over her legs. A flutter of dizziness passed through her, and she grabbed the end of the table.

"Take it slowly, Maggie. Ye hiv been wi'oot food or drink for close to twa days. Yer body is weak from that and from the beating ye took." Moira slid her arm under Maggie's. "Come, let me help ye wi' the pot in here this time. Ye will soon be tending to yerself."

Moira continued talking through every humiliating moment. Maggie knew she was trying to divert her attention and went along with the woman's efforts. In a short time, she was much more comfortable and sitting back near the fire.

"I didn't know you had an extra room in your cottage, Moira. I didn't see it last time I was here."

"I tend the ills of the clan. At times, 'tis easier to bring the sick here than to go to their cottage. My herbs and supplies are close at hand."

Maggie was curious about Moira's relationship with Pol but didn't want to ask outright.

"Ye dinna need to chatter, Maggie. Ye can ask yer real questions."

"I didn't know I was chattering." Subtlety was never her strongest characteristic. "All right, does Pol live here?"

"Aye, he does."

"So, you two are . . . ?"

"Aye, we are. Can ye no' say the word, Maggie? Lovers. We are lovers."

This was worse than everything that passed before. Heat filled her cheeks and she looked down at the floor. "I'm sorry for asking. I'm curious about you . . . and him."

"No need to apologize." Moira put a kettle of water on to boil and returned to her table and began sorting a basket of plants into various piles. "My husband died in the same battle that saw David captured by the English devils. We were no' long married, and I was his second wife. He was a good mon, my Gordon. So, I live here in the cottage that was ours, as a widow."

"And your healing?"

"I hiv been clan healer since I was no' more than Anice's age. My mother was, afore me. She taught me what she ken'd and I hope to pass on my skills to a daughter."

"Will you marry Pol?"

"He hasna asked."

"Do you want to? He seems like he would make a good husband for you. Have you never broached the subject with him?"

"We hiv talked aboot it. Mayhap one day we will. In the meantime," she rolled her eyes at Maggie, "I enjoy his attention and his other attributes and he shares my home."

"You are a wicked woman, Moira." Maggie laughed at her obvious references to Pol's lovemaking.

" 'Tis what some say." Moira dipped into the kettle and poured the hot water over some leaves in a mug. She stirred it, added a few ingredients, and then passed the mug to Maggie. After sniffing it a few times, Maggie sipped the warm beverage.

"Won't I be in the way, here? I mean if Pol and you share your cottage, I don't want to impose."

"Struan wants ye here 'til ye heal, then we're to find ye another place to live."

"Here, in the village? Are there empty cottages?"

"No, lass, and unmarried women do no' live by themselves here."

"They don't? Where do they live?"

"A girl lives in her faither's house until she marries and moves to her husband's. Widows live with their children and may keep their cottage if they dinna marry again.

The only unmarried women living in the village . . ." Moira paused.

Remembering Anice's comment, Maggie completed Moira's statement. "Are the village whores." She stared at Moira and asked, "Are there many?"

"Ah, lass, ye bring the judgments of yer own time here to us. The whores are just women who serve that need for the men here. Although Anice despises them, the rest of the clan kens that they hiv a place here."

"So they are accepted?"

"Weel, by most. Some are cruel, but most ken the whores' work haes a place in the clan. But, that isna yer place."

"Where will I stay?"

"I am thinking aboot that. We hiv some time afore yer healed." Moira continued to keep her hands busy as they talked. She broke up branches, wrapped and hung some herbs, measured others. "Weel, what else do ye want to ken?"

"What happened after?"

"After ye were beaten?"

"Yes. I don't remember it. I mean, I remember counting as she . . ." Maggie shuddered as she thought of the first blows. "Anyway, I passed out and woke up here last night."

"Someone told Alex that Anice was aboot to punish ye and he and Struan went to yer room. They got there just as she finished. Alex took one look at ye," Moira locked gazes with her, "and screamed something fierce. The ones who helped Anice took off, running from his fury, but no' Anice. She stood her ground. She haes grit, that one." Maggie didn't feel like admiring Anice right now. She snorted at Moira's comments.

"Come now, lass. 'Tis said he looked and sounded every bit the warrior ready to slay those who haid done this to ye. Anice walked out of the room wi' her head held high." Maggie shifted on the chair. "Struan ordered a litter to bring ye here, and he forebade Alex to come to ye. As I told ye, Alex did come last night, under the cover of dark, to see how ye fared, in spite of the laird's order. 'Tis all I ken aboot it."

"How did you find out this much?" The woman had to have a great deal of sources within the castle to know the details she did.

"I ken much of what happens to the clan, be they in the castle or in the village."

"Aye, but do ye ken it afore they do?" Maggie imitated the accent that surrounded her daily. It was becoming easier and easier to slip into it. Alex had even started teaching her some Gaelic words and phrases—the interesting ones.

"Ye may pass for a good Scottish lass yet. And no. I mostly find out after things happen. 'Tis only for special things that my gift awakens and I share in the wisdom."

Maggie shifted again and yawned. Just sitting up for this little while had used all of her strength.

"Weel, lass, are ye ready for a bit of a rest? I think that will do ye the most good. Come, I will help ye back to the pallet."

"I want to be awake in case Alex comes."

"Alex willna come here in the daylight, Struan willna allow it. If he is able, he will come this night. So, get yer rest now."

Maggie didn't have the strength to fight the woman. She followed Moira's lead and, in a few moments, found herself on the pallet in the small room. The darkness and warmth of the room called to her. She was aware of Moira putting on more of her ointment, but she was falling asleep quickly.

Alex, will you come tonight?

Chapter 37

HE DIDN'T COME that night. He didn't come the next, either. By the third day, she was feeling well enough to be angry. ''Oh, he was worried about her,'' Jean said when she brought Maggie's clothes and belongings from the castle. He checked on her condition when Moira was called to the keep to treat a few wounded soldiers. Moira told her that he waited to speak with her and asked many questions. But his actions spoke louder than his words in this case.

She stretched up and pulled another shirt from the line strung between the trees. Her blouse pulled across her back, making her wince. Still, it was an improvement over yesterday when the wounds still seeped. She found that if she kept moving, she felt better. Inactivity caused more tightening and stiffness. Folding the air-dried laundry was her therapy. It kept other things off her mind. Alex, however, would not stay out of her thoughts.

She remembered Moira's expression when she refused any more of her homemade brews. Afraid that it would interfere with the amoxicillin hidden in her backpack,

Maggie stopped taking the tea. Moira caught her taking some of the oval tablets and just frowned. When she tried to explain their use, Moira waved her off. " 'Tis no' of my time, lass. Ye keep it to yerself," Moira said. So, Maggie had kept them hidden, following the same regimen she used for her recurrent ear infections. After just two days of the antibiotic and several liberal doses of extra-strength pain reliever, her fever was gone and the sores were healing quickly.

Now, the time when she would move elsewhere was growing closer. It was uncomfortable sleeping in the small house with Pol and Moira. They did not curtail their relationship, so Maggie was left lying awake, fantasizing about Alex. Oh, they didn't make it obvious but, without even a door to separate them, the sounds of lovemaking, avid lovemaking, spread through the compact cottage.

So, maybe she was just jealous.

And hurt.

And hurting.

She moved on to the next row of clothes, carrying the folded laundry in a large, woven basket. She thought Moira's reaction to the medicine was peculiar. She was interested in learning as much as she could about this time and place. Moira didn't seem interested or intrigued about Maggie and Alex's time at all. Other than a few general questions about men's and women's fashions, Moira kept her curiosity to herself.

Now that Maggie's back was mending, Struan said she was to move from Moira's cottage soon, and what the laird ordered was obeyed. Moira was out at the moment making arrangements for a place. Maggie didn't like being in the dark, but she knew Moira would do what was necessary.

Sounds of laughing reached her on the cool breeze. Maggie took the basket inside the cottage and pulled her scarf from her pocket. With it in place, no one could tell that her hair had been cut. It was to save her from shame and scorn in the village that Moira urged her to cover her head when anyone visited. She was getting used to the lightness of her curls already.

Yesterday, with Moira's help, she trimmed her hair to get all of it to the same length. Moira was horrified to learn that in Maggie's time any length *or color* of hair was permitted and encouraged. Moira had shaken her head at that information and muttered under her breath for a few minutes about it.

Maggie approached the door and watched as Moira and an older woman walked down the path from the village. The older woman was tall, with gray hair peeking out from under her kerchief. Maggie opened the door and stood back for them to enter.

"Be a good lass and get us some cool water from the well, Maggie."

Maggie nodded at the other woman's smile and picked up the wooden bucket by the door. They waited for her to leave before continuing their conversation. When she stepped inside, their words halted again. She poured the water into two mugs and set them on the table in front of them.

"Will there be anything else, Moira?"

"Nay, lass. Give us a few moments alone, if ye please."

"Of course, Moira." Maggie didn't want to leave; she knew they talked about her and her future. But she was learning her place here more each day. It was a hard lesson to learn. Here, she had no choice but to follow the rules, fit into the role. After talking with Moira, however, she'd found that women here had much more control over their lives than she had first thought. Most of it was a subtle power, but power nonetheless.

When she got home, well, she had things to think about. Her last experience with a man left her with a bad feeling about men and their need to control. To Don, love meant controlling everything she did, every place she went, everyone she knew. She had let her guard down and before she was even aware of it, Don had firmly entrenched himself in a power position in her life, and it had been a long time before she could take back that control.

Somehow, she could not ever picture Alex doing the same thing. He knew she hated restrictions on her and did his best here to ease her way. In the privacy of their room, in their conversations, in their lovemaking, they were equals. Neither controlled the other. For that alone, she would have loved him.

She wanted to see him to tell him how she felt but was afraid to burden him with her feelings. What if he didn't feel as strongly about her? He had certain things he wanted to accomplish in his life, and she definitely hadn't been on that list. When they got back home, would they go their separate ways? Would he look for another suitable candidate for his wife of convenience? Or would their experience here have as profound an effect on him as it was having on her?

Shaking her head, Maggie decided to keep her feelings to herself for a while longer. Alex was surely having a difficult time on his own in the castle. Looking up, she saw Moira and the other woman walking toward where she sat in the shade of the trees. She stood as they approached.

"Maggie, this is Pol's aunt Torra. She haes invited ye to stay wi' her in her cottage."

Maggie looked at Torra and smiled. "Thank you for offering, mistress. When should I come to your home?"

"Gather yer belongings now, lass, and she will show you the way there. Ye may come to visit whene'er ye hiv time to, Maggie. Torra will need yer help wi' the bairns most of yer days, but yer evenings will be yer own. And join us for supper this eve."

"Help with the children, er, bairns?"

"Aye, Torra watches o'er her son's bairns while he and his wife work in the castle. Since Torra hurt her hip some weeks ago, she needs help to lift and care for the wee ones."

Children? This was wonderful. This was exactly what she should be doing: caring for children.

"Of course, Moira, I would be glad to help." Turning to the older woman, she asked, "How many ah, bairns do you tend?"

Torra started laughing. With a very thick accent, she answered Maggie's question, but she directed it to Moira. Maggie didn't understand any of it.

"Torra doesna understaun yer words. She haes the *Gaidhlig* but doesna speak the lowland tongue."

"How are we supposed to work together?"

"Ye will learn, lass. Haes Alex no' taught ye any of our words in these weeks?"

Maggie smiled and felt the telltale heat creep up her cheeks. Some words, yes. Not words she would use in mixed company here.

"A few, Moira."

"Weel, that's a good start. Go, gather yer things. Oh, I left the small crock wi' the salve in it on the table for yer back. Torra kens of yer injuries and will put it on for ye."

"I'll be right back, Moira."

She went into the cottage and grabbed the canvas sack that held her clothes and backpack. As she passed Moira's worktable, she picked up the crock of ointment and walked back outside to the waiting women.

"I am ready."

"Ye come to me if ye hiv need, Maggie. Keep yer eyes open and yer mouth shut and watch for clues."

"Thank you for everything so far, Moira. Thank Pol for sharing *his* food and *your* home with me." She hugged her friend and stepped away.

"Dinna lose heart, lass. There is a way home, and ye will find it. I ken it."

Maggie followed Torra through the village. She looked at the ground and kept an eye on the woman's bare feet as they moved. The villagers stopped their work and pointed at her as she passed. Although aware of their actions, she didn't want to see their open curiosity any longer, so she kept her eyes lowered. Soon, they entered a narrow alley and stopped at a door. This dwelling looked smaller than Moira's and it was located in a group of cottages. Torra opened the door and motioned for her to enter.

It had the same packed dirt floor, the same small hearth in the main room as in Moira's. A small alcove ran off one side of the room, and a table took up most of its space. A bench and some stools encircled the table, but no other furniture stood in the room. Torra pointed to a small chest in one corner and then to Maggie's sack. Nodding her head, Maggie placed all the things she had in this world on that small trunk.

Maggie looked around and shrugged at Torra. "The bairns?" Nothing, not one word in the reply she received could she comprehend. Maggie laughed. This must be Struan's punishment: putting her with someone who couldn't understand a word she said!

Well, at least Torra seemed like a kind woman. And she was Pol's aunt. She would make do until she could leave. And, she would help with the children. And wait. Watch. Listen.

"It haes been six days, Faither, and I will wait no more."

"Ye will wait until I give ye permission."

"And when will that be? After I am married to Anice?"

Struan clamped his mouth shut and didn't answer Alex's question. That was his plan, then. To force him to wait until the wedding was performed before he could see Maggie. Well, it wouldn't work.

"Ye talk aboot responsibility to the clan. I hiv a responsibility to Maggie. She saved my life on our travels here. I will see to her."

"She is weel, and living in the village. She isna being abused. Ye are free of yer responsibility. As yer laird and yer faither, I hiv taken care of it for ye."

" 'Tis no' that simple." Alex pounded his fist on the

table in Struan's chamber. "I want to see her. Now. Not after the marriage."

"*No!* Ye will obey me, Alex. Ye and Anice are getting along much better since she left. Give Anice a chance to win yer affections. She'll be warming yer bed soon enough." Struan pushed back in his chair and stood, rising to his full height and forcing out his chest. "Now, the MacNab will be arriving in a fortnight. By then, ye and Anice will be chomping at the bit to be together."

Alex glared at him. It did no good.

"If ye are that anxious for a woman, bed her now. It wouldna hurt if ye anticipated yer vows wi' her, Alex, after all, ye are betrothed. If ye hivna yet?"

"God damn ye, she is but fifteen."

"And ye think she isna ready for ye? Ye are wrong in that, Alex. I hiv seen the looks she gives ye, like she could eat ye alive! Her passion is only for ye, dinna waste it while ye pine for yer leman."

"I canna believe ye want me to bed Anice afore the wedding." He paced the wall in front of the huge hearth. "I dinna want Anice. I want Maggie and I will see her."

"I understaun that Maggie is a good lover, but ye can teach Anice the loveplay ye like. She will learn to please ye quick enough."

"Ye dinna understaun, Faither. I love Maggie."

"And what haes that to do wi' bedding and marrying Anice, I ask ye?"

He wouldn't get through Struan's thick head and years of customs. He decided then and there he would make his way quietly to Maggie in the dark of the night.

"Never mind, Faither. Ye willna hear me."

"Alex," Struan approached him and laid his arm on Alex's shoulders, "I hear ye and ask ye to hear me. The woman is safe in the village, making her way by tending to the bairns of Torra's son. She haes recovered from the beating and looks weel. Leave it at that for now." Before he could object, Struan continued, "If ye hiv a need for a woman, seek out Anice. It will go much smoother if ye dinna visit the village until after the wedding.''

Struan steered him to the door and pulled it open. Alex found himself outside the room, looking at Struan in the doorway.

''Heed me, Alex. Dinna think to disobey me in this.'' The door slammed in his face.

Alex pounded on the door. Struan opened it after but a moment.

''This isna the end of it, Faither. I hae obeyed ye afore, but I will no' in this.'' Alex yelled his threat at the stubborn old man.

''It haid better be the last I hear of it, Alex. I willna suffer yer defiance in this. Push me, and I promise ye she will be sent back to England. Ye'll never ken it until it's too late and there will be nothing ye can do.'' Struan shook his fist at Alex. ''And just see if I willna carry through on my promise.''

Alex turned and stalked down the hallway. He had to get out before he exploded. Maybe he would drink with the men in the hall and pick a fight? Maybe go to the loch for a long swim until he could move no more?

''Where are ye going, Alex?''

Alex stopped at Struan's question but without turning this time. ''To the loch.''

''The loch is fine. Dinna go to the village, mark me weel.''

Alex jumped at the force of Struan's words and the reverberating crash of the door, flung against its frame.

Struan didn't want to hear of any disobedience in this issue? Well, fine, he would make sure no word of his visits to Maggie ever reached Struan's ears. But the laird's threats would not keep him from Maggie any longer.

The loch it would be . . . then, on to the village.

Chapter 38

"PSSST, MAGGIE. WAKE up."

He had a better chance of waking the dead, he thought in frustration. Alex picked up a few stones and tossed them at her through the window, one at a time. She didn't seem to move a muscle. He did not want to enter the house and take the chance of being seen by Torra. The woman would report back to Struan by morning and all hell would break loose over this. Knowing Maggie's difficulty to wake, he had a feeling he would be stepping inside quietly in a few minutes.

"Maggie? Can ye hear me, lass?"

No response. Damn.

He climbed through the low window. His leg touched the floor without even stretching. Torra was lying on her side on the pallet next to Maggie. She rolled as he took his first step, turned, and now faced the front of the cottage. Maggie lay on her side, not moving other than to breathe. He crouched next to her and wondered how to do this.

He put his hand over her mouth and waited for her to

react. Her eyes flew open after a moment. She grabbed at his hand and began to struggle. He could tell the instant she recognized him because tears filled her eyes. Alex put his finger to his lips and, when she nodded, he removed his hand. He pulled her to her feet and led her to the window. She yanked her hand free and walked to the corner of the room. Maggie returned to him with a plaid wrapped around her shoulders.

Alex went through first and then lifted her out. Leading the way, he followed a narrow path away from the buildings. As they moved farther from the village, he slowed his pace. Finally, feeling safely away, he stopped and turned back to her.

He opened his arms to her, and she filled them instantly. He wrapped his arms around her, holding every inch of her as close as he could. He'd feared that Struan had sent her away already. He had feared he would never see her again. He had feared that he would never love her again.

Alex looked down at the woman he held in his arms, the woman he loved. She was sobbing, crying silently but so deeply it nearly broke his heart.

"Ah, Maggie, love. Dinna greet so. I'm here." He put his hand on her head and caressed the soft curls. He moved his hand onto her neck and then onto her back. She didn't flinch, so he rubbed there, too.

"Alex," her voice came out in a whisper. "I didn't know if I'd ever see you again. I was so frightened."

"I hiv missed ye, Maggie. So much, I canna say."

"And I have missed you, too. Kiss me, Alex. Please kiss me."

She offered her lips up to him, and he accepted. The touch sent vibrations through him. He slid over her lips softly, then pressed against them until she opened her mouth to him. He licked her lips and then moved his tongue inside to taste and feel her warmth. Oh, he had missed this. Missed her warmth and her acceptance. Her passion. Her love.

His body readied itself for her, hardening, lengthening, swelling. He pressed her closer and she rubbed her breasts against his chest.

"Oh, Alex, I need you. Love me, Alex, make me feel safe again."

He stepped away from her and took the plaid off her shoulders. Spreading it on the ground in front of them, he reached for her hand. She gave it to him, and Alex pressed it on his belt buckle. She smiled and tugged on the belt. It loosened, and the plaid fell to his feet, exposing his desire to her.

Before she could move, he grabbed the edge of her shift and pulled it over her head. They stood, inches apart, and he enjoyed the anticipation of her touch. He didn't have to wait long for it. Maggie reached for his hardness and slid her hand along the satiny smooth surface. Up and down she stroked, teasing the sac below his erection with her fingers. He held his breath when she knelt before him and moved her mouth closer.

He was going to die.

He knew it as he felt her breath on his manhood. He could not allow her to do this—he would explode. The first contact of her tongue sent a jolt through him; his knees buckled, and he couldn't stand any longer. As they slid to the plaid, he gathered her back into his arms.

He would never let her go.

Maggie moaned at the feeling of Alex's hardness entering her body. It had been so long since they joined this way. He filled her emptiness, the one at her woman's core and the one in her soul. As he moved deeper within her, she wrapped her legs around his.

She would never let him go.

She felt the passion building inside her, thrumming throughout her body with every touch of his hands, his mouth, his sex. He throbbed inside her passage, swelling even more than before, harder, longer with each stroke he made. He surged into her and groaned out her name. She felt his release and exploded with her own, pulsing and quivering from inside out. Her breath stopped as wave after wave of pleasure passed through her. Alex collapsed on her, and she cradled his body between her legs.

Seconds, minutes passed them by. Neither one moved. She didn't want to lose the touch of his skin against hers. Alex turned, taking her with him, and wrapped the plaid around them as they rolled.

"Now, snug as two bugs in a rug. Are ye all right, Maggie? Was I too rough?"

She smiled and shook her head at him.

"Nay? I lost control when ye used yer mouth. 'Tis been too long."

"Can you stay, Alex?"

"Brodie said the moon will rise at midnight. I hiv some time afore I maun leave." He laid on his side and she used his arm as a pillow. She could keep touching him while they talked.

"Are you all right, Alex? How are things going in the castle?" As much as she didn't want to admit it, she wanted to hear about Anice. And Struan. And especially about Rachelle and Brodie.

"Am I all right? My God, Maggie, the last time I saw ye, ye were unconscious and bleeding in my bed. Hiv ye truly recovered or was Struan lying to me?"

"I am okay, Alex. Moira took care of me for the first few days until Struan ordered me to move in with Torra."

"And yer back?" He started to roll her over. She knew he wanted to check her back for himself. She stopped him.

"My back is healed. It's fine, really."

"Did Moira's medicines work then?" She heard the worry in his voice. It made her feel loved.

"They started the healing but . . ."

"But what?"

"I used some of the antibiotics and the anti-inflammatory medications I had in my backpack. They worked quickly. A couple of days, and the wounds were better."

"Thank God. Did Moira ken?"

"She saw me taking the tablets but didn't want to know anything about them."

"Ye are lucky ye haid them wi' ye. Ye may hiv gotten verra ill wi'oot them." He held her tighter. "Who is Torra? The woman ye are living wi' here?"

"She is a nice person, Alex. She is Pol's aunt. Moira arranged it, I think. I help her watch her grandchildren during the day. And she's been teaching me Gaelic."

"So, yer safe here."

"For now, I am. But, Alex . . ."

"Aye, Maggie, I will touch ye there." He slipped his hands under her bottom and caressed her there. She felt rather than heard his chuckling.

"You really need to come up with a new line, Alex MacKendimen."

"Really, lass?" His finger spread her thighs from behind and she felt him coming nearer to the place where she ached.

Again.

Already.

Still.

She held her breath, waiting to see what he would do. She was not disappointed.

"That line seem to work fine wi' ye."

His hands worked their magic again, playing her body like a musician plays his instrument. She gave up her control to his and responded to his every touch. Their pace was slower, and she made him as crazy as he made her. Maggie used her body, her hands, her mouth against him, on him. Their climaxes were long in coming this time, and definitely worth the wait.

He stood and wrapped the plaid around his waist, securing it with his belt. She watched his every move from her place on the ground.

"If ye keep looking at me that way, I will just take it off again."

"That would be fine with me, Alex. I don't want to let you go."

"And I don't want to let ye go. But, I maun. The moon is starting to rise and the darkness will no longer cover my travel."

"Will I see you again?" She feared his answer.

"I canna promise, but I will try. Struan haes threatened to return ye to England if I try to see ye afore the wedding."

"Oh, my God, Alex," she gasped. "Why did you do this?"

"I haid to, Maggie. I haid to see for myself that ye were weel. And I haid to see ye for myself, too!"

She laughed at his words. He reached down, took her hand, and helped her to her feet. She picked up her shift and pulled it over her head.

"So, now you know I'm well. You need to follow Struan's orders, Alex. He is in control of this for now. I'll try to get a message to you when I can." She couldn't believe he was leaving so soon. She wanted to clutch him and beg him not to leave, but his staying would be dangerous for both of them.

"I will go now, Maggie, but I amna happy aboot leaving ye here on yer own. I hiv a bad feeling aboot the coming weeks."

"Are you a psychic, now, like Moira?" She tried to make light of his fears.

"No, ye ken I amna. But heed my warning: I haid this feeling afore, and it ended wi' Anice's beating of ye. Be careful." He took her in his arms and kissed her. It was over almost as soon as it started. Then he took a step back and dropped his hands from her shoulders. "Hiv a care."

Her throat tightened, and she couldn't get any words out. She just nodded at him and watched as he turned and ran down the path, away from the village, away from her.

Tears pooled in her eyes, making it difficult to see his progress. She swiped her hand across her eyes and reached down to pick up the plaid on the ground. Shaking out the dirt and grass, she folded it in half and wrapped it around her shoulders. Looking toward the village, the moon's rays began to shine over the rooftops and the houses. He'd left just in time.

Maggie walked quietly back to Torra's cottage and climbed through the low window in the back. Torra still slept, lying in the same place and position as when they left. Torra turned over and shifted a bit as Maggie lay down on her side of the pallet and closed her eyes.

Torra's hand patted Maggie's shoulder and she murmured some words in Gaelic. Maggie recognized them immediately; they were the same words Alex had taught her. The words for what she and Alex had just done in the forest! Torra knew, but would she say anything about this to Struan?

Maggie fell asleep much later, still praying that Torra was on their side.

"Weel, did ye see the lass?" The voice came out of the darkness along the side of the path. Brodie stepped into the rays of the moonlight.

"Aye, my friend, I did."

"See her and more, from the look of ye. Is she wearing the same smile as ye?" Brodie's eyes lit as he continued his teasing.

" 'Twas what we both needed. Thank ye again for yer help in this." Brodie had shown him the postern gate and how to get out of the keep without being seen by the guards.

"Dinna thank me 'til we are sleeping in our beds safely. We still hiv to get back inside."

"Weel, lead the way. The moon is rising fast, and we maun get back as soon as we can." Alex held out his hand, gesturing for Brodie to lead the way. Brodie stepped onto the path. They took off at a trot and left the trail as they neared the castle wall.

"How do ye ken aboot this way in and out of the keep?" Alex asked.

"I told ye—I used this to visit Rachelle when she still lived in her faither's cottage. I hivna used it in a long time and wasna sure it was still clear."

Alex was very pleased the way was still open. He had reached the end of his patience with Struan's refusal to allow him to see Maggie. But, for Maggie's sake, he knew he couldn't afford to antagonize Struan by openly going against his orders. He would appear to acquiesce to Struan's demands about Anice. Well, not about bedding her. He drew the line at seducing a child, whether she wanted to be taken to his bed or not.

He worried though, just as before, because the feeling of unease grew within him. The real Alex must be on his way back by now. How long would it take to reach Dunnedin from London? They had only days left to them, mayhap a sennight. Something would happen soon—before the wedding.

A shiver of warning vibrated through him. Something—or someone—was coming.

Chapter 39

MAGGIE PEERED INTO the darkness. It was the designated time for her arrival but no one stirred inside Moira's cottage. A fire burned in the hearth, flames flaring high. Moira couldn't be far. Turning back, she walked to the back of the house and looked in the area that surrounded the small dwelling. Moira wasn't there, either. This was strange, very strange.

Moira had invited her to share supper this night since Pol would be gone from the village. He had traveled to a nearby clan to exchange some tools and would not return for two days. They could talk freely of their mutual concern and didn't have to watch their words. Moira admitted not feeling good about keeping the truth from Pol, but she knew the blacksmith would be overwhelmed by the knowledge of who Maggie and Alex really were.

Maggie called out, and was surprised to hear Moira answer her in a low voice. She walked into the house and followed the voice to the small side room. Moira knelt next to the pallet, tending to someone ill. Maggie gasped in surprise when Moira leaned back and she saw who the healer tended.

"Rachelle? My God, she looks terrible." Maggie knelt at the sick woman's side and took her hand. She burned with fever and thrashed around, mumbling something in her delirium. "Moira, what is wrong with her? How long has she been this sick?"

"She came to me yesterday, no' feeling weel. The fever grew stronger through the day and now I canna wake her."

Maggie rubbed her friend's hand. "What have you done so far?"

"I gave her some of the tea I make that lowers fever. I bathe her and keep her drinking, but the fever is too strong. And," Moira paused, "she haes the white throat. I'm afraid, lass, that I canna treat that."

"What do you mean 'white throat'?" Maggie searched her mind for a definition. Some kind of throat infection, strep, maybe.

"She haes pustules in her throat. They cover the back of her mouth, too. Soon she will quiet and then . . ."

"Wait a minute. You can't mean she'll die from this?"

"Many do, lass. I canna treat all ailments."

"She can't die. You can't let her die." Maggie glared at Moira through gathering tears. "She was the only one in the clan who accepted me. She's my friend. And what will Brodie do without her?"

"Dying is as much a part of life as birthing, Maggie. Ye maun accept that things here are no' as they are in yer time. If the fates mean for her to live, she will. If it is her time to pass over, she will do that."

"We can't let her die. We have to do something." She heard her voice get louder. Rachelle must have heard her because she turned to her and spoke without opening her eyes.

"Maggie," she whispered hoarsely, "Alex pines for ye while ye live here in the village. He needs ye."

"Rachelle," Maggie leaned over closer to her friend, "rest now. We'll take care of you."

"Aye, Maggie. Tell Brodie . . ." Rachelle drifted off before she could finish her words. Maggie held her breath as Moira checked Rachelle.

"Nay, she isna gone. She is just deeper asleep than afore."

Maggie stood and stumbled from the room. She couldn't just stand by and let this happen. There had to be some way of helping Rachelle fight this infection.

Infection?

She knew what she had to do.

"Moira, I will be right back. I have an idea."

Maggie ran as fast as she could through the village to Torra's dwelling. Torra was at her son's and would not return for hours. Maggie skidded into the corner, pulled open the chest, and grabbed her sack. Fumbling through it, she found the bottle of antibiotic tablets and stuffed them in the pocket of her skirt. Throwing her belongings back in the chest, she slammed the lid and ran out. She was out of breath when she entered Moira's house and found her by the main hearth. She held out the bottle to Moira and met her questioning gaze.

"Nay, lass, I dinna think we should do that." Moira shook her head, refusing the gift from the future.

"I can't stand here and watch her die when these may help."

"Maggie, mayhap 'tis her time to die. Ye would be interfering wi' fate e'en more than Alex haes."

"If it's her time to die than she will, in spite of these, Moira. But, maybe the fates have sent me here to save her life with this medicine."

Moira walked to the fireplace and knelt in front of it. Maggie watched as the woman's body stiffened and her eyes gazed at the flames. The fire flared in colors and spat smoke into the room, forcing Maggie to the doorway for fresh air. Moira still didn't move—the smokiness in the room had no effect on her as she continued to stare at the greenish flames.

She's having a vision!

It lasted for a few minutes longer. Then Moira's whole body shuddered and she sat back on her heels. The smoke now flowed up into the chimney, and the room cleared. Moira blinked quickly and then took a deep breath and exhaled loudly. It took a few moments before Moira looked around the room and noticed Maggie standing nearby.

"I sought the wisdom for an answer, Maggie."

"Did you have a vision? Did you see something in the flames?" The fire looked normal again, no more green or blue colors or strange smoke.

"Aye, lass, I saw."

Maggie edged close to the seer. "Can you tell me what you saw? Are you allowed to share it with me?"

"I share what I want to aboot what I see, Maggie. After all, that is the purpose of the gift." Moira stood and faced Maggie. "I saw Rachelle holding a red-haired bairn in her arms. And I saw Brodie wi' her."

"Yes!" Maggie shouted. "Then we can help her with these." Maggie held out the bottle again.

"Aye, Maggie, 'twould seem so. But, we hivna much time. Tell me how to use these."

After much discussion about the way antibiotics work and the appropriate amount to give, Maggie gave Rachelle a large initial dose. It took many minutes and many tries to get the tablets into the unconscious patient. Waiting for a change in her condition took longer, much longer. The sun was as high as it can reach in the afternoon sky over Dunnedin on the next day before the fever broke.

"Maggie?" Rachelle's voice was hoarse and scratchy but a welcome thing to hear. Maggie's tears flowed as her friend opened her eyes for the first time in over a day.

"Yes, Rachelle, I am here." Maggie held Rachelle's hand tightly and touched her cheek. "How do you feel?"

"Like a herd of cattle walked o'er me. How long hiv ye been wi' me?"

''I came yesterday. You scared me, Rachelle. I thought I might lose you.'' Her tears escaped down her cheeks.

''My throat hurts. May I hiv some water?''

''I'll get you some.'' Maggie stood to go for a cup of fresh water when Brodie brought one into the room.

''Nay, Brodie, ye canna see me like this,'' Rachelle rasped. She struggled to turn away from him but couldn't do it alone.

Maggie smiled and stepped out of Brodie's way. He had been there for hours, waiting, worrying, praying. He needed to be with Rachelle.

''Lass, ye look beautiful to me. Here now, let me help ye to sit up.'' The big man slid his arm behind Rachelle's shoulders and lifted her off the pallet. ''I will hold this for ye. Slowly, now, Moira said to hiv but a wee sip.''

''Brodie, I am going outside for some fresh air. I'll be back shortly.''

She didn't receive a reply—Brodie was so wrapped up in Rachelle he wouldn't know if she was there or not. Maggie picked up the wooden bucket by the door as she left the house and walked to the well.

She filled the bucket with cold water, leaned over, and poured the water over her head. There was at least one advantage to short hair, she thought, as the coolness washed away the sweat and heat from her head.

''Does that feel as good as it looks?''

Maggie peeked with one eye and saw Moira now standing next to her. She twisted her curls, wringing out most of the water. Straightening up, she fluffed her hair by running her fingers through it.

''Yes, Moira, it does feel good. Why don't you try it?''

''Nay, Maggie. I wasna the one inside with the fire roaring, taking care of Rachelle. I am fine.''

''Brodie is in with her now.''

''Yer medicine helped her. And now she and Brodie will hiv that bairn I saw. Did I tell ye aboot the red hair?''

Maggie joined Moira in her laughter. It felt good to laugh after so much worry and fear.

"Maggie, come wi' me now. I want to show ye something." Moira waited for her agreement and then headed into the woods. They hiked a short distance into the thickening forest and stopped in front of a rock formation. Maggie watched, surprised, when Moira lifted a section of branches and twigs and opened an entryway into a cave. "Come inside."

She had to stoop to enter, but once inside, she could stand again. It was a small cave, dry and clean, with no sign of animals or visitation. A small table and bench took up one wall, and there were some vines and herbs hanging from the ceiling. Using a flint, Moira lit a torch set in the wall.

"I use this place for drying and preparing some of my herbs and potions. No one kens of it, or at least no one bothers it. Do ye think ye can make yer way here alone if need be?"

"Why, Moira? Why are you showing me this place?" Maggie's fear grew. This was a place to hide. Why did Moira show her a hiding place that no one in the clan knew about? The vision? What else had she seen in that vision. "What else did you see in the flames?"

"He is getting closer to Dunnedin, Maggie. I ken no' the time he will arrive, but he gets closer each day."

"The real Alex? Is that who you mean?"

"Aye, the clan's Alex. He comes wi' soldiers from England. I saw the chaos of discovery and . . ."

"You're scaring me, Moira. What else did you see?"

"I saw a gallows built for one."

Maggie gasped and then couldn't breathe. Fear tightened its grasp of her and she saw the cave begin to spin around her. A gallows? Someone would hang? God help them!

"Maggie, dinna let fear control ye. Ye maun be ready to hide if the need arises. Be strong. Be ready."

Maggie pulled herself together and looked at Moira. "Will one of us be hanged for this masquerade?"

"I saw only the gallows, no' someone hanging from it. There is every chance that ye may get out of this alive."

"We *may* get out alive? I don't like the sound of this."

"Weel, ye now ken a safe hidey-hole. If there is trouble, get here wi' or wi'oot Alex, and I will find ye. I will do what I can, lass, but ye maun be ready."

"I will be, Moira. Thank you for showing me this place."

"Now, remember our path as we return. Ye may need to make yer way here in the dark." Moira stepped out into the sunshine and covered over the opening. Once done, Maggie could see the aperture only because she knew it was there. "Come, lass, or Brodie will start on that bairn afore we get back."

The walk back took a few minutes, and they found Brodie sitting by Rachelle as she slept. He rose when they entered.

"She is sleeping again. Her throat still hurts."

Maggie reached down and touched Rachelle's cheek—still cool. She patted Brodie's arm. "Just asleep, Brodie, just asleep."

"Can I speak wi' ye outside, Maggie?"

"Of course." She walked outside and waited for Brodie to catch up with her. He stood next to her and took her hand in his.

"I hivna always been good to ye, Maggie, and I beg yer pardon for that. I ken what ye did for Rachelle and I thank ye."

"Brodie, it was Moira who . . ."

He squeezed her hand tighter and said, "Nay, Moira told me what ye did for Rachelle. That 'twas yer ingredients that cured Rachelle of the fever." He choked up and couldn't speak. The lump in her throat grew.

"Maggie, if ye ever hiv need of me, just call on me.

Ye will never ken how much Rachelle means to me or what you did for her, for us. I thank ye.''

She still couldn't talk, her throat was clogged with unshed tears. All she could picture in her mind was that baby yet to be born. She just nodded her head.

''I maun get back to the keep. I will return later to see her. If ye need me . . .''

''No, Brodie, she's fine, really.'' Now that she could get words out, Maggie reassured him.

''Weel, then, until later.'' Brodie nodded to her and trotted up the path, back to the castle.

Maggie thought about his words and prayed that she would never need to ask for his help. Alex was right; something was starting here. Trouble was coming straight for them. They would either get back home or end up dead. Maggie shivered at the choice. She knew neither would come easily.

Chapter 40

"DO YOU THINK we'll ever have a hot bath again, Alex?"

"Brodie keeps telling me that the loch haes been much warmer this year than last."

"Well, that's Brodie. That's the first thing I want to do when we get back to our time—soak in a hot bath until I look like a wrinkled prune. Actually, then I think I'll refill it and soak even more." Maggie laughed. "I will never take my hot water heater for granted again, Alex."

Alex watched as she pulled her blouse on and adjusted her skirt and bodice. It took much longer to get her clothes back in order than it took for him to remove them.

"I'm glad Brodie offered to take my message to ye. I enjoyed this time together." He reached for her hand and entwined their fingers.

"Moira thinks the real Alex will be here soon. I'm worried about what will happen." She stepped next to him and wrapped her arms around his waist.

"She told me the same thing. She warned me to be prepared for the worst, whatever that means." Moira had shared more with him, but now was not the time to worry Maggie. Her fear was growing already.

"Did she tell you about the hiding place? Do you know how to get there?"

"I'm afraid there's no hiding place for me, Maggie. If we're still here when Alex arrives, they will hunt me down, wherever I am. Ye may be safe once they hiv me."

"Alex," she said, laying her head against his heart, "I don't like the sound of that."

"Whatever happens, Maggie, get yerself to that place and stay until Moira comes to ye. Trust no one else."

"Not even Brodie?"

"Brodie will be put in a hard spot when the truth is out. He's been a friend, but only because he thinks I am his cousin."

"Alex, you're wrong. It isn't just your kinship that makes Brodie your friend. You've built a relationship with him in these few months."

"Aye, but I dinna want to test that wi' my life," he leaned down and kissed her, "or yers."

"He may surprise you, Alex."

"Weel, I hope he doesna hiv to take a stand against me, against us. I am getting depressed wi' this talk. Can we no' finish our time together wi' something a bit more pleasant?" He really needed to hold her longer. The dread of what was to come was getting more powerful, even though he tried to make light of it. He just hoped he was ready when the time came. Moira had stressed how important it would be.

Moira also thought that the power of the arch was tied to the phases of the moon. A full moon was due in three days. If things went right, they would try then. But, would the arch work this time? Or would they be trapped here and not return to their time? Since Moira remained hopeful in spite of her warnings, so would he.

"Maggie, let's try that preein' the lips o' again afore ye leave. I need to feel yours against mine."

As always, she opened to him. She gave him her mouth, her body, her heart. In return, she had his heart, even if she didn't know it yet. He would tell her before she left. He wanted her to know the depth of his feelings, new as they were to him. She would help him make sense of it all.

He deepened the kiss, enjoying her taste and the feel of her tongue in his mouth. He held her so closely he could feel her heart beating against his. A pity there was no more time for them. Suddenly, the sound of galloping horses seeped into his awareness, and he broke off the kiss. The clan almost never rode their horses here so close to the village. It had to be outsiders.

"Maggie, get down in those bushes. I dinna ken who is coming this way."

"Alex, it . . ."

"Get down, I said. Do it now." He grabbed his belt and scabbard. "Stay in there until this is over, then get ye to Moira's hiding place." She followed his orders. He watched her scramble under the low shrubs and tuck her feet under her. With the drab skirt, she blended well enough to be hidden. "I am going to draw them away. Dinna make a sound."

With his plaid and sword in place, he was ready. He thought he was prepared for anything—until he faced his double on horseback.

The man before him, one of a dozen men riding together, looked like his twin, and yet he didn't. His hair was short and straight and held back from his face by a gold band around his forehead. No beard covered the face, which was pale from being out of the sun's light. Instead of a plaid with knee-high boots, this man was dressed in leotards. Well, that's what he would call them. A very short shirt topped the tights and short boots covered his feet. A cape, not of plaid, but of some fancy material with slashed edges, covered the outfit.

When their eyes met, the recognition was electrifying.

Not the same person, but very, very close. Of course, he had warning. The other Alex was shocked speechless.

Before anyone could move, another group of riders approached from the direction of the keep. The watch had warned the clan of intruders. Alex took a deep breath and prepared himself to meet the challenge ahead.

"Halt! Who are ye?" Brodie rode at the front of the clan's guards. He hadn't seen Alex standing by the road yet. He watched as Brodie's eyes lighted on the real Alex.

"Who am I? Are ye joking?" The real Alex's voice rose to a girlish pitch.

"I ask ye who are ye, and who is this?" Alex waited for Brodie to recognize the man on horseback.

"Wait a moment, ye are my cousin Brodie," the real Alex said. "Ye have grown bigger than I thought possible, cuz." The soldiers in his group laughed at the insult.

Brodie recoiled, and his horse reared at the movement on the reins. Brodie regained control easily and walked the horse forward. He had finally seen Alex. His eyes, wide with shock and disbelief, went back and forth between the two. The other clansmen also gaped openly at the two similar men. Alex waited, he would put up no struggle in what was to come; he would raise his sword only if forced to defend himself.

"I am yer cousin, Alesander MacKendimen, lately a guest of good King Edward and companion of David, king of the Scots. Since ye are kin to me, ye may call me Sandy." The men in his traveling party all cheered at his declaration.

"Ye canna be," Brodie started. "This is Alex . . ." He stared at Alex, waiting for him to deny this claim.

Alex wouldn't lie to him now. He shook his head slightly so that only Brodie could see it. Brodie's eyes widened as he realized there would be no challenge. Brodie dismounted in a smooth motion and stood before Alex. He grabbed the sword from Alex's scabbard and handed it to another.

"Who are ye?" he bellowed at Alex. "Tell me who ye are!"

"I am Alex MacKendimen," he replied in a low voice.

"*Nay!* There canna be twa of ye." Brodie grabbed Alex by the shirt and yanked him forward. "Now, tell me who ye are."

Alex didn't reply. He stared over Brodie's shoulder, not meeting his look. Brodie roared out and then swung his fist at Alex's face, hitting him in the lower jaw. Alex landed on the ground, dizzy from the force of the blow. Brodie picked him up and backhanded him into the dirt again. His jaw ached, his lip split, and his nose now bled profusely. It was probably broken. Alex wiped the blood with his hand and waited for Brodie's next move.

"Iain, Braden, tie him and bring him to the hall. Struan will straighten out this mess." Brodie mounted and called out, "We ride." The clan guards surrounded the visitors, prepared to lead them to the castle.

Alex was pulled roughly to his feet by the young Iain. His hands were tied in front of him, and the rope was held by Braden. As they kicked their mounts into a trotting pace, he searched for Maggie in the bushes. He didn't see her. Good. She was safe for now if she followed his orders.

Then he was running to keep from being dragged and had no time to think at all.

She waited in the bushes until they all rode away. She had seen and heard it all and only stayed quiet by clamping her hand over her mouth. When Brodie punched Alex, she fought the impulse to go to him. Then Alex was being tied and led away. She saw him glance her way, looking for her.

Maggie knew she had to get to Moira's cave before the whole clan knew of their deception. Searching the ground for anything she had dropped, Maggie scurried out from the thicket and ran from the lake. Skirting the edge of the village to avoid being seen, she found Moira's cottage empty. She gathered a water pouch, a few oat cakes wrapped in a piece of linen, and an extra plaid and left quickly.

A few minutes later, she arrived at the cave. To her surprise, there were more supplies already inside. Moira had brought a pallet, some dried meat and hard bread. Jugs of water and cider stood in the corner. It looked as if she would be staying at the cave longer than she had thought.

She prayed Alex was still alive. Would they hang him? How would Struan react to their deception? Anice? The rest of the clan? Maybe Moira would know what was happening when she came to the cave. She didn't want to just sit there and worry. But, she had no other option. Rushing into an unknown situation at the castle might cost her and Alex their lives.

She would wait.

And worry.

The great hall filled rapidly as the wild tale spread through the clan. The reaction was always the same: one look at him, one look at the real Alex, another look at him. Men and women he had lived with for these last months glared at him now. He stood, trying not to flinch as they yelled their questions at him. He and Moira had decided long ago that it would be best not to answer questions or charges. She had seen most of this in her last vision.

Struan had not come to the hall yet. Brodie was missing, too. The real Alex sat at the high table, eating and drinking with his men. Every so often, they would glance across the room.

This was not what he expected to see in the real heir to the clan. He looked, acted, and sounded more English than Scottish. The silly clothes and hairstyle made him look more woman than man.

And being called Sandy? What the hell kind of name was that for a good Scot?

He wasn't the only one with such thoughts. He saw the expressions of those who watched the real Alex. Many emotions crossed their faces, but the most common was disgust.

They must now be realizing that this was the real Alex they remembered from those years ago. This Alex fit more with their memories: rude, overbearing, a disgraceful heir for the MacKendimens.

Loud voices came from the other end of the hall, and Alex turned to see what caused the commotion at the entranceway. Struan and Brodie, followed by Dougal and Anice, came barreling into the hall. Struan waved away those who tried to speak to him. Alex watched their progress through the crowd until they reached the steps to the dais.

Struan started up the steps, stopped, and then walked over to where Alex stood between Iain and Braden. Struan opened his mouth to say something, but then shook his head. The older man searched his face for a long minute before turning away. He climbed the steps and approached the table.

The real Alex threw aside the chicken leg that he was eating and it landed next to the table in the rushes. After wiping his hands on the table cover, he gulped down the rest of his ale. Then he stood to greet his father.

"Faither, I have come home and found things not right in the MacKendimen keep. Who is that impostor?"

Struan's reply was too low to be heard by anyone but the real Alex. Struan must have made an impression, for Sandy's face reddened and he coughed several times before saying anything more. Then the man walked to the table and gave his companions an order. They resisted at first, then complied, getting to their feet and leaving the table. When the table was empty, Struan sat in his chair and pointed to the stool next to it. Anice, pale as a ghost and shaking with each step she took, moved to her place.

Iain and Braden dragged Alex up the steps and stood with him at the end of the table, facing Struan and Anice. They held onto his arms as the real heir approached.

"I guess I can see how ye could have made the mistake. If he was cleaned up, he would resemble me." He turned to Struan. "I suppose after years apart, ye did not know what to expect."

"Why did you return now?" Struan asked heavily.

"It seems that David received a message from the MacNab, my betrothed's dear faither, offering his thanks to the king for arranging the match. The MacNab also expressed his disappointment that David would not be joining us at the wedding." The real Alex walked to Anice and touched her cheek. She flinched at his touch and he smiled at her reaction. "We did not understand how a wedding could be performed if the groom was in London and the bride was here in Dunnedin. He sent me to investigate."

"So, *Sandy*, do ye hiv proof of yer words?" Struan asked in a mocking tone. Alex could tell that Struan was already disappointed in what he found in his real son.

"Proof? Did ye ask that one for proof on his arrival? If ye had, ye could have saved the clan this humiliation." Sandy had no idea how close Struan was to laying him out in the rushes, Alex realized. "Aye, I have proof. Here," he took parchment sheets out from under his cloak and handed them to Struan, "are the letters from the MacNab and from David."

While Struan looked over the letters, Sandy reached for Anice's hand, pulled her to her feet, and forced her to walk to the end of the table where Alex stood. Alex waited to see what Sandy would do.

Poor Anice. The lass looked near to fainting. What a shock this must be to her, he thought. Looking at Sandy, he pitied the girl and what she would have to bear from this jerk.

"Tell me, Anice, did he fool ye, too?"

She trembled and stuttered, but Sandy interrupted her, dragging her forward. She stumbled at his side until Sandy stopped right in front of Alex.

"Did ye give to him what belongs to me, my dear? Will I find ye still a maiden when I take ye to bed?"

Anice gasped and struck out at his crude remarks. Her slap could be heard throughout the hall. Without hesitation, Sandy struck back at her. The force of the blow pushed her off balance, and she stumbled.

Alex couldn't stand still and watch this. He pulled his arms free of his guards' hold and grabbed at the falling Anice with his bound hands. He caught her arm before she fell off the dais. Brodie, standing at the bottom of the steps, reached them and pulled her to safety.

She started sobbing after Brodie left her side. Struan called to Firtha to take her lady to her chamber. The maid took hold of her mistress and led her away. Anice's weeping echoed through the hall.

"There wasna cause for that, Sandy."

"I but asked a simple question of her. 'Tis my right to expect a virgin as my bride, Faither. I do not want used goods in my bed or another man's leavings in her belly." Everyone who heard the accusations gasped. They may not like everything the lass did, but no one wanted to hear her slandered in this manner.

Sandy walked toward Alex again, but Iain and Braden had just regained their grip on him. One punch would do it, and he intended to get at least one good jab in before they stopped him. Alex knew an insult was coming.

"So, impostor, should I keep her? Did ye teach her anything worthwhile when ye turned her into your whore?"

Alex did the only thing he could in defense of Anice: He demonstrated his complete and utter disgust of this man. He leaned back and spit in Sandy's smug face. Cheers rippled through the assembled clan.

Then all hell broke loose.

The last thing he saw was Sandy charging at him. Iain and Braden both relaxed their hold and he got off one good swing with his bound hands before the whole group landed on the floor. After a few minutes and a few more men joined the fracas, a loud voice interrupted the fight.

"Good God, Struan, what goes here?"

Chapter 41

AMAZINGLY, EXCEPT FOR being at the bottom of the pile, he was uninjured. The fop Sandy fared far worse. He didn't remember being able to rip the fancy clothes or getting to Sandy's face other than the once. As he was pulled back to his feet, hands still tied, he saw the glances and expressions of satisfaction that were exchanged by Brodie, Iain, Braden, and a few others. They took their original positions as this newcomer entered the proceedings.

"Robbie, I didna expect to see ye so soon." Struan's voice boomed over the onlookers. Struan looked over at Alex and frowned. The other man, younger than Struan and with a full head of wild blond hair and a beard to match, limped through the hall to the dais. The MacNab! An entourage followed close at his heels, all of them glancing around the room as they walked.

"No' so soon, Struan? Come now, ye ken'd I, er . . . we, were on our way here. What is this aboot? And where is my daughter?"

An attractive woman came to the MacNab's side and

curtsied to Struan. Anice got her red hair and pretty features from her mother, Alex could see. The woman's face was a picture of worry.

Sandy recovered from his daze and Alex saw him straightening his clothes and searching in his cloak again. As he watched, Sandy walked down the steps and bowed in front of Anice's parents. He held out another parchment to the MacNab.

"I am Alesander, Laird MacNab. Since ye are so soon to be faither by marriage, ye may call me Sandy."

Everyone else saw the look of horror on the MacNab's face. Sandy continued, oblivious to all but himself, "I have just returned from the king's side in London and he bade me give this to you at our first meeting." He pointed to the parchment. "Ye may want to read that before we continue."

Alex watched the MacNab shake himself and open the parchment he held in his hand. The man's mouth dropped open wider with each sentence he read. Lady MacNab grabbed her husband's arm and tried to look at the contents, but he shook her off and finished reading it alone. Alex could just imagine what was in the letter.

"Struan, did ye read yer copy of David's message?"

"Aye, Robbie, I did."

"And what are ye planning to do aboot this mess?"

Alex saw the MacNab catch sight of him and start toward him. Sandy followed close behind. His guards tightened their grips again, expecting trouble.

"Is this the mon, the impostor?"

"Aye, Laird MacNab, this is the mon who despoiled yer daughter and tried to take my inheritance."

"Despoiled my Anice? Do ye speak truly?" The MacNab could shout even louder than Struan. Alex's ears rang from his words.

"Well, Robbie . . ." Sandy changed his address at the MacNab's glare. "I mean, Laird MacNab. He has been living my life here for many weeks . . ."

''And, because, 'tis yer habit to ruin the innocent, ye supposed 'tis his, too?''

Sandy sputtered and tried to make a response, but the MacNab turned his attention to Alex. He walked closer and stared hard at Alex squarely in the eye.

''Did ye? Did ye take my daughter's innocence when it didna belong to ye?'' The MacNab's voice, low and full of malice, was meant only for his ears. Even the jerk, blocked by the MacNab's body, strained to listen.

He could have stayed silent, since that was the plan. But he'd never wanted to hurt Anice and letting this slander go on, letting her parents believe the worst, would devastate her and her reputation. If there was a way out of this for her, he had to protect her name.

''Nay, Laird MacNab, if yer daughter was an innocent when I came here, she was no' ruined by me.''

He waited for a reaction. Alex saw a flash of surprise mixed with respect in the man's face. Anice's father turned his back on Alex and walked back to where Struan stood.

When Alex met Struan's eyes, he saw a jumble of anger, admiration, and confusion in the old man's eyes. He'd surprised Struan by answering this question when he had answered no others.

''Robbie,'' Struan said, ''let Siusan go to Anice. The lass surely needs her maither's comfort. She waits in her chamber.'' Anice's mother followed a woman out of the hall. ''Robbie, come to my chambers, we will hiv privacy for the rest of this.'' The MacNab nodded.

Struan wasn't done yet. He walked toward Alex and Sandy. He ordered another chamber prepared and told another servant to escort Sandy there.

''Sandy, stay in that room until I summon ye.''

''Faither, why should I be punished when . . .''

''Ye heard me, stay in that room.'' Struan's voice made the rafters shake and the clan hold their breath. Alex waited for his next move.

"Brodie, put . . . this mon in the dungeon until I am ready for him."

Alex was not surprised at all; he expected it. Brodie stepped forward and took hold of the rope that tied his hands. He wrapped the length around his hand several times and then tugged hard until Alex moved with him. They moved through the rest of the hall in silence. Alex didn't resist.

As they walked through the doorway leading to the entrance of the dungeon, Alex heard Struan give one more order, one that filled him with terror.

"Find his woman, and bring her to me."

He prayed to God that Maggie had made it to the hiding place. He was glad he didn't know where that safe place was. If he didn't know, then he couldn't tell . . . no matter what they used against his resolve.

They walked down the narrow stairway, down into the lowest level of the castle. Alex felt the dampness grow with each step. The small group reached the bottom floor, and Brodie banged on the door in front of them. If the guard was surprised at the sight before him, his expression didn't show it. He swung the door open and stepped back out of their way. Brodie grabbed a torch from a sconce on the wall as they moved inside.

Brodie tugged on the rope, and they walked deeper into the dungeon, with only the small flame to light their way. Alex heard the scurrying noises made by mice and other scavengers in the darkness. He tried to see ahead of them but could not glimpse anything past Brodie's bulk. Looking to the sides, he saw small cells on each side of the corridor. Most were empty, but a few held prisoners. The light of an occasional torch showed them to be wet and cramped spaces with nothing to sit or lie on but the packed dirt floor. He choked on the horrible odors that escaped from each one.

So, this is where he would wait. He hoped again that Maggie was safe. He could not see her staying in one of these hellish places. They still walked on, past all of these open rooms to the end of the corridor. Iain then grabbed Brodie by the arm and pulled him to a stop.

''Brodie? He canna be put here.'' Iain was furious at whatever Brodie planned to do. ''Struan didna give that order.''

''Haud yer wheest, Iain. He will go where I put him. If ye disagree, go to Struan and ask him.''

Where was Brodie putting him? Could it be worse than what they had already passed? Alex swallowed deeply. Oh, God, what was in store for him?

Brodie opened a door and pulled him inside. He remembered his resolve not to fight, not to instigate another beating or punishment. He had to be alive to get back home, and he would use his head and not his fists.

The room they entered was much bigger than the others on the corridor. And, it was dry! It was also private; the small opening on the door with iron bars across it was the only way to see into the room. A small cot stood by one wall, a table and chair on another. A bucket to be used as a necessary sat in one corner. This must be a place where the clan held important prisoners or hostages. He wheeled around and looked at Brodie. Brodie had brought him here?

''Why?'' he asked.

''I ask the same of ye: Why?'' Brodie threw it back to Alex.

''I canna say,'' Alex answered. He regretted not being able to tell Brodie the truth. He just could not.

''So, be it. Ye will stay here until Struan calls for ye.''

Iain interrupted. ''Brodie, 'tis no' right, him staying in here. No' after what he haes done.''

Alex had misread the situation: Brodie wanted him here, young Iain wanted him in a regular cell. Brodie untied Alex's hands wordlessly and then turned to face the younger soldier.

''Think on it, Iain. What haes he done? 'Twill be easy

enough to move him to another cell for torture. I will inform Struan and await his orders on it."

Alex saw Iain swallow several times at the mention of torture. If he didn't know better, he would swear that Brodie was teasing Iain. The men left, and Alex heard the key turn in the lock. Without the torch, the room fell into complete darkness. Alex stumbled to the bed and collapsed on it. He needed to rest, to regain his strength before he was called to Struan.

He could not fight sleep when it came to claim him. It had been a helluva day. He laughed humorlessly as he drifted into oblivion.

It was late that night when Maggie heard the approach of footsteps outside the cave. She hadn't dared light a fire, so she sat in the dark waiting as the noise came closer and closer.

This was not the first time today that someone came near. Earlier, a crowd passed by, shouting and yelling, searching for the Sassenach whore. She still sat in the darkest corner of the cavern, next to the table and behind Moira's trunk, unable to move for fear of discovery. So far, she was safe.

This time, the person or people outside came nearer. And nearer still. Maggie forced herself to breathe slowly and quietly so she would not be detected by sounds. The branch and twig covering was pulled away, and someone entered. Maggie still waited.

"Maggie? Lass, are ye here?"

"Moira," she cried in relief, "you finally came."

Maggie crawled out of her corner, slowly, because her legs would not move. After hours of sitting curled up, she was stiff and her legs numb. She endured the stinging sensations as the circulation returned to her limbs.

"I canna light a fire for ye or stay long, Maggie. Struan still searches for ye. Others may pass close by here, looking for ye."

"Others have already, Moira, a number of times earlier today. What's happening out there?" Maggie felt her way to the table and sat on the bench. Moira joined her.

"Alex is in the dungeon awaiting Struan's judgment. The real Alex now calls himself Sandy." Moira snorted in disgust. "And he is confined to a chamber."

"Is Alex okay? I mean, is he hurt?" She worried that he would be beaten more once they took him to the castle.

"He fares weel enough. And, Anice's parents hiv arrived."

"Could things get any worse?" She really didn't want an answer, she feared what the answer would be.

"No' much more than this. I got yer belongings from Torra's house and brought them to ye." Moira placed the canvas sack on Maggie's lap. "No one saw me, so it will look as though ye fled the village."

"Thank you for all this. What's next?"

"The waiting."

"What are we waiting for? Will Alex be hanged?"

"We wait for the moon to reach its fullness in just over twa more days. I believe the arch's power will be strongest then."

"Do you think we can return home? Have we done what we were sent to do?"

Moira took her hand and patted it. "I believe that ye hiv, Maggie. The rest is up to Alex. Yer safe return is on his shoulders."

"And there's nothing I can do to help?"

"Ye hiv done what ye could do, lass. Ye hiv offered yer heart to Alex. If he doesna accept yer love and return it, ye are lost."

"Love? You think this is about love?"

" 'Tis for him."

"Moira, does he love me? Do you know?"

"It doesna matter if I ken, he maun recognize that his love for ye is more important than anything else."

"But, Moira, we only just started to feel this way about

each other, it isn't fair to expect him to be completely selfless about his own needs.''

''Fair? This is no' aboot fair. This is aboot the fates teaching him a lesson. He learns or he dies.''

''Will I . . . die?''

''I dinna think so, no' if ye stay here until the full moon. If he learns by then, the fates may let ye pass through the arch and back to yer own time and place.''

''And if he doesn't?''

Maggie's throat choked with tension as she forced out the words. What would happen to them? Would Alex be dead? Tears filled her eyes and her chest tightened. How could she go on if he were dead?

''Weel, lass, we will all learn what fate haes in store for us in the next few days.'' Moira rose and took Maggie with her by pulling her hand. ''Get some rest and dinna leave this place for anything, anyone. I will return tomorrow evening to ye.''

''Wait, Moira. Before you go, I wanted to ask about Rachelle. Is she well yet?''

''She grows stronger wi' each day.''

''Make sure she takes that medicine. If she stops too soon, it may not work.'' Maggie hoped that the antibiotics were more potent in her system because Rachelle had never used them before.

''I will. Now, I hiv to go.''

Maggie listened in the darkness as Moira moved the camouflage and left the cave. A bit more rustling, and the entrance was covered again.

Feeling the way around the table, Maggie found the pallet, rolled up and tied, on the other side of the table. Untying the bindings, she spread out the thin mattress. She picked up one of the lengths of plaid and wrapped it around her body to keep out the chill.

Maggie laid down on the bedding and thought of Alex. Was he hurt? She had seen Brodie punch him before they tied him up and dragged him to the castle. He was in the dungeon. She had never seen the place itself. Just the entrance to it was scary enough to keep her away from it.

More importantly, would Struan really hang him? She thought that Struan genuinely liked the man he thought was his son. But he was probably furious at the deception. Struan had to uphold the clan's honor, and that meant taking harsh retribution against anyone who threatened the clan's safety, prosperity, or reputation. And that meant her and Alex.

Maggie rolled to her side and tried to settle her thoughts. She needed to rest for the coming days. Oh, God, please keep him safe. Please. Please. Alex had to be safe.

Chapter 42

THE COMMOTION OUTSIDE his room woke him. He sat up and rubbed his eyes. The light of many torches invaded the darkness through the space below the door and the sound of many voices prepared him for company. He couldn't tell if it was day or night in the dungeon.

The door flung open and hit the wall behind it. Alex's eyes teared at the light after so long without it. Of all those he expected to come here, this one surprised him. Sandy, accompanied by two of his cronies, came into the room.

"This is where they hold ye? It looks too comfortable for a traitor and a spy. What do you think, Charles, Garrick?"

"Oh, I must agree with you, Sandy."

"Absolutely right."

"I think that a spy and usurper should suffer for his crime."

Alex's gaze never left the face of his true adversary. Sandy was looking for a fight, but three on one did not seem quite fair. He stood and took a position opposite where they stood.

"And, as his intended victim, good friends, I think I should deliver justice."

Alex sized up his opponents and watched for a chance to get out of the room. Unfortunately, they read his intentions and blocked the door with their bodies. He waited for their attack. It was not long in coming.

The three pounced on him and fought him to the ground. While the two others held him down, Sandy pulled out a length of rope and tied Alex's hands behind his back. Then he tied his ankles together and connected the bindings so that Alex felt like a trussed animal.

They didn't stop there, and he was soon on the edge of consciousness from their beating. He blacked out, for how long he couldn't tell. When he came to awareness, he thought he saw Anice's face peek through the open door into the room. *It couldn't be,* he told himself. The doors were always locked in the dungeon, and Anice would never set foot in a place like this.

It could not be.

Anice could not believe what she saw in the dungeon. Sandy had tied Alex up and beaten him mercilessly until he lost consciousness. Her stomach lurched as she pictured the scene again in her mind. Alex's blood pouring from his nose and mouth. The two large brutes standing over him, kicking him in the ribs and stomach. She began to gag but fought the urge to retch.

She now stood before Struan's chamber and wondered how to tell him about Sandy's actions in the dungeon. What could she say?

She smoothed her hair back from her face and took a deep breath. The laird and her father would both be furious to discover that she had gone to the dungeon in the first place. Would Struan even care that the man had been beaten? That fear drove her back to her chamber's door.

She shouldn't be concerned about the impostor held prisoner below. He had deceived the clan and he had fooled her into believing that he was Alex MacKendimen, the real Alex who left with the king five years ago.

She thought back to that time when she was still a girl and he was a younger man. Shaking her head, she remembered hoping that he would turn into her gallant knight when he grew up. They would live happily ever after and rule over the Clan MacKendimen together.

Now, it was obvious that he had spent either not enough or too much time with David in London. All the cruelties and coarseness she recalled were now even more pronounced. The impostor never spoke to her as Sandy had in the hall. Her face flamed as she thought of Sandy's accusation of being a whore in front of Struan and the gathered clan. The impostor had never beaten her, even when she had given him provocation. The man called Alex treated her with respect and mayhap a bit of affection. She had never seen him abuse anyone or anything while he was here.

Alex had also stopped her when she offered herself to him that night in his room. He had tried to protect her then, protect her from herself and her own foolish actions. And she had repaid him by beating the woman he brought with him.

Maggie? Where was she? Was she really his leman? Did they both come from England? Or were they sent by the damned MacArthurs as her father had suggested to Struan? If he was sent to take her as bride and claim her dowry of land on their behalf, the MacArthurs stood to gain much. And the wedge they drove between the MacNabs and the MacKendimens would be even more powerful than the land they claimed.

She leaned against the stone wall and shook her head. Nay, this man had rejoiced when the wedding was delayed. If he was part of a plot, he would have come here and married her quickly, without delay. This made no sense.

Well, while she stood here and tried to figure this out,

he was lying on the dungeon floor, beaten and bloodied. He had defended her yesterday when Sandy asked his crude questions. She knew his hands, bound as they were, had kept her from falling when Sandy slapped her. She owed him at least a kindness in return. She would tell Struan and let him decide what to do. She walked directly to Struan's door and knocked loudly on it.

"Laird Struan, may I have a word with you?"

The door opened quickly and she saw a shocked look on the laird's face.

"Anice, come in. Yer faither will be here shortly. Do ye wish to wait for him?"

"Nay, Struan, I dinna think waiting will help."

He offered her a cup of cider and a stool, but she refused both. Her stomach still clenched tightly with the news she carried.

"Laird, I was down to the dungeon and . . ."

"Down to the dungeon, Anice? Is that such a good thing for my betrothed to be doing?" The voice came out of the shadows at the other end of Struan's chamber. She had not seen him there!

"Sandy! I beg yer pardon, I didna see ye there."

"Obviously. But, pray, continue with your news of the dungeon."

She could not let him know that she had seen the beating. In an instant, she realized that the next one beaten would be her. She might be safe if she did not reveal all that she knew about Alex's treatment in the dungeon.

"Struan, I know that I shouldn't see him, but I had questions to ask of . . . the prisoner. I went there a short time ago and found him in his cell . . ."

"Of course, he's in a cell, my dear, he is a traitor and a *spy.*" Sandy's emphasis on the last word sent a shiver of fear through her tense body.

He knew! He must have seen her there or leaving.

"What I mean is . . . he has been tied and beaten, Struan. I didn't know you had ordered it."

"I didna! When did you see him?" Struan strode to the door and flung it open. His voice reverberated down the hall as he barked out names

Within seconds, the room was jammed with people, all awaiting the laird's orders. Someone was sent for the healer, and the rest of the retinue followed Struan's long, fast steps down to the hall, then down to the dungeon. The guard was nowhere to be found. The corridor of cells was overflowing with torches.

Struan reached the end room first and stopped in his tracks. Anice bumped into the back of him and others into her. She heard his indrawn breath and his whispered "Alex."

"Get back, all of you!" he yelled.

She jumped from the loudness of his command. She would stay, she decided, and took a few steps back into the same alcove where she had hidden earlier.

"Tell Jean to bring hot water and bandages from the kitchen."

"Aye, Struan," came the reply from those closer to the stairs.

Struan took a step into the room, toward Alex, when Sandy's voice stopped him.

"Faither, your concern for this mon 'tis unseemly. So what if a prisoner is beaten before going to the gallows? His pain will end soon enough."

Sandy stood next to her now, his leg and elbow purposely rubbing against her body. She leaned as far away as she could to escape his touch.

"Gallows? Ye hiv decided to hang him then, Struan?" The question was out before she could stop it.

"Of course he will be hanged, my dear. The clan's honor demands nothing less." The son answered for his father.

Struan walked up to Sandy, as close as he could get to the man. She strained to hear his words.

"I will decide his fate, Sandy, not ye."

"I would never think to interfere with your justice, Faither. As long as he pays for what he did to this clan's honor, to mine, and, of course, to my betrothed's, I care not what happens to him." She looked at his face and saw he wore a disinterested expression, but his eyes gleamed with hatred.

"Good. Ye hiv been away for a long time and hiv much to learn afore ye take my place as laird. Now, go from here and await me in the hall."

Sandy made a bow to Struan and held out his hand to her.

"Come, dear Anice. Let us spend some time together and reacquaint ourselves. Our marriage day is fast approaching."

Anice tried not to let her fear show through. Struan took one look at her and his eyes widened.

"Stay in the hall, Sandy. I will hiv need of ye both shortly."

"Of course, Faither."

She let him lead her from the dungeon without comment or incident. She would be courteous and attentive, as her mother had trained her to be. Sandy would not find fault with her wifely abilities or training in the ways of the English court.

As she thought about the look in his eyes, Anice knew it might be the death of her if she ever revealed the person behind the beating. Now that Alex would be tended to, she had to look out for herself.

"Weel, Moira, will I survive?" He cleared his throat but didn't put much force behind for fear of coughing.

"Yer beating? Oh, aye, ye will survive it. The bruises look worse than they are, and the bleeding has all but stopped from yer torn cheek and nose. Ye are lucky that none of yer ribs broke. I hiv bound them tightly. They will feel better soon."

"Will I survive my trip to the Clan MacKendimen?"

He probably should not force the issue with her.

"I canna see that, Alex. Many of things but no' that."

"Why did Struan send for ye, if he plans to hang me?"

"Struan is verra confused now. His feelings for ye and his feelings for his son are twisted together, and he doesna ken what to do. He haes listened to Sandy." She snorted after she said his name and Alex wanted to laugh. The bindings around his chest stopped him. "He haes listened to his kith and kin and e'en the MacNab. His first instinct was to hang ye, right away. He was more angry than I hiv ever seen him to be."

"What stopped him, do ye think?" Alex had his own suspicion.

"Between ye and me? I think that Struan likes ye and the Alex ye are better than the real one who haes returned."

"Ye think so?" Alex shifted on the narrow cot and held his side. He wanted to sit up, but the binding made getting up very difficult.

"I do. Ye were a good Alex for the clan. Unfortunately for us, ye are no' the real one."

"And that . . . fop is?"

"He is the heir to Struan. When ye are gone and Struan is dead . . . Weel, dinna worry, the clan haes survived other, worse lairds."

"There is something that does worry me, Moira." He reached out to her and she pulled him up to his feet. Ah, better, much better, he thought.

"I ken what ye will say, Alex. Ye hiv found a soft spot in yer heart for Anice, hiv ye no'?"

"Aye. The thought of that innocent being in the power of that slime is too much to bear. Do ye think we could try to take her wi' us when we try the arch?" He practiced taking deeper breaths. Standing up was a definite improvement over lying down.

"Nay, Alex. Anice's place and future is wi' the clan. She canna leave."

" 'Twas just a thought."

"She will make her way here fine after ye are gone. She haes grit. It will be difficult for her at times, but whose life isna?"

"Maggie. Ye hiv no' said a word aboot Maggie."

"She is safe and hiding. She isna a verra patient one, I will say that aboot her."

"I hiv to agree wi' ye, Moira. Maggie canna stand a slow pace. Ye hiv my thanks for keeping her safe." He watched Moira gather her bandages and medicaments into a large basket. "There is one more request I would make of ye."

Moira stood and looked at him, waiting. This one request was harder to make than he first thought it would be. Moira had given him no indication of how things would turn out. She insisted she didn't know, but he thought otherwise. If he was not able to escape the gallows, he wanted to make sure that Maggie would be safe.

"If I canna get out of this mess, can ye get Maggie to the arch and make her try it alone?"

"Alone?"

"Aye, alone. I will go to my death easier if I ken that she will at least try to get home. And, if she canna, will ye find her a safe place to live? Watch over her for me?"

" 'Tis important to ye?" She looked him straight in the eyes as she asked. He felt as if she was looking into his heart, his soul.

"Verra. I may no' get a chance to try it, but she maun."

"I will try to convince her, Alex." She walked to the door and called out to the guard.

"It bothers me to ken that I canna protect the woman I love. That I maun ask others to do it for me."

Moira gifted him with a bright smile that didn't match the situation or the atmosphere. " 'Tis what friends are for, Alex. I will do what I can." To the guard, she said, "Send word to the laird that I am done here. He wishes to speak to the prisoner."

"How much can I tell Struan? I dread lying to the mon."

"Tell him the truth of it when ye can. But, 'tis most important that ye no' reveal the truth of who ye really are or how ye came to be here."

Moira left the room, following the guard down the hall. He walked to the chair and straddled it, easing down onto the seat. Struan would waste no time in coming to him now that he was awake and his injuries were treated.

He didn't wait long. He heard Struan's voice giving orders to the guard. He began to stand as he heard the key turn in the lock.

"Ye may stay sitting down."

"Thank ye. It feels better to sit for now."

Tension filled the small room as they faced each other across it. Alex waited. Struan should have the first word.

"Who are ye?"

"I am Alex MacKendimen."

"There is only one Alesander MacKendimen in this clan, and he sits above us in the hall. Are ye a bastard that I didna ken? Who is yer mother? Where does she live?" Struan barked out the questions without pause.

"I can only tell ye that my name is Alex MacKendimen and that we are kinsmen." *Distant relations and dozens of generations apart,* he didn't add.

"Leave that for now. Why are ye here?"

"I canna say."

Alex watched the frustration grow on the man's face. He wished he could settle the confusion, but he had no choice. His truth must remain unspoken.

"Are ye a spy for the MacArthurs? Do ye plot wi' them to take Anice and her dowry from my son?"

"Nay, Struan, I wasna sent by the MacArthurs."

"Who then? Who sent ye?" Struan stalked across the room and stood in front of him.

"I canna say."

Regret at this avoidance of satisfying Struan's need to know tore at his heart. He had grown to like Struan. He respected him. He hated doing this to him.

"Canna? Or willna?" the man shouted.

Alex didn't insult him with an answer.

He watched the laird walk to the door and lean against it, looking out the small, barred opening.

"Who beat ye this morn?"

He wanted to charge the guilty one, but he held his tongue. Sandy would be here after Alex was gone and could cause much trouble for both Struan and Anice. He ignored the question, and asked one of his own.

"Will Anice be safe wi' Sandy?"

"Safe enough." Struan turned back to look at him, and they shared a moment of common disbelief.

"Try to keep her safe from his abuse, Struan. She is an innocent and doesna deserve what he brings to their marriage."

"I will do everything in my power to keep her safe, Alex." Struan frowned. "Ye didna bed her as I suggested. Why no'?"

"She is but fifteen years and wasna meant for me. And, there was Maggie to consider."

"Do ye ken where she is?"

"Maggie?"

Struan nodded.

"Nay, she disappeared when yer son returned and found us at the loch," Alex answered truthfully.

"So ye did disobey my orders and meet wi' her?" Alex could swear Struan's voice lightened a bit.

"Aye, sir, I did."

"Weel, I hope she is safe and long gone from here. Sandy speaks of finding her and using her to get the truth from ye." Alex started to stand, he had to . . .

"Nay, Alex, dinna fret. I do no' hold wi' using women as weapons. The lass never hurt anyone here, and I ended the search for her just after I ordered it."

"Thank ye for that, Struan. She means ye no harm."

"Ye ken what they are demanding for ye?"

Alex nodded. Again he asked rather than answered. "Are ye going to hang me then?"

"If it were just me, I wouldna. But 'tis the clan's honor at stake here. I maun uphold that or I am nothing. Not fit to lead or serve."

"I understaun, Struan."

"And ye willna answer my questions. Give me something to pacify yer accusers?"

"Nay, Struan, I canna. I am sorry."

"Nay, lad, I am sorry. I hiv come to like ye and regret sending ye to yer death wi'oot understauning the why of it."

Struan walked to the door and called for the guard. Alex stood to face the laird one more time.

"If ye change yer mind after ye think on it, tell the guard to come to me. If ye do not, ye will hang tomorrow at noon."

Alex fought the urge to scream out the truth. He didn't want to act the brave warrior in this fantasy come to life. Maybe Moira was wrong. Maybe Struan would understand about the arch. Maybe he would let Maggie come to him and help them to get home.

Moira had not been wrong yet in her knowledge, her wisdom. If he didn't follow her instructions, he feared being trapped in this time and place. He would risk it if he was alone, but there was Maggie to consider.

In the end, he just shook his head at Struan and watched as the MacKendimen left his cell.

Chapter 43

"COME NOW, ANGUS, open the lad's door. I canna carry the torch and open it, too."

"Brodie, are ye sure the laird said this was permitted?"

Brodie softened his voice in speaking to the guard. "Angus, the mon dies on the morrow. Would ye deny him his last good meal and a bit of comfort on his last night in the world?"

Maggie kept her head tilted down so that the hood of her cape hid her face. She held her breath as Brodie convinced the guard to let them enter Alex's room. She spied the opening in the door and fought the urge to peek inside. No, let Brodie get us in. He promised it would work, so she waited. Before the guard answered, she heard Alex moving around the room.

"Let me get him settled inside and then I brought a flask of something verra good for us to share while we wait."

The guard paused, apparently weighing his choices. "Who is it that ye bring to him? Why is she covered?"

" 'Tis Robena, from the village. Angus, ye ken how

Lady Anice feels aboot whores being in the keep. I haid to hide her face to get her past wi'oot trouble.''

The two men laughed loud and long while Maggie waited. The tray of food she carried was heavy. The dirk fastened to the bottom of the tray added to its weight. Maggie shifted her hold on her burden. The men finally noticed.

''Weel, Brodie, she can pass inside, but ye maun stay wi' me.'' Angus took a step closer to her. ''And, I maun search the lass for weapons.''

Oh, God!

''Go ahead, Angus. Ye may find something, but it willna be a weapon.''

Brodie did as he must and so would she. Brodie stuck the torch in the wall and took the tray from her. The guard approached her from behind and put his huge arms and beefy hands around her. He took a breast in each hand and squeezed them.

Maggie forced a giggle to come out, she was supposed to be the village whore who was used to being mauled by these men. She relaxed her body, not fighting or resisting his caresses. He rubbed his body against hers as his hands fondled her.

''No weapons there, Brodie. Now,'' he slid his hands down past her hips, one in front, one in back, ''what aboot here?'' He pushed his hands between her legs and rubbed there. She made herself think of Alex and why she was here. The groping, done through several layers of clothing, was over quickly.

''She can go in now, Brodie. Mayhap I can get a taste of her when she's done wi' the prisoner?'' Angus was practically drooling with lust now—she heard it in his voice and felt him panting behind her.

''Weel, let's see if she can still walk when he gets done wi' her.''

''Aye, I get yer meaning. If 'twas my last night, I would make sure I worked her for all her worth.'' The guard moved to the door and turned the key. ''Come, Brodie and wait wi' me at the door. Bring yer flask.''

Maggie started toward the door when Angus stopped her with a hand on her shoulder. She paused but didn't turn around.

''And try to save a bit for old Angus, would ye, lass? I hiv a penny or twa to spare.''

Brodie grabbed her and shoved her into the room. He pulled the door closed, and Angus removed the key. She looked through the window as Brodie threw his arm around Angus's shoulder and led him back down the corridor.

''Nay, Angus, ye willna pay for her. I hiv paid her for the whole night. It matters no' how many of us take her in that time.'' Their laughter echoed down the passageway.

Still holding the tray, she turned to face Alex.

''Robena, is it? Weel, lass, come and make my last night worthwhile.''

Maggie put the tray down on the small table, pushed back the hood, and got her first good look at Alex since he'd been taken prisoner. His jaw was swollen and his lips and nose bruised and cut. Moira told her she shaved his beard to treat the cuts, so she was prepared to see his face clean-shaven again. He wore his plaid wrapped only around his waist so the bandages around his ribs were visible.

She walked slowly to him. She saw his smile as she came closer, step by step.

''You don't look like a man who could survive a night with the village whore.''

''Nay, but I wouldna mind dying in the trying.'' He laughed and pulled her into his embrace. She tried to be careful of his injuries, but he wouldn't let her. He held her tighter and tighter against his chest. ''Ah, Maggie, I think ye were right aboot Brodie being a true friend.''

''Enough about Brodie, I came for you.''

"I still canna believe my eyes, Maggie. When I heard ye both out there, I nearly died from shock. I canna tell ye how good it feels to hiv ye in my arms again."

"Was it bad? When they captured you?"

He stood holding her for a few moments in silence. She eased her hold on his chest.

"Nay, no' too bad."

"Who did this to you? Moira would not say."

"*Sandy* and his cronies. The heir felt much put upon and took it out on me."

"I was shocked to see what he looks like and how he acts, Alex. He is not what I expected at all."

"He was a bit of a surprise. The clan is in a state of shock, I think. If ye haid seen the look on Anice's faither's face when Sandy introduced himself, ye would hiv laughed yerself silly. It made this almost worth it."

"Anice. I forgot about her. How is she doing with all this?"

"Weel, I'm afraid Anice is in o'er her head wi' no escape. The plans for the wedding are in place. Now that the MacNab has arrived, they'll be married." He paused then added, "after my execution that is."

"I just can't believe that this is really happening, Alex. Do you see any way out of this at all?"

"Our only chance is to get to the arch once the moon is full. Moira tells me that happens just afore dawn tomorrow."

"But the moon won't rise until after midnight tomorrow night, Alex."

"It will reach the full phase sooner than that. Moira tells me that's all we need. Don't ye remember? We came through in the daylight. There's a chance for us if we can reach the arch."

Alex pulled away and peeked under the covered tray. He inhaled over the bowls of food.

"Are you hungry? Have they fed you?"

"I am hungry now. They gave me a bowl of porridge

and a chunk of bread this morn, but I couldna eat it.'' He pointed at the food. ''Will ye join me?''

''Can you eat all tied up like that?''

''The bandages actually feel good.''

He sat in the chair and tasted the stew. Then he drank some of the ale. Maggie watched as he methodically went from bowl to bowl finishing all of the food she brought. There was something of the old Alex still inside. In a few minutes, the tray was empty.

''How long can ye stay?'' He wiped his mouth, wincing when he rubbed too hard on the bruises.

''Brodie said we have about an hour.''

''We need to talk, Maggie.''

She walked to the cot and sat down on it. And waited.

''If I canna avoid this . . .''

''Alex, I came to see you so we could think of a way for you to escape.'' She went over and picked up the tray. Turning it over, she removed the dirk and handed it to him. ''See, now you have a weapon.''

He couldn't talk about not making it. That meant he would die. She couldn't accept that, and neither should he. Tears clouded her vision of him. She swiped at her eyes. Damn it, she never cried before she came to Scotland, and now that was all she ever did.

''Maggie, the dirk may help, but it willna hold off the entire Clan MacKendimen. Give me yer hand.'' She held out her hand, and he clasped it in his. ''Ye maun give me yer word that ye will get to the arch tomorrow.'' He stood, still holding her hand.

''We will find a way to the arch together, Alex. Together.'' She refused to consider any other option. *They* had to go through together.

''Give me yer word that ye will try it tomorrow, wi' or wi'oot me. Ye word, lass.''

She shook her head in refusal.

''Maggie, make this easier on me, I beg ye. I maun ken that ye will try it. Moira haes promised to find ye a safe place to live if the arch doesna take ye back."

"What? What do you mean a safe place?" Her mind would not allow her to think about his not going with her.

"If they hang me, someone here and now needs to help ye. Moira has kin in another village a few days from here. Ye will be safe."

"Alex, please, I don't want to think about you dying. I love you. I couldn't live here without you." She realized what she had revealed. She looked into his eyes and saw her love reflected back at her.

"Maggie, how do ye think it feels to ken that I may no' be here to protect the woman I love in these dangerous times? It grieves me to ken that ye will hiv to make it on yer own."

"The woman you love?"

"Aye, Maggie. I hiv come to love you as I hiv no other afore ye. 'Tis a shame that love haes come to me, to us, at a time when I may no' live to enjoy it."

She had waited to learn the depth of his feelings, and joy warred with sadness that it had to be at this moment, when the future seemed so ominous. She reached up and cradled his face in her hands. Drawing him down to her, she whispered, "And, I love you, Alex MacKendimen. No matter what happens, no matter how or when we are separated, you will always have my love with you."

Maggie reached up and touched her lips to his. He opened to her and her tongue slipped into his mouth, tasting and dancing with his. She leaned against his body, feeling his hardness against her. He tangled his fingers in her curls and held her head still, turning his face and kissing her mouth, her cheeks, her eyes, her forehead. He stopped and rested his chin on her head.

"This is a fine mess we've gotten ourselves into this time, Maggie." He did a great imitation of the Laurel and Hardy line.

"I never got into trouble at all at home, Alex. I was a normal, run-of-the-mill elementary schoolteacher who did normal, everyday things. You must be the bad influence.''

''*Me?* A bad influence? I protest. I was just a law-abiding accountant bringing an elderly aunt to a family reunion. How could I ken the trouble that awaited me here in Scotland?''

''Will we get back, Alex? To our time?'' She needed something to hang her hopes on.

''I hope so, lass, I hope so.''

''Ye canna be a MacKendimen, Alex. A real MacKendimen would've had the lass naked under ye by now.'' Brodie spoke through the grating to them.

''But, Brodie, I am a MacKendimen. I've haid her naked, under me, and dressed again!''

Maggie watched as Brodie entered and Alex offered his hand to the other man. They clasped arms and then hugged.

''I thank ye for bringing her to me. I ken the difficulty and the risk to yerself.''

''I owed her a debt.'' Then he looked at her. ''Ye maun come wi' me now, lass. The festivities in the hall are breaking up, and I fear someone may come down.''

''Brodie, why don't you just knock out Angus and bring Alex out with us now?'' She turned to Alex. ''Hurry, get dressed. Come with us.''

Brodie was strangely silent at her suggestion. His face had turned to stone before her eyes. But, it was Alex who answered.

''Brodie haes been seen by others who will ken his involvement in any escape, Maggie. I canna jeopardize his life and his future wi' the clan. He would be outlawed by the clan and his life would be anyone's to take.''

She looked to Brodie for confirmation of this. He wouldn't meet her eyes but nodded his head in acknowledgment.

''Bringing ye here was one thing, helping me escape

the clan is another matter and no' one he can be part of,'' Alex added.

''I didn't understand, Alex. I was only thinking of you and saving your life.''

It would not be right to place Brodie at risk in order to save Alex. Easier for her, safer, but not right.

''Well, I guess I'd better go with him then.''

She ran to him and he kissed her over and over again. She was determined not to make a scene, not to cry, not to argue. Maggie put her cloak back on and pulled the hood forward, over most of her face. Brodie stepped away from the door, and she walked into the hallway. She had to force her feet to move away from the man she loved.

''Good-bye, Alex. Remember that I love you.''

''Maggie, ye remember, too. I love ye.''

Brodie pulled the door closed and turned the key in the lock. He leaned closer to the grating and whispered something to Alex. Maggie caught a word or two: ''prepared . . . ready.'' What did it mean?

She was not given a chance to ask, for Brodie took her by the elbow and propelled her to the stairway, past the drugged guard, up the steps, and out through a side door. She followed his lead and kept her head lowered again. In a few minutes, they had left the castle and were in the woods nearby.

''Can ye make it back to the cave, Maggie?''

''Yes, Brodie, I know the way.''

''Then go there now and tell Moira, when she comes, that all is ready.''

''What do you mean? What's ready?''

''I canna say. 'Tis for her to tell ye. Go now and be quick aboot reaching the cave.''

''I will, Brodie. Thank you for bringing me to Alex.'' Maggie stood on her toes and kissed his cheek.

''Aye, lass, I could do no less for the woman who saved my Rachelle's life. Now, run.''

She did.

Chapter 44

THE SCAFFOLDING WAS a horrible sight, with its noose swaying in the breeze—a frightening imitation of the Hangman game she played as a child. There would be no amusement with this structure. Clouds covered the sun, and a cold wind blew through the courtyard. Only lightning and thunder could add more gravity to this scene.

Maggie held tightly to the edge of her cloak. No one must see her here. She didn't even know why she came except to prove to herself yet again that this was not a dream—a nightmare but no dream. The area was empty still, with time left before the execution. She reviewed Moira's scheme in her head another time. If everything went as planned, she and Alex would get their chance to try the arch today. If something went awry, either one of them or both could end up dead.

The wind tore down the pathway between buildings and threatened to pull the hood from her head. She adjusted her backpack and made her way to the alcove that Moira told her would be a safe place. Moira insisted that she not be in the courtyard when Alex was brought to the platform. She expressed the fear that Maggie would freeze and not be able to carry out the plan. Maggie agreed silently with Moira's assessment. And nothing, *nothing*, was worth risking the plan to save Alex.

Soon, people began to gather in the area, young and old, men and women. They came to witness clan justice. Most knew all the details of the story—it was impossible to keep anything secret within this extended yet close-knit family. The impostor would hang today. The man they thought they knew, the man who trained with them, ate and drank with them, was an impostor. And, if the tales were true, a spy for the damned MacArthurs.

Maggie heard the questions and the suspicions as she meandered out of the courtyard and toward the arch. Would they really support the decision to hang Alex? She could not believe that those who grew close to him during his time with the clan would call for his death. But, she had never seen Highland justice in action. And, if all went well today, she never would.

After walking toward the construction area outside the wall for a few minutes, she felt the telltale vibrations. She was near the arch, the noise grew in her head and pulsed through her body. It felt different to her today, not stronger, not louder, just different. She stood across from it and stared at it. Would it work? Would they get the chance to try it?

Her stomach clenched in fear.

The night they first found the arch again flashed into her thoughts. It took days to recover from the backlash effect it had on her. If they didn't travel back to their time, she would be a liability to Alex, trapped here in this time and unable to help in their escape.

''Please, God'' became her mantra.

The sounds from the courtyard grew louder and more boisterous. The clan was gathering. They would have but one chance today.

One chance.

Please God, please God . . .

For one more moment before leaving on her mission, Moira paused before her hearth and gazed at the fire. The wisdom called to her, not from the flames but from the arch. The call was different with each, and she knew it would become stronger and stronger. Her plan must be carried out if Alex and Maggie were to return to their place and time.

After Alex's admission to her and to Maggie, Moira felt deep within her soul that the fates would smile on them this day. With a sense of relief, she gathered a few objects in a small bag and left her cottage. She walked past the gate to the castle and walked toward the arch. The call was growing in intensity; it would not wait for the end of things. It called now, and she obeyed.

The arch was warm to her touch. She approached and touched the sacred stones, running her hands over the smooth boulders and waited. Only seconds passed before the scene unfolded before her under the curve of the arch.

Flashes of color and light and sound came from the portal. Her gazed never wandered; she saw the images moving before her. Another betrayal, Maggie in danger, English soldiers, a hidden dagger. Then nothing.

She looked around for Maggie. She should be here by now.

Here and gone?

Had she been discovered by Sandy's cronies? She could waste no more time. She must get to the arch now. Moira ran to the courtyard to avert disaster.

Alex shielded his eyes with his bound hands when they took him into the courtyard. It was not sunny but too bright for eyes accustomed to the darkness of the dungeon. His guards, new ones this day, took his arms and pulled him toward the platform in front of the entrance to the castle.

The crowd was quieter than he expected, none of the jovial behavior he thought he would see at something like this. Of course, this was his first hanging. He shook off the bad humor—it was probably the fear that grew in the pit of his stomach that caused the irreverent thoughts.

The crowd opened a path for him; some met his eyes, some spoke his name, others turned away. He walked up the steps and faced the rope noose hanging from the scaffold. The crowd held its breath as he looked up at it. No sound could be heard, none.

Struan took a place high on the stairway of the castle, where Alex had seen him and Anice for the first time. The man had aged in these past few days. He looked tired and worn down. Anice stood a short distance from Struan, with her parents at her side. Sandy was nowhere to be seen.

"Ye all ken what haes happened wi'in the clan. The impostor is brought to justice this day. He will hang this day for his crimes against the Clan MacKendimen." He paused and looked directly at Alex. "Do ye hiv any last words?"

Alex had not thought this far—he couldn't think of words to say. He opened his mouth but was interrupted.

"What are his crimes, Struan?" a man near the back of the crowd called out. "What haes this mon done?"

"Haes he stolen from the clan?" another yelled out.

"Did he kill anyone while he was here?" One of the soldiers came forward and added, "He trained us in weapons in the yards. Would a mon train his enemies?"

Alex looked from face to face.

They were defending him!

A woman who worked in the castle walked to the steps. Alex thought she was one of the women with Anice when she beat Maggie. "He could hiv beaten the lady Anice to punish her for what she did to his woman, but he didna."

Alex glanced at Anice and saw her blush brightly.

One of the old men called out to Struan, "Do ye really think we should hang him wi'oot proof, Laird? It doesna seem fair, e'en if he is a spy."

The murmuring and hissing grew louder.

" 'Tis no' the MacKendimen way of it, ye ken."

Struan looked as though he had been given a way out of this when another voice entered the discussion.

"Now that we have his whore, he will give us the truth."

Everyone turned at once and gasped at the sight of Sandy holding on to Maggie by her waist. He held a dagger at her throat and dragged her through the crowd. Alex could see her face as she got closer. She was furious and continued to struggle in spite of Sandy's weapon.

"How do you want to do this, Faither? Do we torture her until the impostor breaks or until she gives us what we want?" Sandy's voice was filled with anticipation.

"Struan! Ye told me she would be safe from this. Ye said ye wouldna use her," Alex bellowed in protest and began to struggle against his bonds.

"Is that what he told you?" Sandy asked him. "And, even as he held you in his dungeon, you believed him?" The man laughed while maintaining a tight hold on Maggie. "You are a bigger fool than I thought, impostor."

Sandy pivoted around to face Struan.

"So, shall I begin with the slut here in the courtyard so all can witness the way we treat traitors and spies?"

Struan stood to his full height and bellowed out his words.

"MacKendimens do no' use women in their fights. I willna allow ye to abuse her, Sandy. Let her go."

"I think not, Faither. If you will not torture her, then I will have her. He"—Sandy nodded at Alex"—will have no need of her. He had my woman. I will have his."

Alex looked at Struan and fought against the guards'

hold on him. Struan started down the steps toward Sandy. Then everything descended into chaos.

He watched as Maggie snapped her head back into Sandy's face, hitting the man's nose. He heard the crack of it from where he stood. Sandy screamed in pain, grabbing at his bleeding nose, while Maggie pulled the dagger from his grasp and slashed his hand. He fell to the ground as she moved away.

The crowd ran in all directions, some toward the bleeding man, some away. Maggie disappeared into the fracas. Without warning, Alex was pushed from the scaffold, his fall broken by the strong arms of the blacksmith. Pol took out a knife and cut through the bindings.

"Come, we maun get out of here. Brodie said to use the other gate and meet at the arch."

Alex accepted the man's hand to gain his feet and they took off into the confusion. "What aboot Maggie?"

"She kens where to meet us. She will make her way there, too."

They ran away from the castle, through the little-known gate, and came to the deserted arch before anyone else. Alex approached it from the side. He felt, heard, saw nothing different about it. Maybe Moira was wrong about its power.

The sounds of a chase came closer and closer. A moment later, Maggie ran around the corner. Chasing her were two of Sandy's men, the same ones who had beaten him.

He stood in front of the arch and held out his hand to her. Another second—just another second—and she'd make it. He was ready to take her hand and pull her through with him.

In horror, he watched as Garrick caught up with Maggie and grabbed her cloak from behind. Unable to free the clasp, she was trapped. The second man tripped and fell to the ground.

He was still holding out his hand to her, waiting.

"Go on, Alex," she screamed. "Go through without me." She saw his hesitation and screamed again, "You must try. Now. Go. *Please*." Her last word ended on a sob.

He lowered his arm and shook his head. "I canna go wi'oot ye, Maggie. I canna leave ye behind."

Struan and the MacNab arrived with Brodie and others behind them. Moira stepped out from behind the arch and spoke to Struan in a loud voice.

"Ye maun let them go, Struan."

"What do ye mean, Moira? Why do ye help them?"

"I do what I maun, what I am told to do. Let them pass, Struan, they do no' belong to us."

"I do no' understaun, Moira. Who are they?"

Moira's eyes seemed brighter as her voice rose. "The fates brought them to us, Struan, and the fates call them back. Do no' interfere."

Alex watched as Struan took a leap of faith. Accepting Moira's words, he nodded. Alex turned to see Brodie step behind Garrick and hit him with a cudgel. The man collapsed to the ground, freeing Maggie to run to Alex.

Maggie threw off her cloak and took Alex's hand. They turned to Moira.

"Moira," he began.

"Nay, Alex. 'Tis the fates ye should thank, no' me. Now, the time is right. Go."

He put his arm around Maggie's shoulders and they walked to the opening.

"Alex, do no' forget the lesson. Do no' tempt the fates again."

"I hiv learned, Moira." He looked at the woman he loved and asked, "Ready, lass?"

"Yes, Alex."

Lightning split the air and thunder rumbled around them. He took her hand, held it tightly, and stepped into the curve of stone.

* * *

In the instant that they entered the archway, wisdom was granted to Moira again.

Alex. Maggie. Laughing together, loving. A bairn wi' bright blue MacKendimen eyes. Time-tested love.

He had learned his lesson. " *'S e am gum bidh an dearbhadh de gaol siorruidh, Alex MacKendimen.* Your love has been proven true by time itself."

Chapter 45

I'M BLIND! BLINKING against the complete darkness, her chest tightened in complete terror. Unable to breathe, she tried to rub her eyes, but her hands refused her mind's command to reach up to her face. Oh, God, blind and paralyzed. But how? A few moments . . . minutes . . . hours ago, she was running to Alex. And, now?

There was movement in the darkness that swirled around her. Was it Alex?

As suddenly as it started, it ended. Maggie shielded her eyes from the glare of the bright sun. As soon as her body would respond, she looked around.

"Maggie?"

"I'm here, Alex."

He was standing at her side and reached down to help her up. They were on the ground next to the half-filled archway. Maggie reached out to touch the stones. She felt nothing, no hint of power or the vibrations once present.

"The sword. Let me look for the sword." He ran a few yards away and searched the ground. She watched him pick up the jewel-encrusted sword and slide it back into the scabbard.

"What do we do now, Alex? Any ideas?"

He ran his hand through his hair and looked at their clothing. "We look a bit worse for the wear, Maggie. Do you see anyone around here?"

"Nope. How much time has passed?"

"Do you still have our watches? Are they in your bag?"

She realized it then—his accent was gone, and he spoke English, plain English. No *hivs* or *cannas.*

"Do you hear yourself? Your accent is gone, Alex."

"Is it? I could never really tell it was there. Did you find the watches?" He was pacing in front of the wall.

"Here, Alex, here's yours."

She unzipped a compartment in her bag and took out the timepieces. She held hers up, amazed that the seconds now ticked by, digits flashing forward, as normal.

"Do you remember what time it was when we sat down here?"

"It was about 1:25. Alex, what does yours say now?"

"Mine reads 1:30. Only five minutes have passed? It seems impossible."

"We couldn't have traveled through time. It can't have happened."

"I think we did. Look at your hair—it was much shorter when we met. And mine," she ran her finger through her curls, "was much longer."

"Your back?" She turned to him and he peeked inside the back of her blouse. He just nodded in response.

"Your face." She raised her hand to touch the cuts and bruises. He winced at the sore spots.

"It happened!" They said it at the same time and laughed.

"Well, Maggie, as Moira said, *'S e am gum bidh an dearbhadh de gaol siorruidh.*"

"Alex, you still have the Gaelic?"

"I may have said it, but I don't have the foggiest idea what it means."

"Mayhap I can help?" Mairi reappeared beside the arch. Maggie had not heard her approach.

"Do you know what it means?"

"Aye, lass, it means yer love haes been tested and proven by time and the fates."

Maggie looked at Alex. Those were Moira's words. She had heard them as they passed through the arch, through time.

"I love you, Alex MacKendimen."

"I love you, Maggie Hobbs." He entwined their fingers and he pulled her away from the arch. "Come on. I think we should get cleaned up a bit, and then the family can meet the fiancée of the heir o' the clan. That is, if you'll have me?"

Epilogue

"AND THAT'S WHAT I did on my summer vacation."

You could have heard a pin drop and bounce in the electrified silence of Mrs. MacKendimen's second-grade classroom. Twenty-one small faces, eyes sparkling and mouths dropping wide open, stared in awe at her as she finished reading her composition. A little hand shot up in the back of the group and waved furiously back and forth.

"Yes, Jennifer?"

"Mrs. MacKendimen, wasn't your hair much longer before? My sister told me . . ."

Maggie reached up and tugged at the short but now even curls, laughing at the details children notice.

"Yes, Jennifer, my hair was much longer when I taught second grade last year. I decided to try a shorter haircut."

Another hand went up in the group. She pointed at John and waited for *his* question.

"But, Mrs. MacKendimen, wasn't that just a story you told us? Did you really go to Scotland?"

Looking at the bright, inquisitive students, Maggie wondered just how to answer.

"Well, yes, John, I did go to Scotland and I visited all the places I told you about. Would you like to see the best souvenir I brought back from my trip?"

The twenty-one heads bobbed in unison. Maggie got up from her chair in the center of the room and walked to the door. Opening it, she motioned for someone to come in. The children gasped at the sight before them.

He stood straight, looking even taller to them than the six feet four inches that he was. He wore full Highland dress: saffron shirt, covered with a plaid in hunting colors, and tied with a thick belt at his waist. The plaid encircled his waist and was thrown over his shoulder and secured with a large, jewel-encrusted badge. His knees were uncovered, but his lower legs were wrapped and cross-gartered.

What most drew the attention of every child was the gigantic claymore he carried in a scabbard hanging from his belt. He pulled the sword free and held it up in front of the children, smiling as they ooh'd and aah'd in fascination. Highly polished, it sent thousands of brilliant shards of light sparkling around the room as it reflected the sun. The class crawled forward to get a closer look at the weapon.

"Oooh, Mrs. MacKendimen, you brought back this sword?" asked one blond-haired girl.

"No, Jessica, not the sword." Maggie walked over to the warrior and slid her arm around his waist. "I brought home a real Scottish warrior."

Alex smiled at his wife's words and leaned down to kiss her. "And I brought home the love of my life."